THE RETROSPECTIVE IMAGINATION OF A. B. YEHOSHUA

DIMYONOT דמיונות
Jews and the Cultural Imagination

Samantha Baskind, General Editor

EDITORIAL BOARD

Judith Baskin, University of Oregon

David Biale, University of California, Davis

Katrin Kogman-Appel, Ben-Gurion University of the Negev

Laura Levitt, Temple University

Ilan Stavans, Amherst College

David Stern, Harvard University

Volumes in the Dimyonot series explore the intersections, and interstices, of Jewish experience and culture. These projects emerge from many disciplines— including art, history, language, literature, music, religion, philosophy, and cultural studies—and diverse chronological and geographical locations. Each volume, however, interrogates the multiple and evolving representations of Judaism and Jewishness, by both Jews and non-Jews, over time and place.

OTHER TITLES IN THE SERIES

David Stern, Christoph Markschies, and Sarit Shalev-Eyni, eds., *The Monk's Haggadah: A Fifteenth-Century Illuminated Codex from the Monastery of Tegernsee, with a prologue by Friar Erhard von Pappenheim*

Ranen Omer-Sherman, *Imagining the Kibbutz: Visions of Utopia in Literature and Film*

Jordan D. Finkin, *An Inch or Two of Time: Time and Space in Jewish Modernisms*

Ilan Stavans and Marcelo Brodsky, *Once@9:53am: Terror in Buenos Aires*

Ben Schachter, *Image, Action, and Idea in Contemporary Jewish Art*

Heinrich Heine, *Hebrew Melodies*, trans. Stephen Mitchell and Jack Prelutsky, illus. Mark Podwal

Irene Eber, *Jews in China: Cultural Conversations, Changing Perspectives*

Jonathan K. Crane, ed., *Judaism, Race, and Ethics: Conversations and Questions*

The Retrospective
Imagination of A. B. Yehoshua

YAEL HALEVI-WISE

The Pennsylvania State University Press
University Park, Pennsylvania

Library of Congress Cataloging-in-Publication Data

Names: Halevi-Wise, Yael, 1965– author.
Title: The retrospective imagination of A. B. Yehoshua / Yael Halevi-Wise.
Other titles: Dimyonot (University Park, Pa.)
Description: University Park, Pennsylvania : The Pennsylvania State
    University Press, [2020] | Series: Dimyonot : Jews and the cultural
    imagination | Includes bibliographical references and index.
Summary: "Explores the layers of signification that A. B. Yehoshua
    constructs in his fiction to draw readers into a critical analysis of the
    condition of Israel as well as his representations of place, vocational
    identities, names, holidays, and love"—Provided by publisher.
Identifiers: LCCN 2020035732 | ISBN 9780271087856 (hardback) | ISBN
    9780271087863 (paper)
Subjects: LCSH: Yehoshua, Abraham B.—Criticism and interpretation.
Classification: LCC PJ5054.Y42 Z68 2020 | DDC 892.4/36—dc23
LC record available at https://lccn.loc.gov/2020035732

Copyright © 2021 Yael Halevi-Wise
All rights reserved
Printed in the United States of America
Published by The Pennsylvania State University Press,
University Park, PA 16802-1003

The Pennsylvania State University Press is a member of the Association of
University Presses.

It is the policy of The Pennsylvania State University Press to use acid-free
paper. Publications on uncoated stock satisfy the minimum requirements
of American National Standard for Information Sciences—Permanence of
Paper for Printed Library Material, ANSI Z39.48–1992.

For my Dani, with love

CONTENTS

List of Maps *(viii)*

Preface *(ix)*

Acknowledgments *(xvii)*

Note on Translation and Transliteration *(xix)*

1 Condition-of-Israel Novels *(1)*

2 Mapping A. B. Yehoshua's Worldview *(16)*

3 The Watchman's Stance *(52)*

4 Vocation *(72)*

5 Holidays *(94)*

6 Names *(127)*

7 Love Under the Burden of History *(145)*

Coda: A Telephone Conversation with the Author of *Mr. Mani* *(161)*

Notes *(169)*

Selected Bibliography *(193)*

Index *(201)*

MAPS

1   Global locations of Yehoshua's novels   *(20)*
2   Those who do not return   *(23)*
3   Israel in *The Lover*   *(28)*
4   Israel in *Hesed Sefaradi / The Retrospective*   *(30)*
5   The U.N. partition plan (1947)   *(33)*
6   Debating Israel/Palestine in *Mr. Mani* during the British Mandate era   *(35)*
7   Avraham Mani's Jerusalem   *(37)*
8   Yosef Mani's Jerusalem according to Lieutenant Horowitz   *(38)*
9   Hagar Shiloh explores Jerusalem in *Mr. Mani*   *(39)*
10   Jerusalem in perspective   *(47)*

PREFACE

I have known A. B. Yehoshua ("Boolie") for nearly half my life; over the years he has become almost like a father figure with whom one can argue, laugh, and commiserate. Although, in this age of iconoclastic critiques, such an avowal is hardly the best way to open a critical analysis of a major author's oeuvre, I hope that the chapters ahead can demonstrate that even friendship and admiration for an author may generate an independent critique, as testified by the work of several other fellow scholars whom Yehoshua has also befriended.

Once, the two of us drove to Tel Aviv after a lecture that he delivered at the Ministry of Foreign Affairs in Jerusalem. When we arrived at his destination, I flung open the cab's door and asked his wife, Ika (z"l)—waiting at the curb in front of their apartment building after sending off their grandchildren, who had come there for dinner as they did every Thursday—how could she manage so well with someone so stubborn! This exasperation, likely to be recognized by anyone who has befriended Yehoshua, is invariably mixed with gratitude for his warm and down-to-earth willingness to connect, assist, and explain. Yehoshua may exasperate through his insistent pursuit of an idea—whichever happens to be foremost on his mind at any moment regarding the Jewish question in its many iterations—yet he is extraordinarily available to discuss it.

When I first met Yehoshua, I was a graduate student of comparative literature at Princeton, and he arrived there to teach Hebrew literature during a sabbatical from his regular teaching duties at the University of Haifa. I was interested at the time in characters who argue (in novels) about how to tell a story that reflects their deepest cultural and aesthetic attitudes toward truth and fiction. Yehoshua's *Mr. Mani* (*Mar Mani*, 1990) became part of that project, along with key examples by Cervantes, Dickens, Conrad, and Austen; and from then on, some aspect of Yehoshua's work has stayed on my desk, tempting me to go further into the world of Hebrew literature, both ancient and contemporary. I have been lucky, as well, to have an opportunity to write and teach about literary traditions that are technically much younger than Hebrew, but which have managed to benefit from a more consistent scholarly treatment in modern times. This in turn nourishes our understanding of Yehoshua's work.

All in all, this book offers a rather eclectic analysis of major patterns and techniques that recur specifically across Yehoshua's oeuvre. To illuminate them, each chapter follows its own unique interpretative approach: chapter 2, for example, uses maps to visualize Yehoshua's worldview in relation to the geopolitical settings of his novels; chapter 3 conducts a chronotopic analysis of the watchman's stance across his oeuvre; chapter 6 unpacks the semiotic prompts behind his provocative name choices; and a Manian coda stages an impertinent conversation about Jewish identity with the author of *Mr. Mani*.

The unified argument of this book is simply a call for a more systematic appreciation of Yehoshua's multilayered imagination. To express this, he uses literary techniques that he learned primarily from Agnon and Faulkner; but his multilayered complexity answers to his own total commitment to clarify the condition of Israel at his present time. Yehoshua's style is notable, as well, for its delectable and subtle humor; but in the tradition of the novel in its heyday, he uses it to entice his readers to engage more conscientiously with what he considers to be the most urgent dilemmas facing his current national situation. Yehoshua's tendency to build his narratives on multiple layers of signification is thus a consequence of his desire to psychoanalyze the moral and practical paradoxes underlying the social and political challenges that worry him.

Ideally, Yehoshua's novels should be interpreted on at least four simultaneous levels of signification: according to the psychological troubles of his characters; with close attention to the sociopolitical tensions of individuals from diverse ethnic, religious, and national backgrounds who interact in Yehoshua's novels through their extended families and in their workplace; via the comparisons he draws between secular Israeli life in the present and historical scenarios that throw contemporary Israeli life into perspective; and finally, as part of his preoccupation with Jewish identity as shaped by longstanding historiosophic conversations that go back to ancient times, and that mix theology with legend and actual history in an entanglement that Yehoshua tries to pry apart.

Avraham Yehoshua's coming of age, his bar mitzvah during the winter of 1949 in Jerusalem, coincided with the armistice agreements that were worked out gradually between the fledgling State of Israel and its neighbors in the aftermath of Israel's Declaration of Independence. During the previous two years, bombings, curfews, battles, and a siege plagued the city in which five generations of Yehoshuas had been raised. Thus, at a most impressionable age, Yehoshua lived through a bitter struggle for national survival and independence; and yet, it is remarkable that he rarely speaks or writes about this era in a direct manner, displacing it instead onto transmuted scenarios across his opus and ethos.

Somewhat like his character Yosef Mani—the son of a Sephardic gynecologist at the turn of the nineteenth century in a more compact Jerusalem—the childhood, boyhood, and youth of Avraham Yehoshua in Jerusalem, during the 1940s and '50s, took place between his parents' modern Sephardic household, the secular Ashkenazi learning environment that they chose for him, and the traditional milieu of his paternal grandfather, a distinguished rabbi who at one time headed the Sephardic rabbinical court. Indeed, like Yosef Mani's career, the lifework of his creator has been dedicated to defining his own national identity in relation to the needs and expectations of different types of Jews, Arabs, and foreigners, across boundaries that are more or less permeable.

Yehoshua's Yosef Mani, at the age of twelve, assists in the birth of a baby whose umbilical cord he must cut because his obstetrician father—who had run after Polish visitors, whom he had been trying to convince to stay in Jerusalem—had left his son alone with a birthing mother. At this age, too, Yehoshua had witnessed a birth—the rebirth of Israel—and part of him bitterly resents having been left holding its umbilical attachment to atavistic attitudes, such as diasporic or religious mentalities, which he regards as being both a debilitating and an enriching source of Israeli identity. As Yehoshua repeatedly declares in his public lectures and shows in his fiction, these cultural attachments cannot be dislodged from modern Israeli life without endangering its core values, and perhaps even its survival. Therefore, by every means at his disposal, he anatomizes the vestigial attachments of Jews, as well as Muslims, Christians, and pagans, paying extra attention to the mindsets of secular Israelis, whether Jews or Muslims, whose behaviors he contrasts, rather selectively, with alternative heritages—Spanish, Hindu, Sudanese, Japanese, and so forth.

In his youth, the orphaned Yosef Mani navigates among the representatives of different cultural enclaves in Jerusalem to grasp their worldviews and means of communication: he learns English from Christian clergy at the Scottish mission near the Old City, he acquires French from a family of Algerian Jewish immigrants, he studies *torah* with a Hassidic sect in Mea Shearim, and he chats in Arabic with a sheik who had befriended his grandfather. In his youth, Yehoshua too navigated among people from a variety of European and Middle Eastern backgrounds, many of whom were making a big effort to configure themselves into a new Israeli identity. He was aware of the double pain of German Jews, who after the Holocaust became alienated from their beloved German language and culture; of *Haredi* ultraorthodox who resisted the reinvigoration of a Holy Tongue for secular affairs; and Muslim and Christian Arabs who soon began to master the nuances of Hebrew. This anxious assembly of individuals from diverse backgrounds was suddenly expected to breathe together as a coherent body with a single national identity. To understand the impediments still facing the consolidation of this modern Israeli identity has been Yehoshua's main intellectual preoccupation.

From an artistic point of view, A. B. Yehoshua's life work invites a study of repetition and variation. Certainly, important distinctions do mark the different stages of his career—from his earliest surrealistic short stories, to his provocative novellas and mature novels, as well as theatrical plays, film scripts, children's books, polemical essays, and even an operatic libretto. Nevertheless, in ever surprising ways, Yehoshua reworks the themes and techniques adumbrated in his early stories and honed in his existential novellas of the 1960s into the multilayered novels that he has composed over the last four decades. This book offers a bird's-eye view of his underlying techniques and overarching themes, with special attention to the novels.

Mine is also an integrative project in respect to the vast scholarship that has been produced around the work of A. B. Yehoshua. Although broad and rich in its subject matter, this scholarship has tended to focus on an analysis of individual works, often in immediate response to their publication. I believe the time is ripe to expand this analysis of Yehoshua's individual works into a more systematic awareness of his major themes and compositional patterns.

Readers who wish to become quickly acquainted with Yehoshua's novels and worldview will find in chapter 2, "Mapping Yehoshua's Worldview," a visual synthesis of his national, global, and local settings, illustrated through ten maps prepared especially for this book to highlight his two key preoccupations: his fear that the Jewish people might find themselves again in the same vulnerable condition that Zionism aimed to correct, but then, despite and perhaps because of this fear, his desire to push his readers—first and foremost secular Israelis—to consider alternative cultural scenarios, which put their own contemporary Israeli life into a defamiliarizing perspective. Defining Israeli identity in relation to these alternative diasporic situations across space and time as well as in relation to Israel's constitutive cultures—the different types of Jews, Muslims, and Christians who make up the mosaic of Israeli life—is another core aspect of Yehoshua's vocational mission.

Although Yehoshua may send his protagonists to the farthest reaches of the globe in his bid to illustrate the dangers of national dispersion, he also demonstrates—and in extraordinary detail—the benefits of interacting with people from many heritages. This paradoxical dynamic governs the composition of his global, national, and local settings. We can best observe it over the course of two centuries in *Mr. Mani*, where Yehoshua pays very careful attention to the evolving interactions between representatives of diverse ethnicities, religions, and nationalities, especially in Jerusalem, but also around the entire Mediterranean region. The principal setting of Yehoshua's fiction is usually the State of Israel; yet even within its borders he portrays a mosaic of diverse social identities in constant interaction with one another. At the same time, he has expressed a keen frustration with Israel's lack of clearly agreed-upon geographic borders, a theme that became particularly prominent in *The Liberated Bride* (2001).

Readers already familiar with Yehoshua's major works and worldview may prefer to skip this introductory map chapter and go directly to chapter 3, which explores the "watchman's stance" across his oeuvre. There, I argue that Yehoshua periodically situates his characters at panoramic outposts where their ability to evaluate the demands of the world around them can be tested. Usually located on high places, these lookout scenarios paradoxically expose the *limited* cognition and impaired eyesight of fallible individuals entrusted with important missions of national repair. Much attention has been paid to the watchman's stance in Yehoshua's iconic novella *Facing the Forests* (*Mul haye'arot*, 1963), but many variations of this stance recur across his fiction, to the extent that we could consider it to be his characteristic chronotope.

Several scholars have noted that in *Facing the Forests* Yehoshua employs biblical terminology to link his contemporary watchman with the prophets of yore known as "watchmen over the house of Israel." Scripture presents the missions of these prophets-watchmen as a binding vocation assigned to them from above. In dialogue with this biblical trope, Yehoshua teases his characters with a range of professional and familial assignments that extend, but also undermine, the biblical model of national identity and responsibility. With extraordinary care, he portrays the daily occupations of lawyers, judges, surgeons, teachers, merchants, and engineers; but then he extends their professional duties into a larger mission of national repair that they can barely keep up with. In Yehoshua's hands, the professional abilities of his characters are thus turned into a higher consideration of national responsibilities, carefully layered unto the author's here and now. The construction of this stratified multifocality is what enables Yehoshua to address questions of national identity and responsibility that acquire a heightened urgency in times of national reconfiguration or consolidation, such as Yehoshua has experienced almost incessantly during Israel's first century as a significant political player.

Conceived as a triptych, chapters 4, 5, and 6, on "Vocation," "Names," and "Holidays," showcase how Yehoshua elevates the realistic details of his fictional worlds into a more abstract intellectual discussion. He does this by creatively evoking historical events and processes, and by joining a long-standing historiosophic conversation about mythical concepts and symbols, such as the belief in supernatural redemption or a lingering nostalgia for an Edenic past. The perception of what counts as history rather than myth can indeed change—notably, the establishment of the State of Israel in 1948 turned the mythical longing to return to Zion into a historical reality. But this potentially slippery slope between history and myth fascinates Yehoshua and fuels his quest to clarify the moral and practical responsibilities that accompany this recent reconfiguration of modern Jewish life in the ancient and contested homeland.

As we will see in the first chapter, most scholars recognize that Yehoshua's novels are constructed on several intersecting levels of signification—which in shorthand could be labeled psychological, sociological, historical, and historiosophic. However, their analyses of his works tend to focus, quite deliberately, on just one or two of these levels, in varying permutations. I believe that we can now adopt an integrative approach that slices across Yehoshua's oeuvre to unpack its rich multilayeredness. Thus, we can appreciate more fully the sophisticated way in which he weaves an abstract historiosophic conversation with concrete psychological and sociological issues, while always maintaining a close dialogue with history, especially

Jewish history, as the backdrop against which he assesses his current Israeli situation.

Suggestive names are among Yehoshua's most potent tools for drawing near and far into perspective. In *Friendly Fire* (*Esh yedidutit*, 2007), for instance, when a character named Yirmi (Jeremy) rants against his biblical namesake—Yirmi being short for Yirmiyahu (Jeremiah)—a connection is traced between the beleaguered prophet who ended up in Africa after witnessing the destruction of the First Temple in 586 BCE, and Yehoshua's character, who exiles himself to Africa after losing his wife and son. Ongoing threats to Jewish survival and national stability since ancient times are further scaled down in this novel to a contemporary setting that toggles back and forth between Tel Aviv, Africa, Jerusalem, and Tulkarm in the West Bank. Yehoshua provides an even older perspective against which to compare Israel's contemporary dilemmas by alluding to the prehistoric era through the mission of an African team of anthropologists who are searching for the roots of humankind. Then, on each of its levels of signification, *Friendly Fire* plays with fire, bereavement, and national identity. Fire and bereavement were among the prophet Jeremiah's favorite keywords as he warned ancient Judeans about an impending destruction; but Yehoshua reminds us, too, that fire, domesticated in the prehistoric era, has created the foundation for a human civilization that continues to use and misuse its resources. Each of these frames of reference is further enacted multifocally through the Muslim, Jewish, and pagan characters that populate this novel's alternating settings in Israel and abroad.

In *The Extra* (*Nitzevet*, 2014) and *The Retrospective* (*Hesed Sefaradi*, 2011) other allusive names such as Honi (the "Circle Maker" from midrash) and Yair Moses ("may Moses illuminate") beg for an interpretation of the predicaments of these characters in light of their ancient referents. However, and always avoiding a hermetic interpretative allegory—a caveat one cannot emphasize strongly enough—Yehoshua scales down this national conversation to a pragmatic size, projecting his psychological and sociological scenarios unto a wider historical canvas, and vice versa, to conduct an historiosophic conversation with the reader above the heads of the characters. Extending a paradigm that is associated in Hebrew fiction primarily with the modernist writer S. Y. Agnon, Yehoshua burdens even his love plots with the weight of a complicated past, as shown in chapter 7, "Love Under the Burden of History."

In a similar manner, holiday settings play a salient role in several of Yehoshua's novels. *A Late Divorce* (*Geirushim meuharim*, 1982) takes place on Passover; *Friendly Fire* during Hanukkah, and Rosh Hashanah and Yom Kippur figure prominently in *Mr. Mani* and *A Journey to the End of the Millennium* (*Masa el tom ha-elef*, 1997). The latter engages with Tisha b'Av, too, while Shabbat plays a provocative role in many of his novels. Given that Yehoshua loves to declare at every opportunity that he is an atheist dedicated to reconfiguring the civic and religious components of Israeli identity, it is important to understand how and why he deploys such traditional markers of Jewish identity as names and holidays. These motifs help him pave the way, not only for a clearer demarcation between modern and traditional beliefs, but also for a pragmatic renewal of Jewish values in the State of Israel, since religion, as he puts it, is simply "too important to be left to the religious."

Like Yehoshua's representations of names and holidays, the professional vocations of his characters draw us into a reconsideration of the boundaries between myth and history, which he regards as hopelessly muddled and in need of constant clarification. Even the impaired vision that Yehoshua assigns paradoxically to his blundering "watchmen over the house of Israel" models his plea to separate mythic postures from contemporary responsibilities. Taken together, these recurrent themes and tropes prompt a multifocal evaluation of Israel's contemporary mores in relation to all the alternative historical scenarios through which Yehoshua evokes a stimulating range of cultural options.

Circling back to an open dialogue with this author, my coda interrogates Yehoshua's definition of Jewish identity in a playful imitation of his masterpiece, *Mr. Mani*. This extraordinary novel features five consecutive speakers, who argue with six figures of authority whose opinions the reader must distill mainly from the replies of their interlocutors (because just the words of one conversation partner are provided at any given moment). Thus, Yehoshua's side of our conversation is naturally missing from my coda. I hope, nonetheless, that his point of view will come across as strongly as the positions of Mr. Mani's interlocutors do through the arguments of their conversation partners. Should I fail at this endeavor, Yehoshua's greater merit as a stylistic virtuoso and lucid intellectual will become more keenly evident by comparison.

ACKNOWLEDGMENTS

It is a pleasure to remember all those who helped to shape this book, conceived in Israel about ten years ago. My beloved Dani, impossible to acknowledge the array of your resourcefulness and support, both when the road gets rough and when it is smooth: may we be granted many many more adventures together. To our Tali, Stevie, Ari, and Yoni, for whom Yehoshua is a household name, I hope that witnessing this labor of love will empower you, too, to secure your own suitable vocational paths. To our parents, Bracha, Peter, Mike and Batya, each with their own distinguished vocations—thank you for understanding how mighty hard it is to do so many things at the same time. As well, I appreciate the support of our siblings, and other close and farther relatives, who supplied missing references, kind thoughts, and sound words of advice.

The friendship of good colleagues in my two departments of Jewish Studies and English at McGill has been a source of deep satisfaction since we arrived to Montreal. Between 2012 and 2015, I offered a series of courses on A. B. Yehoshua with the goal of identifying his characteristic patterns of composition. Among the wonderful students who participated in these classes, I must especially mention Vas Gogas, who got so hooked on Yehoshua that he decided to write a master's thesis on the role of history in *The Liberated Bride*; Eyal Moyal, who became a PhD student of Hebrew literature at the Hebrew University of Jerusalem; and Yael Faitelis, who prepared the ten maps for chapter 2 through vital funding facilitated by Eric Caplan and a matching grant from our faculty's internship program. Deena Yanofsky, our librarian expert in Geographic Information Systems, was instrumental in helping us work on the correct cartographic platforms. And finally, Sophie Weiler, gifted student and writer, proofread and formatted the manuscript thanks to funding from the Arts Undergraduate Society.

Beyond McGill, I am happy to have this opportunity to thank Bernie Horn, a fellow traveler on the Yehoshuan road, who graciously reassured me that a thousand interpretations of *Hamlet* have still left room for more. Wisely, he also advised me to keep things as simple as possible, despite the inherent complexity of Yehoshua's multilayered style. More recently, I had

xviii THE RETROSPECTIVE IMAGINATION OF A. B. YEHOSHUA

the joyful experience of sharing my appreciation of Boolie with Dan Miron, an extraordinary scholar and now a friend. Warm thanks as well to Rina Cohen-Muller for her invitation to Paris INALCO during my sabbatical in 2015, and to Nitza Ben-Dov for her extensive scholarship on Yehoshua, and more personally, for welcoming me to the University of Haifa during the second half of that sabbatical trip. It is quite an experience to write about a major living author in the company of the scholarly productions of these and other mutual friends and acquaintances on three continents.

Another debt of gratitude goes to "my old ladies"—the eager lifelong learners who participante in Montreal's many book clubs, and who invite me, every few months, to discuss literature over delicious cakes and coffee in their magnificent homes. Among them I have encountered high school principals, judges, psychiatrists, homemakers, journalists, and even a husband or two. When I write, this lay audience has helped me to conceptualize the intelligent reader with little use for academic jargon; although this book still has its fair share of literary terms, this lay audience kept me from jumping into the deep end.

Today, one can celebrate that the field of Hebrew literature and Israel Studies is far more crowded than it was twenty-five years ago, at a time when Professor Bob Fagles, who for many years headed Princeton's department of comparative literature, advised me to get on that bandwagon as soon as possible. At first, I did not heed his advice, but when I did, Ross Brann, Alan Mintz (z"l), and Gershon Hundert made a place for me on this wagon by inviting me to teach Hebrew literature at Cornell, Brandeis, and McGill. Inspiring discussions with Wendy Zierler go way back when. Ranen Omer-Sherman put in a kind word for the timeliness of this project, and Naomi Sokoloff offered good advice at a crucial turn. Finally, Patrick Alexander has been the approachable publisher that this project truly needed.

I am grateful to the following journals for permitting us to reprint revised versions of three sections of this book: chapter 4 was published as "A. B. Yehoshua and the Novel of Vocation" in a memorial issue of *Prooftexts: A Journal of Jewish Literary History* 37 (2019): 688–710, dedicated to its founder, Alan Mintz; chapter 5 was published as "Hanukkah and Passover in Yehoshua's Opus and Ethos" in *Shofar: An Interdisciplinary Journal of Jewish Studies* 35, no. 2 (2017): 55–80; and chapter 6 first appeared as "The Watchman's Stance in A. B. Yehoshua's Fiction," *Hebrew Studies* 58 (2017): 357–82.

NOTE ON TRANSLATION AND TRANSLITERATION

Whenever possible I cite from the standard American translations of Yehoshua's texts; only when a more nuanced point is required, I provide my own translation, along with page references to both the Hebrew original and the published translation.

The transliteration method used here strives to evoke the most natural way of vocalizing contemporary Hebrew, except in cases where common usage suggests an established format, as in Hakibbutz Hameuchad rather than the simpler Hakibutz hame'uhad.

Some of the English titles of Yehoshua's novels differ substantially from their original Hebrew names. To avoid confusion, I periodically note both names, as in *Molkho / Five Seasons* or *Hesed Sefaradi / The Retrospective*.

CHAPTER 1

Condition-of-Israel Novels

—"Zvi," says the village teacher, recalling the name of the retired engineer who visited him several months ago, "aren't you Zvi?"

—"Yes, Zvi," Luria confirms, full of gratitude and excitement for the name that has returned to him, though grief also swells in his heart.

—"So, here's another Zvi." The teacher grabs Luria's shoulder to turn him southward toward a nearby hill. And really, a deer or stag stands there . . . as if all the light in the world emanated from him. And the village teacher goes back into the ruins, coming out with an old rifle, a hybrid shotgun of unclear origin and parts, and he trains it toward the deer that still seems to be disseminating all the surrounding light, and before Luria can stop him, the teacher shoots one precise shot, and the deer, shocked, tries to escape but the bullet had already penetrated inside him, and he collapses, wounded, slowly dragging himself toward a hidden crevice.

—"Land of the deer," says the teacher to the agitated engineer, "land of the deer."

—A. B. YEHOSHUA, *HAMINHARAH [THE TUNNEL]*, 323

Ancient legend has it that four men entered a mystical orchard: one of them looked around and dropped dead, another went mad, a third damaged the seedlings, and only the wisest among them entered in peace and walked out in peace.[1] The kabbalistic imagination used this story to justify adding an esoteric dimension to the literal, allegorical, and analogical interpretations of scripture that were already part and parcel of ordinary Jewish learning and spirituality. Many centuries later, the modern Hebrew writers who were responding to the nineteenth-century Jewish enlightenment could still assume that their readers were fairly well accustomed to interpreting every story and situation according to several interlinked layers of signification. Although to appreciate A. B. Yehoshua's creative enterprise it is certainly not necessary to claim him as a direct heir of the Haskalah movement or

2 THE RETROSPECTIVE IMAGINATION OF A. B. YEHOSHUA

to a kabbalistic hermeneutics; still, remembering this background helps us take stronger note of his multifocal engagement with questions of Jewish identity and history that he scales down to the psychological struggles and social interactions of his characters. They point, either directly or obliquely, to his concern with Israel's complex existential situation. At the same time, and somewhat paradoxically, he insists on also maintaining a universalized perspective that challenges any narrow political allegiances.

To read Yehoshua, then, is not only to follow the absurd obsessions of his characters and to delight in the wry humor of his style; for beyond the tragicomic texture of his narratives there also lies a deeper preoccupation with contemporary Israeli identity, in relation to a longstanding history and the symbolic concepts that have framed and punctuated Jewish life since ancient times.

Perhaps the easiest way to describe Yehoshua's characteristic style is to imagine his novels as a multistoried house with a main floor, a basement, upper stories, and wings. The challenges facing the characters in their immediate environment are staged on the main floor, while Yehoshua's preoccupations with the people of Israel are discussed partly over their heads, above the main action, in upper stories accessible through references to traditional Jewish concepts and symbols that go back to ancient times, such as Zvi's name in the passage cited above. A deeper psychoanalysis of the characters is worked out in the bowels of the narrative, which, for a lack of a better metaphor, we can imagine as the basement area. And in the wings we are invited to compare Israel's sociopolitical circumstances in the present with alternative places and eras that spin the present into a wider perspective.

Toggling creatively between these four layers of signification—psychological, sociopolitical, historical, and historiosophic (or mythological)—Yehoshua burdens each of them with elements from all the others, constructing tragicomic scenarios whose stakes become weightier as the narrative progresses. This multilayered method of composition is neither self-evident nor easy to explain, so we reach out for spatial and optical metaphors—shadows, drawers, panels, or edifices—in a collective effort to define Yehoshua's ability to complicate his fictional worlds, and perhaps our real world, artistically and ideologically. Let us examine, first, how Yehoshua scholars—himself included, for he sometimes comments insightfully on his own work too—broach this multilayered aspect of his narrative style.

METAPHORS OF MULTILAYEREDNESS

In an early response to Yehoshua's first full-fledged novel, *The Lover* (*Hame'ahev*, 1977), the leading literary historian in Israel at the time, Gershon Shaked, admitted cautiously that Yehoshua "tries here, perhaps, to portray some of the paradoxes of Israeli existence." Shaked described a "vertical" composition of "enfolding shadows" with secondary motifs that amplify the main action by enclosing "a concealed plane within the revealed plane."[2] He recognized Yehoshua's tendency to engage with history and identity through objects drawn from daily reality, such as the grandmother's 1947 Morris—a car that starts off blue but is later painted black, and whose role in *The Lover* invites a reconsideration of Israeli history and culture from the UN vote for the partition of Palestine to the novel's contemporary setting in 1973, during the aftermath of the Yom Kippur War. Two decades earlier, when Yehoshua had begun to publish short stories with a surrealistic flavor, Gershon Shaked had immediately hailed them as a part of a "new wave" in Hebrew literature, which was produced mostly by Israeli writers who had come of age after the establishment of the state and whose style and subjects had begun to appeal more broadly to an international audience.

Shaked's formulation influenced in turn Yehoshua's own propensity to define himself in literary-historical terms. For instance, during a 1998 lecture to commemorate Israel's fiftieth anniversary, Yehoshua presented himself as part of a generation of writers who tried to establish "some kind of interesting balance between the revealed and the hidden. I am talking about hidden, false-bottomed compartments that were within us, drawers that were opened in the course of our creativity, and because of which the writings of Agnon became the source of such multi-layered inspiration for us. Because Agnon is the supreme artist of folding and hidden-away drawers."[3] Truly, S. Y. Agnon is a sui generis artist who never fit squarely into any literary trend, but by linking himself and an entire generation of fellow Israeli artists to Agnon, Yehoshua aligns himself both with an outlier who was already celebrated as the most successful Hebrew writer of his era, while also including himself diplomatically among the peers of his own era—Amos Oz, Aharon Appelfeld, Amalia Kahana-Carmon, Yehuda Amichai, and so on.

In this manner, Yehoshua traces his own lineage to a giant of Hebrew letters and also remains a generous team player among the peers of his own era. It is important to add, moreover, that Yehoshua's preoccupation with national identity positions him also within a much longer lineage in the wider history of the novel, one that has adapted modern ideas about national reconfiguration into complex fictional plots. This endeavor includes Agnon and Faulkner, two of the novelists whose impact on Yehoshua has been strongest. Yet, even within this longer lineage, Yehoshua's multilayered style of composition is exceptionally systematic and sophisticated. Hence it is important to properly recognize this characteristic feature of his style.

In one of his conversations with Bernard Horn, Yehoshua described all literary productions as trees growing in a forest nourished by the common soil of humanity. Only the tree trunks exhibit the distinguishing features of any particular culture, while narrative techniques, which he calls mere foliage, can be easily grafted, Yehoshua claims, from one tree to another.[4] If we consider, however, that Yehoshua absorbed especially from Agnon a tendency to design his fiction on multiple layers of signification, then this feature evidently functions for him as both bark and foliage, since Agnon's own multilayeredness emerges from a Talmudic hermeneutics that maintains a close dialogue with its historical and theological sources.

When elaborating on Agnon's influence on Yehoshua and Oz, Nitza Ben-Dov conjures up a "twilight zone," which shrouds their objects and concepts in a partial darkness—an allusive, dreamlike state of in-betweenness that "casts not one, but two, three shadows and more."[5] For although Yehoshua and his peers found themselves demanding "clarity and plain speech," they also appreciated a literary style full of "complexity and ambivalence." Or, as Amos Oz put it, they were attracted to light while acknowledging "the artistic importance of shadows and twilight."[6]

I contend here that more systematically than any other Hebrew writer before him, Yehoshua constructs his novels on four layers of signification so as to distinguish fantastic desires from pragmatic responsibilities, because he worries that history and mythology are dangerously mixed up in his readers' minds. Reconsidering traditional links between the Land of Israel, the God of Israel, and the Jewish people, Yehoshua dramatizes intimate contacts between individuals from different cultural groups that are commonly regarded as opposite to one another—Jew and Gentile, Arab and Jew, Ashkenazi and Sephardic, secular and religious, native and foreigner—and by historicizing their geographic and political coordinates, he invites us to respond more sensitively to their complex histories and identities.

In a famous interview with the Israeli scholar Nissim Calderon and with Menachem Peri, who subsequently became Yehoshua's principal editor, Yehoshua articulated this propensity "to always look for the intellectual symbolic side, by searching within reality for a general, abstract idea. I have not overcome this tendency, and I don't know whether I shall ever overcome it. This is, really, my deepest genre."[7] When this interview took place in the mid-1970s, Yehoshua was already recognized, both in Israel and abroad, as a virtuoso of surrealistic short stories with a hint of political provocation. And by the time he turned forty and published his first novel in 1977, this propensity to look for the "symbolic side"—to search "within reality for a general, abstract idea"—intensified threefold. Now he began to broaden his psychological plots into elaborate representations of Israeli culture, examining its constitutive subcultures in relation to unfamiliar places and eras. Within this microcosm, every individual struggles for self-actualization, but, crucially, Yehoshua holds each of them responsible for the welfare of everyone else. Not only does he hold every character responsible for themselves and everyone else in their own social environment, he even scrutinizes the extent to which they can be held responsible for anyone they meet in all the places where they travel, as we will see in the next chapter.

I will stress throughout this book that Yehoshua invites his readers to participate in a thoughtful conversation about Israeli identity and history, and that he does this primarily by studding his fiction with provocative symbols of national identity such as names and holidays. Although, unfortunately, such semantic nuances are often the first casualties of literature in translation, in Yehoshua's case, the playful network of cultural allusions is extensive and consistent enough to survive some of this external tampering. To give an example from the mere title of one of his novels—from his fifth novel, *Hashivah mehodu* (*Return from India*, 1994)—its Italian and German publishers preserved the original name, literally, as *Ritorno dall'India* (1994) and *Die Rückkehr aus Indien* (1996), while the English publisher decided to change the title to *Open Heart*, and the French shortened it to *Shiva*. The novel's original title signaled, from the onset, that some sort of relationship would be explored here between Israel and India, while invoking a homecoming motif, so central to the Zionist ethos, through the obvious reference to *shivat zion* (return to Zion). Nevertheless, even when the title is translated literally, this key historiosophic referent may go unnoticed by some readers in a foreign context. Conversely, the allusion to the

6 THE RETROSPECTIVE IMAGINATION OF A. B. YEHOSHUA

Hindu deity Shiva becomes readily apparent only in the short French title, where Shiva evokes nothing other than the Hindu deity, which is indeed worshiped by one of the novel's Jewish characters. Further extending this multicultural interplay, the Jewish custom of sitting shiva upon the death of a close relative takes on a special coloration during the week of mourning for Lazar, one of this novel's main characters. Ultimately, Yehoshua invokes all these referents, inviting us to compare tradition with modernity, both in Israel and in India.

To some extent, Yehoshua wrote *Hashivah mehodu* as a complaint against the enthusiasm of young Israelis who hike in the Himalayas and become attracted to mystical aspects of Hindu culture, preferring it sometimes to a Judaism that may have failed to provide them with sufficient social or spiritual nourishment at home. On the level of a historiosophic conversation with mythological ideas, this novel does not shy away from exploring the paradox of a Hindu deity that symbolizes life as well as destruction, just as the voyage to India facilitates both an exciting new source of vitality and a danger of forgetfulness among Israeli tourists. Tenuously encoded in the novel's original title, all this is ultimately accessible through all its translated editions, even when elided from their covers. However, the name chosen by the English publisher (*Open Heart*) draws extra attention to the protagonist's vocational aspirations—he wishes to become a cardiac surgeon—and to his hopeless love affair with the wife of his boss, a woman practically old enough to be his own mother. This line of analysis directs us in turn toward the basement and main floor of the novel—its tragicomic erotic plot and psychological drama—at the expense of deemphasizing the historiosophic and multicultural conversation going on in its attic and side wings, so to speak, through the references that we just traced to the idea of *shivat zion* and its parallels among different ancient and modern cultures.

In short, even the mere title of a Yehoshuan text can encode the historiosophic, sociological, and geopolitical referents that interest him, over and above the turbulent psychological relationships of his characters. These interconnected spheres of signification are consistent and pervasive enough to transcend individual manifestations, and in this manner they often survive translation, especially when we pay closer attention to the hinging passages, where Yehoshua transitions between his thematic clusters. This is what occurs, for example, when he asks us to reflect on the history of fire (in *Friendly Fire* [*Esh yedidutit*], 2007), or on objects laden with a symbolic and genealogical force, such as the eyeglasses passed down from one generation to the next in *Mr. Mani* (*Mar Mani*, 1990), or the sociopolitical implications of the collapsing 1947 automobile in *The Lover*.

Readers attracted to this allusive dimension tend to be better attuned to Yehoshua's stratified method of composition.[8] Thus, Ziva Shamir, one of Yehoshua's perceptive interpreters, outlined in an early review of *The Lover* its fourfold stratification of "a realistic layer, a psychological layer, a socio-political layer and a mythological layer."[9] Nevertheless, she limits her analysis to two of these strata—the political and mythological—although her interest in what she calls the mythological layer leads her, in the first place, to acknowledge the existence of the other more obvious strata. We might argue, correctly, that writers such as Agnon and Faulkner likewise engaged their readers in mythico-theological conversations about redemption and national progress, yet I would answer that even they did not construct their layers of signification as systematically and deliberately as Yehoshua has done from *The Lover* onward.

Dan Miron visualizes Yehoshua's method of composition as facets or panels (*yeri'ot*) configured in a rising order:

> from an existential chain of motifs grounded in bodily functions, all the way to metaphysical and even religious motifs. Folded upon each other, within this framework, is a panel of existential motifs; a psychological panel of emotions and affect; a historico-political-social panel; an aesthetic panel related to beauty and its role in human life, motifs that may exhibit a poetic or narratological character, especially in connection with the means and aims of storytelling and its creation [a notable aspect of *Hesed sefaradi* / *The Retrospective*, on which Miron focuses here]; and above them all, moral and metaphysical motifs about the essence and meaning of existence. These overlapping facets are laid out in nearly all of Yehoshua's novels, though not always attaining a complete breadth or variegation. Some clustered motifs may obtrude at the expense of others; but while psychological motifs abound in all of Yehoshua's novels, other types of motifs, such as the poetic-aesthetical or metaphysical-ethical, may appear in a limited manner.[10]

Miron, as we see here, outlines five facets. Yet I would contend that the self-reflexive metafictional dimension that he counts as a fifth dimension

8   THE RETROSPECTIVE IMAGINATION OF A. B. YEHOSHUA

is actually folded into all the other four layers of signification through Yehoshua's attention to the vocational responsibilities of his characters, a topic with which I will deal extensively in chapters 3 and 4 of this book. The mysterious writer who types all night in *The Lover*, yet callously ignores his shared wakefulness with the troubled adolescent across the valley, functions as a self-reflexive figure against whom Yehoshua contrasts the attention that he pays to this and other troubled adolescents in that novel. In *A Late Divorce* (*Geirushim meuharim*, 1982), a virgin wife expresses her sexual anxieties by composing stories about spinsters who kidnap babies, while her impotent husband fantasizes about writing a historical treatise that doubles as a self-reflexive frame for the entire novel; in *Five Seasons* (*Molkho*, 1987) and *The Extra* (*Nitzevet*, 2014) musical performances also operate in this self-reflexive fashion, as do the vocational aspirations of Yehoshua's troubled scholars, poets, and cinematographic crew in *The Retrospective* (*Hesed sefaradi*, 2011), on which Miron focuses in the passage cited above.

However, Miron's exposition of the compositional scaffolding of *The Retrospective* emphasizes yet another key aspect of Yehoshua's worldview—his paradoxical logic, which rejects any rigid *either/or* position even if it seems to lead to an ostensibly illogical *both/and* perspective.[11] Like other polyphonic writers before him, Yehoshua likes to stage difficult encounters between characters who hold worldviews that are stereotypically regarded as opposed to each other, but he insists on connecting, as well as separating, these worldviews. This paradoxical position can be observed in his ambivalent attitude toward diasporic Jewry, as well as his propensity to turn his characters into watchmen and watchwomen ironically endowed with an impaired vision, as we shall see in the next chapters.

Yehoshua's multifocality may strike us as less exciting than the psychological dramas that torment his characters, gripping us into his plots. But the tension that he draws between his different levels of signification is actually the matrix out of which he designs his whole narrative, from its opening pages on which he typically spends utmost care, until the end point, usually resolved in his mind from the start.

Reassessing the relationship between ideology, psychology, and sociology in Yehoshua's *Mr. Mani*, Bernard Horn recently suggested that "rather than accept the conjecture that the psychological background of the characters necessarily determines their ideas, we must consider the alternative hypothesis that they *choose* their ideas despite their psychological background, or, to go a step further, that their idiosyncratic psychological dynamics—reinforced by their sociological status as Sephardim—liberate them enough from social convention to enable them—when confronted with a multicultural environment—to be intellectually and morally daring."[12] It is not a coincidence that both Horn and Miron arrive at a deeper appreciation of the relationship between Yehoshua's interlinked levels of signification when they consider the role of Sephardic identity in his opus and ethos. Bernard Horn's "Sephardic Identity and Its Discontents" and Dan Miron's An "Ashkenazi" Perspective on Two "Sephardi" Novels suggest, in parallel ways, that Yehoshua's counterintuitive and paradoxical ethos is generated by his attitude toward sociohistorical identities. On the one hand, Yehoshua invests an enormous effort in portraying the cultural heritages of his characters; on the other hand, he believes that whether they are Sephardim or Ashkenazim, Jews or Muslims, religious or secular, male or female, young or old, should matter less than the need to *climb out* of these limited positions to envision and create a more stable and inclusive consolidation of a common Israeli identity, resting on their essential humanity.

This, of course, is the grand program of Jewish normalization that Gilead Morahg underscores in his extensive analysis of *Mr. Mani*.[13] It is striking, moreover, that Yehoshua's idiosyncratic definition of national normalcy as "nothing but a rich and creative pluralism in which one is as sovereign as possible over one's deeds and where the options on the horizon are vast"—a formulation to which we will return several times over the course of this volume[14]—touches on the same four spheres of signification that he deploys in his novels, though directed more explicitly here toward the national condition, envisioned in psychological terms.

A "rich and creative pluralism" can be observed in the social mosaic that Yehoshua presents through his characters, who come from diverse ethnicities, religions, and nationalities, but who meet through their extended families and in their workplaces. This close contact between members of different social communities enables him to explore whether they are actually capable of assessing the consequences of their interactions, and whether they are "sovereign over their deeds," according to a notion of emotional stability that equates the moral behavior of individuals with the achievement of a national sovereignty (*ribonut*).

When the mythical plan to return to Zion became a historical reality upon the establishment of the State of Israel in 1948, Jews, at least in theory and to a significant extent also in practice, became a nation like any other, according to nineteenth-century definitions of national identity. But, as Yehoshua so often underscores, serious obstacles continue to jeopardize this normalization of modern Jewish identity in its ancient homeland.[15] Many Jews remain outside of Israel, and even within Israel, atavistic longings for *yemey kedem* (days of old) persist in the nostalgia for former lifestyles and religious aspirations of fundamentalists from every side.

If the people of Israel actually "returned to History" when they assumed control over their political sovereignty, as Gershom Scholem famously put it, then what role can traditional myths of national redemption and repair *continue* to play beyond this actual return to Zion?[16] Yehoshua's propensity to search for "the intellectual, symbolic side"—"to open drawers and double-bottomed compartments" in order to test the boundaries of Israeli identity and sovereignty from such multiple perspectives—serves, first and foremost, to challenge this complex entanglement between the aspirations and realities of Israelis and members of other nations with whom they come into contact, in the present time and other eras, both within Israel and around the globe.

IN THE LAND OF THE DEER

Until the 1990s, Israeli writers were expected to address questions of national survival and identity in their fiction.[17] Therefore, when Yehoshua declared in 1976 that his "deepest genre" is the propensity to produce multibottomed narratives, he was positioning himself bravely, not only in relation to high modernists such as Agnon, Faulkner, or Kafka, but also vis-à-vis local writers of the "generation of independence" such as S. Yizhar, whose fiction had dealt more directly with the national situation in the more or less self-critical manner advocated at the turn of the twentieth century by Yosef Haim Brenner. Scorning a utopian "Eretz-Israel genre" that merely praised the beauty of the land and the labor of the early Zionist pioneers, Brenner had called for a serious exposition of the moral and practical difficulties besetting the pioneers at that earlier historical juncture. Certainly, Yehoshua subscribes to Brenner's blatant line of criticism, but his multilayered engagement with historiosophic motifs and symbolic abstractions still aligns him more firmly with what Ortsion Bartana calls "the Agnon school."[18]

Even Yehoshua's earliest surrealistic short stories, with no apparent connection to any recognizable national condition or landscape, grapple with an existential situation that has been increasingly connected to contemporary Israeli problems in ways that are becoming clearer over the years, shedding new light on their unfamiliar and sometimes threatening scenarios. But much more elaborately, the multilayered constructions of Yehoshua's later novels emerge from his subsequent decision to place his fiction at the service of an ongoing process of national repair by constructing a network of social interactions that are ideologically suggestive and historically conscious, but still never reducible—and this is a crucial caveat—to any simplistic political message.[19]

Yehoshua's privately circulated curriculum vitae describes his fiction as "an experiment with literary techniques put at the service of deeply painful national and personal themes."[20] This does not mean that his fiction is autobiographical—though to be sure, some autobiographical elements do play a background role in his fictional worlds, as Nitza Ben-Dov has shown.[21] The "personal" dimension (*tokhen ishi*) to which Yehoshua refers here manifests itself, rather, through the psychological troubles of his characters as they struggle with a tragicomic range of problems at home and at work. Concomitantly, when Yehoshua describes the ideological motivations behind the essays and lectures that he regularly delivers alongside his fiction, he emphasizes his desire "to get to the roots of the Arab-Israeli conflict, to understand the soul of the nation of Israel, and to express non-conventional ideas about the slipperiness and uniqueness of Jewish identity."[22]

Mindful of this agenda, Amir Banbaji asks,

> In what way should an Israeli state be "Jewish"? In exile . . . Judaism did not demand from the Jewish people concrete historical action, so, to cite one of Yehoshua's favorite examples, they could endlessly declare . . . "next year in Jerusalem" without moving an inch towards its realization for hundreds of years. This Judaism has to be set aside, claims Yehoshua, in order to establish a "Judaism" . . . based on pragmatic actions that eliminate dangerous illusions. Yehoshua does not excise traditional Judaism from a modernized Jewishness, but like Brenner . . . he demands that Judaism be collectively released from its noncommittal exilic metaphysics to become instead a . . . "total Jewish reality" [capable of seeping into every element of daily life].

This is an excellent articulation of Yehoshua's ideology because it avoids any reductive political message while nevertheless acknowledging that his brand of realism raises even the most trivial details—"roads, clothing, idioms"—to a "higher ontological or aesthetic level without necessarily canceling their mimetic relevance."[23] In other words, Yehoshua's sophisticated multilayeredness serves his project of national reformation by differentiating and also integrating a variety of points of view and intertexts, which he creatively yokes together while always remaining historically grounded. Brenner, by contrast, was incapable of producing such a panoramic perspective at the beginning of the twentieth century, because he felt that the cultural and material conditions of daily life for Jews in Palestine were not yet ripe enough to generate such an integrative vision.[24] Be that as it may, within Jewish literary history Yehoshua's multilayeredness recalls, to some extent, the allusive methods of earlier Hebrew writers, whose readers were accustomed to approach scripture through several intersecting spheres of signification, and who extended this practice into modern Hebrew fiction by refreshing the language's historical options across all its former genres and ages (biblical, mishnaic, medieval, poetic, and prosaic).[25]

Thus, when we come to decode the cultural attitudes embedded in the names that Yehoshua assigns to his characters, or in the practices and beliefs associated with Jewish holidays, or through the vocational responsibilities that he assigns to fallible creatures, and even in love plots that are burdened with the dysfunctionalities of former generations, we essentially articulate Yehoshua's ongoing attempts to evaluate Israel's geopolitical circumstances and cultural identity in reference to alternative places and eras. *This is a writer who never really takes a break from history because he views every action as history in the making, and his worldview is permeated by a historicized consciousness of how today's shortsightedness might shape tomorrow's landscapes.*

I would like to wrap up this overview of Yehoshua's multilayered imagination by showing, briefly, how his interconnecting layers of signification operate in his most recent novel, *The Tunnel* (*Haminharah*, 2018). As usual, a psychological drama dominates the reader's immediate engagement with the world of this novel—in this case, Zvi Luria's tragicomic struggle with his encroaching dementia. A retired highway engineer happily married to an aging pediatrician, Zvi suddenly finds himself forgetting names and directions, and eventually he forgets even his own name, which is then restored to him, under alarming circumstances, as we saw in the shocking scene at the top of this chapter.

Playing with one of the biblical names of the Land of Israel—*Eretz hatzvi*, land of the deer, land of beauty—this climactic scene at the end of the novel forces a reconsideration of the goals of each of its characters, and the complicated relationships in which they are enmeshing themselves. In a desperate bid to continue practicing his professional talents as an engineer, Zvi Luria assists in the design of a tunnel that aims to surreptitiously protect a Palestinian fugitive who has sought refuge in the Negev Desert, an area in the south of the country for which Ben Gurion had particular fondness and high hopes in terms of its modern development. Yas'ur, the Palestinian fugitive whom Zvi and his friends wish to assist, is hiding from his neighbors because he had given away some land that did not belong to him. Zvi's encroaching dementia, together with Yas'ur's plight, form the basic plot of this novel.

I claimed earlier that Yehoshua never forgets history, but sometimes he does tuck it into tricky places. Here, for example, into the ruins of an ancient Nabatean structure where Yas'ur ensconces himself on a Negev hilltop. Yehoshua subtly juxtaposes the desperate man's bid to survive on this desert hilltop with an ancient culture whose descendants have not survived in any clearly discernible form. In an obvious but unstated manner, he also connects Yas'ur's situation with our contemporary "hilltop youth" in Judea and Samaria, who similarly entice road planners and army officials to cater to their aspirations.

The Tunnel does not take us into any of the tunnels that Zvi had designed during his long career, and even the tunnel that he designs to preserve Yas'ur's hideout in the desert remains in its planning stages when the novel closes. But instead, we clamber with Zvi unto several high posts, from where this octogenarian observes his world from the perspectives of three Palestinians whom he befriends. From the rooftop of a Tel Aviv hospital where his wife works, Zvi admits that on a clear day, it may be possible to discern with one's bare eyes the towns and villages of the Palestinian Authority on the West Bank. From a peak in the Negev, he witnesses the optical illusion that Yas'ur's daughter had captured in one of her artistic photographs—a puzzling image of twin suns apparently rising together from the horizon. And finally, from the Nabatean structure, Zvi realizes that he had placed himself in a very vulnerable position, next to a lonely and embittered armed man.

14   THE RETROSPECTIVE IMAGINATION OF A. B. YEHOSHUA

Noticing a stag in the morning sunlight, the Palestinian fugitive leeringly recalls one of the ancient names of this coveted land—*Eretz hatzvi*, land of the deer, land of beauty—and in so doing, he unwittingly restores to Zvi his own forgotten name, forgotten due to his dementia. In a sudden move that is as shocking to Zvi as to the reader, Yas'ur draws out a strange shotgun and shoots the stag that had been basking in the sunlight a moment ago. This is a bitter ending for a novel so full of generosity and humor, a novel that had tactfully avoided any direct confrontation with current politics to finally hint, nevertheless, that no tunnel can bypass a conflict between people with divergent attitudes toward each other and their common spaces.[26]

To reduce a rich and nuanced novel to a political message is to reduce it to pulp. On the other hand, to pretend that Yehoshua does not engage with the hot political issues of his hour is to obscure his uncanny ability to infuse his ongoing preoccupations with Israeli identity and survival into the symbolic, historical, sociopolitical, and psychological dimensions in his novels—in this case, the pain of two elderly men losing control over their responsibilities toward themselves and others.

Yehoshua's most recent novel was composed at a time of intense personal anguish for its author. He designed it when his wife was still active by his side, but he completed it in the midst of the deepest mourning, after she unexpectedly passed away. One of the questions raised by this novel is whether it is possible, or even desirable, to separate one's personal life from one's public responsibilities. In the prime of his life, Zvi Luria had insisted on keeping those two spheres separate from one another, and therefore he knew almost nothing about the private troubles of his colleagues. Now, due to his encroaching dementia, he begins to disregard those conscientious boundaries that he maintained so carefully in the past.

While writing this novel, Yehoshua almost did succeed in separating his professional activities from his personal life. He managed to carry on with his vocational tasks without allowing the debilitating loss of his lifelong and deeply beloved companion to steer him away from the novel's original design. Remarkably, he maintained the same light and humorous tone with which he had begun, and its bitter ending was actually planned from the start. Such an insight into Yehoshua's deepest processes of composition testifies, once more, to a creative interplay between different levels of signification that is not a mere afterthought, but that constitutes the novel's inherent architectonic plan all along.

Keeping in mind this sophisticated tendency to intertwine historical and historiosophic elements with the sociopolitical background and psychological turmoil of his characters, we can now turn to an overview of Yehoshua's worldview. Ten maps designed especially for this book shall guide us next through a discussion of this writer's attitudes toward identity and place, as manifested in his multicultural representations of Jerusalem, Israel, and the world.

CHAPTER 2

Mapping A. B. Yehoshua's Worldview

A. B. Yehoshua's attitude toward Israel and the world may be called prescriptive, and its tone prophetic, in that it seeks to convey a vision of national improvement beyond the scope of his novels. While not entirely dystopian, his fiction offers a tragicomic picture of Israeli life as a chaotic state of affairs, which he exaggerates in order to advocate for its repair. Repair itself is rarely achieved within the scope of Yehoshua's narratives, though they do tend toward a breakthrough that facilitates some cognitive adjustment in the reader's mind, if not in the fictional lives of the characters. In this manner, Yehoshua guides his reader toward a reconsideration, and even a judgment, of the decisions taken by his characters at every point in their lives.

Via other types of public forums—lectures, interviews, op-eds— Yehoshua delivers more direct prescriptions for national stabilization. These extraliterary statements inevitably affect our interpretation of the worldview that underlies his fiction, yet we must guard against allowing such blunt statements, uttered in the heat of a specific moment, to altogether guide our understanding of his works of art. His literary creations respond to a wide spectrum of aesthetic and intertextual prompts, whereas his provocative public opinions are sometimes targeted pronouncements aimed at illuminating some cultural or political issue that preoccupies him at any given moment.

Compelling us with its sophisticated humor and dramatic energy, Yehoshua endows his work also with a deeper sense of gravity by projecting a multifocal network of allusions, as outlined in the previous chapter.

Therefore, even when we interpret the itineraries of his characters in relation to his extraliterary pronouncements, as I do in this chapter, we need to take into account the political and autobiographic contexts of his ideological statements, in addition to the literary-historical contexts that are particularly relevant to each work. This chapter conveys such background as unobtrusively as possible, but it always informs our understanding of the relationship between Yehoshua's artistry and worldview.

By inviting his readers to imagine better solutions to the complex moral and practical dilemmas in which he embroils his characters, Yehoshua ultimately aims to clarify his contemporary Israeli identity in relation to the experiences of all the diverse cultural subgroups contained within it—ethnic and religious minorities that live within Israel and around its borders, as well as Israelis who have left the country, a particular sore point for Yehoshua, as we will discuss below. To clarify and support a modern reconfiguration of Jewish identity in Israel, he also explores alternative national scenarios in a variety of geographic locations, which he sets both in the present and the past.

The historian Fania Oz-Saltzberger once appealed to Yehoshua during a retrospective of his work, asking him to continue creating historical novels, as he had done in *Mr. Mani* (*Mar Mani*, 1990) and *A Journey to the End of the Millennium* (*Masa el tom ha'elef*, 1997), or at least to continue designing characters who are professional historians, as he had done in *The Liberated Bride* (*Hakala hameshahreret*, 2001) and *A Late Divorce* (*Geirushim meuharim*, 1982).[1] Oz-Saltzberger complained that Yehoshua had lately become more interested in geography at the expense of history. But actually, Yehoshua's treatment of geography is just another manifestation of his historical imagination;[2] for, invariably, he constructs a tight nexus between place and time by sending his characters to interact with representatives of different nationalities, religions, races, and ethnicities in circumstances that are always steeped in an awareness of their distinctive cultural histories.

When Yehoshua sends his Israelis to far-flung locations around the globe—Tanzania, Minnesota, India—he thus paradoxically defines (and refines) his own modern Israeli identity at home by insisting, first of all, on clearer definitions of Israel's borders and responsibilities vis-à-vis other nations. Even inside the homeland, he sends his characters up and down the country to connect with the local representatives of many backgrounds, because such contacts enable him to test the viability of modern Jewish life

18   THE RETROSPECTIVE IMAGINATION OF A. B. YEHOSHUA

in Israel, along with the big challenges to its consolidation. Yehoshua extends this probe to the hardest test case, the city of Jerusalem—Zion's historical center—where every resident and visitor walks in a geography that is loaded with historical resonances that convey longstanding political implications.

This chapter illustrates these core aspects of Yehoshua's worldview by mapping the local and global itineraries of his novels, in light of his commitment to strengthening a modern reformation of Jewish identity in Israel.[3] Compared to the literary cartographies that Franco Moretti and others had drawn to render visible the covert economic underpinnings of literary fiction,[4] the ten maps presented here are simpler itineraries of Yehoshua's twelve novels (to date).[5] Nevertheless, they facilitate an overview of Yehoshua's opus and ethos with special attention to the interactions that he establishes between individuals from diverse backgrounds. Aided by these maps to focus our discussion, we can follow these interactions between Yehoshua's characters on the local, national, and international scope of his novels.

Avidov Lipsker noted that Yehoshua's fiction "sketches the most detailed atlas drawn by any modern Hebrew writer except, perhaps, Agnon." Reflecting on the barriers obstructing Yehoshua's characters during their travels, Lipsker concludes that they travel more like nomads than pilgrims energized by a spiritual destination.[6] It is indeed remarkable that an author like Yehoshua, who rails so virulently against national dispersion—even accusing diaspora Jews of "playing with Judaism" instead of living up to the full range of daily responsibilities for a reconstruction of Jewish identity in the old/ new homeland[7]—nevertheless has chosen to send his Jews on voyages to the farthest corners of the globe, and even those who stay in Israel travel restlessly up and down the country and across its immediate borders, seeking connection, validation, and escape.

One might have reasonably expected that Yehoshua, of all people, would situate his native consciousness in its own immediate locale, as did S. Yizhar, for example, among many other native writers who fought for Israeli independence when Yehoshua was twelve years old.[8] But although Yehoshua portrays the topography and ethnography of his country in great detail, in nearly all his novels he chooses to send his characters on extended trips abroad. Even Yehoshua's earliest surrealistic stories, set in an abstract locale that cannot be associated definitively with Israel or any other place, derive their characteristic shock effect largely from this provocative omission of a geographic specificity. Amos Oz once argued that if one were to pin them down to some specific time and place—which is not particularly hard to do—we would deflate their surrealistic effect and expose a mere shell of existential drama.[9] But indeed, if their shock effect depends so strongly on their geographic ambiguity, then, by the same token, the political urgency of Yehoshua's longer fiction also depends on its recognizable engagement with the geographic and ethnographic dilemmas of Israel. To his credit, in one of his later novels, *The Retrospective* (*Hesed sefaradi*, 2011), Yehoshua returned to wrestle with several of his surrealistic stories—which had virtually become instant classics of modern Israeli literature—now repositioning them within a concrete geography that retroactively enhances their political resonances. All in all, Yehoshua's method of composition works in a paradoxical and dystopian fashion: he exaggerates alarming behaviors in the present and the past in order to advocate for a future repair.

ISRAELIS ABROAD

If we situate the itineraries of Yehoshua's novels on a map of the globe, we see that with the exception of *A Journey to the End of the Millennium*, which takes place entirely in Europe and North Africa, all of his novels are set within Israel with strategic voyages to international locations such as Paris, London, Spain, Berlin, Beirut, the United States, the former Soviet Union, India, Tanzania.[10] In *The Extra* (*Nitzevet*, 2014), Noga even manages to catch a glimpse of the North Pole during her flight from the Netherlands to Japan. Since so many of us long to see the world, it may be difficult to conceive of such voyages as anything but a positive opportunity for cultural interaction and personal growth; in Yehoshua's worldview, however, such travel is both an asset and a liability.[11]

The concert halls of Paris and Berlin, the funeral ghats of the Ganges River or the marketplace of Dar es Salaam, are vital sources of cultural enrichment for Yehoshua's travelers. They sharpen their awareness of spiritual and social challenges that still need to be confronted back home. At the same time, these excursions also pose a danger of centrifugal perdition—an irresponsible loosening of family commitments and a propensity to abandon the homeland. When we remember that family units for Yehoshua function as a microcosm of the nation, we can appreciate the extent to which these long voyages compromise national cohesion.

20   THE RETROSPECTIVE IMAGINATION OF A. B. YEHOSHUA

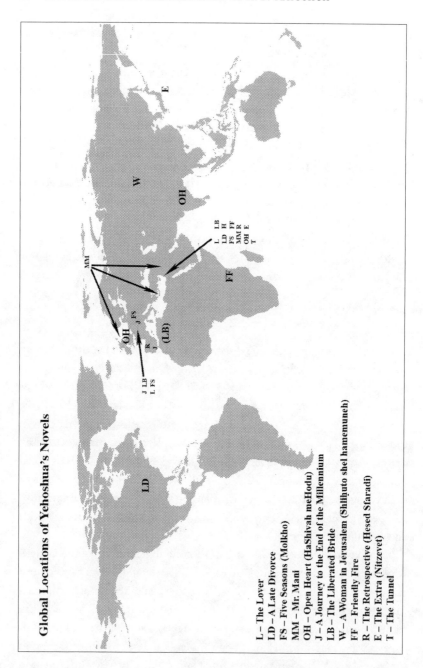

MAP 1. Global locations of Yehoshua's novels.

Like Stephen Dedalus at the end of James Joyce's *A Portrait of the Artist as a Young Man*, A. B. Yehoshua sends his protagonists "away from home and friends ... to encounter for the millionth time the reality of experience and to forge in the smithy of my soul the uncreated conscience of my race."[12] But unlike Dedalus and his autobiographical creator, Yehoshua has remained firmly rooted in his country, taking only measured trips abroad. Moreover, when he sends his people abroad, they are rarely conscious of this deeper significance or their missions. Parenthetically, one may argue that he did in fact abandon the city of his birth, Jerusalem, where several generations of Yehoshua's ancestors from his father's side were born. He chose instead to reflect on it from the calmer perspective of Haifa, and more recently Givatayim near Tel Aviv; but we will return to this argument in the final section of this chapter.

The point I wish to make first is that by sending his characters to far-flung locations, loaded with historical significance, Yehoshua invites selective comparisons between any culture and his vision of a "normal" Jewish identity in the State of Israel. Like India, portrayed in *Open Heart* (*Hashivah mehodu*, 1994), Israel too has dealt with the legacy of British colonialism and a never-ending tension between its modern aspirations and ancient cultures. Like Spain in *The Retrospective*, Israel too is struggling with a reformation of religious attitudes toward all the groups that form part of its multicultural fabric.

According to Yehoshua, the way to forge a "normal" national identity is to facilitate a responsible relationship among Israel's diverse inhabitants and between Israel and its Palestinian rivals for the national space. At the level of individual psychology, he understands this normalcy as assuming full control over one's personal actions, while from a sociopolitical perspective, as we saw, he defines national normalcy as "nothing but a rich and creative pluralism in which one is as sovereign as possible over one's deeds and where the options on the horizon are vast."[13] On both levels, his emphasis falls on a moral duty to choose a path of self-control in relation to other individuals and groups around us.

Thus, when Yehoshua sends his characters abroad with no clear mission or date of return, a dilemma immediately arises regarding their responsibilities toward their family and homeland. Yehoshua usually distinguishes—and this is a crucial point—between Jews dispersed around the world (diaspora) and foreign nations whose influence he portrays as largely positive. As in

Theodor Herzl's *Altneuland*, the *Jewish* diaspora for Yehoshua is ultimately "no place," a space that condemns Jewish life to a precarious and even negative development.[14] Compared to this frustration with Jewish dispersion, the nations of the world appear here as a source for emulation and exciting collaborations through plots that feature intimate meetings between Israelis and African anthropologists, Spanish priests, Dutch musicians, Indian doctors, and even retired Soviet generals, who equip the reader, and sometimes also the characters, with new insights for repairing their trouble spots at home. In Yehoshua's fiction, the world can be a dangerous magnet that pulls Jews away from their national and familial responsibilities; at the same time, any nation around the world becomes a source of invigorating comparative perspectives that elucidate the goals and requirements of a modern Israeli identity.

"You Jews are always at the airport," jokes the Arab-Israeli maître d'hôtel in *The Liberated Bride*. "Always coming and going. You can't sit still. It will make you sick in the end."[15] Einat Lazar does get sick in India (*Open Heart / Hashivah mehodu*). She contracts hepatitis, and the dashing Dr. Benjy Rubin, who accompanies Einat's parents to retrieve her from India, also gets "sick" during this trip—in the sense of falling desperately in love, not with this damsel in distress, but rather with her middle-aged mother, the pampered wife of Benjy's boss. In the grip of his thwarted desire for this older woman, the young physician goes so far as to contemplate suicide. Yet out of this powerful experience of impossible love—facilitated by an encounter with itinerant Israelis searching for spiritual nourishment in India—the young Dr. Rubin begins to heal from psychological illnesses he did not even know he harbored. This experience cures him of his former single-minded devotion to professional goals, it cures him of an oedipal complex he had never acknowledged, and it awakens him from the social and spiritual stupor that had permeated his life. Yehoshua has often declared that gaining a stronger grip on life does not justify flirting with perdition.[16] Yet, time and again, his novels explore this dynamic from both positive and negative angles.

Why do Yehoshua's characters leave Israel? Why do they stay away or return? Do they fulfill the original goals of their journeys? To give an overview of the ways in which Yehoshua weaves the itineraries of his novels with the psychological profiles of his characters and Israel's current national concerns, I will focus on three characters from three novels—Michaela

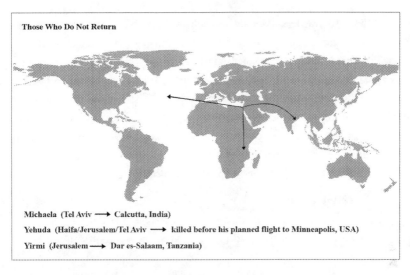

MAP 2. Those who do not return.

(from *Open Heart*), Yehuda (from *A Late Divorce*), and Yirmi (from *Friendly Fire*)—whose enervated attitudes toward the project of national reconstruction are mirrored in their weakened family units as a microcosmic social warning. This engages as well with key references to the historiosophic identity of the people of Israel though myths and symbols that have shaped them since ancient times.

Michaela—a lover of Hindu culture to whom Dr. Benjy Rubin gets callously married in his bid to conceal his love for the wife of his hospital director—does *not* get sick in India. On the contrary, she thrives in this environment, freed from the social expectations of both her distant homeland and her hosting nation. Michaela is a seasoned traveler who had begun visiting India in her early twenties like so many young Israelis who marvel at its vast landscape and exotic culture. However, unlike most Israelis who spend a few months hiking in the Himalayas before starting college, Michaela has no vocational direction at home, while in India she exerts herself on behalf of other travelers, even helping to nurse local inhabitants too. Benjy's mother concludes that Michaela's attraction to India and Hinduism had been "reinforced by the simple human experience of working with the sidewalk doctors of Calcutta, which gave her a feeling of worth and led the Indians to regard her as almost a doctor herself, even though she had never graduated from high school."[17]

24   THE RETROSPECTIVE IMAGINATION OF A. B. YEHOSHUA

Michaela is portrayed empathetically in the novel, so that her reluctance to create a stable role for herself in Israel exposes the wider challenge of offering secular Israelis the spiritual nourishment they may seek in foreign experiences, in this case through India and Hinduism. At the end it still remains unclear whether Michaela's sense of responsibility toward her infant daughter would supersede her attachment to India. By contrast, her mother-in-law returns from a furtive trip to Calcutta—having completed the round trip in only seventy-seven hours—to retrieve little Shiva, who had contracted a mild illness there. As Benji relates:

> mother left on Tuesday morning and returned Friday evening. . . . As dusk began to fall I was already racing to Jerusalem. . . . The lights were on in all the rooms, and I quickly saw that there were new lines on my mother's exhausted face, but also a new radiance. Shivi, whom my mother now insisted on calling Shiva like Michaela's Indian friends, was really in pretty bad shape, though not at all critical. She was thinner and browner, and in her little yellow sari, with the third eye (which my mother had not wiped off during the entire journey home) shining between her eyes, she reminded me for a moment of the Indian children who had run after me when I went down to the Ganges. In our time apart, she had learned to walk and . . . she began tottering toward me. . . . All this time I had thought of her as being a part of Michaela, and I hadn't realized how much she was also a part of me.[18]

Indeed, *this* return from India—as emphasized in the novel's Hebrew title, *Hashivah mehodu*—reinvigorates Benjy's commitment to his family and nation under the sign of a central marker of Jewish time: "Friday evening . . . as dusk began to fall . . . racing to Jerusalem . . . the lights were on in all the rooms, and I quickly saw that there were new lines on my mother's exhausted face, but also a new radiance." Yehoshua, a staunch atheist, keeps insisting as we shall see, on the need for a thoughtful reengagement with traditional markers of Jewish identity such as holidays. He therefore closes *Open Heart* with a homecoming gesture that takes place under the sign of Jewish time—the onset of Shabbat—during a dramatic ascent to Jerusalem where Benjy's parents reside, and even the language describing the heroic mother "with a new radiance" recalls the traditional welcoming of Shabbat. The extent to which any of this may constitute a rehabilitation of Benjy's family is left up to the reader's consideration as the novel closes.

Earlier on, Michaela and Benjy debate what name to give their child, a debate that foregrounds the challenges of configuring a modern Jewish identity that is attuned both to its own heritage and to other cultures. Michaela insists on naming the baby Shiva. Her husband agrees, but on condition that, in Hebrew, the name be spelled with a *bet* rather than a *vav* (שיבה rather than שיוה): in Jewish liturgy, Shiva with a *bet* denotes return and atonement, while Shiva with a *vav* refers to the Hindu deity Shiva (whose statue Michaela venerates). But, "Shiva with a *vav*," she argues, "is also connected to the word *shivayon*, equality, or even . . . to something religious like *Shiviti elohim l'negdi*, 'I have set God before me' . . . but never mind, let it be with a *bet* in the meantime, and when she learns to read and write she can decide for herself how to spell her name."[19]

Playing such games with the itineraries and names of his characters, Yehoshua explores similar challenges to Jewish identity and cohesion. For example, Yehuda from *A Late Divorce* (1982) and Yirmi from *Friendly Fire* (2007) struggle, like Michaela, to escape from the demands of their families and nation. Regarding Yehuda, we must remember that already since ancient times, the term *yehudi* (a Jew) ceased to refer to just the members of the largest Israelite tribe (the tribe of *yehudah*, Judah); from the time of the first exile to Babylonia following the destruction of the First Temple, the name gradually adhered to all the House of Israel—that is, to all the Israelite tribes.[20] By attributing to Yehuda Kaminka from *A Late Divorce* a propensity to leave Israel, Yehoshua thus ironizes this unclear relationship between the seminal identity of *am Israel* (the people of Israel) and its long exilic history as a Jewish people.

In *Friendly Fire*, similar onomastic references to the fire-and-brimstone prophet Jeremiah (Yirmiyahu), through his namesake Yirmi in the novel, remind us of this prophet's exhortations to adhere to the Sinaitic covenant or suffer the destruction, which according to the biblical heritage, did indeed materialize during that prophet's lifetime. But while the biblical Yirmiyahu lamented the fall of the First Temple and refused to join the exiles to Babylonia, Yehoshua's Yirmi announces that he wants nothing more to do with Israel or its covenants in any iteration, and promptly leaves Israel. After the loss of his wife and son—the latter from a "friendly fire" incident during an incursion into the West Bank—Yirmi decides to take "a rest" from Jewish identity; to release himself "from the whole messy stew, Jewish and Israeli," by altogether moving to Tanzania, and supporting himself there as an assistant to a team of African anthropologists.[21] As he explains to his shocked sister-in-law when she visits him:

> Here there are no ancient graves and no floor tiles from a destroyed synagogue; no museum with a fragment of a burnt Torah; no testimonies about pogroms and the Holocaust. There's no exile here, no Diaspora. There was no Golden Age here, no community that contributed to global culture. They don't fuss about assimilation or extinction, self-hatred or pride, uniqueness or chosenness; no old grandmas pop up suddenly aware of their identity. There's no orthodoxy here or secularism or self-indulgent religiosity, and most of all no nostalgia for anything at all. There's no struggle between tradition and revolution. No rebellion against the forefathers and no new interpretations. No one feels compelled to decide if he is a Jew or an Israeli or maybe a Canaanite, or if the state is more democratic or more Jewish, if there's hope for it or if it's done for. The people around me are free and clear of that whole exhausting and confusing tangle. But life goes on. I am seventy years old, Daniela, and I am permitted to let go.[22]

I quote this passage at length because it summarizes so well the "whole messy stew" of Jewish history and Israeli identity that so infuriates Yirmi after the loss of his wife and son. However, much of what he alleges as absent in Africa—"they don't fuss about assimilation or extinction, self-hatred or pride . . . there's no struggle between tradition and revolution. No rebellion against the forefathers"—applies only to his subjective perception of this illusory safe haven. In Africa, he devises for himself a state of temporary freedom—an escape from the pressures to which the Africans themselves are of course far from impervious. After visiting Yirmi in his Tanzanian hideout, his sister-in-law concludes that it is indeed preferable that he should stay far away from her family, for the resentment he had accumulated against them and Israel could poison it; for his sake, too, she concludes that it would be healthier for him to stay in Africa and perhaps establish a liaison with the sensitive Sudanese nurse who seems interested in him.

Like Yirmi, Yehuda Kaminka (from *A Late Divorce*) leaves Israel in the wake of a family catastrophe: his schizophrenic wife had lunged at him with a kitchen knife and was institutionalized. Just as Yirmi's sister-in-law blames him for not shielding her sister from the pain of losing their son, Yehuda's sons accuse him of driving their mother to insanity and provoking the family's dissolution. Surely Yehuda Kaminka is among Yehoshua's least likable figures; he exacerbates the pecuniary difficulties of his married children and causes great sorrow to the women who love him. After his wife's institutionalization he moves to America, where he meets a middle-aged Midwesterner who becomes pregnant by him, and only then he returns to Israel for a brief visit—not out of concern for his children or grandchildren, but rather to enlist their help in obtaining his divorce from their mother.

"Homeland can you be a homeland"—with no accompanying question mark—and "I'm leaving for America soon" are the refrains that churn around in Yehuda's mind during his week in Israel.[23] But he never manages to board that flight back to America. Having signed away his share of the family's apartment to gain his freedom, he attempts to sneak back into his ex-wife's insane asylum with the intention of stealing back the house deed that he had granted her in exchange for the divorce. He then slips into one of her dresses to scurry away through a hole in the fence, but an anxious inmate, feeling threatened by the ambiguity of this wo/man before him, pitchforks him to death[24]—a very grim end for the *yored* (emigrant from Israel) in this novel.

"Emigration has no place in the conceptual space of Zionism," notes Rina Cohen Muller in her analysis of *A Late Divorce*.[25] Yet as Gilead Morahg further clarifies, Yehoshua's attitude toward emigrants has softened in subsequent works.[26] While Yehuda Kaminka's ambivalence toward the homeland ends so violently, in later novels Yehoshua allows Yirmi, for example, to organize for himself a comfortable retirement in Africa, and Michaela thrives on the sidewalks of Calcutta. Still, their outlying situation refocuses the responsibilities of their family members, who visit them and elect by contrast to strengthen their own commitments to family and nation.

BOUNDARIES OF SEPARATION AND INTERACTION

"Traveling," as Yehoshua told Vered Shemtov in an interview, "is one expression of the desire to cross boundaries." To David Herman he added that traveling provides a sense of perspective: "different place . . . different

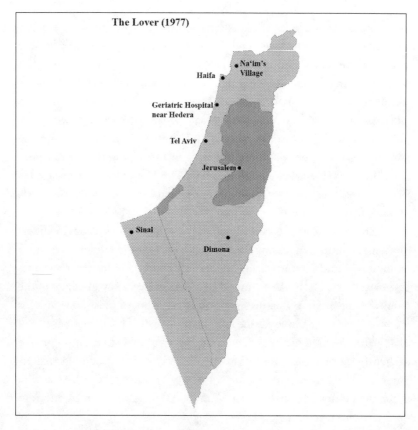

MAP 3. Israel in *The Lover*.

angle."[27] Yehoshua's main method for providing a historical and cultural sense of perspective is precisely through interactions between individuals from diverse national, religious, and ethnic groups, who meet each other within Israel or beyond its borders.

The plot of Yehoshua's first novel, *The Lover* (*Hame'ahev*, 1977), is set in motion when Gabriel Arditi returns to Israel after a long sojourn in France. He returns merely to collect an inheritance from his grandmother, who is lying in a coma in a geriatric hospital near Hedera and staying alive longer than had been expected. While waiting, however, Gabriel has an affair with Asya, before being suddenly whisked away into a battle with Egypt when the Yom Kippur War of 1973 breaks out. *The Lover*'s itinerary provides a fairly typical snapshot of the locations through which Yehoshua's protagonists move within Israel and across its immediate borders. From Haifa, where his grandmother's apartment is located, Gabriel is taken to the Sinai battlefields; from there, he escapes to Jerusalem to hide under the protection of an ultraorthodox sect, until Asya and her husband find him, and return him to their apartment in Haifa.

In search of the elusive lover, Adam, Asya's husband, a mechanic by profession, crisscrosses the country in his tow truck, scanning the highways all night, and making inquiries from Tel Aviv to Dimona. Absurdly and tragicomically, this cuckolded husband does not pursue his wife's lover in order to get rid of him; he wishes, rather, to return him to Asya—the geographic entity on whose edge Israel is located—so that what appears tragicomic on the level of genre and family dynamics becomes pathetic on the level of national history. However, aside from Gabriel, there is another important lover in this novel, the Muslim youth Naʿim, who arrives from his village in the Galilee to work in Adam's garage. Naʿim joins Adam's absurd search for Asya's lover, and in the process, he becomes the lover of Adam's teenage daughter. The novel ends after they make love for the first time.

If we now glance at the Israeli itinerary of one of Yehoshua's later novels, *The Retrospective*—which includes two voyages to Spain marked on the global map above[28]—we again see a broad movement across different sectors of Israel's geography, and toward its borders. *The Retrospective*'s principal character is a film director, Yair Moses, whose name literally means "may Moses illuminate"—but this is a rather tall order for an aging man who lives alone in a Tel Aviv skyscraper, and from where he travels to Spain, Jerusalem, and various locations in and around Israel connected with the production of his earliest films. Yair Moses takes several trips to the south of the country: to Beersheba to meet his former producer, and to a *moshav* near the border with Gaza, where he seeks a reconciliation with his former screenwriter, a creative, but bitter, Sephardic man who had inspired the Ashkenazi Moses to become a movie director but then quarreled with him. Moses decides also to revisit the location of their earliest films, which had been produced together with the actress Ruth and the cinematographer Toledano in the Negev Desert and the Judean Hills.

Every outing here sets the stage for an ethnographic survey of Israeli society, which Moses compares to the 1960s, when his crew had produced their initial films. As is quite typical for Yehoshua, the common prototypes of Sephardic and Ashkenazi Jews, religious and secular, rich and poor, Jews and Arabs, old-timers and newcomers, are all delicately scrambled to reveal

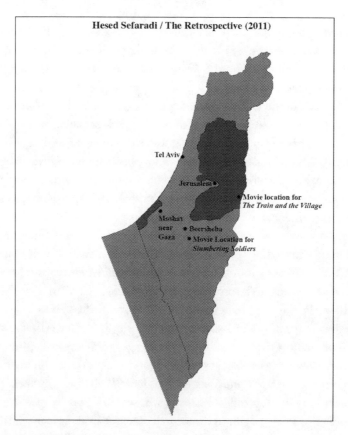

MAP 4. Israel in *Hesed Sefaradi / The Retrospective*.

alternative definitions and modes of interaction.[29] The two trips that Moses makes to Jerusalem open up a window into his childhood and youth, in what was then a divided city, when the eastern sector was in Jordanian hands and barbed wire ran near his home. Coinciding with Yehoshua's own adolescent experiences in Jerusalem of the 1950s,[30] this historical background invites the reader's reevaluation of the state of the nation in the twenty-first century, compared with its foundational years.

Aside from Moses's two international trips to Spain—where he befriends Catholic clergy, meets veiled Muslim immigrants, and participates in a surrealistic meeting with a resurrected Don Quixote—the most picturesque sites that Moses visits are the Israeli and Palestinian locations connected with his early films. He drives down to the Negev in search of the crater where his crew had filmed *Slumbering Soldiers*—a rewrite of

Yehoshua's own early story "The Last Commander," which is now endowed with a disconcerting new twist at the end. When Moses reaches his spot in the desert, he is shocked to find a military installation, out of which he is guided by a Bedouin woman, veiled from head to toe, who helps him navigate through the dunes that surround them.[31] The actress Ruth later accompanies Moses to the Judean Hills, where they had shot their most dramatic film, *The Train and the Village*—an allusion to Yehoshua's own early story "Yatir Evening Express." At this location, which used to mark the border between Jordan and Israel, they are surprised to find a new fence now marking the boundary between Israel and the Palestinian Authority.

A Palestinian border controller lets them hike over to the spot where they once filmed the Judean Hills using long-range cameras, for at that time this area was in Jordanian hands and not otherwise accessible. The encounter with the Palestinian at the border facilitates a friendly interchange that quickly escalates into remonstrations, though ironically not as harsh as those that Moses absorbs from the actress Ruth and his estranged scriptwriter, Trigano. The dialogue between Moses and the Palestinian clarifies their mutual expectations: when the latter suggests that his village is entitled to profits from Moses's old movie, the cinematographer retorts that "the movie did well with the critics, but at the box office we had only losses . . . and if we're opening accounts, we can also sue you for losses you dealt us a hundred years ago."[32] All of Moses's trips set the stage for similar meetings between representatives of different ethnicities, nationalities, and religions. These encounters clarify their mutual identities and terms of interaction, a process that facilitates potentially creative contacts often marked by actual border crossings.[33]

During the commemorations of Israel's fiftieth anniversary in 1998— when there was still hope in the Oslo Accords—Yehoshua emphasized the importance of defining Israel's borders in relation to the aspirations of both Palestinians and Israel's nationalist religious parties. Invited to name the attributes of his own generation of Israelis, he mentioned their internalization of the historical transition between a mythical Land of Israel (*Eretz Israel*) and the concreteness of belonging to a State of Israel (*Medinat Israel*).

> This . . . provided us with a clear consciousness of boundaries, and . . . the security that comes with knowing borders. If I had to define Zionism in a single word I would say: *boundaries*.[34] We were the

generation, the only generation, I would almost say, in the two-thousand-year history of Israel till then, which possessed a clear consciousness of the physical boundaries of our country. It was we who understood what existed within the area of its authority and responsibility and what not. . . . The cornerstone in the foundation of *Yisraeliuth* . . . remains this consciousness of boundaries, which crystallized in particular between 1956 and 1967.[35]

During yet another speech that he addressed that year to Israeli historians, Yehoshua added that "the Zionist movement encompassed and still contains many different and opposed ideological positions . . . [yet] it does not delineate a position toward any subject in the world except one thing: the establishment of a Jewish State in the land of Israel—it does not even adopt a specific position regarding territory or the borders of that state."[36] Seven years later, he would go as far as to argue that anti-Semitism is a neurosis triggered by the fuzziness of Jewish identity, including its unclear geographic parameters.[37] This preoccupation with the clarification of boundaries—both geographic and in terms of social responsibilities—plays a key role in Yehoshua's literary imagination. As we have seen, Yehuda Kaminka's foray into his wife's insane asylum to steal the house deed—a breach of several boundaries, including an attempt to pass off as a woman when he slips on her dress—triggers the hysteria of one of the inmates and results in Yehuda's death. But stronger references to national borders became a more explicit theme in Yehoshua's public statements at the turn of the millennium in response to the collapsing negotiations between Israel and the Palestinians. In his fiction, this theme reached its most creative format in *The Liberated Bride* (2001), as we shall see below.[38]

It is important to underscore, however, that Yehoshua's preoccupation with borders does not stem from a desire for insularity. On the contrary, "the fact that a state has borders does not mean it has no contact with its environment, that its borders have no crossings or gateways," he explained to Marshall Berman during their heated interchange.[39] Indeed, as Risa Domb puts it, Yehoshua's borders may be "fixed, but one can cross them."[40] We saw already how the border crossing in *The Retrospective* facilitates an Israeli-Palestinian conversation that potentially enables a mutually validating interaction. These are the permeable borders to which Yehoshua aspired at that time.

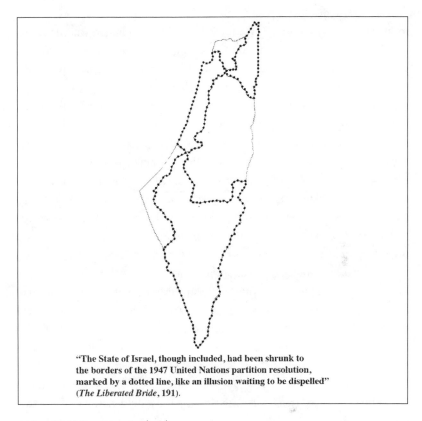

"The State of Israel, though included, had been shrunk to the borders of the 1947 United Nations partition resolution, marked by a dotted line, like an illusion waiting to be dispelled" (*The Liberated Bride*, 191).

MAP 5. The U.N. partition plan (1947).

On the other hand, a bleak portrayal of the threat posed by instable national borders can be found in *The Liberated Bride*, which he began to compose in 1998 during the Oslo process but completed in the midst of the suicide bombings that marked the Second Intifada. Several scholars have noted that this novel explores the consequences of an unclear attitude toward moral and political boundaries,[41] a theme that Yehoshua projects here through all its interrelated representations of individual psychology, family microcosm, national history, and his critique of the mythical longing for a lost Eden.

A map of the 1947 United Nations resolution recommending the partition of Palestine plays an interesting role in *The Liberated Bride* when the historian Yochanan Rivlin, the novel's protagonist, visits the home of one of his Arab-Israeli students and notices on her cousin's desk a map that marks the Jewish sections "by a dotted line, like an illusion waiting to be dispelled."[42] The owner of this map, however, is a Muslim citizen of Israel, a young man who exerts himself indefatigably on behalf of his family and its acquaintances, including Professor Rivlin himself; by assigning to this earnest young man a document that places Israel in such a precarious position, Yehoshua thus encapsulates not only the existential threat to Israel but also the plight of its Arab citizens who are caught between conflicting allegiances. Rashid, the owner of this map, is an amiable young man for whom Rivlin and the reader can feel nothing but sympathy, but to satisfy his grandmother he attempts to smuggle his sister and nephews into Israel from the West Bank, and the outcome is a terrible disaster. At the turn of the twenty-first century, as soon as he completed this novel, Yehoshua took to the public stage to urge a clarification of the borders of each of these entities.[43]

The most dramatic representation of national borders in Yehoshua's oeuvre can be found in *Mr. Mani*, a masterpiece that spans more than two hundred years of Jewish history presented through five conversations, each of them set in a different locale and period. At the heart of this novel we find a "map scene" that encapsulates Yehoshua's attitude about the consolidation and definition of a modern Jewish national identity. The scene takes place in 1917 on the outskirts of Jerusalem, right after Yosef Mani learns that Lord Balfour had declared that the British government would view with favor the establishment of a Jewish homeland in Palestine. As a native Jerusalemite with a sharpened political awareness, Yosef Mani surmises that the real intention of the British is to wield control of the region after defeating the Ottoman Empire; he therefore disguises himself as an Arab shepherd, goats and all. In exchange for divulging military secrets to Turkish and German soldiers fighting against the British, he obtains access to local Arab villagers, upon whom he urges a national awakening.

"Get ye an identity," he shouts at them in the middle of the night from an improvised podium, "Awake! . . . before it is too late! All over the world people now have identities, and we Jews are on our way, and you had better have an identity or else!" At this point, Mr. Mani shows them a map of what would soon be the British Mandate for Palestine, cutting it lengthwise with his scissors to indicate that half should be for Arabs and half for Jews. He hands them "the half with the mountains and the Jordan" and keeps "the sea and the coast," but "it rather distressed them to see it snipped up like

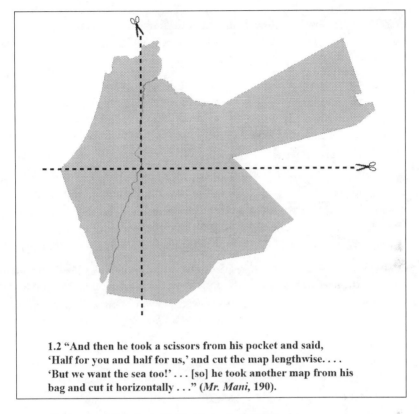

1.2 "And then he took a scissors from his pocket and said, 'Half for you and half for us,' and cut the map lengthwise.... 'But we want the sea too!'... [so] he took another map from his bag and cut it horizontally..." (*Mr. Mani*, 190).

MAP 6. Debating Israel/Palestine in *Mr. Mani* during the British Mandate era.

that, and they pressed forward.... 'But we want the sea too!' At first that stunned him, made him lose his temper; then, irately, he took another map from his bag and cut it horizontally."[44]

This scene sums up Yehoshua's appeal for a clarification of national borders as a precondition for defining national identities and responsibilities. The exact borders are not important to him. Rather, what concerns him is this: If Israel's borders are unclear, where do Israelis cross the line between home and abroad, and for which inhabitants can Israel be held responsible as a modern state? To what extent does the idea of Israel as a Holy Land continue to be relevant from an international and ethnographic perspective? And what role does Jerusalem play in this dynamic of interaction and separation, which we traced so far on the national and international scope

36 THE RETROSPECTIVE IMAGINATION OF A. B. YEHOSHUA

of Yehoshua's novels? We will now turn to Yehoshua's representation of Jerusalem both as a mythical concept and as a setting for daily life, especially in *Mr. Mani* but also in other novels.

TERRESTRIAL JERUSALEM

"Jerusalem is becoming impossible, impossible!" Yehoshua told Bernard Horn in the early nineties. "People complain all the time about my leaving Jerusalem. . . . And I am so happy that I do not live there . . . this city, the place from which the destruction of Israel could come."[45] Despite this negative personal attitude toward the city of his birth, Yehoshua's *literary* attitude toward Israel's capital, a holy city to the citizens of many nations around the world, is nuanced and complex. Jerusalem threatens and also fascinates him in part because it is impossible to trace a clear boundary between the myths that surround it and the political exigencies of any given moment. Yehoshua does not deny the symbolic and political importance of Jerusalem, but he responds to its power by disentangling the city's historical, ethnographic, and mythic components in order to minimize their potentially chaotic combinations.

Especially in *Mr. Mani*, Jerusalem figures as a powerful magnet that pulls all the characters toward it but rarely retains them. According to Y. Cohen, the city develops in this novel as a "heroine" capable of adapting herself to the demands of each new generation, as if she were the main protagonist of a bildungsroman spanning more than two hundred years.[46] Most of Yehoshua's novels gravitate toward Jerusalem in one way or another;[47] but in his chef d'oeuvre, *Mr. Mani*, this city becomes a site of intense interaction between all the different ethnicities, religions, and nationalities portrayed in the novel.

So far, we have been following the portrayal of these interactions through the national and international itineraries of Yehoshua's novels. Here, three maps of Jerusalem highlight this multicultural interaction across three of the five historical periods encompassed by *Mr. Mani*: the walled mid-nineteenth-century city that Avraham Mani visits in 1848, when he arrives to investigate his son's marriage to a local Jewess (map 7); Yosef Mani's Jerusalem as described in 1918 by Lieutenant Horowitz to Colonel Woodhouse of the conquering British Army (map 8); and finally, *Mr. Mani*'s contemporary Jerusalem, visited by the kibbutznik Hagar Shiloh in 1982

MAPPING A. B. YEHOSHUA'S WORLDVIEW   37

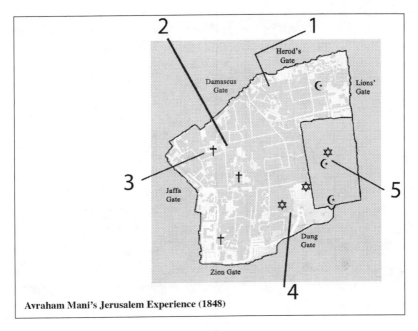

MAP 7. Avraham Mani's Jerusalem in *Mr. Mani*.

(map 9). I did not map two other periods dramatized in this extraordinary historical novel: the Holocaust, which Yehoshua sets in Nazi-occupied Crete, and Dr. Moshe Mani's Jerusalem at the *end* of the nineteenth century, because it is almost identical to the layout that Lieutenant Horowitz encounters two decades later. Much more significant changes occurred between the three periods drawn below.

Avraham Mani's Jerusalem in the middle of the nineteenth century is an enclosed space with its boundaries clearly marked off by the rampart walls that surround what today we call the Old City, which at that time constituted the entire town. Within the circumference of this wall, various ethnic, religious, and national groups lived in juxtaposition to each other, amidst a tenuous *convivencia* that occasionally erupted in violence toward the weaker parties. Although the physical boundaries of the city were clear enough, the historical claims of Jews and Christians were muted. Yet even here, as across his oeuvre, the "rich and creative pluralism" that Yehoshua defines as an optimal form of national normalcy is envisioned as a means of *balancing and stabilizing* a sovereign Israeli identity that does not erase any of the historical heritages of its constitutive subcultures or condone

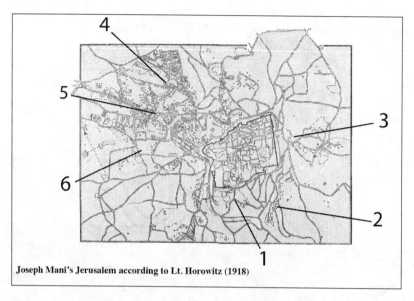

MAP 8. Yosef Mani's Jerusalem according to Lieutenant Horowitz in *Mr. Mani*.

any of their mythical yearnings for a religious or ethnic supremacy. Rather, Yehoshua's vision of social creativity celebrates a dynamic *interface* between mutually validating identities, capable of adjusting together to every new historical challenge.

I will first introduce our three mappings of Jerusalem, and then we can return to contextualize the itineraries of Yehoshua's characters within *Mr. Mani*'s multicultural dynamics.

In 1918, the Jerusalem that Lieutenant Horowitz describes to Colonel Woodhouse in the aftermath of the British conquest of Palestine from the Turks had long expanded beyond the rampart walls as a result of increased Ottoman permits for real estate investments by Jews and Christians throughout the second half of the nineteenth century. One can still easily spot the parallelogram delineating the Old City, along with considerable northwestern expansion beyond the Old City walls (map 8).

By the end of that century, the city that Hagar visits in 1982 had become a sprawling urban center with Muslim neighborhoods mainly to the east, Jewish neighborhoods to the west, and a Christian minority then residing mainly in the Old City itself (map 9). This is a city of many days and many denominations.[48] Yehoshua's fiction celebrates this ethnographic diversity,

MAPPING A. B. YEHOSHUA'S WORLDVIEW 39

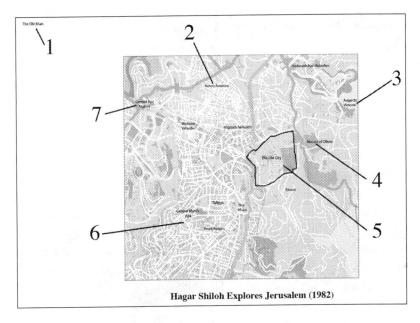

MAP 9. Hagar Shiloh explores Jerusalem in *Mr. Mani*.

while at the same time criticizing a self-serving multiculturalism that works against the consolidation of a common Israeli identity.[49]

So, how do the contacts that Hagar Shiloh establishes with different types of Jerusalemites in 1982 convey Yehoshua's vision for a pragmatic stabilization of Israeli identity? Let us look more closely into "her" Jerusalem, starting at the northwestern corner of the city's outskirts by the ruins of the old Khan, which had once been a roadside inn (#1 on map 9), where she fantasizes about "all the travelers who must have stopped there on their way from Jaffa to Jerusalem."[50]

Like most travelers who come up to this city, Hagar too winds her way up from the Mediterranean coast to the ancient city on the Judean mountains. Hagar has come to visit her boyfriend's father—a middle-aged Sephardic judge whose ancestral relationship to Jerusalem fascinates her. He lives in an apartment in the southwestern part of town (#6 on map 9), but farther north he owns a building that he inherited from his great-grandfather, "a famous gynecologist who ran a maternity clinic ninety years ago, in which all the women of Jerusalem, Jews and Arabs, came to give birth" (35). Located in Kerem Avraham (#2 on map 9), this clinic had been described by

Lieutenant Horowitz in 1918 as "a small lying-in hospital," run by Dr. Moshe Mani with the aid of a "tough old Swedish woman . . . who had come to the Holy Land on a pilgrimage and . . . had taken up free thought and midwifery" (166). In its heyday at the end of the nineteenth century, it is also described by a young Polish visitor, Dr. Efrayim Shapiro, as "an open . . . multiethnic, syncretistic, ecumenical clinic, which it has to be in order to survive" (256).

"Ecumenical" is the key word here. The original Hebrew translates more literally as "multiracial, nonreligious, and multicultural"—but in Hillel Halkin's translation the term aptly highlights Yehoshua's endorsement of a syncretic pluralism attuned to a broader common good (247).[51] Tragically, Moshe Mani's clinic does not survive, first because he cannot raise enough funds to keep it going, and second because he falls in love with a young Polish Jewess, Linka Shapiro, and commits suicide when she abandons him. This combination of misfortunes stresses the precariousness of even this ecumenical and pragmatic brand of Zionism in the initial years of the Zionist Congress. Yet although Dr. Mani's enterprise collapses, he leaves two descendants, along with his vision of an ecumenical Zionism. As Hagar further learns, three of Gabriel Mani's ancestors lie buried on the Mount of Olives on the eastern side of the city, where Hagar accompanies her boyfriend's father to pray at the graveside of his recently deceased mother (this cemetery on the Mount of Olives figures in #4 on map 9, #3 on map 8, and just outside the eastern walls on map 7).

In her exploration of this city, Hagar appeals to Arabs as well as Jews. When she fancies that she is suffering a miscarriage, she stresses a human and vocational claim to the Arab staff of Augusta Victoria, a hospital in East Jerusalem (#3 on map 9): "If I had landed in their hospital," Hagar insists, "the least they could do was examine me and see what was wrong" (60). In the evening, the nurse who had initially tried to send her away is eager to offer her a ride back to the Western part of Jerusalem: "down . . . from the opposite direction . . . through . . . Arab neighborhoods and villages inside the city" (62–63). But thanks to this closer interaction with local Arabs, Hagar feels that "this day had made a real Jerusalemite out of me, an old-time Sephardi with a touch of Arab" (64).

The next morning, her boyfriend's father, a "stocky, pleasant, Mediterranean-type man," whose relatives seem to come "straight out of some Greek or Italian movie" (19), takes her to visit the *kotel* (the Western Wall) and the *shuk* in the Old City (#5). Hagar becomes so obsessively attached to Gabriel Mani, and to Jerusalem through him, that she returns to his apartment uninvited three nights in a row. This apartment, she notes, is located near a street with a name that "only a Jerusalemite could live in ... no Tel-Avivian could stand for it" (21)—Emek Refaim, Ghost Valley (#6 on map 9). Yet, at the end of her Jerusalemite experience, Hagar does not return directly to Tel Aviv, where she has been living and studying. At Jerusalem's Central Bus Station (#7 on map 9) she hops instead onto a bus to visit her mother in their family's kibbutz near Beersheba in the Negev Desert. This southern area of the country, for which Ben Gurion had the highest hopes for new Israeli developments, is where Hagar tells her mother about Gabriel Mani's Jerusalem and her now expanded appreciation of the multicultural life of her country.[52]

But what can be the connection between Gabriel Mani's sprawling multiethnic, yet still compartmentalized, Jerusalem in 1982 (Hagar's Jerusalem) and Avraham Mani's underdeveloped and walled-up city in 1848? Avraham Mani's sojourn with his daughter-in-law, Tamara, in the middle of the nineteenth century takes place under Ottoman rule, when Muslims, Jews, and Christians of various denominations—Armenian, Greek Orthodox, Roman Catholic, Anglican—interacted with each other mostly for commercial and administrative purposes within the four cramped quarters of the walled space. Avraham Mani finds it to be "a city in which all places are connected," and even if there really isn't "a way around *every* obstacle," one could in principle avoid the crowded alleys "by going from house to house without once stopping out into the street" (340, my emphasis).

Avraham Mani comes to Jerusalem from Salonika in 1848, a year known to historians as the Spring of Nations. Yehoshua's hint in choosing this year is that when Europeans were busy staking modern national spaces, Jews around the world were invested in promoting their partial assimilation and emancipation among those nations, rather than reclaiming their own indigenous national life. Avraham comes to Jerusalem "to shore up a marriage" that he thought "needed consolidation" because he soon realizes that the union between his son Yosef and a local Sephardic beauty, Tamara Valero, had not yet been consummated, either because of Yosef's sexual immaturity or because of his political fantasies, or a combination of both. Uninterested in Tamara, Yosef cares only about convincing local Muslims that they formerly were Jews converted to Islam; he therefore expects them to convert back to Judaism. His father, horrified, cares only about the propagation of his seed. To this end, he rents "half a stand from an Ishmaelite

42   THE RETROSPECTIVE IMAGINATION OF A. B. YEHOSHUA

in the Souk-El-Kattanim" (#1 on map 7). Displaying on it the spices he had brought from Salonika, "from time to time I took [the young wife] with me to my spice-and-sundry stand" (329, 334).

As Avraham later informs his rabbi, Jerusalem under a weakened Ottoman rule had suddenly become a city that Christian ladies could visit while being "royally put up" at the British consul's home (#2 in map 7). As a protégé of this consul, and the one who guides these British ladies through "the churches of Bethlehem . . . the mosques of Hebron," and the tomb of King David's rebellious son, Absalom," Avraham Mani's own rebellious son also likes "putting everything into perspective, and then passionately, by the end of the day, scrambling it all up again," much to the consul's delight (329). This is a Jerusalem to which Russian pilgrims come "crawling on their knees," filling up "the square of the Church of the Holy Sepulcher and the streets all around" (343; #3 on map 7).[53] It is also a Jerusalem where, according to Yehoshua's wild imagination, Yosef completes a minyan for his father's prayers by rounding up eight Muslims and insisting that they are Jews who "just don't know it yet. . . . From time to time he went down on his knees and bowed like a Muslim so the Ishmaelites would understand" (321–22).

Yosef's father, however, wants nothing to do with this conversionist enterprise, inspired by the British consul's own schemes through the British Society for the Conversion of the Jews. Avraham prefers to stick to his own kind by praying for the continuation of his seed among "the worshipers in the Stambouli Synagogue" (#4 on map 7), who "let me read from the Torah every Monday and Thursday . . . [until] I was becoming a true Jerusalemite, rushing up and down the narrow streets for no good reason, unless it were that God was about to speak somewhere and I was afraid to miss it" (329).

Finally, this is an environment where the errant bridegroom makes his way to "the great mosque on the Haram-el-Sharif"—the golden-domed mosque built on the site of the ancient Temple Mount (#5 on map 7). "And there, on the steps leading up to the Dome of the Rock, he had his throat slit . . . butchered like a black sheep" (318).[54] Later on, Avraham discloses to his mentor, Rabbi Haddaya, that he had in some unclear manner assisted in this murder of his son, whose wife he then impregnates and abandons, for "what was I to do . . . I was down to my last centavo, and all out of the spices I had brought from Salonika, and had I [remained in] Jerusalem as a pauper, I would have had to join the roster of Ashkenazim to qualify for [their] dole . . . would His Grace have wanted me to Ashkenazify myself?" (314).

Ethnic and religious separation with limited interaction is the desired way of life for this Mani, this Avraham who differs widely from his creator, for whom interaction is the substance of life. For Yehoshua, on the other hand, multicultural interaction serves, first, as a means of clarifying distinct identities, and commutatively, from a position of clear identities, as a way of facilitating creative and mutually validating relationships between members of different religious, ethnic, and national communities. This intercultural dynamic informs Yehoshua's worldview, not only through his representation of Jerusalem across the ages but also on the global and national itineraries of his novels, as I have shown in the opening sections of this chapter.

Jerusalem's geographic and ethnographic borders were quite clear in 1848—a cramped walled-up town where no Jew dared to spend the night outside the gates, and where contacts between the members of different religions and ethnicities—even among Sephardim and Ashkenazim—were primarily commercial exchanges. Sixty years later, the boundaries of the town that Lieutenant Horowitz encounters in 1918 are already fuzzier, both geographically and ethnographically. During those seven decades, Jerusalem changed dramatically (see map 8): it expanded beyond the Old City walls, and by the middle of the nineteenth century the majority of its population was Jewish. Nevertheless, the ecumenical program to which Dr. Moshe Mani's birthing clinic had aspired at the end of the nineteenth century hardly fares better in Yehoshua's novel than the exclusivist or conversionist enterprises of Dr. Mani's ancestors or the push for independence advocated by Dr. Mani's son in the aftermath of World War I.

According to information that Lieutenant Horowitz provides to Colonel Woodhouse in 1918 on the eve of Yosef Mani's trial for treason against the British forces, the first independent decision that this defendant—whom we can call Yosef ben Moshe to distinguish him from Yosef ben Avraham— took as a young orphan after his father's death was to "study languages . . . roaming the streets of Jerusalem until he found the Scottish Mission . . . and its School of Bible, a very Christian Institution" (#1 on map 8), where he wished to learn English rather than religion; afternoons "found him in the nearby village of Silwan, where a chum of his father's, an old Arab sheikh, agreed to chat with him in Arabic" (#2 on map 8); and in the evenings "he sometimes frequented an Algerian family to help mind the children and pick up a bit of French" (they would more likely have lived in the Jewish quarter of the Old City than in the northwestern part of town) (170). On the map,

44   THE RETROSPECTIVE IMAGINATION OF A. B. YEHOSHUA

the Scottish Mission and the Arab village of Silwan, located south from the Old City, appear to be far from Yosef Mani's home in Kerem Avraham at the northwestern part of town (#4 on map 8), but it is a walkable distance of about forty minutes for a vigorous boy.

When his bar mitzvah approached, the orphaned boy "betook himself to one of your little Jerusalem sects"—Hasidim living in the Mea Shearim neighborhood (#5 on map 8)—"one of those black-coated, fur-hatted, curly-eared lots," who "taught him the proper chant notes, and even saw to the refreshments.... [But] it's not as if he belonged to them or could have, even if he wished to: first, because he's a Sephardi; second, because he's a freethinker; and third, because he's a Zionist" (171). The members of this ultraorthodox Ashkenazi sect nevertheless feel responsible for this orphaned Sephardic boy, and even when he is imprisoned by the British later on, they continue to worry about him.

By this time, Western Jerusalem had developed considerably thanks to European construction projects and the earlier determination of locals such as Yosef Rivlin to take the risk of dwelling outside the crowded Old City. Arriving with the conquering British army, Lieutenant Horowitz notes that several buildings (especially in area #6 of map 8) had been immediately appropriated by the British: "policemen and officials and statesmen and politicians were scurrying everywhere; the Jews were exultant; the Arabs in shock," but according to Horowitz, the Jerusalemite Yosef Mani merely said to himself, "Aye, the foreigners have come to replace the foreigners" (186).

During the Great War, this Mani had been "boning up on the living and the dead and studying maps and keeping track of the progress of the war and the lines of battle." He then embarks on a new "identity shuttle": "Mornings are spent in an Arab coffeehouse in the walled city, arbitrating petty tiffs and composing writs for the courts ... afternoons he ... call[s] on a German-Jewish professor in the new city to teach him Arabic grammar; and from there to his Sephardic synagogue for the afternoon prayer; and then to his [Hasidim] to translate some English correspondence; and then back again home for dinner with his wife and child; and then off again ... to the Zionist Club ... sometimes rising to ask ... a question of his own" (177–78). Now responding to the upheavals caused by the World War, Yosef ben Moshe assumes the role of a "*homo politicus*," and a subtle change now comes upon him (172). As Gilead Morahg has observed, Yosef ceases to move in a neutral manner among the city's cultural identities and begins to articulate an independent political position in the name of the local and native inhabitants of the land.[55] It is from this perspective that he conceives the aforementioned program of approaching Muslim villagers with a map that he cuts vertically or horizontally, any which way, in an effort to persuade them to partition the land with the Jews (map 6). With this goal in mind, he heads north, past Ramallah, toward "the houses of an unfamiliar Arab village that . . . must be el-Bireh . . . and begins to speak in Arabic. . . . 'This country is yours and it is ours; half for you and half for us'" (189). But the British soon discover that Yosef Mani had been acting against their interests, even relaying military secrets to their opponents, and it is only with tremendous subtlety that Lieutenant Horowitz manages to circumvent an almost certain death sentence into an extrajudicial decree of exile. Ironically, this Yosef Mani ends his days in Crete, captured by a Nazi soldier whose battalion had conquered that island.

Given the vast network of multicultural contacts that Yehoshua establishes in *Mr. Mani,* and indeed in all his novels, I do not think it is possible to conclude that his work centers on any particular group or any particular neighborhood, as Saranga and Sharaby have argued.[56] On the contrary, Yehoshua is interested in portraying ethnographic *interactions* among *many* groups on the local, national, and international settings of his novels. I agree that Jerusalem functions as a formidable conceptual locus in his works. But even this is a corollary of his larger preoccupation with the long-term stability of a democratic Israeli identity, within which Jerusalem is the most difficult test case. His attitude toward each of the city's cultural groups is therefore space-dependent and historically contextualized, and the relationships that he traces between Jews and Others, as well as between varieties of Jews, tend to be multivalent and tragicomic in every locale.

If we could stack *Mr. Mani's* Jerusalems on top of each other, and imagine all its characters walking simultaneously across the city, we would notice that they converge at several locations, including the *kotel* (Western Wall), the cemetery on the Mount of Olives, and the Manis' property in Kerem Avraham. This again recalls James Joyce, with his method of crisscrossing the paths of his characters in *Ulysses's* Dublin on June 16, 1904, where the principal characters actually do converge at the Blooms' home at the end of the day. *Mr. Mani's* protagonists live in separate historical moments, and cannot actually converge, though they all turn toward Jerusalem in one way or another. But even if they could meet, their ideological differences would

46 THE RETROSPECTIVE IMAGINATION OF A. B. YEHOSHUA

make it very difficult for them to sit together and endorse a common agenda. This is precisely the situation Yehoshua would like to repair, a situation that in recent years has become, again, more difficult to imagine.

JERUSALEM FROM ABROAD

Yehoshua can be a contrarian, or to put it more politely, he wishes to raise our self-awareness so that we will not delude ourselves about our circumstances in the past or the present. His representation of social diversity, as we have seen, contributes to this goal by historicizing his contemporary Israeli society, while also comparing it explicitly and indirectly to other regions, cultures, and eras, using Jerusalem as the most challenging test case. Yehoshua may rail against Jerusalem—"I am so happy that I do not live there ... the place from which the destruction of Israel could come"[57]—but he always pays careful attention to its status and development and admits its spiritual power, as portrayed, for example, in his late novella *A Woman in Jerusalem* (*Hamemuneh 'al mash'abei enosh*, 2004):

> I am not a religious person. In the deep sense of the word, I am not religious. But a certain religious energy erupted . . . through the beautiful foreign woman. . . . I tried to restore meanings that we have lost. The meaning of Jerusalem. The spiritual meaning of Jerusalem. Suddenly I noticed that Jerusalem had become rather tattered with the Jewish-Arab conflict and that both we and the Palestinians are completely losing its global dimension. I have to say that the conflict here will not be resolved without a resolution in Jerusalem. And a resolution in Jerusalem means upgrading it to a spiritual level. It means restoring the city's original spiritual depth.[58]

Is this the same writer whose narrator rails bitterly "against Jerusalem" (נגד ירושלים) in the 1965 novella "Three Days and a Child," which calls for "a clear stand in respect to Jerusalem. One cannot traverse her in silence. I maintain: Jerusalem is a hard city. Sometimes extremely harsh. Do not trust its modesty, its softness that is not soft; it is enough to glance at its sealed stone homes"?[59]

In 2004, by contrast, the frustrated human resources manager of *A Woman in Jerusalem* (*Hamemuneh 'al mash'abei enosh*) learns to recognize and acknowledge the spiritual impact of his hometown when he travels to

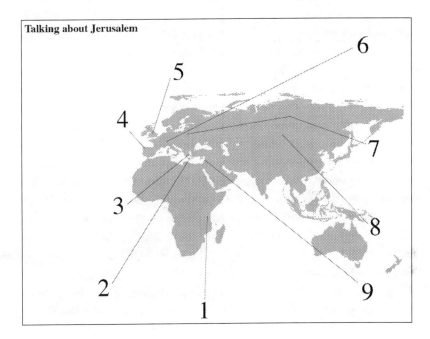

MAP 10. Jerusalem in perspective.

a former Soviet republic and meets devout Eastern Orthodox Christians who kindle in him a renewed appreciation for the "suffering city he had left just a week ago," now suddenly "bathed in a glow of importance, as it had been in his childhood."[60]

When does Jerusalem become a place whose name nobody wishes to mention, and when is it an awe-inspiring force of spiritual invigoration, as it becomes for the human resources manager at the end of his journey to the steppes of Europe? Anxious to conceal his Jewish identity from a Nazi captor, Yosef Mani, exiled to Crete, declares that his birthplace is just "some small desert city in Asia" (109), whose name might mean nothing to his captor: these are the last words that he utters before dying in an ancient Minoan urn (#2 on map 10). It is almost as if by denying his origins, which of course makes perfect sense under the circumstances, he also extinguishes his life.

Nonetheless, in this and countless other ways, Yehoshua's characters precariously renegotiate their relationship to this city. We especially feel this in a tragicomic scene from *Mr. Mani*, at the end of the nineteenth century, when cashiers at a Swiss train station (#6 on map 10) are mystified by Efrayim Shapiro's request to purchase an *actual* ticket to a destination that

48 THE RETROSPECTIVE IMAGINATION OF A. B. YEHOSHUA

they had imagined not as "a place on the map but a location in the Bible" (236). To assess Jerusalem's spiritual and historical importance, Yehoshua portrays it ethnographically across many eras, while also describing it from the defamiliarizing perspectives of many cultures around the globe, thus teasing out, and also taming, its mythical power.

Our final map in this chapter showcases the multiperspectival statements uttered about Jerusalem by nine Yehoshuan characters around the globe. When Efrayim Shapiro returns to Poland in 1899 (#7 on map 10)—after visiting, and mortally disappointing Dr. Moshe Mani in Jerusalem—he notices that the peasants on his parents' estate approach him as if he had turned into a holy man: "Mrazhik actually went down on his knees . . . Church bells? . . . No doubt . . . Lights in the village? . . . Of course . . . it is their Holy Land too . . . Jerusalem and all the rest of it" (208). Conversely, when Yair Moses in *The Retrospective* visits the cathedral of Santiago de Compostela in Spain, the third most popular Christian pilgrimage after Rome and Jerusalem, their host is "determined to prove to his guests that the holiness of the place they have come to is in no way inferior to the holiness of the land from which they come" (#4 on map 10).[61] And when in *Friendly Fire* African anthropologists explain their mission to an Israeli visitor, they similarly remind her (and the reader) that Israel is not the only place in the world that is historically laden: "In Africa they do not have artistic masterpieces nor historical memories of ancient battles and wars that changed the face of the earth . . . and yet . . . humanity began here" (#1 on map 10).[62] In other words, Jerusalem may be the womb of culture, but Africa is the womb of humanity at large.[63]

"The city itself, sir," explains Lieutenant Horowitz to Colonel Woodhouse while they discuss Yosef Mani's impending trial,

> What does it have to offer? Jolly little, Colonel. One renowned and quite impressive mosque. . . . A few important churches. . . .
> . . . The Jews have little to offer except themselves. . . . It turns out that they are a majority here. . . . And of course, there's that big, white wall . . . a remnant of their Temple." (151)

Since Colonel Woodhouse is nearly blind and cannot see with his own eyes the famous sites that his army has just conquered (#9 on map 10), Lieutenant Horowitz describes the Holy City for him. But while Horowitz's Jewish background is hardly a secret between them, he still strategically employs the third-person plural when referring to the city's Jewish dimension to attenuate his own connection to it. Paradoxically, by thus appearing to cut himself off from Jerusalem's Jews and the "remnant of their Temple," this Anglo-Jewish soldier paves the way to intercede on behalf of a fellow Jew whose life is endangered.

What Horowitz achieves, in such an oblique manner, mirrors to some extent Yehoshua's own propensity to maximize the Christian connections to the city in order to attenuate both the Muslim *and* religious-Jewish claims upon it, thus minimizing their explosive friction: "Jerusalem doesn't belong *only* to Israelis and Palestinians, or to Muslims and Jews, but to the world," he explained to Maya Jaggi back in 2006. He then suggested that one square kilometer of the Old City should be run "as a kind of Vatican" by representatives of the monotheistic religions, while the rest of the city's Eastern and Western neighborhoods could be partitioned between Israelis and Palestinians.[64] In other words, rather than embrace or deny the religious importance of Jerusalem, Yehoshua would delimit its power in ways familiar to citizens of polities with more tangible separations between church and state.[65]

The *kotel*, the most important remnant from the ancient temple, strikes Avidov Lipsker as an ultimate barrier in what he views as the otherwise boundless itineraries of Yehoshua's characters.[66] Yet although it is true that in *Hakir vehahar* (The Wall and the Mountain) Yehoshua complained that "if this remnant of Jewish spirituality were a column, a gate, or even a wall around which one might turn to gain a sense of perspective, then something dynamic and liberating might change its arresting essence,"[67] I would counter nevertheless that, in his fiction, Yehoshua *does* manage to transform this spiritual and historical marker into "a column, a gate, or even a wall around which one might turn," precisely by describing it from the *defamiliarizing* perspectives of characters who are culturally, emotionally, or geographically distant from Jerusalem. This minimizes Jerusalem's iconic power, subsuming religion and religiosity under the civic task of creating a modern national identity in Israel.

What Yehoshua told Vered Shemtov about revisiting the past in order to "get rid" of its negative impact applies just as much to his diffusion of religious myths and symbols in order to tame them.[68] For Yehoshua the Western Wall is a distracting relic, almost a fetish, that anchors but also jeopardizes the task of rebuilding a national Jewish identity in Israel. He would therefore like to cordon it off, to control its power, in a way that recalls the discomfort expressed by ancient prophets toward the temple in its standing heyday (for more on this topic see the end of the next chapter).

Minimizing both the Jewish and the Muslim allegiances to Jerusalem, Yehoshua prefers to emphasize the religious importance of the Holy City through a Christian perspective. During a stopover in Athens (#3 on map 10) after abandoning his new young family in Jerusalem, Avraham Mani informs his rabbi's wife that the city of her birth "is shaking off the dust of centuries now that Christendom has rediscovered it and given new hope to the Jews" (310). And, as we already saw, the human resources manager from *A Woman in Jerusalem* travels to "the end of the world" to learn from devout Eastern Orthodox Christians that his native city and religion are inspirational: he needs to go outside his own city, outside his country, outside his daily routines, to acquire through the power of alienation, a deeper consciousness of the impact of his actions in the place where he was born.[69] In a snowy village of a former Soviet Republic, he is then informed that he should not have returned the corpse of Yulia Ragayev to her hometown (#8 on map 10) but should rather have buried her in the Holy City that attracted her, though it had also killed her. These last words in that narrative—actually located on its opening page, so that they seem to frame the manager's mission by looping the conclusion of his journey into the beginning of his story—express a transcendental epiphany that reenergizes him toward a more meaningful future.

In this chapter, I have tried to give an overview of Yehoshua's opus and ethos by mapping the local, global, and national itineraries of his characters as they come into contact with a variety of ethnic, religious, and national communities in Israel and abroad. Together, this presents a network of cross-cultural exchanges that challenge Yehoshua's readers to clarify the boundaries of the State of Israel as a modern Zionist entity at the heart of which lies the city of Jerusalem, Zion itself, with its ancient history and mythic power, exalted by some and disparaged by others. To complete this overview of Jerusalem in Yehoshua's opus and ethos, let us evoke a powerful scene from his very first novel, *The Lover*, where the abandoned Sephardic grandmother, who had been lying in a coma for many months in a geriatric hospital near Hedera, suddenly reawakens to life by becoming conscious of her memories of Jerusalem:

Usalem.... An important place, a hard place—Rusalem....

... Find it.... Find it, it's important....

... Where was she born?—Rusalem. Where are they from?

... —Rusalem? Not that.... A little different....

... What's its name? Not Usalem—Rusalim.... Something at the beginning. Gerusalem, Sherusalem, Merusalem, Jerusalem. Oh, oh, oh, Jerusalem. Jerusalem, Jerusalem. Exactly, but no. I weep. Great pain. Jerusalem. Simple. Ah, that's it. Jerusalem.[70]

Yehoshua's attitude toward Jerusalem is not uniform: harsh words written in its dispraise in 1965 are followed a dozen years later by this graceful recognition of its power to almost raise the dead. He is painfully aware of the significance of the city of his birth, but he fiercely contextualizes it from a historical and ethnographic perspective to inoculate us against its force.

Paradoxically, he is a staunch nationalist who sends his characters to explore all nations of the globe. In Israel, he celebrates a multicultural mosaic while calling attention to the dangers of centrifugal allegiances. Zion's centerpiece, Jerusalem, elicits from him the careful attention of a historian, a poet's imagery and a prophet's frustration. In an effort to tame its religious importance, he breaks down its components by putting them, too, into a comparative perspective. If we map the settings of Yehoshua's novels and follow the itineraries of his characters, we thus obtain a quasi-dystopian vision of Jewish affairs and modern Israeli life, which he exaggerates in order to advocate for its repair. To read Yehoshua's fiction is therefore to accept an invitation to imagine alternative itineraries and unconventional solutions to the absurd and chaotic problems that his characters confront, for his vision of national normalization is projected toward the future, beyond the scope of the novels.

CHAPTER 3

The Watchman's Stance

> Yes, Doña Elvira, beyond the manifest reality lurks a dark abyss, and we
> must rip open the screen and look straight into it, for only then will we
> know how best to handle what is known and apparently understood. But
> we must not become addicted to it, for then despair will sap our strength.
>
> —YAIR MOSES IN *HESED SEFARADI / THE RETROSPECTIVE*, 152

Much has been written about the watchman in Yehoshua's iconic novella *Facing the Forests* (*Mul haye'arot*, 1963), where an observation post is an obvious feature of the plot. Yet other such lookout stances that mediate precariously between the characters and the world around them recur across Yehoshua's oeuvre. This chapter argues that these lookout scenarios expose the *limitations* of Yehoshua's watchmen: instead of endowing them with a comfortable sense of control over their surroundings, he tests and undermines his lookouts' abilities to respond to complicated and often absurd situations that he develops around them. The myopia of his typically bespectacled protagonists signals this limited perception, along with the more extensive imagery of lost and broken glasses on which Yehoshua scholars have often remarked.

Like the threshold scenes that Bakhtin recognized as a distinctive chronotope in Dostoevsky's fiction—a device that concentrates a narrative's emplotment of time around key physical locations—Yehoshua's lookouts mark a time of reckoning and decision-making in the lives of his protagonists.[1] Yet unlike Dostoevsky's threshold scenes, which Bakhtin defined as a moment of *dehistoricized* crisis,[2] Yehoshua's chronotopic observation posts promote a greater sociohistorical awareness in the reader and sometimes also in the characters' sense of belonging; this therefore resembles Goethe's approach to an evolutionary identity-in-progress more than the moral crises in Dostoevsky, which transcend "ordinary biographical . . . time."[3] Indeed, starting with *Facing the Forests*, Yehoshua's lookout stances reveal a trace of the past that is suddenly exposed on a watchman's horizon, demanding action and responsibility. And yet Yehoshua only grants his lookouts an abstract and uneven access to the past due to broken links among the generations and a complicated entanglement between myth and history, which Yehoshua strives to pry apart.

Any lookout stance is by definition extrospective; however, paradoxically, Yehoshua's observation posts facilitate an *introspective* "time-out" from the regular din of life. This experience grants his watchmen and watchwomen an opportunity to reevaluate their responsibilities according to new social contexts that put their habits into a new perspective. Yehoshua believes that every rational person is responsible not only for his or her own deeds but also for clarifying the national collective in relation to all the subcultures that constitute it; he moreover insists, quite radically, on a complex triumvirate of "freedom-responsibility-choice," which he applies to both the individual and the collective—an individualism that acknowledges, but at the same time also transcends, any narrow allegiance to cultural subgroups.[4] This dynamic appears in concentrated doses in Yehoshua's chronotopic lookout scenarios, thus making them productive nuggets of analysis for the way that he organizes his narratives from a moral point of view.

The watchman's stance in Yehoshua's fiction presents a situation of impaired cognition where a watchman is overloaded with pressures from a variety of contexts (psychological, socioeconomic, historical, historiosophic).[5] Some of these forces, especially mythic or historiosophic references, are conveyed over the heads of the characters, in ways that invite the reader to see further than the myopic watchmen and watchwomen, who are struggling to make sense of a situation that requires a new mode of moral judgment and action.

One would assume that watchmen stationed at high posts, surveying the horizon, have a powerful advantage. But Yehoshua's panoramas befuddle his watchmen, exposing their limited ability to deal with the complicated situations unfolding around them. Often occluded, their knowledge of the past is not readily accessible; nevertheless, Yehoshua does grant his watchmen and watchwomen an *opportunity* to develop a deeper sense of historical perspective and a more balanced mode of social interactions with acquaintances and even intimate family members. All this contributes to the process of national normalization that he defines as "nothing but a rich

54 THE RETROSPECTIVE IMAGINATION OF A. B. YEHOSHUA

and creative pluralism in which one is as sovereign as possible over one's deeds, and where *the options on the horizon* are vast."[6]

Yehoshua's observation posts are situated at strategic locations from which his watchmen can gain a firmer control over their environment, if they succeed in developing a mutually validating relationship with individuals from different cultural groups that they meet. These socializing opportunities are sometimes seized by the characters but often missed, as Gilead Morahg has underscored in a much broader context.[7] Indeed, within a broader dynamic, the special function of Yehoshua's lookout scenes is to interrupt the habitual routine of the characters and compel a more careful assessment of their political realities and historical backgrounds; on the other hand, the ability of Yehoshua's watchmen and watchwomen to establish creative and pragmatic connections with individuals from different age groups, races, ethnicities, and religions is always mediated by the foggy consciousness of each character and the foggier world that s/he glimpses from the observation post. This is not necessarily a special Israeli deficiency revealed by Yehoshua's narratives; it is rather an inherent human condition that, in a neo-Kantian vein, he wishes his countrymen to acknowledge and accept.

The most obvious lookout stance in Yehoshua's fiction is that of the procrastinating student who becomes a forest watchman in *Facing the Forests*, but a similar tense mediation between self and world through windows, hilltops, crossroads, and balconies can be traced across the rest of his stories and novels too, and even in the voyeuristic plots of some of his theatrical plays.[8] Usually located on high points—geographic and architectonic—Yehoshua's lookout scenes typically dramatize an *attempt* to clarify the watchman's degree of responsibility for the events around him. What especially interests Yehoshua is *the gap* between what his characters see and do and what they ought to have seen or done. From their observation posts, especially in his later novels, some of Yehoshua's watchmen and watchwomen manage to reconnect to their world in life-affirming ways; in his earlier stories, fire and chaos tend to take over. Still, even in his most optimistic novels, the abyss functions as an antithesis to the observation post—the cliff, for example, from which the cinematographer Toledano slips to death in *The Retrospective* (*Hesed sefaradi*, 2011), which illustrates the danger into which a careless observation stance can lead.

FROM THE FOREST WATCHMAN'S STATION
TO THE ROOFTOPS OF TULKARM

Even before *Facing the Forests*, Yehoshua had already made strategic use of a lookout scenario to organize the flow of his short stories, for example in "Flood Tide" (Ge'ut hayam, 1962), where a warden and his prisoners are locked into a mutual observation stance: "They watch me with tranquil eyes," reports the prison warden, "always . . . facing the corridor, as though waiting. What are they waiting for?"[9] When the warden believes his prisoners will drown in a flood, he brings them out of their cells to explain "the law" to them, but the watchful prisoners naturally seize the opportunity to lock up their watchman, condemning him to a horrible death.

In "Yatir Evening Express" (Masa ha'erev shel Yatir, 1959), another early story, the villagers' habitual evening activity revolves around an observation stance violently disrupted by the story's denouement. Every evening Yatir's inhabitants *ritually* prepare for the spectacle of an express train whizzing past their village without ever stopping:

> At five-thirty Mrs Sharira would open the shutters of her window overlooking the wide bridge that spanned the wadi, and bring a few chairs out on to her balcony. . . . By six o'clock, all the small windows overlooking the track would be open, with heads peering out of them.
>
> . . . All eyes accompanied the train along the length of the bridge, until it disappeared at the first bend. After that the people would look at each other stealthily, wordless, with an uneasy sense of gravity. . . .
>
> So it was every day. So it is every day. So it will be forever.[10]

But one evening this observation stance is exchanged for a criminal yet ostensibly sympathetic interaction with the dying and wounded passengers from a train derailed by some of the villagers. The railroad had been designed to include Yatir, but the train schedule persists in bypassing it. Therefore, the villagers act out a fantasy of inclusion by forcing a violent interaction with a train that is now *their* train, too.

Interestingly, accompanying the lookout stance in these early stories is a sense of imprisonment that Yael Zerubavel intuitively attributed to the student-watchman in *Facing the Forests*.[11] This is not a panoptical system of surveillance designed to inflict mental punishment on its subjects, as in Foucault's analysis of Jeremy Bentham's famous design.[12] The problem in Yehoshua's stories is rather one of neglect and inadequate surveillance, which leads to greater misunderstanding and chaos. In "Flood Tide," where the setting is actually a prison, the old jailbirds watch the young warden as much as he watches them, and when he naively releases them, they condemn him to a cruel death. Even in these early works, Yehoshua's lookout scenarios expose the inadequacies of the lookout as much as they expose the inadequacies of the system in which the lookout is caught.

In *Facing the Forests*, which Yehoshua published in his late twenties—and where he began to signal his readiness to become a more politically engaged writer[13]—a thirty-year-old procrastinating student, originally destined for brilliance, but who has not managed to even complete his degree, goes off with a suitcase full of books to work as a forest ranger in the north of Israel. Worrying about fires now becomes his new means of procrastination—except that he does stir himself to encourage a local Arab caretaker to burn a lush forest that had been planted around the Arab's ruined homestead.

As Mordechai Shalev immediately emphasized, from the moment that the student arrives at the national forest, he is called *Hatzofeh* (a scout or watchman), in language that recalls the biblical trope of a prophet/watchman invested with responsibility for guarding the house of Israel (as in Ezekiel 3:17, *Hatzofeh lebeit Israel*).[14] In Yehoshua's story, however, the student is not the sole watchman. Hanan Hever noted that the Arab caretaker observes the watchman carefully as soon as he realizes that the latter is interested in the ruined homestead.[15] The manager of the forestation project is also a watchman by proxy—an overseer of rangers and caretakers—whose ability to delegate responsibility turns out to be inadequate. We could even say that the Arab caretaker's daughter becomes a watch girl who is literally chained to the job while the older parties roam around the pine forest. From his elevated station in the midst of the forest, the student-watchman glimpses the flames he has fanned, and the following morning the distraught manager surveys a disaster he might have prevented had he paid more attention to the pent-up frustrations of the staff of his forests, instead of courting foreign donors. Indeed, the story's allusion to the biblical motif of the prophet-watchman invites a broader reassessment of the goals of modern Zionism in light of the worldview and responsibilities of the ancient prophets (and vice versa).[16]

THE WATCHMAN'S STANCE   57

These same references are then reactivated in Yehoshua's late novel *Friendly Fire* (*Esh yedidutit*, 2007), which echoes his iconic *Facing the Forests* conceptually and onomastically. Fire, exile, and the abyss with which the prophet Jeremiah threatened the people of Judea prior to the fall of the First Temple are mapped in Yehoshua's fiction—as in the Bible—upon the topography of the land of Israel, where mountaintops served as altars for competing modes of worship and the valley of ben-Hinnom was associated with the child sacrifices of Moloch worshippers.

In *Friendly Fire*, Daniela Ya'ari—whose last name literally means "my forest"—conveys these bundled references to her husband when she returns to Israel from visiting their brother-in-law in Africa. Daniela reports that their brother-in-law, Yirmi (short for Jeremiah), is angry at the ancient prophets, especially his namesake, for engineering a cultural attitude that he blames for the untimely death of his son. Daniela's husband, Amotz, retorts that Yirmi is then "angry a bit against himself too" (ktzat gam neged atzmo).[17] This dialectic between individual Jews and the Jewish collective, as well as between Jews and Gentiles across space and time, is organized in that novel around four high posts overlooking Tel Aviv, Jerusalem, Tanzania, and Tulkarm.

Friendly Fire opens on top of a Tel Aviv skyscraper, the Pinsker Tower, named after the Russian Jew who called for auto-emancipation a decade before Herzl launched his program of national revival. Amotz Ya'ari comes to this building to investigate why one of the elevators that his engineering company had installed there is making unbearable noises. Yet as he stands on a high balcony, "shivering, hypnotized by the sunrise that expands the broad horizon," he pays less attention to his elevator responsibilities than to an airplane hovering above, carrying his wife to visit their brother-in-law in Africa: "His discerning eye has already picked out one deviant craft that is gracefully bending to the south. It's *her*, he thinks excitedly. . . . Then he relaxes. Yes, his wife will arrive in peace and return in peace. And he leaves the tiny balcony, locks the engine room, and calls the elevator to take him down to the car park."[18] Only later in the week does he find the moral and practical resources to deal with his share of responsibility for the peace and quiet of the tenants of the Pinsker Tower.

It is not uncommon for novels to open or close with a panoramic bird's-eye view of their social and geographic settings, sometimes drawing attention to the anxieties of a troubled observer.[19] Think, for instance, of

Mrs. Dalloway on the morning of her party, throwing open the French windows, "feeling as she did, standing there at the open window, that something awful was about to happen."[20] But Yehoshua uses this device intensively as a means of connecting the inner and outer worlds of his characters at key junctures in the plot. *Friendly Fire*'s opening scene is situated in the anxious mind of Amotz Ya'ari during an introspective moment in which he reaches out toward another being (his wife) while she moves toward an invisible world beyond the horizon (their brother-in-law in Africa); from that moment, Amotz becomes saddled with duties that extend beyond his professional problems at the Pinsker Tower, to encompass the entire past and future of his family members in Tel Aviv, Jerusalem, and abroad.

From downtown Jerusalem, the psychoanalyst Dvorah Bennett begs him to repair the private elevator that Amotz's father had installed in her bedroom when she and the elder Ya'ari were lovers during the early years of his widowhood. This contraption zooms from the psychoanalyst's closet to the roof of her building, allowing her who allegedly sees into human minds to also take stock of the city that had grown around her. Amotz's father had promised a "lifetime guarantee" on this private elevator, but at this point he shakes from Parkinson's and cannot honor his former commitment without an absurd degree of assistance. Still, this exposure to the old man's desire to honor his promises, encourages the son to deal more ethically with his own problem at the Pinsker Tower, though it stretches his already strained ability to help his family members with all their assorted difficulties.

The past, as remembered from Dr. Bennett's Jerusalem rooftop, encompasses not only her personal relationship with Ya'ari senior, but also the history of a fledgling state—because from that rooftop she observed the comings and goings of the first Knesset during its heyday. As soon as this national history is brought into focus, however, it is shooed back into the background: "better not to romanticize the purity of the past; better to concentrate on the present," declares Amotz. Still, he continues to probe Dr. Bennett's memories of the old Knesset until she insists that "the sun out here is too strong for history."[21] It is only when Amotz accompanies his father to take personal responsibility over the old man's "lifetime guarantee" that the son relaxes without shirking accountability: "from this moment on, I am but a silent onlooker. He brings a wicker chair from the kitchen, stands it beside the big bed, sits down and crosses his legs and closes his eyes."[22] For one moment, he can loosen control over his anxious duties.

Meanwhile, Ya'ari's wife arrives at a colonial farmhouse in Tanzania, which serves as the headquarters of a team of anthropologists to whom her brother-in-law attaches himself in an effort to escape the unbearable weight of his double bereavement: his son was killed during a military ambush in Tulkarm, and his wife, Daniela's sister, died soon afterward.[23] From the window of her brother-in-law's bedroom on top of this farmhouse, Daniela Ya'ari surveys the African plain, and on his desk "the skull of a young monkey a few million years old," a *memento mori* so remote that it doesn't disturb her relative's desire to escape from history.[24] Daniela learns that on this African plain, the dead "are not buried . . . but rather left exposed in the wild . . . reabsorbed into the natural world that gave them life."[25] Echoing this attitude, she later accuses her brother-in-law of failing to absorb the death of his son into the world that gave him life, thereby hastening the end of her sister.

On the last night of her visit, Daniela "looks out at the dark universe," lit by a "sliver of moon, a Muslim crescent, that may illuminate the path somewhat."[26] Yehoshua's selection of a modal verb here—a Muslim crescent that may (or may not) illuminate Daniela's path ("she'ulay yatzliah leha'ir me'at et hadereh")[27]—connects this lookout to the novel's fourth and most dramatic observation point: Yirmi's reaction to the worldview that he glimpses from a Palestinian rooftop in the town of Tulkarm, at the place where his son had been killed by "friendly fire" several years earlier.

Yirmi's son had been had been stationed as a lookout on this rooftop during a military ambush and was shot by one of his own comrades when he unexpectedly jumped down from his post to clean a bucket into which he defecated during the night.[28] Twice, the bereaved father visits this place where his son spent his final hours—looking "out to the west," where "Israeli lights are . . . so close, close enough to touch."[29] And although on his first visit "the tenants did not seem surprised that again the Jews wanted to see the world from the Palestinian rooftop," on a second visit a young Palestinian woman berates Yirmi with such bitterness that he flees all the way to Africa.[30]

How, then, can the light of an embittered Jewish star, or Muslim crescent for that matter, "illuminate the path somewhat"? In *Friendly Fire*, as in *Facing the Forests*, this is a difficult question to answer;[31] but Yehoshua invites his reader to deepen the connections that he traces between all the different observational stances that coordinate his narrative: how *can* the worldview from a rooftop in Tulkarm relate to the view from Jerusalem or Tel Aviv, or to the African plain, where carcasses are left to blend into "the natural world that gave them life," while a team of anthropologists digs below the surface in an effort to uncover mankind's oldest prehistoric roots?

The relationship between Jews and others on the axis of time (history) and space (geopolitically) is a fundamental concern in Yehoshua's fiction and public outreach. In *Friendly Fire*, Amotz Ya'ari manages to pinpoint the exact degree of his responsibility for the noises that disturb the residents of the Pinsker Tower, and, on a broader scale, the novel shuffles among diverse environments to demonstrate that partnerships everywhere entail a long-term commitment that requires a careful forecast of responsibilities.

HAZY VISION, BIFOCAL GLASSES, AND THE ABYSS

While Yehoshua's lookout stance exposes the *limited* cognition of his characters in ways that test their control over their environment, this trope (as a rhetorical device) stimulates the reader to evaluate the watchman's degree of responsibility for a situation unfolding on the horizon, demanding clarification.

Ziva Shamir's attention to visual vocabulary in a discussion of Molkho's bifocals (in Yehoshua's third novel, *Five Seasons* [*Molkho*], 1987) helps us appreciate the hazy vision and impaired cognition that Yehoshua typically attributes to his characters: "Molkho observes the world through bifocal lenses. Usually he only sees what happens right under his nose and is completely focused on his own navel, but sometimes he extends his vision toward greater distances, for example, to Vienna or Berlin (although there he mainly tours the spaces of the past). Between his narrowest and furthest spheres of vision, dim expanses spread out, which Molkho does not notice."[32] Molkho's bifocals signify that he has trouble accurately discerning what lies near him, as well as what stretches further in time and place. Still, he manages to act responsibly and even nobly toward family members and acquaintances in every situation in which his pedestrian life places him. His limited perception—narrated in a third-person mode but filtered through Molkho's naive and therefore comic consciousness—enables Yehoshua to conduct a deeper conversation with the reader behind the protagonist's back, thus driving a wedge between Molkho's observations and a broader range of cultural issues that Yehoshua reveals to the reader above the limited cognition of his character.

Molkho looks out from various observation posts—some of them intimate and local like the view from the bedroom window that he shared with his wife during her seven-year battle with cancer; others involve artistic events, like the operas he watches in Paris and Berlin after his wife's death. These experiences during his first year of widowhood help Molkho recalibrate the distance that now separates him from his deceased wife. From their bedroom window overlooking the Carmel wadi, he reexamines the lush view that he had come to associate with decay, because his wife faced this landscape during her long illness, but as Risa Domb notes, the view from the window is in flux—it changes in response to Molkho's moods and the seasons.[33] Curious about European operas, Molkho attends a performance of *Orpheus and Eurydice* in Berlin, and when he watches Orpheus's futile attempt to drag his beloved out of Hades, he learns to reassess his newfound freedom in relation to his wife's lingering influence upon him.[34] Molkho's current responsibility—an *ability* to *respond* to life anew—takes the form of a clarification of these new boundaries between his present, past, and future.

The subtle healing process that Molkho achieves despite his rather simplistic understanding suggests that, to some degree, his impaired cognition is just a "normal" human limitation that must be acknowledged and overcome in a Kantian manner, as a basic status quo for all human interactions with the universe. More dramatically, however, a dependence on eyeglasses, binoculars, and other devices signaling the limited vision of Yehoshua's characters[35] condenses Yehoshua's wider and more elaborate use of the watchman's stance to highlight dangerous blind spots in his character's introspective/extrospective relationship with the world around them. On a historiosophic plane, as mentioned, this dynamic echoes the angry recriminations of biblical prophet-watchmen who lamented their inability to control those whose "eyes cannot see and whose ears cannot hear."[36]

The student-watchman in *Facing the Forests* establishes a relationship with an Arab caretaker whose tongue cannot speak, but who nevertheless acts in ways that result in disaster for him, as well as for the little girl for whom the Arab caretaker is responsible, and for the forest. Most scholars emphasize the limited cognition of the student-watchman, noting, as Gil Hochberg does, the half-visible forces that clamor for his attention:

> Moving back and forth between "seeing clearly" and "failing to see," the protagonist struggles to distinguish between optical illusions

and obscured realities. . . . Realizing there is no fire, he concludes that "the spectacles are to blame." Even after the forest is actually burned, visions overcome reality as the "green forests continue to grow in front of his angry eyes." . . . With this focus on visual deficiency, Yehoshua prepares to ask what I believe is the novella's main question: What kind of seeing (or compromised seeing) is required in order to see . . . [what] remains visible only in its invisibility?[37]

In this iconic novella, Yehoshua shows that to connect optimally with one's environment, it is not sufficient to survey the horizon through binoculars or walk among the natives.[38] It is necessary to also take into consideration the subjective positions of every relevant social body entangled in a web of conflicting needs and desires. In this novella, just as in *Friendly Fire*, Yehoshua questions the degree of mutual responsibility required from individuals and groups whose lookout stances are interconnected, and whose existential agendas are juxtaposed or even opposed to each other. Nevertheless, achieving an accurate vision from any of these observation posts appears to be an almost insurmountable challenge.

In *Friendly Fire*, Daniela Ya'ari's habit of wiping her glasses contrasts with her futile attempt to clean the bug-splattered windshield through which her brother-in-law wildly drives his jeep on the African plain; his lax responsibility tallies with his general attitude toward the surviving members of his family. By contrast, Daniela's husband, Amotz Ya'ari, is one of Yehoshua's few protagonists with good eyesight, yet even he requires the aid of an expert endowed with supernatural hearing to determine the extent of his company's responsibility for the "winds" that howl through *his* "forest." (As mentioned, Ya'ari means "my forest," and the winds that disturb the residents of the Pinsker Tower hint at some problem in the process of constructing the edifice of Jewish auto-emancipation advanced by the ideologue Leon Pinsker in Jewish history.) These onomastic analogies, added to the fire symbolism and the prominent role accorded to the four lookout stations in *Friendly Fire*, emphasize how much this novel, published in 2007, echoes Yehoshua's *Facing the Forests*, published in 1963, with their extended invitation to consider the worldviews of the ancient prophets in light of the responsibilities of modern Zionism, and vice versa.

Yehoshua relies on observation posts staffed by watchmen and watchwomen with impaired cognition in the rest of his novels, too. And although

THE WATCHMAN'S STANCE 63

there the lookout scenes become more smoothly integrated into the plot, they still function as a chronotopic tool for exposing and historicizing the *limited* judgment and the precarious response *abilities* of the main characters.

For example, in *The Liberated Bride* (*Hakala hameshahreret*, 2001), a deficient lookout stance draws attention to the protagonist's inability to discern the object of his quest, even though he arrives to the place most intimately associated with the secret that eludes him. A historian by profession, Yochanan Rivlin is obsessed with discovering "the truth" behind his son's divorce so that he can help him overcome this broken relationship. Yet although Rivlin's investigations lead him to the very agent and location where his son had witnessed a damning secret about his ex-wife's family, it remains impossible for Rivlin to fathom what his son had seen, and what nobody wishes to tell him outright.

This episode interests me because when Rivlin arrives at the site most intimately connected with his son's explosive discovery (an incestuous relationship between the ex-wife's sister and father), Rivlin's vision is technically impaired in a manner that exacerbates his natural handicaps without sharpening his senses. At this crucial point in his quest, Rivlin ironically finds himself in a truly semiblinded condition—earlier that day, his own wife, Hagit, furious that he had concealed from her a previous visit to their son's ex, had crushed Rivlin's spectacles. Nitza Ben-Dov argues that Hagit's action highlights the moral myopia of *both* spouses in a reiteration of an "Astarte paradigm" that she traces across Yehoshua's fiction, as we shall discuss in more detail later.[39] Rachel Albeck-Gidron emphasizes the Freudian symbolism of a metaphoric blinding that is sandwiched between incest and female spousal violence (two breached taboos).[40] When we further consider Rivlin's "blinding" in terms of Yehoshua's recurrent use of the watchman's stance, we notice that Rivlin's hazy quest encapsulates his overall struggle to understand and control his personal, familial, and professional responsibilities, in ways that ultimately prove victorious.

When Rivlin visits his optometrist to fix his broken glasses, he learns that both his distant and his near vision have deteriorated. If distant vision, as we noted in relation to Molkho, corresponds to historical vision and long-term commitments, while near vision is essential for clarifying intimate details in a synchronic manner, then the historian Rivlin, deprived of his customary seeing aids until his new bifocals arrive, is suddenly forced to concentrate on his immediate environment in order to function with any degree of safety. He thus physically experiences the lack of confidence that had plagued him ever since he realized that he had failed to foresee both a crisis looming near him (in his son's life) and one farther away (where he did not expect an outburst of civil war in Algeria, his field of academic expertise).

What relevance, then, applies to the limited vision and hazy cognition of a sophisticated scholar, a historian who specializes in Algeria yet who nevertheless—like the ordinary Molkho and indeed like all of Yehoshua's characters—must strain equally hard to recalibrate the relationship between what lies near him and what unfolds far away? Professor Rivlin's personal immersion in the Israeli-Palestinian environment, which lies relatively near him, affects his interpretation of Muslim fundamentalism and guerrilla warfare in the more distanced Algeria; at the same time, his professional responsibility toward Algerian history enhances his involvement with local Israeli-Arab students and neighboring Palestinian acquaintances in the West Bank.

At home, Rivlin looks out of his office window obsessively to keep track of an elderly lady across the street, who reminds him of his deceased mother. In a liberating move at the end of the novel, he crosses the street to meet this specter of his cantankerous mother, thus consciously enacting a *bifocal* move that clarifies what he did not discern from afar: the differences between his mother and this neighbor; in other words, the differences between the present and the past. Having managed to indirectly help his son lay to rest the specter of his failed marriage, Rivlin now achieves greater inner peace and self-control.

Yehoshua situates his observation posts on hills, tow trucks, balconies, and even in the incestuous basement where Rivlin senses but cannot grasp the clues that he has been seeking. But behind the blundering characters stationed at these lookouts, the author enjoins the reader to judge the extent of each watchman's responsibility for the psychological and sociopolitical forces that lie smothered or hidden, exerting a force that at any moment can rise to the surface to wreak havoc.

Before moving on to examine some lookout stances in Yehoshua's more complicated "Faulknerian" novels, I would like to bring a final example from one of his later third-person narratives, *The Retrospective*, where a lookout stance is again tied closely to the professional identities of its characters. As a film director, Yair Moses is quite accustomed to anticipating and controlling the reactions of the spectators of his films. But at one point toward the middle of the novel, he watches the actress Ruth (his longtime collaborator and lover) rehearsing teenagers in her private acting studio. She instructs Moses to conceal himself behind a curtain so that his presence will not disturb the teenagers. From this hidden and mute position, Moses begins to judge his lover from a new perspective: suddenly he appreciates how her Stanislavskian method elicits emotions from the actors by forcing them to watch each other: "Yes, watch," Ruth instructs one of her students, "but not as an outside observer. If you're dressed like them, you'll participate with your body and not just by looking. . . . This will help build the character you'll be playing."[41] Moses observes Ruth's manipulations of her students' feelings and postures—now *she* is in control—and begins to warm up to the idea of allowing himself to be guided toward concessions to his former screenwriter, with whom he had quarreled forty years earlier and with whom he now seeks reconciliation.[42]

By contrast, the relationship between the actress Ruth and the cinematographer Toledano, who had been infatuated with her since childhood, had ended in a fatal loss of control when he perched himself up on a cliff to photograph her naked body sprawled below and then "carelessly lost his footing and crashed to an untimely death," leaving behind a widow and three orphaned children.[43] During a speech that Moses delivers forty years later at a Spanish retrospective of their films (see the epigraph to this chapter) he explains that "beyond the manifest reality lurks a dark abyss [*tehom afela*], and we must rip open the screen and look straight into it, for only then will we know how best to handle what is known and apparently understood."[44] He warns, however, that addiction to such voyeurism (such as Toledano's) can lead to an uncontrollable fall.

The abyss functions in Yehoshua's novels as a counterpoint to the observation post: it signals a total loss of control, in contrast to the watchman's blundering but continuous reassessment of his responsibilities toward the world around him. Peering into the abyss—very carefully—usually leads to a liberating reassessment of the boundaries between the possible and impossible in ways that revitalize Yehoshua's watchmen and women. After all, Rivlin, Molkho, Moses, and others peer into an abyss, but they step back to realign themselves toward family and friends with renewed creativity. But occasionally, Yehoshua's abyss denotes a full stop of death or disaster into which he allows some of his characters to slip or derail others, as a warning.

THE LIMITS OF RESPONSIBILITY

Yehoshua's reliance on the watchman stance diminishes, but by no means disappears, in his Faulknerian novels. *The Lover* (*Hame'ahev*, 1977), *A Late Divorce* (*Geirushim meuharim*, 1982), and *Mr. Mani* (*Mar Mani*, 1990) follow Faulkner's narrative style to a greater or lesser degree,[45] the gap between what the characters see and what they are unable or unwilling to see is taken to an extreme. Indeed, here this gap functions as a structural and thematic device through which character development and narrative events are diffused into overlapping perspectives that are presented from the voice and inner consciousness of each character. This means that there is a lesser need for extrospective probes into the characters' relationship with the world around them, which is the primary function of the watchman's stance in Yehoshua's third-person narratives, as we saw in the previous examples.

In Yehoshua's Faulknerian novels, the inner life of each character is *already* transparent—although in *Mr. Mani* he constructs a double and triple layer of consciousness through a sequence of storytellers who discuss "their" Manis with interlocutors whose attitudes *also* affect the narrative perspective. Yet despite this dispersion of narrative control, I would argue that a chronotopic lookout still encapsulates *Mr. Mani*'s preoccupation with national cohesion and responsibility. By contrast, Yehoshua's earlier Faulknerian novels, *A Late Divorce* and *The Lover*, do not have any chronotopic pattern that works as a cohesive center of gravity in the manner we have been tracing in his more integrative third-person narratives. These distinctions help us appreciate the function of the lookout stance across Yehoshua's oeuvre.

We noted how even in *Facing the Forests*, the watchman's stance is to some extent dispersed among all the characters, although only the student-watchman's cognition is focalized; in *Friendly Fire*, too, four lookout stances are (unevenly) distributed among Yirmi, Amotz, and Daniela, but Amotz emerges as the principal focalizer. This dispersion is taken to an extreme in Yehoshua's Faulknerian novels, where the narrative is fragmented into an extraordinarily large number of overlapping positions: *The Lover* is told through six different consciousnesses, while *A Late Divorce* presents ten—including the family's dog, whose section was initially omitted by the publishers but was later restored to a new Hebrew edition of the novel; *Mr. Mani* includes five narrators who inhabit completely different historical

THE WATCHMAN'S STANCE   67

periods and discuss different generations of Manis with interlocutors who in turn judge the storyteller, as much as the Manis that form the main topic of each conversation.

As Henry James famously put it, the "house of fiction" is a structure with a million windows from which different consciousnesses look out on intersecting slivers of reality.[46] Faulkner took this modernist attack on omniscience and coherence a step further, turning fragmentation and indeterminacy into both narrative method and theme of his experimental work. In an important interview, Faulkner declared that *The Sound and the Fury* had grown out of his desire to explain "the little girl's muddy drawers, climbing that tree to look in the parlor window with her brothers that didn't have the courage to climb waiting to see what she saw."[47] Nevertheless, he did not grant that girl a voice in "her" novel: instead we must gather Caddy Compson's story piecemeal from the discontinuous narratives of her three alienated brothers, and Dilsey, the family's caretaker. This extreme narrative fragmentation and indeterminacy overturns the panoramic perspectives of a Rastignac at the end of Balzac's *Père Goriot*, for example, where Rastignac stands at a high point, overlooking Paris, utterly disgusted at the cruelty and hypocrisy of upper society but resolved nonetheless to manipulate it to his advantage. Rastignac's extrospective/introspective moment merely sums up what the plot had already shown all along.

By contrast, Yehoshua's pervasive use of the watchman's stance organizes plot and character development, especially serving to draw attention to blind spots reached by nobody's foresight, under nobody's responsibility, which therefore pose a danger comparable to that of unresolved neuroses that threaten to derail a rational judgment. Yehoshua's attention to the watchman's stance also stems from his desire to criticize and, at the same time, co-opt the traditional position of a "watchman over the house of Israel," whose authority he puts into a historicized perspective.

A Late Divorce, Yehoshua's most pessimistic and disjointed novel, tells the story of Yehuda Kaminka's return to Israel from America to divorce his schizophrenic wife. A farcical lookout scene in this novel exaggerates the difficulty of a harmonious integration of perspectives, and it occurs precisely in the chapter initially omitted by the publishers but restored to a later Hebrew edition, though it still remains unavailable in translation. This is the chapter narrated from the perspective of the family's dog.

68 THE RETROSPECTIVE IMAGINATION OF A. B. YEHOSHUA

The Kaminkas' dog wanders around the country; in Jerusalem he feels obliged to adopt an elevated prophetic discourse that turns into a tragicomic dialogue when he begs the author to help him "explain Jerusalem" by conveying him to "a high and lofty place, overlooking the entire city, from which I will bark it with all my might."[48] The selected lookout is Mount Moriah—the site of the Dome of the Rock, where the temples once stood in connection with Avraham's readiness to sacrifice his son Isaac—the story of the 'akedah, which Yehoshua views as an ultimate act of irresponsibility toward one's offspring, and which Yael Feldman has described as a reversed oedipal complex in Yehoshua's thought.[49] Since a lack of responsibility toward one's children is indeed the main problem in this novel, as it is in most of Yehoshua's works, we can argue that the dog's lookout on Mount Moriah denotes a time of farcical *irresponsibility* from which *A Late Divorce*'s overall plot and characterization flow. The fact that this episode is assigned to a dog validates moreover a postclassical belief that *any* consciousness is entitled to occupy the position of an important spectator—a privilege that "depends not upon qualitative distinctions of 'better' and 'worse' points of view, but rather upon quantitative distinctions between more and less distance. It is a privilege available to anyone who is willing to travel."[50] The dog has traveled all the way to the national center of consciousness, and from there he barks at the horizon with the help of a "translation" supplied by the implied author. By contrast, the family's patriarch, who has traveled back to his homeland to get divorced, is not assigned any distinct lookout stance from which to reconsider *his* responsibilities toward family and nation. Instead, he fantasizes about escape to America and is able to engage with the family's problems about as effectively as the family dog.

Like *A Late Divorce*, *Mr. Mani* is fragmented into many narrative perspectives, which in this case span five historical periods covering more than two hundred years. However, Yehoshua brilliantly balances this extreme fragmentation with a set of recurrent motifs that generate a sense of cohesion. Commenting on this balancing act, Gabriel Zoran notes that narrative aspects commonly tied to the axis of time (memory) are conveyed in this novel via spatial means (eyesight and geographic locations) and vice versa—in other words, *Mr. Mani* historicizes geography and spatializes history so as to create recurrent and unifying motifs.[51] The typical short-sightedness of Yehoshua's characters—which Zoran classifies as a spatial element because it connects characters physically to their surroundings—is passed down in *Mr. Mani* from one generation to the next, along with a stash of old glasses. A recalibration of near and distant vision is further conveyed in *Mr. Mani* via a nuanced interplay between the Manis' limited knowledge about their own family's past and the transgenerational knowledge that Yehoshua conveys to the reader over the heads of the confused characters. This dynamic extends to a recurrent lookout site that emphasizes this gap between short and longsighted attitudes toward family life and national (ir)responsibility.

In *Mr. Mani*, Yehoshua distilled his usual concern with personal and collective responsibility into a series of observation posts dotting the road between the historical center of Jewish identity in Zion and the rest of the world. On this road leading up to Jerusalem (and away from it), travelers from every era are invited to reassess their commitment to the city and its inhabitants. For example, in 1982 Hagar Shiloh spends three days tagging after Gavriel Mani all over Jerusalem, as we saw in the previous chapter, and she then recounts this adventure to her mother, who lives on a kibbutz in the desert. According to *Mr. Mani*'s unusual narrative scheme, Yehoshua presents only Hagar's side of the conversation, so that the reader must imaginatively reconstruct her mother's responses:

> [I] headed for that old ruined building there, you know, the one where the road starts climbing back into the mountains . . .
>
> —Yes. Someone once told me it was an old Arab khan where travelers to Jerusalem stopped to rest their horses. . . .
>
> . . . I'm not so alone anymore but part of a much bigger story that I don't know anything about yet. . . . And I was even beginning to enjoy that old ruin, which *everyone sees from the highway but no one ever bothers to explore*. . . . And I began to imagine all the travelers who must have stopped there on their way from Jaffa to Jerusalem, because a hundred years ago it was the place in which they all spent the night—and all at once, Mother, I had this feeling of great peace inside me.[52]

This place that "everyone sees from the highway but no one ever bothers to explore" is explored in *Mr. Mani* as a vital link between Jerusalem and the rest of the world because *here* a choice must be made to leave or return—to contribute to familial, national, and international relationships, or to give up on them.

A hundred and thirty years earlier—on what was then a narrower road between Jaffa and Jerusalem—Avraham Mani accompanies his son up to Jerusalem, and just a year later he descends toward the coastal port again, abandoning his newly widowed daughter-in-law and her baby (actually his own son, incestuously sired): "When I was sure that now she would bid me farewell and return with a caravan ascending to Jerusalem from Beit-Mahsir, she suddenly swore that she would do no such thing until she had seen the sea that I was about to embark on. And so we climbed to the top of the hill and saw the sea from afar, and I thought, 'Now her mind has been set to rest,' and I took my leave."[53] Although one wonders why this young woman might feel pacified by a glimpse of Avraham's escape route, he imagines it so. And, as if their son were acting out a delayed reaction half a century later, this next Mani—by now a Jerusalemite gynecologist with a family of his own—accompanies his visitors the Shapiro siblings, down this same road from Jerusalem on their way back to Poland via Jaffa and Beirut, and, under Efrayim Shapiro's indifferent gaze, this Mani throws himself under a train in despair over their departure.

Thus, through the lookouts that dot the path between Jerusalem and the world, Yehoshua dramatizes his characters' opportunities to reconsider their relationships and responsibilities to Jerusalem and its inhabitants; these opportunities are occasionally seized (Hagar clings to her Manis) and more often abandoned (Avraham Mani and the Shapiros leave the country), so that again, Yehoshua's chronotopic lookout scenarios function as a pivotal moment of judgment and misjudgment capable of recalibrating each watchman's relationship to what lies relatively near (familiar places and people) and what lies far (history, and further, myth).

As a trope that dramatizes a hazy or impaired vision, Yehoshua's watchman's stance invites his reader to see *further* than the characters who are responding to complicated and urgent challenges on their horizons. Overall, Yehoshua's lookout moments offer an opportunity to embrace new viewpoints, which the characters sometimes internalize in positive ways; just as often, however, they shirk away when they realize that a difficult situation has spun out of control. These lookout scenarios thus function as heightened moments of introspection that lead, especially in his later novels, to a potential improvement in the communal and personal relationships of the characters, while revealing always a dangerous blind spot of irresponsibility.

By using this device to expose the limitations of his watchmen and watchwomen, Yehoshua evokes, as well, the biblical posture of prophet-watchmen expected to guard over the house of Israel; he rejects their reliance on God and mocks their high-handed attitudes, but he echoes their complaints about blind and deaf people who refuse to conform to their prophets' guidance. Yehoshua positions his myopic characters at strategic observation posts that force them to reassess their relationship with the national past and the different cultural modes that surround them: although their judgment may be impaired, they still find themselves invested with great responsibility over situations they can barely control. He thus models scenarios where responsibility, understood as an ability to respond to new problems on the horizon, is jeopardized. However, the reader is placed in an optimal position from which to evaluate the watchman's options and is thus invited to consider alternative solutions to the problems that face the characters. In a rhetorical manner, Yehoshua's watchman's stance equips his readers to imagine better solutions for the crises dramatized on his fictionalized horizons.

CHAPTER 4

Vocation

> Was Ben Attar nothing more than a merchant? ... No. ... [He was] a man
> disguised as a merchant. ... A loving man, a philosopher and sage of love.
> —A. B. YEHOSHUA, *A JOURNEY TO THE END OF THE MILLENNIUM*, 133–34

When Yotam Reuveni inquired of A. B. Yehoshua how he manages to learn so many details about the daily routines of the merchants, judges, scholars, doctors, and engineers that populate his fiction, Yehoshua proudly admitted that he makes every effort to acquaint himself with the labor of these specialists, because "it is important to integrate occupation as much as possible within a novel. ... It's a core aspect of one's psychology ... of the way one behaves toward other people."[1] Elsewhere he ventured that people are characterized "first and foremost by their professional identities."[2]

In other words, rather than narrowly project upon his characters his own occupation as a writer and public intellectual,[3] Yehoshua presents an extraordinary range of professional activities in his fiction: doctors, scholars, filmmakers, musicians; judges and lawyers; teachers galore; accountants and homemakers. And yet all of them, in one way or another, are *memunim*—managers who have been charged with supervising or repairing something or someone: *memunim* turned into repairmen, and repairmen who become *memunim* (in the singular, *memuneh*).

In Yehoshua's fiction, this pattern can take the form of a mechanic who owns a large garage, as Adam does in *The Lover* (*Hame'ahev*, 1977), or a character actually may be called *hamemuneh*, as in *A Woman in Jerusalem* (*Shlihuto shel hamemuneh 'al mash'abei enosh*, 2004), where Yehoshua dispensed altogether with proper names for all but one of his characters, labeling them instead only according to their family functions or professional identities: factory owner, journalist, night-shift manager, secretary, neglected children, ex-wife, aging mother, and above all, the *memuneh* over human resources who is charged with ferrying the corpse of Yulia Ragayev from Jerusalem to her former Soviet republic.

The idea of vocational responsibility in that novel is signaled already by its very unusual title, which reads, literally, "The Mission of the *Memuneh* over Human Resources." Quite tellingly, the English-language publisher decided to rename it *A Woman in Jerusalem*, precisely to avoid being misshelved among business management manuals.[4] In a moment, we will return to take a closer look at this novel, along with Yehoshua's notions of a *memuneh*. But first, let us recall briefly the role of vocational tropes throughout literary history, so as to appreciate the choices that are readily available to Yehoshua within this wider lineage.

As noted, Yehoshua's attention to the professional identities of his characters certainly endows them with a greater sense of psychological depth, and it also facilitates significant social interactions within their workplaces. However, such vocational themes also invoke a "higher calling" that transcends the daily requirements of modern life. Rooted in the vocational errands of biblical prophets who were entrusted with divinely ordained missions, the ancient idea of an exalted vocation was subsequently secularized and incorporated into the modern novel during the eighteenth and nineteenth centuries, chiefly via the European bildungsroman. Yehoshua can connect to the biblical model directly through Jewish tradition, but his plots are also shaped in response to normative narrative expectations associated with the bildungsroman.

A standard bildungsroman recounts a young protagonist's quest to make his or her way in the world by finding a suitable employment and a compatible love partner.[5] Starting with Goethe's *Wilhelm Meisters Lehrjahre* during the second half of the eighteenth century, such novels of education advocated for an expansion of opportunities available to the members of the bourgeoisie. In no small measure, this attitude stemmed from an adaptation of the Protestant belief that every person "has been called by God to a specific worldly vocation and that his success is a token of salvation," as Alan Mintz observed in his study of *George Eliot and the Novel of Vocation*.[6] However, the prototypical bildungsroman demonstrates that no matter how eccentric an individual may be, he or she must still adapt to an existing social order by establishing a stable family unit within it, and conversely, society, too, must acknowledge the talents and special circumstances of its individual members, by removing fossilized impediments to their personal

74 THE RETROSPECTIVE IMAGINATION OF A. B. YEHOSHUA

growth. This attitude was then imagined as crucial for the progress of an entire nation and extended even to "the progress of humankind."[7]

The bildungsroman's attitude toward vocational responsibilities hence mimics, but at the same time also reconfigures, the errands of the biblical prophets, who in ancient literature were responsible for warning against a potential dissolution of the collective welfare. Of course, their vocational duties were neither chosen nor optional: they were authoritatively imposed from above, often with very little suitability between the *memuneh* over God's words and the tasks that God imposes upon him. Furthermore, neither the prophets nor the people of Israel were encouraged to blend into the world around them, as occurs in the standard bildungsroman. Instead, the prophets remind the people of Israel to behave as a nation set apart to be God's wife. If a biographical model operates here, as Ilana Pardes has argued, then it is one that narrates the development of a specific nation as it struggles to live with its God in a challenging world.[8]

From Goethe's prototype of the genre, through Balzac's *Illusions perdues*, Dickens's *David Copperfield*, and Charlotte Brontë's *Jane Eyre*, these modern fictionalizations of vocational identity also intertwine their protagonists' professional quests with a search for true love. Even in George Eliot's *Middlemarch*, which Alan Mintz regards as the ultimate "novel of vocation," the professional success of its characters still hinges upon their romantic interests. We are shown again and again how any misguided love choices obstruct vocational aspirations, while compatible love partnerships enable professional success.

Now, to get back to our subject, it is crucial to note that unlike the youthful protagonists of a standard bildungsroman, Yehoshua's principal characters tend to appear in their middle age, rather than in the flower of their youth. Usually, they already have a successful professional occupation, but all of a sudden they are confronted with new professional demands, coupled with a conjugal crisis that challenges their overall identity and stability. The professional identities of Yehoshua's characters are therefore *not* simple expressions of their psychology, but rather another means of constructing the multilayered social, historical, and historiosophic texture of his novels.

In fact, Yehoshua enjoys creating provocative *discrepancies* between the private behaviors and professional identities of his characters. For instance, Molkho, an accountant for the Ministry of the Interior who had dutifully nursed his wife for seven years until she died from cancer, feels compelled to

VOCATION   75

establish a new romantic relationship immediately after her death. However, as Avraham Balaban discerned, Molkho approaches every potential love affair as an accountant rather than as a sex-starved widower and therefore fails to establish any viable new relationship.[9] Although Molkho's private behavior is comically aligned with his professional identity as an accountant, he ironically *miscalculates* the depth of his attachment to his wife and his own readiness for sexuality and love.

Across Yehoshua's fiction one finds many such interesting discrepancies between the professional identities and private behaviors of his overwrought characters. Hagar Shiloh is shocked to find Judge Gabriel Mani presiding cheerfully over his municipal court the morning after he allegedly tried to commit suicide in his apartment; in public, Judge Mani behaves in a dignified manner that contrasts with the erratic chaos that Hagar had noticed in his home at night. Similarly, in *A Late Divorce*, the charismatic historian Asa Kaminka develops a theory about shortcutting political catastrophes, but although he has been married for several years, he has not yet managed to consummate a sexual relationship with his wife. And Asya in *The Lover*— an energetic high school teacher, PhD student, and mother of a teenage daughter—accepts the pathetic lover that her husband brings her instead of striving to create a romantic, sexual, and intellectual partnership at home.

If Yehoshua really believes that human beings are defined first and foremost by their professional identities, why, then, does he introduce such provocative discrepancies between the professional images and private behaviors of his characters? Asya's husband, Adam, is a garage owner and mechanic whose "dirty hands and overalls" clash with the upper-middle-class milieu of his wife and daughter. This discrepancy, which questions the continued validity of the State of Israel's socialist ideals, is never discussed openly in their family, but Adam's teenage daughter consoles herself with the thought that at least her father's long beard sets him apart from the common stereotype of a manual laborer:

> That beard of his is something remarkable, growing wild, making him look like an *ancient prophet or an artist*. Something special, not like all the others, not like a laborer anyway.... When they asked me "What does your Daddy do?" I used to say innocently "Daddy works in a garage," and at once I felt that they were a bit disappointed. Then I started saying "My Daddy has a factory." "What kind of factory?"

they'd ask. "A garage" I said and then they'd explain that a garage isn't a factory. I used to say "My Daddy has a big garage" because it really was a very big garage. . . .

But then I thought, oh, to hell with it, why should I need to apologize. . . . When somebody particularly irritated me with this question I used to say "My Daddy is a garage hand" and look him full in the eyes, enjoying his astonishment. Because in our class most of the pupils' parents are professors . . . architects, scientists, executives in major companies, army officers.[10]

By assigning to Adam a professional identity that requires such complicated explanations and even apologies, Yehoshua draws attention to a lack of harmony between the different facets of this family's life. In high school, Adam had followed a "calling" to become a garage owner when he stepped into his father's business and was thereby jolted out of his age group and alienated from his former classmates. He then attempts to repair this rupture by marrying a former classmate who had become a teacher, indeed a perennial student, but their liaison, as we previously saw, does not result in an optimal match.

Adam's business flourishes, yet he too does not see himself primarily as a mechanic or a businessman. He declares that his true vocation is to help people repair their lives, and not just their cars: "People put themselves in my hands sometimes . . . they throw themselves at me as if saying—'Take me,' and sometimes I take them."[11] But precisely because he views himself as responsible for "repairing" people, he allows himself to sometimes misuse this calling in immoral and even criminal ways, as when he has sex with his daughter's neglected friend. Adam's misguided attempt to repair everything results in the greatest catastrophe, when he redesigns the hearing aid of his deaf son, inserting an off switch, and the child is then run over by a car.

Do such discrepancies between the professional identities and the personal abilities of Yehoshua's characters undermine the fundamental link that the bildungsroman draws between a modern vocational identity and a "higher calling" expected to promote a wider national well-being? Is Yehoshua readapting the vocational responsibilities of an ancient nation that perpetually finds itself worried about its prospects, behavior, and morals? And more simply, why does Yehoshua ask us to judge Adam, not merely as a mechanic, garage owner, and paterfamilias, but also as a *memuneh* charged

VOCATION   77

with troubled lives, which Adam often manipulates, disastrously, and not to his advantage?

Interested only tangentially in raising our greater sensitivity toward blue-collar laborers or wealthy garage owners whose parents had imposed a limiting professional path upon them—that is the story of *Wilhelm Meister's Apprenticeship*—Yehoshua in *The Lover* is concerned rather with a reconsideration of the Labor Zionist ideology of *torat ha'avodah* and its *livnot ulehibanot* ethos (to build and be rebuilt), the ideology that had guided the modern Zionist effort in its early years, as Eric Zakim has shown.[12] Even this ideology is ultimately a secular adaptation of the biblical *hashivenu venashuvah* (return us to You and to the land, and we will *then* follow Your commandments—i.e., Eicha 5:21), where the prophet conveys to God a plea for redemption as a prelude for atonement. From his earliest short stories to his most recent novels, Yehoshua has been interested in this relationship between redemption and self-repair (a secularized variation of atonement). And the ultimate repair that preoccupies him is the transition in Jewish history from a state of dispersed vulnerability to a modern Israeli sovereignty envisioned as a stable, inclusive, and creative entity. By stressing the weakest links between the private and professional troubles of his characters, Yehoshua shows that his *memunim* over the collective welfare can only rise up to an adequate degree of responsibility if they are also willing to repair themselves.

THE *MEMUNEH*'S MISSION

Yehoshua's engagement with the Labor Zionist ethos of "build and be rebuilt" comes across most sharply in his early story "Sleepy Day" (Tardemat hayom), which tells about two construction laborers who shock their site manager by announcing that they are going home to rest instead of working under icy rain conditions.[13] The *memuneh* over the construction project—such is the only name that Yehoshua assigns to this character—plays a very minor role in this story, which focuses rather on the leading rebel's decision to be *memuneh* over his own personal needs and actions (or inactions). The dilemma that Yehoshua tackles here, as in several of his other early stories, is this: Under what circumstances can individual desire take precedence over collective responsibilities? When is it urgent to invest in basic infrastructure, and when is there an opportunity for individual development and privacy?

78   THE RETROSPECTIVE IMAGINATION OF A. B. YEHOSHUA

To what extent does the social and material infrastructure enable or impede personal bildungs?

To this debate, so familiar to students of Zionism, Yehoshua contributes a plea for weaker individuals who may falter when attempting grander enterprises. He hints at the danger of inaction, while also criticizing any frenzied action that disregards individual welfare. Within the "build and be rebuilt" ethos, Yehoshua emphasizes a labor of *self*-repair that depends on social contacts that are especially vital during times of increased stress (icy rain or catastrophes of different kinds), so that psychological repair becomes a strategy for regenerating the collective strength and goodwill. While in some of his early stories solipsism and a shell-shocked laxity are portrayed as legitimate responses to a frenzied materialism and militarism, in his novels, especially the later ones, Yehoshua searches for a middle ground between the dangerous extremes of frenzy and laxity. In this manner he invites a reevaluation of national goals and their means of implementation as a responsibility assigned to various *memunim*, whose negligence or over-zealousness can generate concentric ripples of damage.

Yet as in a standard bildungsroman, in Yehoshua's novels too it is never enough to be just a doctor, garage owner, merchant, or musician. It is also necessary to be a committed lover, with all that this entails: in other words, a spouse *and* a parent *and* a responsible caretaker of a family that functions as a nucleus of a nation. This is a tall order for representatives of a nation that so recently returned to sovereignty after a hiatus of over two thousand years. But in Yehoshua's view, and more generally in Judaism's, such is the individual and collective labor necessary to achieve a national reconstruction.

To better understand Yehoshua's attitude toward vocational identity and responsibility, it is worth dwelling, therefore, on his strange term *memuneh* to designate minor characters in "Sleepy Day" and *Facing the Forests*, and more extensively, the hero of his short novel *A Woman in Jerusalem*. The English translations of *Facing the Forests* and *A Woman in Jerusalem* refer us to "managers"—a human resources manager and a forestation manager—even though the actual functionaries who occupy these managerial positions in Israel are normally called *menahel* (director) or *ahra'i* (responsible person). Yehoshua's selection of the less common term *memuneh*—which connotes an external assignation, as for someone who has been *charged with* a task—alerts us to the main significance of this nomenclature: a *menahel* directs

VOCATION   79

but a *memuneh* is directed: he is appointed from above (by whom? why?), assigned specific tasks (which?), and there are limits to his obedience, responsibility, and control.

This dynamic comes across most clearly in the novel whose English publication, as mentioned, was retitled *A Woman in Jerusalem* to avoid being confused with a business management manual. Like most of Yehoshua's characters, its main protagonist—the human resources manager (*hamemuneh 'al mash'abei enosh*)—reaches what could have been the prime of his life, if he had been less psychologically and socially impaired. Suddenly he is placed in a situation that demands a redefinition of his professional and personal capabilities. Known to us exclusively by his job title in a Jerusalem factory that bakes bread and also produces paper goods on the side, the human resources manager is responsible for all the employees of both factories, including a foreign worker, Yulia Ragayev, whom he had hired as a cleaner but whose absence is not noticed when she dies from a terrorist attack in the marketplace. Although Yulia is the focus of most of the hopes and worries in this novel, only the *memuneh* is charged with responsibility for her afterlife.

The labor that defines this head of personnel in a Jerusalemite bread-and-paper factory is, significantly, *not* his chosen vocation: he had not educated himself for this task, nor does he like it. Nevertheless, he grows into this new responsibility over the course of the plot. In his youth, he had dropped out of a BA in philosophy to become an officer in the army, yet due to his individualistic personality and a lack of interest in the military, he did not get very far there either. After marrying and becoming a father, he finds employment as a globe-trotting salesman for the paper factory, where his efforts to expand its international markets are indeed appreciated by the elderly owner. But now that he has finally found an enjoyable and productive employment, its travel demands prove incompatible with his family life:

> When [his] marriage was on the rocks, in part because of his frequent travels, the old man [the factory owner] reluctantly agreed to appoint him temporary head of the human resources division, a job that would allow him to sleep at home every night and try to repair the damage. Yet the hostility engendered by his absence was only distilled into a more concentrated poison by his presence, and the chasm between [husband and wife]—at first psychological,

then intellectual, and finally sexual—continued to grow of its own accord. Now that he was divorced, all that kept him from returning to his old job, which he had liked, was his determination to stay close to his daughter.[14]

And then, just as the unfortunate *memuneh* is attempting to find a new mate and at least salvage his relationship with his teenage daughter, he is suddenly assigned extra responsibilities by the factory owner: "Surely he understood that his responsibility was to deal not just with vacations, sick leaves, and retirements, but with death as well."[15]

The factory owner decrees that for the sake of the factory's reputation, the body of the foreign worker Yulia Ragayev, which had lain unclaimed in the morgue for several days, should be accompanied by the *memuneh* back to her home country. "There isn't any choice," the factory owner announces, and this becomes the slogan with which the old man manipulates the *memuneh*, who in turn manipulates others into ferrying the embalmed corpse through the steppes of Eastern Europe until they reach Yulia's mother, who angrily tells them that her daughter should have been kept in the Holy Land, where she had chosen to live. The shocked *memuneh* then decides to return the corpse to Jerusalem, at his own expense, together with the old mother and her orphaned grandson. "There's no choice," he tells his boss, insisting that this dramatic return, which will be reported in a local newspaper, might "benefit a city we've despaired of."[16]

The *memuneh*'s reasons for dragging the body back to Jerusalem are quite absurd, but his ability to grow into the requirements of this new responsibility transforms his temporary assignment into a genuine vocation that brings him renewed self-respect. To be sure, while he is manipulated by Yulia's mother and son, he nevertheless feels empowered, and this helps him reconnect emotionally with his daughter and ex-wife. Now he is ready to take control over his own destiny and to respect the destinies of others. Having assessed the limits of his responsibility, he now appoints himself head of the return journey, which he also expects will put him in the headlines of a newspaper, whose conscientious reporter had invoked biblical admonitions about Israel's responsibilities toward foreigners when he raised an outcry against the factory's obliviousness to the missing worker. Yulia Ragayev, however, evidently reneged on her own responsibilities toward her teenage son by abandoning him to a life of truancy in her native country.

After meeting this son, the *memuneh* steps up and declares that he will be responsible for him too, though it is unclear for how much or for how long. What, then, are the limits of this *memuneh*'s responsibility? He had learned from the factory's owner that no fixed boundaries are attached to his duties, but his private decision to take control of Yulia's family is a radical move with unpredictable consequences.

The *memuneh*'s decision to return Yulia's body to Jerusalem also functions as a reminder of Christianity's relationship with that city. Yulia's corpse is marked with stigmata—"the only visible damage was a few small puncture wounds in her hands and feet and a scratch on her skull"—and her Russian Orthodox mother declares that Jerusalem belongs to them too, as much as to anyone.[17] Ironically, rather than diminishing the *memuneh*'s relationship to the city of his birth, this attitude enhances the importance of Jerusalem in his eyes, so that when he absurdly prolongs his responsibility over Yulia's body, he also feels, as we have seen in chapter 2, that Jerusalem is "once more bathed in a glow of importance, as it had been in his childhood."[18]

Reinvigorated, the *memuneh* ceases to automatically obey the factory owner who had invested him with professional responsibilities in the first place. Now he independently hones the tools of his trade to their fullest capacity. This is his private bildung: he grows into old responsibilities and steps up to new ones. In so doing, he manages to take fresh control over his relationships at work, within the family, and publicly, through the newspaper articles that will be written about his mission to the end of the world and back to Jerusalem with a corpse in tow. He thus embraces his ultimate vocation as someone who is truly capable of rising to the demands of a sensitive and complex situation.

THE JUDGE VERSUS THE HISTORIAN

While the human resources manager is rejuvenated through his journey with a corpse, Professor Rivlin in *The Liberated Bride* (*Hakala hameshahreret*, 2001) is reinvigorated by his investigations of a dead marriage, as we saw in the previous chapter. Five years after the sudden divorce of his son Ofer from Galya, Ofer's stagnating romantic life torments Rivlin. Nobody asks him to repair his son's broken romantic life—on the contrary, both Rivlin's wife and his son demand that he refrain from approaching Galya's family with inquiries—but Rivlin cannot dance at other people's weddings, or conduct his research on modern Algerian history, while remaining perplexed and troubled by the collapse of his son's happiness.

Ofer contends that he knows very well why his marriage collapsed, and his mother, a district-court judge, upholds Ofer's right not to divulge those reasons. Nevertheless, half a decade after the divorce, Rivlin concludes that, unassisted, Ofer is simply unable to pull himself out of his protracted romantic stagnation and self-imposed exile in Paris. As well, Rivlin's quest to discover "the truth" behind the collapse of his son's marriage is also tightly associated with Rivlin's vocation: "I have to know," Rivlin declares. "That's how I am. I need to know the truth even if it's useless. . . . It's what motivates any historian—otherwise he's in the wrong profession."[19] Rivlin aligns himself with neither Israel's "new" nor "old" historians—from his point of view they are all legitimate types of investigators[20]—but at the end he holds all members of his guild collectively responsible for a clarification of "life-and-death issues affecting our lives and the lives of our children."[21]

It is remarkable, however, that by drawing so much attention to the historian's quest for truth in this novel, Yehoshua temporarily distracts us from the conventional association of truth with justice, though a judge is featured in this novel through Rivlin's wife, Hagit. Provocatively, then, by pairing this judge with a historian, Yehoshua wrenches away from the former a monopoly over "the truth, all the truth, and nothing but the truth," and instead assigns the deeper responsibility for extracting the truth to a historian (rather than a psychoanalyst or a detective). Who, then, is *memuneh* over the "truth"? And what game is Yehoshua playing with the professional, familial, and national responsibilities of a judge and a historian, whose arguments are staged here not only within the intimacy of a couple but also in the overbearing space of a courtroom?[22]

As Gilead Morahg puts it, "both Rivlin and Hagit obviously love their son, so the opposition between them is an opposition between two sensibilities with conflicting normative views on how best to exercise this love. Rivlin's sensibility is empathic, truth seeking, and convention defying. . . . Hagit is much more circumspect and pragmatic. . . . But Hagit turns out to be wrong."[23] Indeed, it becomes clear eventually that to liberate Ofer, it is essential to expose him to the source of his confusion. By moving the quest for truth and good judgment away from the judge and assigning this task instead to a historian, Yehoshua defamiliarizes and expands the range

VOCATION   83

of response *abilities* expected from different types of *memunim* over the private and public welfare.[24]

It is also significant that the pithy definition of Rivlin's professional identity—"I need to know the truth even if it's useless. . . . It's what motivates any historian—otherwise he's in the wrong profession"[25]—appears in a section called "The Judgment Seat," in which Rivlin and Hagit come to physical blows in the empty space of her courtroom, where he has come to help her tidy up her drawers on a weekend. Oddly, Yehoshua stages this conjugal fight as a struggle between a docile male and a judge in her own powerful domain, a variation of the gendered paradigm that Nitza Ben-Dov identifies as an "Astarte paradigm" across Yehoshua's work, wherein a powerful woman dominates a docile man who worships her.[26]

> "Tell the truth [she admonishes him]. That's all I'm asking. The whole truth. It's not as hard as all that."
>
> "I'm not a defendant in your court."
>
> "It has nothing to do with my court. I'm your wife. I'm open with you about everything. And you keep things from me like a coward. . . .
>
> "Don't change the subject. It's not Ofer, it's you. I'm asking you plainly. What did you say to him, and what do you know, and what are you up to?
>
> . . . ["]Speak the truth, man! Let's have it. I'm your wife. What are your afraid of? Even if you were foolish enough to try putting them in touch again, which could only cause more pain, that's not a crime. The crime is not sharing it with the only person who shares everything with you. Please, don't force me to squeeze the truth out of you bit by bit. . . . What have you done? What have you said?"
>
> "All right. All right. Just stop threatening me as though I were a traitor or a murderer."
>
> "You are. You've betrayed me. You've murdered the trust between us."[27]

The crime, we must bear in mind, is that Rivlin had stealthily visited their ex-in-laws. And Hagit's overreaction is of course as problematic as Rivlin's fear of his wife, as if he were a child disobeying his mother. Although justice is traditionally painted as a blindfolded woman to indicate impartiality, this judge ironically "blinds" the "defendant" during this heated altercation by angrily crushing his glasses and rendering him unable to drive or type for several days, as we saw in the previous chapter.[28]

Their disagreement stems in the first place from Hagit's unwillingness to allow Rivlin to investigate the causes of their son's failed marriage; she insists on drawing firm barriers between themselves and their son, as well as between themselves and their ex-in-laws. But since Rivlin contravenes her, she breaks out of the common bounds of domestic discourse and allows her professional identity to flood their conjugal disagreement: "Watch out," she threatens when he twists her arm after she slaps him. "You don't know what you're getting yourself into by assaulting a judge in a courtroom. I can press an alarm. . . . You'll be locked up in solitary before you know it. It will be a week before you can open your lying mouth to anyone."[29] Allowing this family disagreement to spill into professional discourse dramatizes Yehoshua's comment that professional identity is "a core part of one's psychology, of one's personality . . . of the way one behaves toward other people."[30] On the other hand, if, as a judge, Rivlin's wife is expected to be fair, impartial, and levelheaded, then her tyrannical and somewhat hypocritical behavior here is totally *out* of character, or at least unprofessional.

By contrast, we get a glimpse into Hagit's professional integrity when she returns from conducting a trial abroad, whose details she is not allowed to disclose:

> "I don't have much to tell. We went to a primitive place at the end of the world to listen to the fantasies of either a psychopath or a highly sophisticated liar. I honestly don't know whether someone in the district attorney's office or the Mossad thought they could put one over on us or they're so naive that they think the man is telling the truth."
>
> "What did the other judges think?"
>
> "They didn't see it that way. . . . But you don't put someone away for fifteen years without better proof."
>
> "Fifteen years?" His curiosity was piqued.
>
> "It could be. There are charges of treason."
>
> "What kind of treason?"
>
> "Never mind. There's not much I can tell you. . . . I'm fed up with the whole trial."[31]

Here we see that Hagit's reticence to disclose details about this trial actually belies her declaration that she shares "everything" with her husband; this time she does maintain professional discretion even in an intimate environment. On the other hand, when she disagrees with her colleagues, she does not hesitate to express her dissenting opinion, as a conscientious judge must do, though at home she makes it almost impossible for her husband to follow any dissenting course.

In conversation with his son, Rivlin anatomizes the differences between himself and his wife: "Your mother is a judge. It's her job to settle the past by issuing a verdict. I'm a historian. The past for me is an inexhaustible mine of surprises and possibilities." To which Ofer replies, "It's not a verdict she seeks. She wants boundaries. And that's something you're a world champion at crossing and getting others to cross."[32] Here it is important to keep in mind that when Yehoshua was writing *The Liberated Bride*, at the turn of the millennium, he was also advocating for a clearer demarcation of the boundaries of the State of Israel despite the collapse of the Oslo Accords. The novel's engagement with questions of borders was therefore of particular interest to its first wave of interpreters.[33] Yehoshua's insistence on firm geopolitical borders obscures the fact, however, that in both his fiction and his extraliterary comments he imagines boundaries as markers of separation to be empathetically *transcended*. In other words, Yehoshua's tendency is to combine Hagit's insistence on firm boundaries with Rivlin's propensity to transcend them.

After months of stagnation in his scholarly work, Rivlin reaches the conclusion that "a scholar with some integrity doesn't just closet himself with old documents and materials" but "reads the newspapers and connects the past to the present." His job is not just to describe the past but also to "show that today's developments have their roots in yesterday's."[34] And to do so, the historian too must cross boundaries, at the very least between the present and the past. Like a judge's, the historian's insights are expected to rest on firm evidence, but while a judge examines evidence from the past to issue a practical judgment—who is guilty and what to do about it?—the historian can examine evidence from the past mainly for the sake of providing a reliable academic investigation. Whatever he or others subsequently choose to do with these discoveries corresponds just to their own interests as individual citizens, creative artists, or ideologues.

In his lecture "Five Recommendations to Historians from a History Lover," which he delivered in celebration of Israel's fiftieth anniversary in 1998, Yehoshua enjoined Israeli historians to

> *hook* us to the past so that we can forge creative connections with it—for art provides the best means to preserve and dialogue with the past. . . .
>
> . . . Hooks that entice an artist who is not learned to link his creativity and inner world to history. Please prepare such hooks for us in the course of your academic research—draw attention to them and package them in an attractive manner . . . in order to entice and attract the artist's interest and imagination.[35]

He thus entices historians to empower creative writers, while acknowledging their need to keep within the stricter boundaries of their discipline. As a fabulist, Yehoshua can, and indeed must, imaginatively embellish his fictional worlds according to his own ideological "inner world." From historians, he expects accurate and balanced research.

Though Rivlin is never allowed to learn the truth behind his son's divorce, in the course of liberating his son he ironically rediscovers his own vocational integrity. Previously, Rivlin had believed that historians "must write as if the present did not exist"; now he accepts a new "scholarly obligation to search for a connection between the examined past and the experienced present." This change in attitude results from his embarrassment at having failed to detect not only a crisis in his own family but also the eruption of a bloody civil war in Algeria, his area of expertise. In the end, Rivlin breaks out of his professional misgivings by proposing "a third approach," one that *neither* blinds itself to the present *nor* projects the present unto the past but rather suggests points of connection—"an arc" that draws together divergent "poles of interest."[36]

This constitutes a fairly close description of Yehoshua's own artistic method for connecting the different levels of signification in his works, as when he establishes points of divergence and convergence between the professional identities and personal behaviors of his characters in the contexts of their workplaces and family troubles, and then associates them, in turn, with symbolic references to national and historiosophic concerns that go back to ancient times.

VOCATION   87

While discussing his research with Arab acquaintances in the West Bank, Professor Rivlin explains that his "job is to know, not to help."[37] But later, his growing desire to help his son, along with his worry that a variation of the Algerian catastrophe might spread to his own country, lead him to become interested in causes as well as solutions for the historical problems that are clearly still impinging upon the present. To some extent, this expansion of Rivlin's range of responsibilities is a positive breakthrough that facilitates both a liberation of his son and a refreshingly new approach to his Algerian research, yet this is also a dangerous expansion that can lead to professional and personal breaches of conduct, a free-for-all attitude where personal interest, hasty conclusions, and wishful thinking may easily override a careful inquiry.

In the novel, Hagit never acknowledges her own limitations or the benefits of her husband's willingness to breach uncomfortable boundaries, but we see that in her professional realm she upholds reasonable doubt as a core component of her vocational responsibilities. Ideally, the judge *within* the historian and the historian *within* the judge should balance each other to keep their labor honest and effective. Both are *memunim* over the pursuit of truth via different disciplinary constraints, but to be fully effective in their professional capacities, as well as in their family circle, Yehoshua's judge and historian require different measures of flexibility and control at different junctures in their lives.

PILOT OF THE SOUL

What happens when an assessment of the optimal balance between knowledge and action is placed in the hands of surgeons and other healers who literally hold life and death in their hands, yet still depend on the efficacy of the tools of their trade to make such crucial decisions? Yehoshua explores this question in *Open Heart* (*Hashivah mehodu*, 1994), where the surprising death of Lazar, a hospital director, occurs after he undergoes a relatively uncomplicated heart surgery in his own hospital. This character's name evokes Jesus's resurrection of Lazarus, but Yehoshua's Lazar, who confidently places his body in the hands of his top physicians, dies with no modern miracle to resurrect him.

The eulogy delivered by a contrite chief surgeon celebrates their director's legendary "knowledge of details" alongside his modest "acknowledgment of

88   THE RETROSPECTIVE IMAGINATION OF A. B. YEHOSHUA

limits": "There wasn't a detail in the life of the hospital, from the numbers of doctors absent on leave to a broken cogwheel in the dialysis machine, that Lazar considered beneath his notice, and the moment he knew something he turned it into his responsibility. But the vast scope of responsibility that Lazar was prepared to take on himself . . . never blurred his awareness of the precise limits of his authority."[38] Lazar nonetheless dies in the care of his staff because he blurs the boundaries of his authority by allowing too many specialists to interfere in his case. In his youth, Lazar had wanted to be a doctor, but, like Adam in *The Lover*, he was forced to abandon his studies when his father fell ill. However, the youthful vocational option that closed down for Lazar opened up another professional path that eventually turned into an expansive responsibility for an entire hospital.

In parallel to Lazar's vocational trajectory, *Open Heart*'s central character, Benjamin Rubin, is a handsome young doctor who dreams of becoming a surgeon, scalpel in hand, adrenaline pumping at the prospect of reconstituting a human body. However, when the medical residencies are assigned, Benjy is invited to become an anesthesiologist instead. "Believe me," the chief anesthesiologist, Dr. Nakash, tells him, "I've been through a lot of surgeons in my time. Who knows them as I do? And I'm telling you, I've seen you at work, and it's not for you. Your scalpel hesitates, because it thinks too much. Not because you're inexperienced, but because you're too responsible. And in surgery too much responsibility is fatal. You have to take a risk; to cut a person up and still tell him it's good for him, you have to be partly a charlatan and partly a gambler."[39] Disappointed, Benjy accepts Dr. Nakash's offer to learn the art of anesthesiology. "The technical side was simple and could be quickly learned, and the main thing was not to abandon the patient, to think of his soul and not only of his breathing."[40] Just a few months earlier, such "soul talk" would have irritated Benjy, but ever since Lazar and his wife enlisted him in an emergency trip to India to rescue their sick daughter, Dr. Rubin's worldview had changed, and he had become more interested in life's spiritual dimensions.

The trip to India had exposed Benjy to alternative attitudes toward physicality and transcendental time, jolting him out of his old habits of thought. He witnessed Hindu rites on the Ganges River and tried to understand why backpacking Israelis felt so drawn to the rhythms of the Far East. In this state of mind, he had become galvanized by love—not for the damsel in distress that he was expected to rescue, but for her middle-aged mother,

VOCATION 89

Lazar's pampered wife. The shock of finding himself desperately in love with this unsuitable partner, and the authenticity and irreversibility of his sensations, revolutionize Benjy's inner world.

Thus, when the oriental Jew, Dr. Nakash, talks about piloting souls, Benjy has a new frame of reference from which to interpret these remarks. Prior to the Indian trip, such discourse would have been incomprehensible to him and might have even offended his enlightened sensibilities. But now, after many months of unrequited love, Benjy's sexual and mystical awakening teaches him that an aching soul may be undefinable and illogical, but the pain and longing are real. The novel ends without full closure, yet one senses that Benjy will assume his place in Israeli society as a stable citizen with a functional family and a healing profession.

Among Yehoshua's novels, the plot of *Open Heart* comes closest to a standard bildungsroman, in which a young person progresses, socially and emotionally, through romantic and vocational choices. Dr. Rubin does not actually *choose* to love Lazar's wife—he falls in love with her uncontrollably—but all his subsequent decisions revolve around a deep need to explore this path. He had wished to become a cardiac surgeon, but this desire is denied him, and instead he is invited to become an anesthesiologist.

Yehoshua does not provide a glimpse into Benjy's earliest "moment of vocation," as Alan Mintz calls the moment in which the self "seizes its identity" by a passionate commitment to a particular type of work.[41] Therefore, we can never know exactly why Benjy became interested in being a doctor in the first place. Still, Yehoshua offers a beautiful "moment of vocation" when Benjy embraces the opportunity to become an anesthesiologist, and this too arrives by way of the oriental Jew, Dr. Nakash, a hybrid eastern-westerner:

> "If you're getting bored," Nakash whispered to me in the middle of the night in his heavily accented Iraqi Hebrew, "think of yourself as the pilot of the soul, who has to ensure that it glides painlessly through the void of sleep without being jolted or shocked, without falling. But also to make sure that it doesn't soar too high and slip inadvertently into the next world." I had heard him speak like this about his role before, but now, in the depths of the night, a little groggy after long hours of intent concentration on the changing monitors of the anesthesia machine, with the skull and brain not actually before my eyes but only flickering grayly on the suspended

video screen, I felt his words were true. I had turned from a doctor into a pilot or a navigator, surrounded by nurses.[42]

Here we have a synthesis between East and West, which poeticizes a scientifically monitored control over vital connections between mind and body. Finally Benjy understands that it is not enough to repair the body: there may be great excitement in exposing living tissue to the surgeon's skill, but there is also a subtler responsibility for the nervous system, which Dr. Nakash calls the soul, that renders a complicated physical repair possible and contributes to the healing process.

Having failed to get himself appointed to a leading position at the operating table, Benjy becomes responsible instead for a patient's consciousness of pain: he has become the *memuneh* over a patient's lifeline from the corner of the operating table. This is a responsibility that he learns to relish thanks to his new openness to the ebb and flow of his own emotional life and his new awareness of the limits of everyone's ability to manipulate the world according to his or her own desires and expectations.

REPAIRING THE NATION

The ultimate healing process that interests Yehoshua is the historical transition from a state of dispersed Jewish vulnerability to a modern sovereignty envisioned as a stable, creative, and moral identity. In his 1995 essay for *Tikkun Magazine*, written during the heady days of the Oslo Process, when final agreements between Israelis and Palestinians seemed near at hand, he listed four major Israeli problems that were overshadowed by the Arab-Israeli conflict: relations between Israeli Jews and Israeli Arabs, a yawning gap between the rich and poor, a lack of communication between religious and secular sectors of the population, and a redefinition of the Jewish "vocational mission," which he imagines as a joint Israel-diaspora "education corps" dedicated to aiding developing countries in a practical manner: "The talk about the 'mission' of the Jewish nation among nations of the world and of our unique destiny—that is, about our need to be 'a light unto the Gentiles' or 'the Chosen People,' continues to perplex us. . . . Where does this need, this quest for a vocation, come from, to speak of being 'Chosen' and of being 'a light unto the nations?' The answer, I believe, can be found in the unique way in which religion and nationality are integrated in the Jewish nation."[43]

Acknowledging the *vocational pressures* felt by a nation scripturally defined as "the Chosen People"—viewing themselves as *memunim* over God's message to humanity—Yehoshua makes an effort to *reduce* the mythic components of this formulation to fit a modern sociopolitical mission, rather than a religious call for a redemption of the land and people. Reflecting nonetheless on his own polemical efforts to define Israeli identity, Yehoshua explains his own responsibility as a continuation of the vocational work of the ancient prophets: "We, the writers of Israel, see ourselves continuing a kind of tradition, a kind of obligation, a kind of duty towards our forefathers, writers who helped create Zionism." For Yehoshua, "the involvement of Israeli writers in public affairs" is in "the tradition of the prophets[,] . . . who spoke against the king, against the people from time to time. [They were] trying to correct the people by saying to them: you are not going in the right way."[44] Yet, like many writers, Yehoshua has refashioned prophetic discourse into a worldview that opposes the biblical worldview in fundamental ways.[45] In other words, the struggle against the forefathers, as Mordechai Shalev pithily put it, is ironically conducted through models inherited from the forefathers.[46] Even when theology is taken out of the equation, the supervisory role attributed to God and his delegates is still an object of struggle among the various *memunim* striving to demarcate new boundaries between their overlapping areas of responsibility and control.

While the mission of the ancient prophets was to *fuse* private and public life into one national identity regulated by the Sinaitic covenant, Yehoshua's mission has been to *disentangle* religious and civic life, so as to reinforce a Jewish identity still connected to the past, but in a corrective manner: "I fear how much the past dominates the present. How much we are bound to the past. And how much we cannot liberate ourselves from the past. [I wish] to understand the past, in order to correct it."[47] To reconfigure this connection between the present and the past—the national body and soul—Yehoshua turns himself into a "historian" with a "prophetic" agenda, who judges the past in light of a desired future. In this path, he follows the vocation of prophets of yore, but he redefines core components of their worldview to fit modern ideals of national behavior.

The American poet Allen Tate once received a questionnaire about creative writing as a career. "I do not think of literature as a career," he replied. "It is a vocation. . . . A writer, I think, must risk everything. If he is moderately intelligent, he will know that the chances of failure are overwhelming. He is a writer because he cannot be anything else."[48] Yehoshua, however, could have excelled as a lawyer or a historian: "I wanted to be a lawyer," he told Bernard Horn during one of their conversations.[49] But as a citizen with a public platform, he has, in a sense, found a way of investigating the past and advocating for social justice through a combination of fiction writing and extraliterary comments about his national situation. He views this activity as a civic responsibility: "People have said to me: you are damaging your writing by being so involved in writing articles. I don't regret it; perhaps I have damaged my writing and so have my colleagues. But it was important to do my duty as a citizen, because first of all, I'm a citizen and only secondly a writer."[50]

Ultimately, I would contend that Yehoshua views himself as a national repairman, and that this is a vocational mission that he projects unto his characters, as we have seen in this chapter. Regardless of their professional identities as judges, mechanics, doctors, or historians, Yehoshua's characters become *memunim* over all sorts of repairs; their responsibility usually includes a reassessment of shifting boundaries between their control over their assigned tasks and their relationship with all those with whom they come into contact in their family and workplace.

A standard bildungsroman ends with a more or less harmonious balance between society and a protagonist who has struggled to find a mate and a vocational path suited to his or her dreams and possibilities. Yehoshua's fiction rarely ends with such tidy closure, though it often does hint at a practical means of attaining this stability. In *Open Heart*, Dr. Rubin finds a niche for himself as an anesthesiologist, and it is suggested that he might reintegrate himself into a conventional family life, having acknowledged the hopelessness of his attachment to Lazar's wife. In *The Liberated Bride*, Ofer never discloses to his parents the cause of his divorce, but he reassures his father that a genuine healing process has begun. In turn, his father's academic research becomes reinvigorated by Ofer's liberation, and the relationship between the judge and the historian is placed on a more balanced footing. Although the *memuneh* in *A Woman in Jerusalem* is unlikely to repair his broken family and may even lose his job for breaching too many professional boundaries, for the first time in his life he believes in himself. And he is now ready to appreciate the power of love and beauty.

The attention that Yehoshua grants to the professional lives of his characters enhances their psychological depth and facilitates a wide range of social contacts in their families and workplaces, but at the end of the day, the professional identities of Yehoshua's characters function less as an expression of their inner psychologies than as a pretext for sending them on grander missions of national repair. However, these grander missions in Yehoshua's fiction finally return to take the form of small, intimate adjustments in the intersecting spheres of the family and workplace.

CHAPTER 5

Holidays

> Not to attack religion as such, the ritual and prayers, all that small stuff,
> which do no harm so long as they give people comfort or provide structure
> for anxious souls. But those souls must not be dragged into the fear of
> something hidden and invisible, of a God who is abstract, jealous, and
> aggressive. . . . If I was incapable of destroying that supremacy, I could
> at least play tricks on it, make it hazy, mock it, put it to sleep, expose its
> wickedness, its instability, inject into it elements that contradict its holi-
> ness—pagan, absurd elements. . . . Because . . . hedonistic secular culture
> . . . is basically a thin, brittle crust that at a time of crisis or conflict crumbles
> before the terrifying power of transcendence.
>
> —TRIGANO TO MOSES IN A. B. YEHOSHUA'S *HESED SEFARADI /*
> *THE RETROSPECTIVE,* 292–93

Declaring himself both a "total Jew" and a "secular Israeli," Yehoshua has
been advocating since the early eighties for a recalibration of a balance of
power between the religious and civic components of Jewish identity. As a
politically engaged intellectual, he laid out in "Golah: The Neurotic Solution"
his basic assessment of an intrinsic entanglement between *dat* (religion)
and *le'om* (ethnicity) in Jewish identity.[1] Noting that both religious and
national/ethnic elements have always, jointly, informed the definition and
behavior of the Jewish people in exile and as a sovereign entity, he insists on
the need to carefully recalibrate their balance, so that creative, pragmatic,
and pluralistic forces of civic Jewish life in Israel will not be overrun by
religious influences.[2] In order to explore whether secular Israeli culture
can ever be more than "a thin brittle crust that at a time of crisis or conflict
crumbles before the terrifying power of transcendence," Yehoshua regularly
stages fictional plots in which his characters celebrate Jewish holidays under
particularly stressful circumstances. Such scenarios enable him to critique
traditional practices and current attitudes, not so much to dismantle religion

as to demonstrate a need for national reformation that includes the revision of seasonal markers of identity and time such as holidays.

Two of his novels, *A Late Divorce* (*Geirushim meuharim*, 1982) and *Friendly Fire* (*Esh yedidutit*, 2007), revolve around a holiday setting: *A Late Divorce* races toward a Passover seder and engages with this holiday's theme of freedom. *Friendly Fire* takes place during Hanukkah, and tallies the number of candles that Amotz Ya'ari lights with his family in Israel, while his wife lights none with their brother-in-law in Africa. Yehoshua's two historical novels, *Mr. Mani* (*Mar Mani*, 1990) and *A Journey to the End of the Millennium* (*Masa el tom ha'elef*, 1997), incorporate the High Holiday season into their plots, paying particular attention to Yom Kippur, the holiest day of the Jewish year. This generates a historiosophic conversation similar to what he evokes through the naming strategies we will trace in the following chapter, since proper names, like holidays, are key markers of identity that link the present with the past, extending traditional beliefs into our modern contemporary lives.

Michael Bell and Pericles Lewis, among others, have argued that the prevalence of religious motifs in works by nonreligious and antireligious modernists such as Kafka, Joyce, and Proust enabled modernists to paradoxically frame and tame an anarchy that they feared was threatening to uproot civilization from its former sources of coherence.[3] Of course religion most likely emerged in the ancient world from a primeval desire to tame natural phenomena perceived as chaotic or unexplainable. Modernists do acknowledge this primeval impulse and therefore adopt ambivalent attitudes toward foreign as well as homegrown myths, relying on defamiliarization and Freudian symbolism to contrast their present societies with other cultures in the present and the past. In Hebrew fiction, this kind of ironic confrontation between modern national life and traditional ideologies is most pronounced in the works of S. Y. Agnon.[4] Yehoshua's treatment of holiday scenarios, and religiosity in general,[5] is indebted to Agnon, and also to other modernists such as Faulkner, Joyce, Woolf, and Kafka. In *A Late Divorce*, which we discuss next, he draws most strongly from the style and the structure of William Faulkner,[6] especially *The Sound and the Fury*, where a holiday setting serves to accentuate the moral status of each character.

96 THE RETROSPECTIVE IMAGINATION OF A. B. YEHOSHUA

DANGEROUS DETACHMENTS

Indeed, from its opening epigraph, *A Late Divorce* acknowledges its relationship to *The Sound and the Fury* by citing directly from it: "Benjy knew it when Damuddy died. He cried. He smell hit. He smell hit."[7] Three-fourths of Faulkner's masterpiece occur between Good Friday and Easter Sunday, and this engagement with the suffering and resurrection of Christ through the holiday setting magnifies the resilience and moral fortitude of the servant, Dilsey, in marked contrast to the inadequacies and disintegration of her employers, the Compson family. The Easter sections, which encompass three-fourths of Faulkner's novel, are titled "April Seventh, 1928," "April Sixth, 1928" and "April Eighth, 1928," while a fourth chapter, set eighteen years in the past, features the suicide of Quentin Compson on "June Second, 1910." Yehoshua's *A Late Divorce* follows a similar calendrical method of titling its chapters in reference to a holiday, and it also adds an extra chapter set three years in the future, to clarify the core plot.

At first, Yehoshua's chapter headings evoke an apparently neutral reference to a "Sunday" and "Monday," but soon they begin to acquire thicker meaning as Shabbat approaches. Thus, "Friday, Four to Five PM" evokes a densely liminal atmosphere that separates the hectic week from an approaching Shabbat. It is during this hour that Zvi Kaminka prefers to visit his therapist in a feeble effort to explore his traumatic adolescent experiences, when his mother had slipped into schizophrenia. Another chapter queries the "Shabbat?" itself, because Yael Kaminka, who narrates this day—each chapter is narrated by a different character, as in Faulkner's novel—had lost her ability to keep track of Jewish time in the chaos generated by her father's visit. "Passover Eve" is followed by "The First Day of Passover"—a total of precisely nine days leading up to a *hurban*, the shocking murder of the family's patriarch, Yehuda Kaminka, just a few hours before his scheduled departure from Israel, as we noted earlier in chapter 2.

Discussing this novel with Bernard Horn, Yehoshua explained that

> the holidays and the festivals . . . are always, for Christians, for Muslims, for Jews, for everyone, concentrations of the personal neurosis as well as the general national neurosis . . . more is demanded of people. . . . So the festivals—the *hagim*, in Hebrew—always symbolize a crossroads, a very, very emotional crossroads, and this is the reason that, during the *hagim*—this is what Ika [Yehoshua's wife,

a clinical psychologist] tells me—more and more people come to mental hospitals, to escape some of the emotional burden and stress that they are suffering.[8]

Significant portions of *A Late Divorce* are in fact set in an insane asylum, where Naomi Kaminka had been confined since her attempt to stab her husband. She still claims that the attack was carried out by her alter ego, Elohima ("Godina")—a condensed female version of the theological forces against which Yehoshua struggles.

The "love" triangle that Yehoshua creates between Elohima, Naomi, and Yehuda has been importantly interpreted by Gilead Morahg as an allegorical manifestation of the oedipal triangle that Yehoshua sets up between God, the Land of Israel, and the people of Israel in his prominent essay "Golah: The Neurotic Solution," composed shortly before *A Late Divorce*.[9] Yehoshua contends there that, since ancient times, the people of Israel have developed a neurotic relationship with their homeland, distancing themselves from it in an effort to escape from the aggressive deity that had been imposed upon them by the prophets. According to Yehoshua, this deity interferes with the people's natural connection to their land, alienating them from it: "The mother-land-earth is given to the people by the God-father, and he lays down the rules of the giving and stipulates its conditions. . . . Nothing was more abominable in the sight of the prophets than the cult of the earth. All the agricultural rites had to undergo transformation, screening, and sublimation by the godhead system." The result was fear of God and alienation from the natural homeland.[10]

According to Yehoshua, since God's power feels less threatening beyond the homeland, escaping to the diaspora (the *Golah*) becomes the "neurotic solution" that the people of Israel devised to circumvent this uncomfortable power dynamic. As well, Yehoshua underscores that the biblical moment of birth of the people of Israel (as a national entity) is traditionally located in exile, during their desert wanderings, after they had just been delivered from slavery and awaited reentry to a land granted to their forefathers by a God to whom they are now freshly and more intimately indebted.

This is the very complex ideological background that informs Yehoshua's representation of Passover in *A Late Divorce*. Before looking at the actual representation of Passover here, I just need to emphasize that Yehuda and Naomi's divorce proceedings (on Passover eve) mark a rushed but also a belated split-up that, rather than resolving their problems, obliquely reveals the precariousness of any attempt to sever the two components of Jewish identity—the two "codes" that Yehoshua regards as inseparable yet conflicted—the civic *and* religious systems, each focused on different goals: "here is a normal system functioning in accord with the basic needs of national existence within a specified territory, and here is a spiritual system setting spiritual goals for the people and trying to make its existence subject to religious-spiritual demands. These are two different codes."[11]

Yehuda Kaminka ends up murdered the day after his divorce. If we keep in mind that this character stands for "the people" (according to Morahg's interpretation of Yehoshua's Freudian triangulation of land/God/people), with Naomi as "the land," while her alter ego, Elohima, represents God, then their divorce evidently results in a very troubled solution to their conflict. It merely represents a wretched failure to negotiate these conflicting codes. Moreover, since Yehuda Kaminka's plan was to escape to the diaspora in order to "rest" from the difficulties that had plagued him at home, his murder is a drastic elimination of the diaspora option, as we saw in chapter 2. More radically than he intended, Yehuda Kaminka thus reneges on all his responsibilities both toward his original family in Israel and his new family in America.

However, as we shall see through the following discussion, it is perhaps more illuminating to interpret *A Late Divorce* in closer contact with the symbols and themes of the Passover holiday. Indeed, in "Golah: The Neurotic Solution," Yehoshua expresses his hope that religious reformers—*metakney dat* (מתקני דת), as he calls them, "religious repairers"—will arise in Israel to recalibrate the relationship between its two inherent yet conflicting codes: "To put it bluntly, religion is too important to be left to the religious. Secular Jews, or those so called, must make their way into religious matters, not as *baalei tshuvah*, romantic penitents [who seek theological guidance], but as courageous reformers."[12] To this day, American-style Reform and Reconstructionist movements remain feeble in Israel (although modern orthodox *kippah srugah* wearers and the kibbutz movement had long adjusted traditional practices to modern life in Israel, even prior to the establishment of the state).[13] Nonetheless, it is mostly to secular Israeli Jews "or those so called" that Yehoshua addresses this plea for religious reformation: he argues that such a reform does not merely imply "an easing of the burden imposed by religion" or "an easing of the burden of the commandments," but rather their full exposure "to the complexities of life, to observe them while changing them."[14] This chapter will showcase Yehoshua's program of national reformation as played out through the holiday scenarios of *A Late Divorce* (Passover) and *Friendly Fire* (Hanukkah), and in his two historical novels, *Mr. Mani* and *A Journey to the End of the Millennium* (Yom Kippur).

WILTED LETTUCE

If holidays "demand more" from people, the detailed representation of preparations leading up to them exposes the difficulties besetting families, individuals, and communities strained in their observance. Yehoshua's bleakest novel, *A Late Divorce*, portrays a chaotic family that has to make an enormous effort to organize itself to celebrate the Passover holiday. Despite not heeding the commandment to abstain from leavened bread for seven days or worrying too much about retelling the story of the ancient deliverance from slavery, the Kaminka-Kedmi family finds that this holiday still demands a great effort from them, in part because after a long sojourn in America, their patriarch has just returned home to Israel to celebrate the seder with his children while formalizing his separation from their mother.

Mirroring Faulkner's *The Sound and the Fury*, which opens with the inner consciousness of Benjy, a man whose understanding had never progressed beyond that of a three-year-old child, *A Late Divorce* starts with the inner consciousness of a child, seven-and-a-half-year-old Gaddi, whose family pressures had made him, conversely, sadder and heavier than warranted by his tender age. His grandfather Yehuda has not visited Gaddi since the boy was a toddler, when his grandmother Naomi was institutionalized and Yehuda left the country. In America, Yehuda finds a new partner, now rumored to be pregnant and about to give birth to their child. Therefore, Yehuda now returns to Israel to obtain a divorce from Gaddi's grandmother.

"Grandpa really has come," Gaddi thinks to himself the morning after his grandfather's arrival, which is also Gaddi's last day at school prior to the Passover break. Since his mother had stayed up late to welcome their guest, Gaddi's father tries to take care of the morning duties alone. This is Gaddi's perception of the situation:

> It was already past seven-thirty. I finished eating and went back to my room to pack my schoolbag. . . . I went to mom and dad's room

and touched mom she opened her eyes right away she smiled but dad was right behind me leave her alone Gaddi hands off let her sleep what is it that you want?

"I need matzos, lettuce and wine. We're having a class seder this morning."

"Why didn't you say so yesterday?"

"I told mom."

"Maybe you can get along without it. Borrow some from another boy."

"I'm getting up," said mom.

"You don't have to. I'll take care of it. Come on, just get a move on."

He went to the kitchen and wrapped two matzos in a newspaper he looked in the closet and found a bottle of old wine he tasted it and made a face *he looked at me and said what difference does it make* you won't drink it anyway it's just symbolic and he poured some into an old jar that used to have olives in it. Forget about the lettuce he said you can borrow a leaf from someone. So I started back toward mom don't be stubborn he said it's getting late but I said I need lettuce so he searched in the vegetable bin and found some old leaves and gave them to me was he sore. Since when did you get so religious? I put it all in my schoolbag my watch already said ten to eight.

"What else do you need?"

"A snack for school."

"What about the matzo?"

"It's for the seder at the end."

"Okay, I won't let you starve." He cut two thick slices of bread in a hurry and put chocolate spread on them. . . .

. . . On the way out I passed grandpa's door I opened it quietly and saw him sleeping by a suitcase full of clothes but nothing in it seemed to be for me.[15]

Less challenging to read than the monologue that opens *The Sound and the Fury*, Gaddi's stream of consciousness still requires us to decode the world as perceived by a child's mind. A measure of cultural knowledge is also expected here—an awareness, for example, that children in Jewish schools rehearse the seder with their classmates, prior to the full celebration at home.

"What difference does it make" is precisely the question that the youngest child at every Passover table is enjoined to ask—*ma nishtanah?*—how is this night different from all other nights? How is our life different from the lives of our ancestors? To answer these questions, we are indeed encouraged to pour old wine into new jars—but this is supposed to be a finely aged beverage, not the rancid undrinkable stuff that Israel Kedmi pours into a discarded olive jar for his son, claiming that "anyway it's just symbolic." Of course everything on the seder plate is "just symbolic," and this precisely is the nature of its importance. Pouring rancid wine into an old olive jar is itself a symbolic act, which in the context of Yehoshua's novel denotes Kedmi's lack of attention to the traditional rituals, especially to the role of the child within this holiday.

If holidays "demand more" from people, then here Gaddi's father misses a golden opportunity to transmit to his son a deeper interest in a holiday commemorating freedom and marking the birth of the people of Israel as a nation. What Ahad Ha'am once quipped about the Shabbat—that more than Jews keeping the Shabbat, the Shabbat kept the Jews—can be applied also to the Passover celebration, which helped to keep Jewish identity alive despite the perils of the Inquisition, the Nazis, or the KGB. Without entering into a fuller discussion about the actual historical background and formats in which ancient Passover commemorations were celebrated,[16] this holiday's antiquity, if not its foundational myth, is itself worth a measure of respect that Kedmi dismisses offhand.

Instead of exposing the holiday's commandments to the "complexities of life, to observe them while changing them," Kedmi prefers to get rid of the holiday's responsibilities as hastily as possible, although, as a litigation lawyer, he is perfectly capable of spinning new interpretations. "Borrow some from another boy," he advises his son, who insists on assembling his own lettuce, matzah, wine, and snack. But borrowing from "some other boy" is exactly what Yehoshua identifies as the main problem that plagues secular Israeli attitudes toward religion: instead of crafting meaningful relationships to traditional themes and symbols, secular Israelis accept wilted versions of religious practices associated with orthodox beliefs and are therefore more comfortable granting that political sector a disproportionate responsibility (*memunim,* as defined in the previous chapter) over religious life in the civic sphere.

102   THE RETROSPECTIVE IMAGINATION OF A. B. YEHOSHUA

That wilted leaf of lettuce that Kedmi fishes out from the bottom of the fridge is the saddest symbol of a decayed transmission of values, not only among secular Israelis but even among ultraorthodox Jews, who may not use the holidays, particularly this holiday, to ask fresh questions. Even if this lettuce, or any other symbol placed on the seder table, may have wilted under centuries of interpretation[17]—and even if core segments of the history commemorated in this holiday are a myth—the discussion of the very boundaries between myth and history (a primary concern for Yehoshua) has a place of honor during this holiday that invites its celebrants to discuss the story of exodus far into the night and to imagine ourselves in every generation "as if we personally had been delivered from Egypt." Instead, like the suitcase that is lying open next to Gaddi's sleeping grandfather—"full of clothes but nothing in it seemed to be for me"—the message conveyed to the boy is that this holiday is full of *shmattes* with nothing in it for him.

THE PRICE OF FREEDOM

How, moreover, does Yehoshua approach the disturbing message of a holiday that commemorates God's redemption of a people from slavery, so they can choose, paradoxically, to serve him? In various strands of its plot, *A Late Divorce* engages with the theme of freedom, notably through the tragicomic prison break of a young man accused of murder, who escapes from jail to celebrate the seder with his parents; there is in addition a sermon about freedom preached by a born-again Russian rabbi to the inmates of Naomi's insane asylum on the night of the seder, and, of course, the catastrophic outcome of Naomi and Yehuda's newfound liberty after their divorce.

Yehuda Kaminka returns to Israel to free himself from it, so that he will be able to settle down more comfortably elsewhere. In other words, the primary goal of his visit is not to spend quality time with his grandchildren—his main goal is to actually *abandon* them, divorce in hand. By contrast, Yoram Miller, a young man accused erroneously of murder and awaiting trial, breaks out of jail to spend a few stressful hours of freedom with his distraught parents. Miller has not committed the crime for which he had been apprehended, but his lawyer, Israel Kedmi, Yehuda's son-in-law, instead of listening to what the defendant is trying to explain, fantasizes about the brilliant speeches that he will deliver in court. When the real perpetrator is discovered, the dejected Kedmi, admitting his inadequacy as a defense lawyer, decides to give up his private practice and goes to work instead for the district attorney.

Kedmi's family habitually refers to Miller as "Kedmi's murderer." After the young man's escape from jail, they ambush him in the streets near his parents' house, so that Kedmi will not lose an opportunity to demonstrate "what a real lawyer was. How his clients obeyed him unquestionably. How they had perfect faith in him."[18] It is actually Kedmi's father-in-law, Yehuda, who manages to convince the escaped prisoner to turn himself in to his lawyer after the seder, so as to reduce the infraction of his escape.

Thus, instead of the ever-expected prophet Elijah arriving at the door at the end of the seder, in walks the escaped prisoner accompanied by his parents:

> "Well, well, well, what an honored guest! Just look at what we have here, everyone! Now that we've made two happy people of father and mother, it's time to cheer up the police. . . . We'll have to think quick if we're to keep this night of yours from costing you another two years."
>
> The young man stood silently, sullenly in the doorway, recoiling from Kedmi's grasp, a great fatigue in his eyes. . . .
>
> "This way, please, Mr. and Mrs. Miller. Come right in, it's no imposition at all. I'm sure God won't mind if we take a break and finish the seder later. Come in, have a seat."[19]

A comic scene ensues when a policeman who comes to collect the prisoner clamps down his handcuffs on the lawyer instead. But then again, the actual prisoner was erroneously arrested in the first place, while his lawyer is guilty of negligence. When the arrest warrant is clarified, Kedmi yells at the sergeant to "sign a statement that I'm turning him over to you of his own free will"—but the policeman refuses to sign, because "the last statement I signed cost me two more years of waiting for my sergeant's stripes."[20] Apart from enlivening *A Late Divorce*'s underlying tragedy, this comic interlude highlights the idea that freedom entails responsibility. Miller jeopardizes his case by taking his freedom into his own hands, while Kedmi does not control his gruff manners, Naomi and her three children have yet to heal themselves, and Yehuda abandons them to conduct their lives in growing disarray.

Meanwhile, at the insane asylum, Naomi listens to a sermon delivered by a Russian rabbi who had escaped from Soviet communism to become a fundamentalist believer through his newfound liberty in Israel: "*Nu*," he interrupts the Passover story to address the inmates. "You are chosen, do you know? Also you have a spark of holiness. Also you belong to God's covenant . . . all of you." He sweeps his hand over all the inmates in the dining room. "A-a-a-ll of you, even who do not want, who do not believe. All . . . everyone."[21] He is committed to a theologically oriented worldview that simplifies the tension between the joined codes of Jewish identity—civic and theological—by spreading a uniformly religious mantle over *all* aspects of Jewish life.

It is this rabbi with a foreign accent who articulates succinctly the key link between the story of redemption from Egyptian slavery (celebrated at Passover) and a permanent enslavement to the commandments accepted at Sinai (celebrated at Shavuot): "*Nu, nu.* . . . In every generation we seek freedom, but only kind of freedom . . . only kind of freedom . . . is freedom to be slaves . . . freedom to be slaves of God. Is freedom inside. Only there. Is freedom outside worth nothing."[22] This pithy definition of Jewish identity emphasizes its core link between divine redemption and a covenantal relationship with God.[23] Any attempt to wiggle out of this theological embrace subsequently constitutes an escape from the national commitment, which also doubles as commitment to God. Here, then, is the source of the intertwined civic and religious components of Jewish identity—a knot that may be loosened but cannot be pried apart.

Earlier on that Passover eve, right after the divorce, Naomi had begun to feel the symptoms that heralded a return of Elohima, the alter ego that destroyed her married life. Nevertheless, she welcomes its return: "now is the time for a visit from her to tell me what she thinks."[24] In the past, this alter ego had spoken with the voice of Naomi's mother, but now Naomi wonders "if I'd be able to talk to her, if I still remembered how. . . . And then suddenly I felt the old throbbing, the urge to have her be part of me again like a heavy backpack, the joy of her wild otherness."[25]

This alter ego reveals herself fully when Naomi seats herself around the seder table to listen to the rabbi's commentary: "now I see him from behind and give a start why it's a woman disguised as a man I hardly can breathe. . . . How didn't I notice before that it was her? It's her disguised as a rabbi! Desperately I turn to all the people watching him. Hasn't anyone seen? From a far table he starts to sing again he returns to his seat and signals us all to join in the melody. It's true, then. She's back. She's right here. And I bolt outside in a panic."[26] Suddenly the return of Elohima ("Godina") is not so welcome to Naomi anymore, for now she grasps that this alter ego is hardly different from the fundamentalist believer who is now sermonizing her. Suddenly she turns against the shadow that had been lurking in her psyche and begins to chase it away: "Shut up," she tells the voice in her head.

> I'm telling you that's enough!
> ... I'll fight.
> ... I'm not listening. I'm through with you. Go back to the desert. Die![27]

But these are not the last words of the novel. The next morning, Yehuda returns to the asylum with the intention of retrieving the house deed he had granted to Naomi in exchange for his freedom. In an awkward attempt to steal back the family's property, he dresses in Naomi's frock and runs toward the asylum's fence, triggering intense anxiety in a gigantic inmate, who advances toward Yehuda with a pitchfork and kills him. This murderer seems to be a Jew named Musa—Arabic for Moses—but he is neither a deliverer nor a lawgiver, unless his pitchfork is the law. He is an ambiguous creature—childish yet huge, obedient yet impulsive, considered Jewish but bearing an Arabic name. He represents those agents of destruction that in his essay "An Attempt to Identify the Root Cause of Antisemitism" Yehoshua characterized as insecure personalities, whose own anxieties are triggered by an exposure to unclear identities and behaviors.[28]

Continuing its engagement with the Passover intertext, Yehuda's post-humous child in *A Late Divorce* is also ironically named Moses. Three years after Yehuda's murder, the toddler appears one morning with his American mother at the Kedmis' doorstep. The mother inquires about events leading up to Yehuda's death and then promptly leaves her child in the care of his half-sister, with no clear indication of her intentions. Stuttering in English and dressed bizarrely in red, this little Moses is deemed "cute" by his relatives, and yet his sullen disposition radiates inauspiciousness. Harold Bloom interpreted this minor character as a "hint and wish that a new Moses might rise among American Jewry and lead it back to Israel."[29] But Yehoshua's two unpublished screenplay adaptations of *A Late Divorce* show rather that this dubious savior evokes W. B. Yeats's ominous "The Second Coming," a poem to which Yehoshua alludes in the second epigraph of his novel: a hybrid creature poised to wreak havoc on his path, like the madman who killed the child's father.[30] This name choice thus functions here as another reference to what Yehoshua views as a frustratingly unclear Mosaic identity.

After Yehuda's death, Naomi lapses into a catatonic state. Her final struggle against Elohima hence amounts to nothing, for she had struggled too late to generate any positive outcome. Still, it can be argued that Naomi re-earns the name of isra-el—a name assigned in Genesis to Jacob after he struggles with a divine entity in the dark wilderness: "You have wrestled with God and men, and you have won."[31] Naomi does not win, but she has wrestled. And from this point of view, the entire people of Israel can be defined as a nation that intrinsically *struggles* with God; from this point of view, we can also better understand Yehoshua's argument that although he is a staunch atheist, he is obliged to wrestle with religion and religiosity in the name of a secular Israeli identity that remains anchored in an ancient relationship with God.[32]

Thus, when Yehoshua says that "religion is too important to be left to the religious," he envisions a *process* of religious reformation aimed at strengthening Israeli identity by diminishing the gap between its secular and religious elements, without relinquishing either tradition or choice. He therefore defends the Jewish identity of the State of Israel,[33] while also insisting on a vital need to clarify the boundaries between its religious and civic components (*dat/le'om*).[34]

His most pessimistic novel, *A Late Divorce* suggests, however, that any drastic attempt at separation would be fatal. After all, Yehuda Kaminka's murder is a consequence of his inability to accept the final terms of his divorce. He won't let go of his relationship with his (ex-)spouse, which had initially foundered due to his refusal, at the onset of her madness, to help her grapple with her Elohima. To retrieve the house deed that he had signed away, he decides to sneak back into the insane asylum—into his wife's bedroom, into her closet, and into her dress—with fatal consequences, as we saw. Yet without trying to reduce this multidimensional novel to any point-by-point equation with Yehoshua's extraliterary statements, it is still important to note, as Gilead Morahg does, that *both* Yehuda and Naomi are escapists rather than problem solvers: she flees to insanity and he to America, two facets of the "diaspora neurosis" that Yehoshua condemns as a pathological escape from a "normal" commitment to national/familial life.

HOLIDAYS 107

One of Yehoshua's two unpublished screenplay adaptations of this novel ends with the little posthumous child winking to the audience and asking, "ma nishtanah?" (what has changed?). In the novel itself the child merely stutters, incomprehensibly, like the Haggadah's fourth child—*she eino yode'a lish'ol*—a young child incapable of fully participating in the seder yet who still lacks the linguistic capacity to express himself. Yehuda Kaminka's grown children resemble the other three children described in the Haggadah: the dutiful oldest daughter undertakes whatever is demanded of her without arguing (a dubious *hakhamah*), the innocent Asa develops a brilliant theory about bypassing catastrophes while his private life lies in shambles (the *tam*), and the self-centered Zvi extorts financial information from a married man in exchange for sexual favors (the *rasha*).

A *Late Divorce* does not reveal whether the Kaminka-Kedmi seder ends with the traditional hope to celebrate "next year in Jerusalem." On the contrary, Yehuda sits at this seder imagining himself flying off to Minneapolis with no desire to return to either Jerusalem, Haifa, or Tel Aviv. Those who add "next year in the *rebuilt* Jerusalem" allude to the absence of the ancient temple, whose destruction is commemorated on the nine days leading up to the Ninth of Av. Indeed, Yehuda's visit lasts exactly nine days, and it ends with a *hurban*: the catastrophe of his murder, as well as the total decline of his (ex-)wife, and the abandonment of his children, on both sides of the Atlantic. Nevertheless, like the Ninth of Av, this catastrophe includes a seed of redemption, for despite the collapse of their elders—or perhaps as a reaction to it—the next generation of Kaminka-Kedmis has a chance to repair itself. During the last visit to his therapist in Tel Aviv, Zvi had begun to tell the truth about his feelings toward his parents. In Haifa, Yael's marriage bonds strengthen despite her husband's gruffness, for, after all, Israel Kedmi is a dependable family man. In Jerusalem, the bedroom struggles between Asa and Dina represent another variation of the struggle between the secular and religious worldviews that so preoccupies Yehoshua, since Dina comes from a religious background and is reluctant to commit to "normal" life with Asa, while his own dysfunctional childhood inhibits him from coaching her into a healthy coupling. Still, as we see in the explanatory chapter that takes place three years after Yehuda's murder, the next generation of Kaminkas has an opportunity to readjust their priorities in view of the outcomes of the choices made by their parents. The sensitive grandson Gaddi, who nearly has a heart attack on the night of the seder, is saved; Asa and Dina begin to

108 THE RETROSPECTIVE IMAGINATION OF A. B. YEHOSHUA

repair themselves, and Yael and Kedmi remain devoted to each other and their children.

MA'OZ TZUR, ROCK OF STRENGTH FOR ALL ERAS?

Just as *A Late Divorce* relies on traditional Passover themes and symbols to spark a fresh engagement with the significance of this holiday, Yehoshua's ninth novel, *Friendly Fire*, appeals to Hanukkah to explore the current relevance of its themes and customs. Immediately, through its subtitles, it becomes clear that *Friendly Fire* intends to keep track of the number of candles that Amotz Ya'ari lights during this winter festival with members of his family and their associates—"Second Candle," "Third Candle," and so on. And the novel ends with a debate between Amotz and his wife Daniela about whether or not to sing "Ma'oz Tzur."

Daniela has just returned from visiting their brother-in-law in Africa, where she was shocked by his announcement that he had decided to radically extricate himself from that "whole messy stew" of Judaism and Israel, for Yirmi, as we mentioned before, had lost his son during a military ambush in the West Bank, and became further embittered by the events that followed this bereavement.[35] When Daniela offers him a stash of Israeli newspapers that she brought from the airplane, he "rushes to the boiler, opens a small door revealing tongues of bluish flame, and without delay shoves the entire bag into the fire." As soon as he notices that she brought Hanukkah candles too, "with the same quick, slightly maniacal movement, he opens the little door and adds the candles to the smoldering Israeli newspapers."[36]

After this summary treatment, Daniela is eager to catch the tail end of this eight-day holiday upon her return to Tel Aviv:

"It's not too late." And she sticks eight candles of various colors into the menorah, adding a red shammash.

"You do it," [her husband] says, not budging from his chair. "Because you didn't light a single candle, I'm letting you light all eight."

"All right, but turn down the TV, we can't make the blessing like this."

"You want us also to do the blessings?"

"Why not? As always."

HOLIDAYS 109

"Then you do them. We live in feminist times, you're not exempt. There are women rabbis out there who go around in prayer shawls and phylacteries."

"But where are the blessings?"

"They're printed on the box."

"So simple and handy."

He lowers the sound on the television, but he leaves the picture on. She lights the shammash with a match, shares its flame with all the other candles, and reads the blessings by their light. Come, she orders him, now we'll sing. He rises reluctantly from the armchair. But please, he insists, just not "Maoz Tsur." It's a song Nofar [their daughter] also hates.

"What's to hate in a song like that?" she protests. "You sound like Yirmi."

"Like Yirmi or not like Yirmi, I don't like that song."

"But it won't do you any harm to sing it along with me, a duet."[37]

Friendly Fire, subtitled *A Duet*, ends with this appeal to reconsider one tiny aspect of a holiday commonly associated with dreidels, jelly donuts, and candle lighting, "all that small stuff, which do no harm," as Yehoshua's Trigano argues in another novel, quoted in our epigraph to this chapter—harmless, he contends, unless instilling "a fear of something hidden and invisible, of a God who is abstract, jealous, and aggressive."

Indeed, "Ma'oz Tzur," which is sung to a majestic tune after the lighting of the Hanukkah candles, was composed at the time of the Crusades in an elevated and archaic Hebrew nearly incomprehensible to our contemporary Hebrew speakers. It features a deity praised for rescuing his people and enjoined, in a generic formula of ancient times, to slaughter their opponents because Hanukkah, we recall, commemorates a historical moment in which the identity of the Jewish people was seriously imperiled, when the Hellenized king Antiochus insisted on suppressing Judaism in the second century B.C.E. An unlikely Maccabean victory of the few against the many enabled a rededication of the Second Temple, followed by a hundred years of Judean independence until the conquest of the Romans and the total destruction of the temple in 70 C.E.

Without specifying whether he objects to its words or tune, Amotz Ya'ari pleads against singing "Ma'oz Tzur," in response to which his wife accuses him unfairly of being like their brother-in-law Yirmi. While the embittered Yirmi had chosen to detach himself from his family, and altogether from the "whole messy stew" of his heritage, Amotz, by contrast, had taken the holiday as an opportunity to strengthen his bonds with every member of his extended family and those who surround them.

On the second night of Hanukkah, he visits his widowed father, who suffers from Parkinson's disease. They light their menorah, together with members of a Filipino family employed by Ya'ari senior in his home. The six-year-old Filipino boy had learned about the holiday in the same school that Amotz attended as a child, and though the Filipino family is presumably Catholic, their son is nevertheless eager to participate in this local holiday. He therefore stands "beside the trembling grandfather, an unlit candle in his hand and a kippa on his head." "Don't overdo it," Amotz says and attempts to remove the skullcap from the boy's head, but the old man allows the child to wear it. Little Hilario sings the Hebrew blessings and lights a clay menorah that he himself had made at school, after which Amotz invites him to repeat the entire procedure on the grandfather's menorah. "His face aglow with excitement," the boy requests permission from his mother to also sing a Hanukkah song. To Amotz's relief, it is not "Ma'oz Tzur" but an old song "whose melody is modest and pleasing to the ear," and Amotz reinforces it "with some humming of his own."[38]

Two things may strike us in this scene: first of all, the integration of a Catholic child into a Jewish ritual that has religious as well as national-historical connotations, and secondly, the attitudes of each character to the ceremony itself. Hilario, the Filipino boy, lives in an Israeli neighborhood and identifies with Jewish customs, and although the blessings contain nothing offensive to a Christian believer—"Blessed are you, Lord, our God, sovereign of the universe, who sanctified us with His commandments and commanded us to light the lights of Hanukkah" and "Blessed are you, Lord, our God, sovereign of the universe, who performed miracles for our ancestors in those days, and at this time"—the first person plural refers specifically to Jews, who, from ancient times, have been distinguished from Christians by a persistent allegiance to traditional commandments that Christianity dispensed with. Finally, although the holiday is meaningful to some extent to both Ya'ari senior and junior, neither of them feels compelled to light his own menorah. They are happy basking in the general atmosphere of the festivities.

Another evening, the fifth night of Hanukkah, Amotz lights the candles with his grandchildren at their apartment, where his two-year-old grandson has a terrible tantrum because he had been allowed to light only two candles, while his older sister lit three. To conciliate him, Amotz refills the menorah with another five candles, but the angry toddler "knocks the smoking menorah over and shoves it to the ground."[39] The contrast between this agitated Israeli toddler and the respectful Filipino boy is striking here, offering another dimension of Yehoshua's employment of holiday scenarios to stage familial and sociological situations in which the Jewish characters are stressed to the utmost.

The next day, Amotz visits his son, the father of this toddler, at an army base where his son is fulfilling mandatory reserve duty. Recalling Yehoshua's description of the rabbi who officiates at Naomi's asylum, this rabbi also "takes the opportunity to begin with a sermon about the wonders and miracles of the holiday, waving the huge shammash like a torch."[40] But even Dr. Dvorah Bennett, a psychoanalyst who is an old friend of Amotz's father, receives Amotz with refreshments arranged on a table that holds that evening's menorah with all its candles. In other words, a winter holiday with national, historic, and religious roots that even Jung, whose photo decorates Dr. Bennett's elevator, would have approved.

Amotz begs his daughter, who volunteers at a hospital, to spend "a little time" with him and "light the candles together."[41] She arrives on condition that they dispense with "Ma'oz Tzur" and indeed every Hanukkah song— for as her mother puts it, she is "boycotting all lights of happiness till she exhausts the grief in her heart."[42] Like her uncle's dejection in Africa, her own grief too stems from an attachment to the cousin who had been killed in a military operation on the West Bank. Nonetheless, she responds to her father's appeal and comes to celebrate the holiday with him.

On yet another night, Amotz lights seven candles with the workers of an elevator factory owned by his father's business partner. There he is shown "a menorah fit for the factory, composed of nine tiny models of elevators, with a small bulb installed in each"—a miracle like this, boasts the factory owner, "would have astonished even the Maccabees."[43]

Is Yehoshua poking fun at Hanukkah celebrations in Israel? Is he offering a realistic portrait of Israeli life during the winter holiday? Or is he stressing the need to pay more careful attention, as he had done with the Passover intertext of *A Late Divorce*, to traditional commemorations that harried modern families may not be living up to with full responsibility? Each of these attitudes guides Yehoshua's representation of Hanukkah in *Friendly Fire*, but I believe that in this case the holiday functions primarily as a backdrop for Israeli life at the turn of the twenty-first century in ways that engage us implicitly in an ongoing conversation about problems of Jewish identity that extend all the way back to ancient times.

In a meditation on S. Y. Agnon's finessed relationship with God and Jewish religion, Amos Oz recalls an episode from Agnon's *Tmol Shilshom* (Only Yesterday), where the protagonist—wavering between his secular and religious tendencies—overhears an anecdote about a Hanukkah celebration held at Bezalel's Art School in Jerusalem. The aspiring artists had created a life-sized effigy of Matityahu, father of the Maccabees, and had danced around this idol all night. Agnon clarifies, "If the spirit of life had been breathed into the statue, it would have come down off its pedestal and stabbed them all with the sword in its hand. For Matityahu the Hasmonean was an iconoclast and a zealot for his religion [which prohibits idols]. Indeed, all the time the Greeks enslaved his nation, he didn't budge; only when they moved to forbid the practice of religious commandments did he rebel."[44] Hanukkah commemorates the deliverance of the Jewish people from an oppressor truly bent on eradicating Judaism, yet the Hasmonean rebellion started when Matityahu struck down a Hellenized Jew who was willing to accept the pagan practices that Antiochus was forcing upon the Jews. The Maccabean rebellion was therefore waged against Antiochus's army as well as against assimilationist Jews, and this *continuing* internal conflict between assimilationist and conservative Jewish forces, preoccupies Yehoshua as much as it did Agnon. Agnon tried to balance these opposed forces by maintaining an active allegiance toward orthodox religious observance while engaging, artistically and intellectually, with the work necessary to achieve a national modernization. On his part, Yehoshua supports a more radical reformation of Judaism that nonetheless remains grounded, as we have seen, in Jewish tradition and history.

Committed to endowing the modern State of Israel with a Jewish character, Yehoshua, like Agnon, challenges his readers to reconsider which manifestations of Jewish identity are most appropriate for an old-new homeland. Admittedly, there is a huge gap between Yehoshua and Agnon's knowledge of halakhic Jewish observance: Agnon was a freethinker allied with the Labor Zionist movement, but also a religiously observant Jew with an exceptionally deep and broad knowledge of Jewish texts and lore.[45] Yehoshua, also allied primarily with the Labor Zionist movement, is familiar with orthodox practices mostly through his early Sephardic upbringing in Jerusalem, where his grandfather was a respected rabbi and his parents kept a kosher household,[46] Yehoshua's parents encouraged him to join a secular Israeli environment that relegated religion to occasional selective practices; but studying the Bible, rather than Talmud, continued to play a significant role in this secularization of Jewish life.[47]

Despite their different levels of Jewish observance and knowledge, Yehoshua, like Agnon, promotes a dialogue between the forces of tradition and modernization. In his public lectures as well as in his fiction, Yehoshua may attack the theological worldview that Agnon so subtly ironized, but even Yehoshua does not believe that religion can or should be eradicated from Israeli life. Rather, he seeks to reinforce a modern Israeli identity that is nourished by traditional markers of Jewish culture, such as holidays, though not dominated by a theological worldview that at any moment might drag "anxious souls . . . into the fear of something hidden and invisible."[48]

From Agnon as well as from Faulkner, Yehoshua learned to project apparently trivial details of daily life onto a broader canvas of local history. Thus, traditional themes and symbols associated with a holiday setting offer Yehoshua a readily accessible cultural intertext through which mimetic trivialities connect with historiosophic ideas that carry weighty moral concerns. Faulkner's Easter setting in *The Sound and the Fury* had similarly enabled this postbellum southern writer to intertwine Christ's passion and redemption with the fall of the Compson family and the comparative resilience of their devoted caretaker, Dilsey. The holiday reference in Faulkner's masterpiece thus injects a higher and deeper moral significance into his tragic representation of family dynamics as an insight into the history of Mississippi before and after the Civil War. Agnon, on the other hand, deals more directly with the same conflict between conservative and reformist forces in Jewish life that greatly preoccupies Yehoshua; it is therefore thematically through Agnon, and structurally and stylistically through Faulkner and other modernists, that Yehoshua gleaned the means of generating multifocal dialogues between his modern national identity and religious history in his literary representations of Jewish holidays.

"WHO BY FIRE AND WHO BY WATER,
WHO IN DUE TIME AND WHO BEFORE HIS TIME?"

"Yom Kippur," Yehoshua explained to Gidi Weitz and Dror Mishani, "is important to me. It's important to me that Yom Kippur should have a certain character within the Jewish community. . . . This community has a character of its own, it has a memory of its own, it has holidays of its own."[49] His attitude toward this holiest day in the Jewish calendar becomes clearer through his criticism of Israel's founding prime minister, David Ben Gurion, whom he faults for secluding himself at home during the fast to read Spinoza, instead of wielding his influence to endorse "an Israeli-style Reform synagogue." Religion, as Yehoshua forcefully puts it, is "too important to be left just to the religious."[50]

Although it is impossible in the space of this chapter to offer a comprehensive analysis of the High Holiday season across Yehoshua's oeuvre, I would like to at least indicate how he deals not only with commemorations of national liberation such as Hanukkah and Passover but also with holy days of a primarily religious orientation. Yom Kippur, in particular, is not amenable to secularization: its confessional prayers are expressed collectively—*ashamnu* (we sinned) *bagadnu* (we betrayed)—but this Day of Atonement does not atone for transgressions against individuals; acts of atonement toward fellow human beings may be *facilitated* by the atmosphere of introspection and repair that stretches throughout the month of Elul to Tishrei, but social acts of atonement require an entirely separate halakhic repair, addressed to the wronged individual(s) and offering a reasonable restitution.

What role, then, can a religious holiday such as Yom Kippur play in the opus and ethos of a secular and self-professed atheist writer, who insists, on one hand, on maintaining the Jewish character of the State of Israel, yet, on the other hand, demands a clearer demarcation of boundaries between its civic and religious components?

Shachar Pinsker has examined the presence of Yom Kippur in Hebrew fiction before and after the turn of the nineteenth century, as an index for tracking the changes in its representation of the tension between modernizing and traditional forces in the lives of European Jews at that time.[51] He notes that in Berdichevsky and Feierberg's stories, it is specifically at the synagogue during Yom Kippur that their protagonists act out a rupture with traditional religious life; in so doing they offend their congregation, with devastating consequences for themselves and the community. By the beginning of the twentieth century, however, in works by Shofman and Gnessin and to some extent also in Brenner and the young Agnon, a struggle against naive piousness turns into a more private psychological drama: the process of introspection and atonement (or lack thereof) is now depicted surrealistically through dreams blending the holiday's symbols with the private anxieties weighing on the minds of the protagonists. Although this interiorization still exposes a keen ideological struggle between the forces of tradition and modernization, it does so without enacting necessarily a full-blown public rupture between the protagonist and the community.

A hundred years later, Yehoshua similarly rose to the challenge of depicting Judaism's holiest day of the year—not in the context of his own secular Israeli society as he does with Passover in *A Late Divorce* and Hanukkah in *Friendly Fire*, but in the more remote historical setting of Jerusalem at the end of the nineteenth century in *Mr. Mani*, and medieval Europe and North Africa during the year 999 in *A Journey to the End of the Millennium*. A nuanced integration of the High Holiday liturgy and customs into the plots of these complicated historical novels actually reveals the extent to which this Israeli author holds himself personally responsible for grappling with the resources of his national heritage, including its theological aspects. In other words, Yehoshua's fiction demonstrates his recommendation "not to lighten the commandments but to expose them to the complexities of life, to observe them while changing them."[52]

In both of these historical novels a celebration of Yom Kippur occurs during the last year of a secular century, even during the last year of a Gregorian millennium, as if to indicate that at that moment a new leaf *might have been* turned in Jewish as well as in Gentile history; in other words, their future (which is our present) could have been configured rather differently at those historical junctures.

Mr. Mani's fourth conversation is set during the last hours of the nineteenth century. It is presented from the perspective of Dr. Efrayim Shapiro, a young and cynical Polish Jew, who tells his father about the ten extraordinary days that he and his sister Linka had spent as guests of the gynecologist Dr. Moshe Mani in Jerusalem. Efrayim and Linka had met Dr. Mani at the Third Zionist Congress in Basel, where he had come in hopes of raising funds for his birthing clinic in Jerusalem, as we saw in our overview of Yehoshua's

Jerusalem in chapter 2. In a logical continuation of the congress's rhetoric, the Shapiro siblings accompany Dr. Mani back to Jerusalem, but ultimately Efrayim is not interested in committing himself to any society anywhere; he also refuses to get married. Nevertheless, through his double and even triply alienated perspective as an idiosyncratic Polish-Jewish free-floater, we learn about Moshe Mani's suicide and about the High Holiday liturgy and customs of the Sephardic community of Jerusalem at the end of the nineteenth century.

To fully understand Dr. Mani's decision to commit suicide the day after Yom Kippur, one must flash back, however, to the world of Avraham Mani, who had been a guest in Jerusalem during another Yom Kippur, half a century earlier. Avraham Mani had come to Jerusalem to check up on his son and new daughter-in-law, and he recounts to his rabbi how "the air was tremulous in that subtle way it is in Jerusalem on Yom Kippur, as if the Merciful One, the chief judge Himself, had secretly returned to the city from His travels and was hiding in one of its small dwellings, in which He planned to spend the holy fast day with us, the signed list of men's fates—'Who by fire and who by water, who in due time and who before his time'—already in His pocket, although He was afraid to take it out and read it."[53] Unlike the freethinking and idiosyncratic Efrayim Shapiro, Avraham Mani is intensely religious and fanatically exclusivist. He is a "pure" Sephardic Jew for whom the continuity of his name and seed is of such paramount importance that he sacrifices his only son to exert control over the Mani genealogy. Soon after arriving in Jerusalem, he realizes that his son has not yet consummated his marriage to a local Sephardic beauty, in part because his son is obsessed with a desire to "remind" local Muslims that they might be former Jews converted to Islam. In a vague reenactment of both the banishment of Ishmael and the biblical binding of Isaac, Avraham facilitates the murder of his wayward son, and,[54] as soon as this unruly youth is out of the way, engenders a new Mani with his willing daughter-in-law, Tamara.[55] The product of this liaison is Moshe Mani, the future gynecologist. As if in a delayed reaction to these transgressions, Dr. Mani throws himself under a train fifty years later, precisely the day after Yom Kippur.

Yehoshua establishes deeper connections too between the lives of these characters and the liturgical process of atonement and redemption associated with the Days of Awe. First of all, Avraham Mani views the holy days literally, as a divine opening of the Books of Life and Death on the eve of Rosh Hashanah—where God inscribes the name of each congregant—followed by ten days granted for repentance, until a judgment is sealed for that year when the gates of heaven close at the end of Yom Kippur. Avraham acknowledges to his rabbi that he has sinned and that his sin deserves a verdict of death, but since death has not come of its own accord, he wishes to know whether, by taking his own life, he denies himself a portion in the world to come.[56] He chooses, however, not to take his own life, and instead wanders from one synagogue to another until he dies of natural causes in the town of Ur—the very spot where the biblical Avraham crushed his father's idols before becoming the founder of an abstract monotheism.

Paradoxically, Avraham Mani's confession to his elderly rabbi becomes yet another transgression because it deliberately hastens the death of the old man; moreover, neither this confession nor Avraham's alleged repentance contributes to the well-being of the new Mani he had taken so much trouble to engender. Finally, although Avraham wonders whether his transgressions merit death (in this world), he does not kill himself because he is afraid to lose his chance to be resurrected in the afterworld. This is a legalistic mindset that understands the commandments as a system of threats and promises full of loopholes that are not fully transparent.

By contrast, the child born to Avraham and his daughter-in-law does commit suicide, by throwing himself under a train on his fifty-first birthday, the day after Yom Kippur. On the level of his personal psychology, Dr. Moshe Mani's suicide can be chalked up to a midlife crisis with its characteristic sexual and professional frustrations, but from a diachronic perspective it represents an additional installment in a perpetual family crisis of which the victim is only partially aware. As Avraham Balaban notes, Moshe Mani had been born just a few hours after Yom Kippur, and his decision to commit suicide on his birthday, is therefore a continuation of the actions that had brought him into the world.[57] The immediate cause of Moshe Mani's despair is the departure of the Shapiro siblings—especially Linka Shapiro, with whom he had fallen in love; he also despairs over the financial difficulties encumbering his birthing clinic. Nevertheless, by killing himself, Dr. Mani leaves two new orphans and two widows, his newly widowed wife, and his elderly mother, Tamara, who was herself widowed and abandoned by Avraham half a century earlier.

Death is hardly an uncommon occurrence in Yehoshua's novels: we saw how Yehuda Kaminka is pitchforked to death the morning after the

118 THE RETROSPECTIVE IMAGINATION OF A. B. YEHOSHUA

Passover seder, and *Friendly Fire* revolves around the pain of a bereaved family. Many of Yehoshua's works, including his earliest short stories, involve either a dramatic or a potential loss of life, so indeed it is hardly exceptional that death should also occur in the context of Yehoshua's representations of the Day of Atonement. Still, the fact that the threat of death forms such an integral part of Yom Kippur's liturgy—"Who by fire and who by water, who in due time and who before his time"—certainly adds an extra layer of significance to Yehoshua's engagement with the themes and symbols of this holiday in *Mr. Mani* and *A Journey to the End of the Millennium*.

Dr. Mani's suicide the day after Yom Kippur is actually one of two deaths clustered around the Day of Atonement in that novel; the first occurs in his clinic, exacerbating his overall sense of dejection and amplifying the ominousness of the Days of Awe. As soon as Moshe Mani had returned from the Zionist Congress to Jerusalem on the eve of Rosh Hashanah, accompanied by Linka and Efrayim Shapiro, he had first of all taken them to see his birthing clinic, where an efficient Swedish midwife had just delivered "a tiny, yellowish little Muslim," as Efrayim Shapiro recounts later to his father; "one of those premature babies you don't expect to last a week," yet "by some miracle it hung on, and on Yom Kippur it was still alive, measuring me with a friendly glance of its little, coal-black eyes.... If it takes good care ... [it] may live to see the tail end of the next century."[58]

In contrast with this Muslim offspring, who thrives despite his shaky health, the labor of a Jewish pioneer from a neighboring farm, ends tragically on the eve of Yom Kippur. Efrayim Shapiro recalls how frustrated Dr. Mani felt by his inability to understand the cause of death of this stillborn baby girl born to the Zionist pioneers:

[I] went to their synagogue. There were candles burning everywhere, and it looked like a mosque with all its carpets and cushioned benches along the walls. The boy [Dr. Mani's son] led me to his father's seat and I was given a prayer shawl and wrapped in it, because the Sephardic men wear prayer shawls even before they are married. And so I abandoned myself to their merry hymns, ... only to look up halfway through the service and see Mani at my side, in his prayer shawl with bloodstains on his fingernails. "The baby died and I don't know why," he whispered to me morosely. I felt I should say something; but before I could, he added, "It wasn't the cord."

After that he was silent except for joining his voice to the cantor's now and then.[59]

When the service ends, Dr. Mani rushes back to the clinic with Dr. Shapiro in tow—and here it is crucial to remember that Efrayim Shapiro is himself a doctor, actually trained in pediatrics:

> in the big room, which was lit only by faint moonlight, we saw the woman lying with her face toward the wall; her husband leaned over her, trying to get her to look at him. Mani walked by them without stopping; he handed his prayer shawl bag to the midwife and led me by the hand to see the dead child in the delivery room. . . . Mani picked her up and shook her, slapping her back as if still expecting a cry, and laid her so carefully down on a bed that you might have thought he hoped there was another baby inside her that might yet be born alive.[60]

This dead baby, "perfectly formed, her eyes shut as though fast asleep," is a soul that had committed no transgression, unless we insist on reading this episode as a post-Zionist judgment of primal Zionist sin against a local Muslim population.[61] Notice, however, that the baby's mysterious cause of death (her blue hue indicates suffocation, but we are specifically told she did not die from the umbilical cord—that is, not from the connection with the mother) points to other sources of blame for this baby's missed breath of life. Efrayim Shapiro, who had trained as a pediatrician in Europe's best schools, might have been able to save this baby, if he cared enough to become involved in Mani's enterprise; however, even during his short visit, he lodges in Christ Church so that he can detach himself easily from the Manis and their problems, and he does not feel responsible for anything other than his sister and their family estate. In this, he differs from the rest of Yehoshua's physicians, and altogether from most of Yehoshua's characters, whose vocational profiles, as we saw in the previous chapter, are a core aspect of their personalities. Dr. Mani, by contrast, is thoroughly immersed in his vocational duties, as well as in the holiday service, though he makes the ultimate escape by committing suicide.

Yom Kippur, like the Passover seder, ends with a traditional affirmation of the hope to celebrate "next year in Jerusalem." Yet as soon as Efrayim Shapiro hears the final shofar blow and sees the watermelons carried into the synagogue to break the fast, he feels "most happy, because I knew that as of that moment my homeward journey had begun"—back to Poland.[62] The following morning Efrayim prevails on his sister to leave Jerusalem. This becomes the breaking point for Dr. Mani, who then throws himself under their train in a doubled act of despair *and* vengeance, both on them and on the grand/father who formerly abandoned him and Jerusalem. Thus, in terms of a commitment to the homeland, Dr. Moshe Mani's suicide is a kind of inversion of Yehuda Kaminka's gruesome murder, which we discussed under "those who leave" in chapter 2.

Moshe Mani had established an ecumenical clinic in Jerusalem to help women from all religions and denominations give birth as painlessly as possible. But although he worked there harmoniously with a Swedish nun turned midwife, his attempt to raise vital funds for this clinic at the Zionist Congress in Basel failed. Filled with joy when at least the Shapiro siblings had decided to follow him to Jerusalem, he despairs when they leave.

Like the stillborn baby's mother, who turns her face to the wall, Moshe Mani therefore feels that his labor has failed miserably too and wishes himself dead, but by acting out this death wish, he becomes guilty, like his grand/ father, of abandoning wife, children, and mother. Although ultimately, following this novel's genealogical scheme, the judgment against Moshe Mani is deflected toward the grand/father who abandoned him at birth, it also points just as harshly toward the Shapiro siblings, who witnessed his need and left him in despair. Indeed, according to Yehoshua's ethos, as we have seen, the two cardinal sins are abandoning family and homeland: whereas Avraham Mani is guilty of both of these transgressions, Efrayim Shapiro is guilty of detaching himself irresponsibly from the enterprise of his Jerusalemite colleague. In the next generation, Dr. Mani's son exhibits the consequences of his father's abandonment, while every single Shapiro descendant perishes in the Holocaust. We hereby see, yet again, how the main effect of Yehoshua's engagement with a holiday setting is to move the discussion *away* from a preoccupation with divine reward and punishment and toward a reassessment, instead, of the practical responsibilities of individual Jews toward Zion, toward each other, and the world.

Yehoshua's most dramatic representation of a death on Yom Kippur occurs in *A Journey to the End of the Millennium*, where Ben Attar's young wife perishes in terrible agony during the final moments of the Day of Atonement. Her death however also conveniently frees Ben Attar from an excommunication judgment that had been pronounced against him ten days earlier, the day after Rosh Hashanah.

In this historical novel, a North African Jewish merchant, Ben Attar, travels with his two wives from Tangier to Paris, and later to the heart of Ashkenaz, to convince his nephew's wife that she should not try to sever her husband's relationship with his uncle and longtime business partner, just because she feels threatened by the bigamous practices of Jews from Arab lands. The outcome of a direct confrontation between these two cultures is the excommunication of the North African partner, whose second wife had brazenly declared in court that she too would welcome having two husbands. Her death on the Day of Atonement thus reaffirms, as if from heaven, a strong judgment against this boundless multiplication of desires, as we will see in more detail in chapter 7. Yet at the same time, the life of this young second wife becomes the sacrificial dove that reinstates the severed partnership between Ben Attar and his nephew.

In *A Journey to the End of the Millennium*, the High Holiday season plays a key role from the moment that Ben Attar's wagon reaches the city of Worms at the heart of Ashkenaz on the eve of Rosh Hashanah, to his reappearance on the Parisian doorstep of his nephew the first day of Sukkot, to announce that his bigamous lifestyle has ended. The cause of death of Ben Attar's second wife is quite clear to her medieval physician—"in the learned tongue of the ancient Greeks," he diagnoses the powerful spasms raking her back as tetanus[63]—but the symbolic context of her death of course activates several interrelated layers of significance beyond their realistic sociohistorical context.

This young woman had caught the tetanus bacteria when the judge who excommunicated her husband had inadvertently dragged her across the rusty nails on the floor of his synagogue while she was clinging to his legs, pleading for a reversal of the verdict. Everything is symbolic here, including the rusty nails—something corroded that becomes inadvertently dangerous. On a metaphysical level, moreover, and despite halakhic reassurances to the contrary, a death at the end of Yom Kippur inevitably suggests some kind of divine judgment against transgression.[64] The testimony given by this young wife had resulted in her husband's excommunication, and hence she interprets her illness as an act of divine punishment, though Ben Attar hastens to exonerate her and initially blames his nephew's wife for a "repudiation" that "had begotten death."[65]

At the end, however, Ben Attar admits that he himself is primarily responsible for taking his wives away from their children and relatives in what proves to be an overly perilous journey.[66] Realizing that he had brought destruction on his young wife, years before her time:

> A terrible dread filled Ben Attar's heart, for he did not know what he would say or how he would excuse himself to her father, his childhood friend, who had trusted him and given her to him as a girl in the tender first flower of youth. Now he could not even offer her father a grave upon which to prostrate himself. And how would he comfort his son . . . who had been left with his grandfather and grandmother in Tangier and who would require satisfaction from his father for the many days he had dreamed of his mother's return, when she had already departed this life.[67]

In addition, it is possible to argue that had Ben Attar been capable of accepting his young wife's deepest desires, then her fate could have been different, even in the midst of her illness. At sea, she had become attracted to the widower Rabbi Elbaz, brought along to plead the merchant's case in Ashkenaz. When during her illness she sees Elbaz praying at her bedside, "a spark of life flared in the sad amber-colored eyes" and "a fancy began to float in her desperate mind that if she tried to . . . arise from her sickbed, Rabbi Elbaz might accept, in return, if only symbolically, the role of her second husband. . . . This fantasy strengthened her will to recover."[68] This will to recover is immediately cut short, however, by Ben Attar's renewed demonstration of his never-yielding "right of a loving husband, to caress her cheeks and kiss her feet. . . . If this were not a holy day, when marital acts are forbidden, he would have offered her proof positive that in his eyes she was neither tainted nor enfeebled but a healthy, whole woman deserving of love."[69] Counterproductively, Ben Attar's alleged proof of love leads the second wife to a disappointed point of no return.

Unlike the legalistic judgment against the bigamous North African family, Yehoshua's representation of divine judgment as part of the High Holiday liturgy creatively blends the customs of Mizrah and Ashkenaz in a manner that put his current sociopolitical tensions into a broader perspective.[70] To gather a *minyan* of ten men for the Yom Kippur services on the outskirts of Verdun, Ben Attar's Sephardic rabbi enlists seven Ashkenazi

Jews from Metz, telling them that their prayers are needed for "a Jewish wayfarer whose sister-in-law, his wife's sister, had fallen sick."[71] These pious volunteers soon grasp the true relationship between their North African coreligionist and the sick woman, but, "fearful of rendering null and void the prayers they had prayed so far in the company of a banned Jew and a lying rabbi," they postpone the "full explanations until after the conclusion of the [Yom Kippur] service."[72]

Since Rabbi Elbaz was unable to assemble a quorum of ten Jewish men, he devises an expedient solution to complete the required number: he decides to "convert" a young Berber into a nominal Jew for the duration of Yom Kippur. This pliable youth—originally pagan, then converted to Islam and circumcised prior to the voyage—is immersed in a pool of water by Rabbi Elbaz, first "to wash away his idolatrous delusions" and then "to purge him for his reception by the chosen people," after which he is declared kosher for the *minyan*.[73]

Along with this tragicomic conversion, which the youth accepts with exemplary decorum, Yehoshua depicts the medieval practice of swinging white fowls over the heads of each member of a household prior to Yom Kippur, as a symbolic transfer of their sins onto a pure creature. Ben Attar decides to enact this animistic custom on all the members of his traveling party, including two Muslim sailors who had agreed to repurpose themselves as wagon drivers:

> A strange idea flashed through his mind of atoning for them too, so as to fortify them on the Day of Judgement that was fast approaching, in case the powers above mistook them for Jews. He told them to approach and bow their heads before him, and out of the large sack he took two more doves, and holding them by the legs he circled them three times above the egg-shaped black skull of the young idolater and three times above the grubby blue turban of the mariner-wagoner. So they would not suspect him of black magic, he also circled the doves above his own head, and he provided a shortened translation of the formula into rich Arabic.[74]

Beyond these holiday preparations, Yehoshua also presents a progressive bid to integrate the prayer styles of Jews from Muslim lands with those of the Jews from Christian lands, who agree to pray together:

124   THE RETROSPECTIVE IMAGINATION OF A. B. YEHOSHUA

It was evident from the first moment that two different prayer rites would have to be combined somehow in the course of the holy day. . . .

Therefore the two rites were attentively and respectfully blended together, and even the melodies adapted themselves to each other, and all was done cautiously, quietly, and properly, so as not to attract undue attention from the Verdun folk.[75]

This reconciliation of prayer styles offers an interesting model of how such an enterprise might be enacted in real life between the customs of Sepharad and Ashkenaz. It is quite ironic, too, that this process of liturgical integration is imagined *davka* by a secular Jew who has no use for the prayers of either side—though perhaps his detachment is precisely what enables him to regard this as a practical problem rather than a hallowed activity. Initially, the Jews of Metz are uncomfortable with the prostrations of Jews from Muslim lands: "But slowly their souls were won over by the splendor of the rhymed and ornamented verses, and obeying the passionate rabbi's gesture, they rubbed their foreheads repeatedly, if cautiously, on the reddish soil of Verdun, in the hope that such deep and humble prostration in the company of one banned Jew, one lying Jew, and one black Jew of doubtful Judaism might be added to the afflictions of the fast and fortify the virtuous act they had committed in making up ten for prayer."[76] The extraordinary injection of humor even into the grave religiosity of this majestic day enlivens Yehoshua's accurate portrayal of High Holiday customs. In his original Hebrew edition, the lines from the prayer book are highlighted in bold and interspersed into the narrative in a manner that evokes Yom Kippur's characteristic atmosphere and tempo. Yehoshua in part drew here on his childhood experiences alongside his father and grandfather at their Sephardic synagogue in Jerusalem, as well as from his adolescent visit to his mother's relatives in Morocco.[77]

As Yom Kippur advances toward sunset, "the seven Jews from Metz were seized by fear and trembling at the approach of the concluding service, when the gates of repentance in heaven would be closed, and they sought to remove the rabbi from the office of cantor and chant the all-important concluding prayers themselves according to the rite and melodies of their own dear, distant congregation."[78] At this point, Ben Attar again steps out from his "holy of holies"—as he has been referring to his wife's sick chamber, which he had been approaching all day with mounting trepidation, like a high priest in ancient times entering the inner chamber of the temple on Yom Kippur. But as soon as Ben Attar realizes that his young wife had drawn her last laborious breath, he decides that the *neilah* prayer has no further "power to eradicate the guilt of the death" that he had brought upon her and shifts instead to begging "the Lord of forgiveness to pity and to inscribe in the book of life his only remaining wife, who would soon need not only comfort for the death of her companion but also renewed assurance."[79]

It is interesting that although Ben Attar now realizes that he had generated great suffering, he does not pray for himself but only for each of his wives. Rabbinically and counterintuitively, despite the holiday's liturgical threats of death, a death at the end of Yom Kippur, as mentioned, is considered a sign of purity on grounds that the holiday had atoned for the sins of the individual and the entire congregation (Babylonian Talmud, *Ketubot* 103b). Still, the death of Ben Attar's second wife functions here as a shocking resolution to the problem generated by his double marriage, and it even seems to "atone" in a practical manner for the shortcomings of the men and women who surround her.

Ultimately, then, if holidays "demand more from people," as Yehoshua told Bernard Horn, they also demand more from a novelist who portrays the shortcomings and resilience of individuals, families, and communities, as they attempt to negotiate the requirements of an ancient holiday under unusually stressful conditions. The preparations for the Passover holiday in *A Late Divorce* are complicated by the arrival of a grandfather who demands an urgent divorce from his children's mother so that he can marry the mother of his next child. The Hanukkah celebrations in *Friendly Fire* are complicated by Daniela Ya'ari's trip to Africa, during which her husband is left alone to cope with the needs of their extended family throughout a hectic holiday season. Congregational participation in Yom Kippur services both in *Mr. Mani* and in *A Journey to the End of the Millennium* is complicated by the extraordinary arrival of travelers from foreign realms, a meeting of diverse outlooks that mingle ambivalently during the holiday.

Modeling such stressful moments in the lives of families and individuals striving to cope with the demands of a holiday, these scenarios in Yehoshua's fiction demand more from the reader, too: they demand an active evaluation of the options available to each celebrant, and they demand a critical judgment of the ways in which the strained characters cope (or fail to cope) with their traditional practices and ancestral beliefs. To some degree, this dynamic parallels the evaluation processes that Yehoshua generates through the watchman's stance, noted earlier in this volume, where we followed Yehoshua's visually impaired characters as they interrupt their habitual routines to survey their new horizons and reassess their attitudes toward the world around them. His holiday scenarios similarly draw the reader into an evaluation of choices available to these celebrants as they struggle through messy situations that demand from them an extraordinary degree of responsibility and self-control.

Yehoshua's holiday scenarios are more than a mere backdrop draping his fictional worlds with a Jewish time frame; they are not just a spice that endows his fiction with a folkloric flavor. His careful engagement with the themes and rituals of each holiday activates a systemic reconfiguration of the mythic and historical components of Jewish identity in ways that position Yehoshua's work in a pragmatic conversation with traditional preoccupations about Jewish identity in an old-new world.

By incorporating holiday traditions into his plots, Yehoshua undermines, yet at the same time also reinvigorates, the relevance of traditional markers of Jewish identity for contemporary Israeli life. When he insists that ancient attitudes toward the divine are an integral part of his heritage, he thus paradoxically *defamiliarizes* the divine to wrestle against the power of "something hidden and invisible, of a God who is abstract, jealous, and aggressive," in an effort to earn for his people, once again, the ancient name of *isra-el*.

CHAPTER 6

Names

A character, first of all, is the noise of his name, and all the sounds and rhythms that proceed from him.
—WILLIAM GASS, *FICTION AND THE FIGURES OF LIFE*, 49

What significance can we glean from the Hebrew sound and meaning of the names that Yehoshua selects for his characters? What is the deeper relationship between these concentrated nuggets of identity and the psychosocial attributes of the literary beings to whom he attaches these symbolic tags? What is the effect of an "act of naming" performed *indirectly* by a novelist, when he lets his characters rename themselves, or name others, within his fictional worlds?[1] On multiple occasions within this book we have noted already that names are the smallest units that expose Yehoshua's multilayered style of composition.[2] As cultural signs, they indicate an association with a specific group—an ethnic, religious, class, or gendered identity—or, on the contrary, they may obfuscate such identifications to invalidate stereotypes. On a historiosophic level, these subtle onomastic allusions enable Yehoshua to project traditional Jewish conceptions of history onto the sociological and psychological layers of his texts. When we decode Yehoshua's name games, we thus recuperate a constellation of references that flicker through the sound and sense of these cultural nuggets of signification, but these references are grasped so intuitively by Yehoshua's contemporary Hebrew readers, including scholars, that they rarely stop to examine their significance in depth. To continue illustrating Yehoshua's multilayered style of composition, now through his name games, this chapter will therefore dwell on one notable example, Yigal and his replacements in Yehoshua's *The Lover* (*Hame'ahev*, 1977), a moniker that functions as an interpretative key to that novel.

128   THE RETROSPECTIVE IMAGINATION OF A. B. YEHOSHUA

Before launching into this analysis of name games, it is wise to recall James Phelan and Peter Rabinowitz's warning against searching for abstractions that erase the richness of a narrative: "Symbol-hunting is a surefire method for transforming the complex experience of reading narrative into a deadening search for neatly packaged Hidden Meaning."[3] Although we should not brush aside the intertextual and sociological connotations attached to loaded signs such as names, one way to protect ourselves against a reductive search for "hidden meaning" is to distinguish, in Yehoshua's case, among the psychological, sociological, historical, and historiosophic levels of his texts, so that we can appreciate every dimension in its own right, along with the rhetorical and associative strategies that bind it all together into a holistic narrative.[4]

The majority of names that Yehoshua chooses for his characters enhance their sociological profiles in a realistic manner. Thus, Rafael Calderon in *A Late Divorce* (*Geirushim meuharim*, 1982) suits the image of a Sephardic Jew with a high position in a Tel Aviv bank at the end of the twentieth century, while Joseph ben Kalonymos in *A Journey to the End of the Millennium* (*Masa el tom ha'elef*, 1997) bears the name of a distinguished medieval clan of Ashkenazi scholars and poets. But occasionally Yehoshua comes up with names such as Honi in *The Extra* (*Nitzevet*, 2014) or Hagar in *Mr. Mani* (*Mar Mani*, 1990), names that are so uncommon from a sociological point of view that they beg for an interpretation based on their biblical or talmudic references. Neither Honi nor Hagar is a name typically associated with the sociological profiles that Yehoshua assigns to these characters; they therefore evoke a sense of defamiliarization and wonder, which the author partly addresses within the text itself. We are informed, for example, that in a Negev kibbutz in the 1960s, Hagar's parents decided this could be "a fitting name for a girl born in the desert."[5] The biblical expulsion of Avraham's concubine and son, and the fact that the biblical Hagar is not regarded as part of the Jewish people, is not addressed in the text, but this background is necessarily invoked, as Mordechai Shalev pointed out, by Yehoshua's unconventional name choice.[6] Similarly, in *The Extra* Noga asks her elderly mother why her brother was named Honi and is informed—at the age of forty!—that she herself had picked this name for her new brother after she learned in kindergarten about the Tanna known as "Honi the Circle Maker," who had successfully prayed for rain.[7] Such statements beg for an interpretation of these texts in relation to their relevant intertextual references.[8]

Yehoshua's sensitivity to these onomastics leads him sometimes to withhold proper names altogether, as in *Facing the Forests* (*Mul haye'arot*, 1963) and other shorter works, including *A Woman in Jerusalem* (*Shlihuto shel hamemuneh 'al mash'abei enosh*, 2004), where, as we saw in chapter 4, he labels all but one of the characters according to their vocational function or family status—factory owner, human resources manager, journalist, old mother, delinquent son. This enhances the historiosophic dimension of the text while minimizing its sociopolitical contexts.[9] On the flip side, Yehoshua often invokes the names of the ancient prophets, chiefly Moses, to address the responsibilities of his own contemporary Jeremiahs and Moses, as we noted in the previous chapter on holidays. Indeed, Yehoshua circles around Moses in many of his essays about Jewish identity and in several of his novels, while he criticizes Jeremiah in *Friendly Fire* (*Esh yedidutit*, 2007) through a modern namesake who blames that ancient prophet for imposing on the Jews a jealous and exclusivist God.[10]

In addition, significant acts of naming and renaming are staged as part of the actual plot of the novels themselves. We noted already how Benjy and Michaela in *Open Heart* (*Hashivah mehodu / Return from India*, 1994) argue about whether to name their daughter Shiva with a *beit* (שיבה) or with a *vav* (שיוה), since the former means atonement or return while the latter refers to equality, but also to a Hindu deity that stands for both destruction and regeneration.[11] In *The Retrospective*, the actress Ruth defends her youthful decision, forty years earlier, to change her name from Nehama to Ruth, thus signaling a move away from her Mizrahi margins to an Ashkenazi cultural center, though readers attuned to Yehoshua's biblical references will also realize that this name change recalls the momentous decision of Ruth, the Moabite, who chose to adapt herself into Israelite culture and who gave birth to the lineage that produced King David. Through Nehama's new name choice, Yehoshua thus indicates that even the most exalted lineage in Jewish history is a product of a multicultural adaptation, a topic of central concern to both the Israeli and Spanish historical contexts of *The Retrospective / Hesed sefaradi*.[12]

From a literary-historical point of view, Yehoshua's name games greatly improve upon the nineteenth-century tendency of Haskalah writers to clunkily incorporate references to holy texts into their fiction, a tendency later critiqued and refined by Abramowitz, Bialik, and other novelists and poets who endeavored to create a richer and more smoothly integrated

130   THE RETROSPECTIVE IMAGINATION OF A. B. YEHOSHUA

Hebrew—a new *nusach* capable of conveying realistic representations of the world in a modern context.[13] Among Yehoshua's direct influences, Agnon activates biblical names as well as Yiddish word games, for example in the troubled relationship between 'Akavia Mazal and Leah Mintz in *In the Prime of Her Life* (*B'dmi yameha*, 1923), where, like the patriarch Ya'akov, 'Akavia is caught between two women, while Leah is pushed to marry *mintz* (coins) according to a monetary transaction that blights her life.[14]

William Faulkner, the second-strongest influence on Yehoshua, uses such onomastics sporadically but to great effect, as with Joe Christmas in *Light in August*, or by hinting at an incestuous fraternal relationship at the heart of *Absalom, Absalom!* in reference to that biblical story, which otherwise remains entirely external to this novel's plot. Another of Yehoshua's strongest influences, Kafka, drastically changed the literary name game by using sociologically neutral characters called "K" or left entirely unnamed. Yehoshua occasionally adopts this route too, but even then, he invests his unnamed characters with such a marked sense of vocational identity that this enhances a wider intersection between the narrative's historical, historiosophic, sociopolitical and psychological elements, as we traced in chapter 4 regarding the characters who are invested with the responsibilities of a *memuneh*.

To show in greater detail how Yehoshua relies on such name games to create a higher level of interpretation for his texts, I will concentrate here only on *The Lover*. Here Yehoshua restricted himself to six major characters, each of whom is easily recognizable through separate monologues labeled according to their names, and set within the relatively self-contained time frame of Israel in 1973, during the dismal aftermath of the Yom Kippur War. As occurs in most of his subsequent novels, here too, Yehoshua includes self-reflexive comments about some of his name choices, a practice that serves as an effective base from which to decode his larger conversation about the condition of Israel at that moment, in relation to other eras.

As in Faulkner's *As I Lay Dying*, where Addie Bundren's life story and burial are described through a series of monologues by a dozen characters, in his first novel, *The Lover*, Yehoshua recounts the life and death of Veducha Ermozo from the perspective of six characters through their monologues. To a certain extent, *The Lover* is dominated by Adam's inner consciousness—but most of the events are retold from the perspective of his daughter, Dafi, as well as through the consciousness of the Arab teenager Na'im, who works in Adam's automotive repair shop. The same events reappear, albeit more vaguely, in the dreams of Adam's wife, Asya, and everything ultimately revolves around the appearance and disappearance of Gabriel Arditi, Veducha's grandson.

Asya's sections are transcripts of her dreams. We are never privy to her rational thoughts, and her behavior is filtered through the family's attitudes toward her. Concomitantly, Veducha's stream of consciousness appears first as a poetic transcription of a comatose mind: "A stone laid on a white sheet. . . . They turn the stone wash the stone feed the stone and the stone urinates slowly. . . . Quiet. A stone weeping."[15] At this stage, Veducha feels herself to be a stone, then a plant, and then an animal. But eventually she wakes up from her long coma and Yehoshua unfurls her character in all its brilliance. Indeed, as we shall see, she reawakens to humanity by remembering her name and the name of her place of origin.

The basic plot of this novel recounts Adam's absurd search for his wife's lover, Gabriel, a weak young man (Veducha's grandson) who had disappeared during the initial days of the Yom Kippur War. Gabriel had returned to Israel only a few weeks earlier, having been notified that his grandmother was about to die. We meet him for the first time when he shows up in Adam's garage, pushing a tiny broken-down Morris that he claims is missing just "a little screw" (89). In Hebrew, "missing a screw" refers to a mental imbalance rather than to sexual deprivation, as the English suggests, yet the absence of sexual relations between Asya and Adam is indeed a central problem here, so in this instance we gain something in translation.

At first it seems obvious that Gabriel is the lover indicated by the novel's title, as mentioned in Adam's opening words: "And in the last war we lost a lover. We used to have a lover, and since the war he is gone. Just disappeared" (3). But gradually it emerges that there is more than one lover: Na'im becomes Dafi's boyfriend; Adam has illicit sexual relations with his daughter's classmate, and this proliferation of cases turns into a call for a closer inspection of the concept itself: What is a lover in contrast to a spouse, a stranger, or a mere acquaintance? How can "we" (collectively) lose or have a lover, as Adam declares? Whose lover is it, and does he really love anyone at all?

ADAM

One could argue that Adam is himself *The Lover*'s principal lover—one that is missing and delinquent on several counts. First of all, he brings to his wife not only a sexual but also an intellectual substitute for himself. Gabriel translates for Asya the French documents that she needs for her dissertation on the French Revolution, and he also gives her the sexual satisfaction that Adam withholds and that she too had kept at bay in a marriage that, from the start, was not particularly passionate or romantic. After the tragic death of Yigal, their firstborn, it had turned into the mere shell of a relationship. Even earlier, when Adam and Asya met as teenagers in the same classroom, his attraction to her was quickened by an awareness that *another* boy was in love with her. Now Adam attempts to rekindle his vicarious attachment to Asya through Gabriel.

From a sociological point of view, Adam's name does not reveal to us anything about this character's ethnic, economic, or religious background. He appears to be Ashkenazi, but why is he then portrayed, rather uncharacteristically, as an owner of an automotive repair shop? (See chapter 4 for a discussion of this issue.) Adam had dropped out of high school to repair cars under his father's tutelage and inherited the business soon afterward. When the novel opens in the fall of 1973, his business is flourishing, and he employs mechanics mainly from an Arab village near Haifa.

The biblical name Adam is actually not a traditional Jewish name, even though in recent years it has become popular among diaspora Jews. It is rarely given to Jews in Israel, for in Hebrew it simply means "human" or "everyman" in a politically incorrect masculine inflection. Yehoshua's assignation of this name to an Israeli character is therefore unusual. Moreover, the omission of Adam's family name—indeed the omission of this novel's central family name—further reinforces Adam's status as an Israeli everyman. He owns a successful business, but he is associated ideologically with his wife's Labor Zionist background; he had dropped out of high school, but he is married to a hyperintellectual teacher; he is neither religious nor bohemian, but he grows a long beard that casts him as a prophet or artist; he is a paterfamilias, but his tiny family is tottering on the verge of dissolution. He is thus a cluster of contradictions without any clear sense of direction.

The biblical Adam knew that "it is not good for a man to be alone," so initially he rejoiced in the wife that God made for him (Genesis 2:18).

Yehoshua's Adam is a sad and lonely man despite the company of his wife and daughter; essentially a mourner expelled from a paradise that he never knew. From a psychological point of view, he is an average middle aged man tied to an inadequate and stale relationship with a woman and a place—indeed a woman who *is* a place, as we shall see—they live in the same household but barely interact physically or intellectually, yet they are preoccupied and even obsessed with each other nonetheless.

But on the historiosophic level of this novel, the main significance of Adam's name revolves around his (vicarious) relationship with the reality of Asya/Asia. This is a somewhat counterintuitive point because in *The Lover* it is Gabriel, rather than Adam, who represents Yehoshua's nemesis—the Jew who has abandoned the homeland, as we saw in chapter 2. While Adam stays put, Gabriel abandons both his grandmother and Israel, returning only briefly to claim their inheritance. Gabriel also absconds from the battlefield and hides among those who do not serve in the army. And yet it is through Adam that Yehoshua chose in this novel to explore the fault lines of an allegedly feeble relationship between an average Israeli "everyman" and his Asiatic homeland. How is Adam (an Israeli everyman) connected to Asya (the Asiatic homeland)? What is the original basis of their relationship, and what would be the consequences of its collapse?

ASYA/ASIA

Asya's name is spelled in Hebrew exactly like the continent on which Israel is located (אסיה), and its semantic and phonetic connotations create an ironic relationship between this sad Ashkenazi schoolteacher and the sunny Mediterranean port town in which she lives.[16] The name is quite common among Slavs and Greeks and Turks, as well as among Jews of Eastern European origin, though, like Adam, it is not a traditional Jewish name. If accented on the last rather than the first syllable and given a slightly different spelling (עשיה), the same Hebrew phonemes turn into "action," energetic action, doing things. Indeed, Yehoshua's Asya is always doing things—mopping the floor, cooking dinner, grading high school exams, studying European history, but mostly busy dreaming.

Her body is in Asia; she teaches Jewish teenagers who must fight to remain in Asia; she hosts Na'im, an Arab Israeli from a local village, who like Veducha and Gabriel is a native of the region, but although she raises a small family in Asia, her own ideological framework is tilted toward Europe. Gilead Morahg describes her as an embodiment of the *"transition* between the European Diaspora to the Asian homeland,"[17] but to her husband and daughter she represents the irrelevance of a Labor Zionist ethos in the 1970s because she continues to adhere to its ideology, without registering her husband's improved financial possibilities or engaging afresh with the social relevance of that foundational ideology.

Twenty years after drawing such a precarious relationship between Asya/Asia and her Jewish everyman, Yehoshua posed the following question to a group of Israeli historians: "Do you intend to sit with your gaze toward the sea and sky, traveling three times a year to New York, London and Paris, considering yourself part of Western culture, or are you also locals, real neighbors who have arrived to your first but also your final home?" He urged Israeli historians to turn their gaze, "not only militarily, but also economically and maybe even culturally and scientifically—to the Middle Eastern region where you live."[18] When Asya meets Na'im in Yehoshua's novel, she asks him about his high school curriculum in the village, and he is surprised to discover that she knows very little about his lifestyle, so close to her home. With Gabriel, Asya shares an interest in European culture, but it is fair to note that Yehoshua himself follows a blend of European and American models in his writing. Thematically, grandmother Veducha was the first Sephardic character that he created, and Na'im his first full-fledged Arab character, though Yehoshua's own Sephardic Jerusalemite roots always informed his attitude toward the multiculturalism of Israeli society.

Going back to the biblical context of Adam's wife, Genesis 3:20 describes Eve (חוה) as the mother of all living creatures (אם כל חי). In Yehoshua's novel, Adam's wife is the mother of one living creature, a sixteen-year-old daughter, who feels isolated and neglected and wanders sleeplessly each night to the curbside where her brother, Yigal, had been run over by a car before she was born. The death of this child was not an entirely random accident—he was a deaf child allowed to bike by himself at age five, outfitted with a hearing aid that he could switch off to enjoy total silence—but Asya and Adam do not blame each other for his death. Instead, their tragic history binds them together, without drawing them closer.

Roberto Faenza's Italian cinematic adaptation of Yehoshua's novel (*L'amante perduto*, 1999) ends romantically with a revitalized marriage when Asya acknowledges Adam's patient devotion to her. On this big screen, the spouses are sexy, Gabriel is playful, and Dafi is troubled but sweet. To be sure, Yehoshua's original text does not entirely eliminate the possibility of a rapprochement between the spouses, but Asya strikes Adam as drab and gray: "something in her fatigued me" (50). (In his later novels, by contrast, Yehoshua has been increasingly portraying aging women as highly arousing.) But here the affair that Adam orchestrates between Asya and Gabriel fails to rekindle his sexual interest in her, and it remains unclear whether Adam's criminal sexual encounter with his daughter's classmate can dispel his years of mourning for the lost Yigal and the disappointed realization that even Dafi could not redeem them.

DAFI

As Michael Ragussis has argued, acts of naming, renaming, or unnaming of offspring in a family novel operate as way of controlling and binding the child's behavior, or conversely, as an attempt to release children from a specific heritage by marking or unmarking them with a social code.[19] In *The Lover*, Yehoshua did not dramatize the process of choosing a name for a child, as he did in *Open Heart* and other novels where he draws concerted attention to this issue. Nonetheless, a name such as Dafi, and much more strongly, Yigal (the brother that she was expected to replace), resonate in the Israeli context of this novel not only as a common name, but also as a "default" historiosophic mode that paradoxically contravenes its actual meaning.

Yigal or Yiga'el (יגאל) literally means "will redeem / will be redeemed." In Jewish tradition, it evokes messianic expectations of a divinely sanctioned return to the homeland, a passive attitude that modern Zionism ostensibly dismissed in favor of a pragmatic and immediate return. From a modern Zionist point of view, this name nonetheless became extremely popular among Israelis after the establishment of the State of Israel. Even earlier, as Anita Shapira observes in her biography of one of Israel's Labor Party leaders—born in 1918 to a family of Galilean farmers right after Lord Balfour's endorsement of a Jewish homeland—Yigal Allon's new Hebrew name signaled that this child had arrived in "heady times of great expectations." Until then, Yigal Allon's father "had given his children traditional Jewish names. He now outdid himself. . . . No more dispirited Diaspora names, such as Moshe or Mordekhai. . . . 'Yigal'—the redeemer—suggested new times, a different sort of life experience, high hopes, and a commensurate

136 THE RETROSPECTIVE IMAGINATION OF A. B. YEHOSHUA

self-confidence."[20] By the time Yehoshua chose the name Yigal for Adam and Asya's firstborn, it was already a trendy name, associated not only with the statesman Yigal Allon but also with many other prominent Sabras, such as the popular writer Yigal Mossenzon and the archaeologist Yiga'el Yadin.[21] However, Yehoshua uses this name ironically in order to draw attention to a gap between the hope encoded in that name—the idea of rescue and redemption—and the series of mistakes that had led to the loss of Adam and Asya's Yigal.

Adam longs for a second chance, a "replacement" child. But instead of an introverted child with a handicap, he gets an extroverted girl born with all her senses intact, and they do not name her Ge'ula (גאולה), the female version of Yigal, but rather Dafna, a laurel plant, which is native to the Mediterranean; in short, Dafi. Yet even this sociologically realistic name—which was a trendy name among secular Israelis at the time[22]—can be loaded with extraordinarily significance, simply by its not being a traditional Jewish name like Sarah, Rachel, or Deborah, or a diasporic name like Fruma or Veducha. Like Yigal, Dafna is an ancient Hebrew term that acquires renewed meaning through the revival of a Jewish relationship with the ancient homeland and with its distinct Mediterranean flora and fauna, thus reinserting Israel into the regional normalcy to which Yehoshua aspires.[23]

Yehoshua is aware of the power of Hebrew names, including deceptively uncomplicated ones like Dafi. In an interview with S. Shifra for the *Davar* daily in 1975, when Yehoshua was already immersed in writing this novel, he talked about the unavoidable significance of even the simplest modern Hebrew names, given the irregular development of the Hebrew language: "The baggage carried by French and English names like Pierre or John has sunk into common usage, its meaning blurred through a continuous use that has become completely technical. But new Hebrew names, or revamped versions of biblical names that did not have the opportunity to develop in a continuous fashion over hundreds of years, are loaded with evocative meaning because their connotations are still too fresh. They have not become 'common' names in a technical manner."[24] By default, even a lighthearted nickname like Dafi is loaded with the heaviness of a three-thousand-year-old tradition that only recently began to fill in the gaps of its discontinuous relationship with an ancient historical heritage, which now requires a reexamination of every Hebrew concept that is layered with old-new resonances.

VEDUCHA

The opposite argument can be made about the ethnic label that Yehoshua assigned to the names of the first major Sephardic figures in his literary career, Veducha Ermozo and her grandson Gabriel Arditi. At first, this ethnic label seems to *liberate* them from the weightier onomastics of a name like Asya or Yigal. The main significance of a name like Veducha (pronounced "Vidúkha") is simply to identify this character as a Sephardic woman—likely an affectionate variation of Chayaleh or Chaimkeh (life), since *Vida* means "life" in Spanish.[25] Her last name, Ermozo—from the Spanish *hermoso*, which means "beautiful"—celebrates and also makes fun of an ancient lady whose external state of preservation impresses the nurses at the geriatric hospital when she lies unconscious for many months. Her nicely preserved external condition—like that of her 1947 car—is misleading: a few months after her recovery, she passes away at the same time that her newly refurbished car collapses at the edge of an Arab village. To what extent, then, does Veducha come "back to life" from her coma, and to what extent is her life "beautiful"?

"It's a wonder," marvels the nurse at the geriatric hospital where Adam searches for Veducha's grandson. "She was born in 1881. . . . Do you know any history? That was when the first Bilu settlers arrived in the country . . . *Hibbat Zion* . . . the beginnings of Zionism" (139). But of course, Jerusalemite Sephardim like Veducha—together with Arabs, Christians, and Ashkenazim of the Old Yishuv—were living in Ottoman Palestine long before the "beginnings of Zionism," and thus the narrative of *Hibbat Zion* as an alleged beginning is both affirmed and contested through Veducha's biography. Her background puts the modern Zionist impetus into perspective by reminding us that Jewish life in this place long predates modern movements. On the other hand, Veducha had fallen into a stupor, forgotten, abandoned, and irrelevant, like Adam's deficient relationship with Asya/Asia. This imperfect juxtaposition between Veducha's lifespan and the heyday of the Labor Zionist movement, which had led to statehood, thus extends *The Lover's* broader inquiry into the continuing relevance of Labor Zionism in the aftermath of the Yom Kippur War fiasco and a rising right-wing voice.

Veducha finds herself alone in this world, abandoned by her grandson and disconnected from her Jerusalemite background. At the age of ninety-three she had lost consciousness, only to regain it a few months

138   THE RETROSPECTIVE IMAGINATION OF A. B. YEHOSHUA

later, reawakened by the sight of Adam's beard, which triggered childhood memories of walking in an Arab marketplace with her own grandmother among Jerusalem's bearded Jews. She then gropes for "a word that will open it all" (118), and this word, the door to her consciousness and her identity, is a name, the name of her place of origin:

> How did they say it? How did they say it?—Usalem. Oh, I have it.
> ... An important place, a hard place....
> Usalem? Usalam? But not so heavy.... Rusalim. I'm sure they called it Rusalim.
> ... What? ... Usalam has returned.... Rusalem.... Where was she born?—Rusalem. Where are they from?—Rusalem. Next year where?—in Rusalem. But did they really say—Rusalem? Not that.
> ... A little different. I've forgotten. Must rest.
> ... What's its name? Not Usalem—Rusalim. But there was something at the beginning. Gerusalem, Sherusalem, Merusalem, Jerusalem. Oh, oh, oh, Jerusalem. Jerusalem, Jerusalem. Exactly, but no. I weep. Great pain. Jerusalem. Simple. Ah, that's it. Jerusalem. (142)

Recovering the name of her original place brings great relief to Veducha, as well as great pain. Afterward, she weeps for several days, in a daze, not functioning as a coherent human being, but no longer comatose. To regain full control over her life, she also needs to remember her own name:

> All that is missing is my name. Someone has only to remind me of my name and the rest will fall into place. I smiled at the dusky nurse and she smiled back, a little scared and a little astonished to find me smiling now and no longer weeping.
> I said to her, "What is your name, my child?" and she told me. "And what is my name?" I asked. "Your name?" She was utterly bewildered, thought I was playing games with her. "Your name ...?" and she came closer to the bed, searching for a piece of paper down there among the latticework, glancing at it and saying in a shy whisper, "It says here Veducha Ermozo."
> That was all that was missing. I heard the name and at once my head opened. The card with my name had been hanging there on the bed all the time and I, foolish woman, had not seen it. Now I knew

who I was and I remembered other things too. All at once I understood everything. I felt dizzy with all the knowledge returning to me. Mother, Father, Hemdah and Gabriel, the State of Israel, Golda, the house, the bay, Galilee, Nixon. My neighbor Mrs. Goldberg, *Yediot Ahronot*, my little Morris, the Jewish people. (175)

Veducha Ermozo is a psychologically coherent character in an absurd story that hinges on Adam's search for his wife's lover, Veducha's errant grandson. On a sociohistorical level, her ethnic background enriches the novel's cultural context at a time when identity politics had not yet become a trendy subject in Israel. It even surpasses the conventional overview of modern Zionist history recited by the geriatric nurse—from "*Hibbat Zion* . . . the beginnings of Zionism" (139)—by reminding us that Veducha's family, for example, was rooted in Jerusalem long before those "beginnings."

A few months after her miraculous recovery, Veducha dies in her apartment, padded by all the newspapers that she had loved to read. In a reversal of her previous condition, her body now turns to stone but her mind remains lucid, concentrated, once again, on a recital of relationships and names: "I think of what I want to think knowing it all my name and my parents' name and my grandson's name and my daughter's name remembering them all recalling all" (345).

Her errant grandson will now inherit both her apartment and her broken-down car, but what will he do with them? Will they merely provide him with funds to survive a few more years in Paris? Will he stay in Haifa and maintain a relationship with Asya and Adam? What kind of relationship is this, anyway, and what are his other options?

GABRIEL

A name can be a metonym, a clue, a history; especially in a work of fiction, it recalls a web of references. But not all these references are equally activated by the author or accessible to his interpreters; for example, the biblical and midrashic contexts associated with Gabriel's name do not strike me as pertinent to *The Lover*, although, for whatever it may be worth, Gabriel happens to be Yehoshua's own middle name, given in honor of his grandfather.[26] Unlike most of the other names in this novel, it is a very common Jewish name, used in all eras and among all Jewish groups. On the other hand, Arditi, Gabriel's family name, identifies him as a Jew of Sephardic background with an Italian twist, rather than the direct Spanish connection preserved in his mother's last name, Ermozo. We are told that Veducha raised Gabriel after her daughter was killed by a stray bullet during the siege of Jerusalem. His father then left Jerusalem for Paris, and Veducha moved with the orphaned boy to Haifa to start a new life there. She describes her grandson as a "lonely, bewildered child . . . a creature of the night" (182), attached to nothing and pining away for his father. His charm stems from the honesty with which he admits his weaknesses.

Gabriel's symbolic function in *The Lover* does not run through his name but rather through the network of substitutes for Adam and Asya's lost son, Yigal, which generates in this novel a conversation about Zionist values, especially in the decades following the establishment of the state. After the death of their little son, Adam had insisted on conceiving a second child to replace Yigal; he gets Dafi, although Asya has no interest in building a family, and both of them had ceased to regard themselves as sexual partners. Years later, Adam brings to Asya another kind of replacement—both for Yigal and for himself—and she accepts this substitute. In one of her dreams it dawns on her "that this wasn't Yigal but some kind of replacement that Adam had brought here for me. But I didn't mind this, it seemed wonderful and right to bring me a substitute. I just waited for him to grow tired of cycling around and around so I could see him close up, touch him, embrace him. But he didn't look, didn't hear. . . . I started walking the streets searching for the 'replacement' [התחליף] and growing more and more dispirited" (180–81). In Yehoshua's original text, Asya's acknowledgment of "the substitute" is even encircled in quotation marks, thus highlighting this concept for the reader.[27] Gabriel's double role as a *replacement* for the missing son, as well as for the deficient husband, is approached in the novel from other angles too: Dafi is shocked to discover that her mother had taken a lover, but she hardly imagines that the new "assistant" is also a replacement for her lost brother. On the other hand, Adam immediately connects Gabriel with the dead boy when Gabriel faints from hunger in his garage; when lifting the "light warm body" he is instantly brought back to the afternoon of the fatal accident (96). Nevertheless, by the end of the novel, the hope for a vicarious redemption invoked by the name of Yigal evidently remains as elusive as ever.

NA'IM

As soon as Dafi lays eyes on Na'im, the Arab teenager employed in her father's automotive repair shop, she thinks of Yigal: "something about him, some similarity. . . . And if I tell them they'll say, 'Nonsense, what do you know about Yigal, you never saw him'" (168). And yet Adam, too, when he first sees Na'im, is "reminded of Yigal, I don't know why, something about those dark eyes" (127). Thus, when Na'im is lightly wounded while tightening a car's brakes, Adam becomes hysterical, reinforcing the link that now encompasses Yigal, Na'im, and Gabriel, who had collapsed earlier in Adam's garage: "Suddenly . . . you see a boy . . . covered in blood. . . . The cuts aren't deep, but all that blood scares me. . . . This isn't the first time you've seen a boy lying in a pool of blood" (147).

In Hebrew, "Na'im" means pleasant, as befits this sensitive, handsome, and intelligent adolescent. In Arabic, the name means tranquility and comfort, one of the attributes that Islam associates with God. Thus, whereas Yehoshua's choice of the common Israeli name Yigal serves here to *defamiliarize* the concept of redemption by assigning it to a dead child, his assignation of the Arabic name Na'im to a very endearing Arab-Israeli character *familiarizes* the connection between Israeli Jews and Arabs across permeable boundaries on a variety of levels, including Dafi and Na'im's blossoming love.

During the early stages of their acquaintanceship, she shows him a path that winds down Mount Carmel, but when they meet two of her classmates, Dafi begins to wonder, "how far am I going to walk with him? To his village? And I parted from him. He could look after himself now" (190). One of those classmates, Yigal Rabinowitz—who, judging from his last name, is an Ashkenazi Israeli—emerges as yet another potential redemptor in what is becoming a tragicomic chain of substitutes for the necessary but deferred work of personal and national repair.

The positive connotations that Yehoshua attaches to Na'im's personality and name are one of the ways through which he familiarizes contacts between the representatives of different backgrounds in the social mosaic that he presents in this, and all, his novels. When he composed *The Lover* in the mid-1970s, there were relatively few Muslim characters in Hebrew fiction.[28] According to his own admission, Yehoshua based this character partly on Na'im Araidi, a Druze poet and former student of Hebrew literature at Haifa University, who eventually became a professor of literature and Israel's ambassador to Norway.[29] A few years before Yehoshua wrote this novel, Araidi published a collection of Hebrew poems entitled *Is Love Possible?* (1972). Yehoshua's Na'im decides that love *is* possible and thus becomes the antithesis to Adam, whose vicarious love for Asya seems to have run its course.

At home in both Hebrew and Arabic, Na'im is sent to live with grandmother Veducha, to keep her company and be ready for the nightly searches for her grandson. Having grown up among Jerusalem's Arabs, Veducha shares many elements of Palestinian culture with Na'im; she is the only Jewish character who communicates with him in his native language, though they are somewhat wary of each other too. Veducha is delighted to feel useful again by attending to Na'im's food and clothing, but her joy is tempered by anxiety about her absent grandson and the alarming reports that Na'im reads to her from the newspaper as the war winds down. Na'im's brother, the reader learns, is a terrorist who had tried to blow up Haifa University, but Na'im, by contrast, becomes the redeemer of this lonely old woman in need of comfort. Abandoned by her grandson, she admits that, through him, there's "light in the house again" (208).

On his part, Na'im is not so excited about spending his days and nights in the company of an old lady in Haifa's lower city. Initially he was happy to scour Israel's highways in a tow truck with Adam and Dafi, learning how to repair stranded vehicles that they rescued while Adam scanned the horizon for Gabriel all night. In this manner, Na'im becomes an expert mechanic. But suddenly Adam suspends the nightly searches, and Na'im is left stranded in Veducha's apartment, without work or school. His father was the one who insisted on pulling Na'im out of high school, though he was a star student there, and his cousin Hamid brought him to work in Adam's garage. But only when Adam discovers that Na'im has become his daughter's lover does he drive the youth back to his village with instructions to "tell your father to send you to school." Relieved, Na'im is "suddenly so full of hope" (350, 352).

GOING BACK TO THE ORIGINAL NAME

In his exasperated remarks to the American Jewish Committee during their centennial celebrations in 2006, Yehoshua explained that "a Jew can survive with his identity, no problem. . . . I want to change the conception of the survival, and put it on another level, on the [level of] the content of survival, on the totality of the elements that you are responsible for."[30] This is a reconfiguration of national responsibility that hinges, according to Yehoshua, on an affirmation of the original name of the Jewish people (*'am israel, bnei israel*) in ways that drive a wedge between Israel and the diaspora, while reinforcing a link between Israelites and modern Israelis, as well as between Israelis of different ethnic and religious backgrounds.

> If Moses would enter this hall, if Isaiah would enter this hall, if Jeremiah, if David, you would ask them, "Identify yourself—who you are?" They would say, "*We are Israel, the sons of Israel.*" . . . The name of the people [is] People of Israel. . . . The name of the land is the Land of Israel. . . .
>   . . . When I say I'm an Israel[i] . . . I was just returning back to my original name.[31]

Veducha's awakening, as we saw, is triggered by her childhood memories of Jerusalem and completed by the retrieval of her full name: "That was all that was missing. I heard the name and at once my head opened" (175). But although she miraculously awakens to take responsibility over herself, and to look after Na'im's food and lodging, she dies soon afterward.

From the point of view of Yehoshua's onomastic conception of national history, we can therefore return now to the question posed at the top of this essay regarding the identity of "the" lover, who at first seems to be Gabriel but then splits into as many possibilities as there are characters in this novel. In Jewish lore, notably in the exilic interpretations of the Song of Songs and in the book of Lamentations, composed after the destruction of the First Temple, the relationship between God and the people of Israel is portrayed as a broken one in which God leaves his wayward wife. Accordingly, Jeremiah imagined the loss of national sovereignty as a kind of divorce from God.[32] It was understood, however, even by the morose Jeremiah, that redemption and restoration could be imminently expected.

When Yehoshua assigns a common but weighty name such as Yigal ("will redeem / will be redeemed") to a vulnerable child of a deficient family, he pushes against any smug conception of an easily achievable Zionist dream, whether driven by religious or pragmatic motives. Not only was Adam and Asya's deaf son killed due to a series of lapsed responsibilities, but his replacements are also vulnerable: Dafi's classmate Yigal Rabinowitz is the worst student in her class; the Arab adolescent Na'im is a good student but his father pulls him out of school and dumps him on Adam; Gabriel appears and disappears willy-nilly and depends on the mercy of others; Dafi, despite all the efforts of her parents to maintain a stable household, becomes an insomniac who is kicked out of school.

The expectation of an external redemption encoded in the name of Adam and Asya's lost child, and through the network of substitutes woven around him, thus holds this novel together conceptually by exposing the absurdity of Adam's search for a redeemer. Mocking these elusive redemptive expectations, *The Lover* retells the classical story of modern Zionism by scaling down its difficulties to the level of character psychology, family dynamics, and the cultivation of a historical consciousness, where a dead end can occasionally generate the potential for a new beginning.

CHAPTER 7

Love Under the Burden of History

> Even if I'm still tied to her in my thoughts, and maybe in my feelings,
> I'm morally a free man.
>
> —A. B. YEHOSHUA, *THE LIBERATED BRIDE*, 560

Among Yehoshua's papers archived at the National Library in Jerusalem—a repository for his documents and manuscript drafts—I came across this rather silly plan for a novel that he never wrote, at least not in this exact manner: "*Masterplan*: Meshulam follows Blume and reaches Eretz Israel. Hirshl and Toyber follow suit to stop him and match him with someone else. *Hakhnasat kalah. Tmol shilshom. Bidmi yameha. Sipur pashut.* Do they bring along the intended bride??? *Blvav yamim* for the overseas journey."[1] This "masterplan," which essentially outlines a sequel to Agnon's *A Simple Story* (*Sipur pashut*, 1935), is called on one page "A Simple Story in the Land of Israel," and on another page "Not a Simple Story: A Literary Exercise." In addition to extending the plot of Agnon's *A Simple Story*, it also invokes elements from other Agnonian novels and novellas, including *The Bridal Canopy* (*Hakhnasat kalah*, 1931), *Only Yesterday* (*Tmol shilshom*, 1945), *In the Heart of the Seas* (*Bilvav yamim*, 1934), and *In the Prime of Her Life* (*Bidmi yameha*, 1923).

Yehoshua extends *A Simple Story* in two ways. First, he wants to bring several of its primary and secondary characters from Galicia to Jerusalem, as Agnon himself had done in three of the aforementioned stories; in particular, Yehoshua mentions Hirshl and Blume (the star-crossed lovers), Meshulam (Hirshl and Minna's son), and Toyber (the matchmaker who had endeared Minna to Hirshl, deliberately separating him from Blume). Secondly, Yehoshua wants to extend Agnon's love plot into the next generation, imagining an erotic attachment between Meshulam and Blume—that is, between Hirshl and Minna's now grown-up son and Hirshl's original beloved. In Agnon's novel, Hirshl had become confused and torn between the three women in his life (Blume, Minna and his mother). He succumbs to a bout of madness, from which he eventually recovers and learns to live affectionately with Minna.

In fact, Agnon's novella is already quite complicated from an inter-generational point of view: Blume's mother had been expected to marry Hirshl's father, but, like her daughter a generation later, she too was pushed aside by the machinations of Hirshl's wealthier family members. By extending these historicized entanglements into yet another genera-tion of dysfunctional love triangles, and by moreover bringing Meshulam into a direct sexual contact with the woman his father had desired and lost, Yehoshua thus intensifies the oedipal tensions already present in Agnon's text. Then, by actually bringing the lovers all the way to Jeru-salem, he reinforces some of the faint links Agnon had drawn between Hirshl's indecisive love for Blume and European Jewry's indecisive love for Zion, a topic that stands at the center of so much of Agnon's work, as Anne Golomb Hoffman has shown.[2] In other words, Yehoshua's sequel would have rendered Agnon's usual symbolic engagement with Zionism more explicit.

Apart from fantasizing about rewriting Agnon's novels, Yehoshua occa-sionally approaches them from a scholarly point of view. In so doing, he likes to highlight their oedipal elements, along with references to the biblical story of the binding of Isaac (the *akedah* episode from Genesis 22)—a conflation of motifs that in turn brought greater attention to their role in Yehoshua's own fiction. For instance, when considering the unsatisfying ending of *A Simple Story* and wondering why the sickly baby Meshulam is sent away to grow up with his grandparents, Yehoshua explains this decision psychologi-cally as Hirshl's unconscious way of exorcising his lingering desire for Blume, along with his mixture of bitterness and desire toward the mother who had driven true love away (and who, according to Yehoshua, had always denied Hirshl any genuine affection). In other words, by "sacrificing" Meshulam, Hirshl bypasses his discomfort with a lifestyle that has trouble nurturing healthy children. By means of this psychoanalytic interpretation Yehoshua also explains Hirshl's bout of madness as a reaction to unprocessed emo-tions toward his mother, so that only by getting rid of the evidence of his illness—embodied in the sickly child—Hirshl can bring himself to accept Minna as a mediocre replacement for his mediocre mother.[3]

To appreciate Yehoshua's projected sequel to *A Simple Story*, we can also recall his interpretation of yet another famous Agnonian love story, *In the Prime of Her Life*, where sixteen-year-old Tirtza insists on marrying the man whom her mother had desired, yet rejected, two decades prior. In a compelling analysis of that exquisite novella, Yehoshua interprets Tirtza's oedipal relationship with her mother's rejected lover as an akedaic ploy designed by her elders to bind the girl to their baggage of guilt and bereavement.[4] Whether this is true or not about Agnon's novella, certainly all the intergenerational love triangles that characterize Yehoshua's own love plots do bind vulnerable creatures like Tirtza and Meshulam to the desires of their elders. This paradigm allows him to trace the inherited burdens that complicate and sometimes impede the establishment of independent and thriving new relationships.[5] We may catch a whiff too of Yehoshua's psychoanalytic interpretation of the Golah, the Jewish diaspora, which, as we mentioned before, he views as a "neurotic solution" that circumvents a normal attachment to one's ancestral homeland, due to an inordinate degree of interference from a religious code.

A "neurotic solution" is also the terminology that Yehoshua applies to Hirshl's expulsion of baby Meshulam at the end of Agnon's novel.[6] If we consider, as Nitza Ben-Dov has done, that Meshulam's name means "paid for," then a further question arises regarding the *apparent* normality achieved between his parents, Hirshl and Minna, after they get rid of baby Meshulam at the end of Agnon's novel.[7] Since this arrangement greatly disturbs Yehoshua, and he interprets it as an immoral purchase on normality, we can better understand why in his imagined sequel to *A Simple Story* (the "masterplot," to which we return in a moment) he draws together the two rejected creatures—Blume and Meshulam—and brings them to the land of Israel in an effort to reevaluate their personal happiness within the larger question of national redemption.

Across Yehoshua's oeuvre, by the way, love triangles threatening the well-being of a child can be found already in his 1965 novella "Three Days and a Child," his first work to have reached an international readership. In that novella, the sharp critic Mordechai Shalev immediately identified akedaic allusions that generate a faint degree of intergenerational drama.[8] The protagonist of "Three Days and a Child," Dov, is partnered with Yael, a young woman desired by her classmate, Zvi, more than by Dov himself. Then, for three whole days, Dov is unexpectedly placed in charge of a little

148   THE RETROSPECTIVE IMAGINATION OF A. B. YEHOSHUA

child, the toddler of a former girlfriend whom he still fancies, while she and her husband prepare for their college admission exams. Throughout this child-care experience, Dov entertains revengeful fantasies against the little boy's mother, even putting him in actual danger. Thus, from start to finish, the reader is unlikely to identify neither with Dov's murderous fantasies nor with his love problems, and in any case, none of the characters gets any closer to an emotional or erotic fulfillment.

Yehoshua's later novels, by contrast, lull us into accepting some absurd quest or obsession that motivates the characters. In *The Lover* we root for Adam as he tirelessly searches for his wife's pathetic lover—not to kill him or beat him up, as we just saw, but just to bring him back to Asya in a comical effort to rekindle Adam's weak attraction to his wife, an impaired attachment that resonates, more seriously, as a symbolic equation between the homeland and the wife. Similarly, in *Open Heart* (*Hashivah mehodu*, 1994) we feel sorry for the talented Dr. Rubin when he falls in love with the pampered wife of his boss; this misdirected passion compromises the young man's career, as well as the safety of his daughter with Michaela, whom he had married mainly to conceal his real passion. So, too, in *A Journey to the End of the Millennium* (*Masa el tom ha'elef*, 1997) Yehoshua temporarily suspends our Western rejection of bigamy by impressing us with Ben Attar's gallant efforts to provide equally for each of his two wives, in bed and in every other way. This medieval North African merchant goes to extreme lengths to convince his nephew's Ashkenazi wife that a marriage to two beloved women can be just as wholesome as attachment to a single partner, but in the end, the fault lines of his reasoning are exposed.

Even after several rereadings, Yehoshua can still sometimes lull us into setting aside our initial mistrust of his heroes' motives and situation, so that during each narrative's climax he can shock us anew with an alarming volte face that, in its full incontrovertible force, reveals the nefarious consequences of unhinged desires. Typically, this involves an existential threat to children or other vulnerable creatures who are jeopardized by the irresponsible behaviors of their elders. As Adia Mendelson-Maoz has shown, Yehoshua's close attention to the moral buildup of a literary work—a subject to which Yehoshua devoted an entire collection of essays[9]—attunes us more carefully to the manner in which he orchestrates a moral awakening in his reader, as much as in his characters.[10] The historicized love plots that we analyze in this chapter show in greater detail how such problematic behaviors, repeated from one generation to the next, serve as Yehoshua's means of showcasing inherited (ir)responsibilities that are difficult to identify and repair.

Yehoshua never did write that sequel to Agnon's *A Simple Story*, nor can he remember exactly when he dwelled two or three weeks on that plan, until his wife and Amos Oz, with whom he used to discuss all his projects, persuaded him to lay it aside.[11] Nevertheless, one can argue that regardless of when exactly he worked on this idea, Yehoshua *did* in fact redirect major aspects of this masterplan into virtually all his love plots, from *The Lover* to *The Tunnel*. They all have elaborate triangular relationships that to a greater or lesser degree encompass more than one generation and jeopardize the well-being of a child. This is a plot scheme that perfectly suits the multilayered narrative style that Yehoshua favors, because it easily evokes questions of national identity and survival, which resonate beyond the simple emotional and erotic attachments of the characters.[12]

In the preceding chapter we saw how in *The Lover* a dysfunctional love triangle in one generation (Adam/Asya/Gabriel) is followed over the next generation by a fainter love triangle between the Arab youth Na'im, Dafi, and her classmate, Yigal Rabinowitz. When she bumps into Yigal on the street at the early stages of her acquaintance with Na'im, Dafi wonders how far to accompany the Arab youth, who eventually becomes her lover: "how far am I going to walk with him? To his village?" (190). Barely noticeable, Dafi's alternative relationship with Yigal Rabinowitz is nevertheless remarkable because, as we explained in chapter 5 in detail, that boy's name—which technically means "redeemer"—echoes that of Dafi's brother, who had been killed in a preventable accident when he was five years old. Throughout this novel about lovers and potential lovers, Yehoshua connects the lost child to each and every lover, thus exposing a fruitless search for external solutions to internal problems—in other words, an illusory search for a "redeemer." Employing this suggestive vocabulary, Yehoshua opens up a wider conversation about Jewish identity and survival that ultimately seeks to clarify the goals of Zionism in part by questioning whether the modern Zionist revolution had ended with the establishment of the State of Israel, or if it remains a work in progress until its moral and pragmatic objectives are achieved, both within Israel, and between it and its neighbors.[13]

When we turn to Yehoshua's historical novel *Mr. Mani*, his most impressive literary achievement to date, we see again how sexual and ideological tensions built up over several generations reach a climax in congruence with oedipal and akedaic motifs. As Yehoshua strongly stressed, its final episode recounts how Avraham Mani undresses and impregnates his son's wife after collaborating, in some vague manner, in the murder of his son at the very site where the biblical Avraham had (nearly) sacrificed Isaac. Avraham Mani reveals all this to his elderly mentor Rabbi Hadaya, who is now paralyzed and bound in diapers, but while recounting this sordid affair, Avraham also undresses his old mentor, thereby hastening the death of the old man through a combined physical and emotional onslaught that has its own oedipal characteristics.

Not only this, but, in keeping with the pattern we have been tracing here, an oedipal assault on a figure of authority—where Avraham Mani literally unbinds his elderly mentor—appears together with allusions to the binding *and* unbinding of Isaac on Mount Moriah. Indeed, Yehoshua has vigorously maintained that in *Mr. Mani* he tried to "cancel out" the hold of the akedah on his own imagination and that of his compatriots, by "acting it out" through Avraham Mani's collaboration in the murder of his son.[14] However, as Yael Feldman brilliantly demonstrated, this *alleged* akedah—a father willing to sacrifice his child to an ideal—turns in Yehoshua's hands into an oedipal situation.[15] Not only does Avraham Mani use his recent akedaic experience as a weapon against his father-like mentor, but the widowed daughter-in-law welcomes the sexual advances of her husband's father and is happy to be impregnated by him. From a Freudian point of view, things get even more complicated when we consider that both Avraham Mani as well as his late son had been attracted to Doña Flora, Rabbi Hadaya's wife and Tamara's look-alike aunt. Avraham Mani's adolescent son had actually slept in Doña Flora's bed when the rabbi traveled abroad, and Avraham himself had wanted to marry Doña Flora.[16] This historicization of family relations thus layers oedipal upon akedaic impulses in a series of misdirected desires that amplify their underlying thwarted needs.

To follow this historicized paradigm of misdirected desires in some detail, let us turn now to *A Journey to the End of the Millennium* (1997), which I will compare first to Yehoshua's discarded Agnonian master plan and then to *The Liberated Bride* (*Hakala hameshahreret*, 2001), composed right after *A Journey to the End of the Millennium* and which surprisingly reveals a departure from the Agnonian paradigm of endlessly inherited dysfunctionalities.[17] As cited in the epigraph to this chapter, *The Liberated Bride*'s troubled son eventually asserts his power to free himself from the traps of his elders, but

LOVE UNDER THE BURDEN OF HISTORY   151

ironically, it is only thanks to the tireless and unwelcome efforts of his father that Ofer is able to acknowledge a need to free himself from the debilitating attachment to a mythologized past.

Before proceeding, I would like to note very briefly one final literary historical point regarding the commonalities not only between Yehoshua's triangulated love plots and those of Agnon, but also in relation to the historicized love plots of William Faulkner. If all three of them use biblical motifs to endow their dysfunctional families with a greater degree of moral and historiosophic resonance,[18] this is in part because they are heirs to literary techniques developed in the eighteenth and nineteenth centuries by the creators of historical romances,[19] who imagined historical processes as romantic and domestic relationships that model different options for national reconfiguration—although Faulkner's tragic and disjointed plotlines totally reject the social harmony envisioned by those positivist models.[20] The central love story in Faulkner's *Absalom, Absalom!*—whose title, as mentioned, alludes to the intergenerational and fraternal problems plaguing King David's court—revolves around the murder of a young man by his own brother, due to a triangulation of incestuous and homoerotic desires compounded here by the racist mindset of the Old South. These "love" triangles extend back several generations in Faulkner's novel, yet there is no incestuous overlap between parents and children. Rather, as in Faulkner's *The Sound and the Fury*, there is rivalry and triangulated attraction between siblings, which results in the family's utter dissolution. By comparison, Agnon's and especially Yehoshua's intergenerational love plots, despite their alarming transgressions of various types,[21] tend to engage more humorously and optimistically with biblical and midrashic traditions of national restoration and repair, while nonetheless stressing how much the past continues to exert a dangerous pressure on the present.

"DUPLICATION INEVITABLY LEADS TO MULTIPLICATION, AND MULTIPLICATION HAS NO LIMITS" (*A JOURNEY TO THE END OF THE MILLENNIUM*)

A Journey to the End of the Millennium opens in the year 999, when Ben Attar travels to Europe from North Africa, with his two wives, in pursuit of his nephew, who is also his business partner, but with whom his relationship has reached a crisis point.[22] Yehoshua's discarded sequel to Agnon's *A Simple*

Story similarly imagines Hirshl traveling with a retinue in pursuit of his grown-up son from Europe to Jerusalem. The intent: to pull Meshulam out of the arms of Hirshl's first love (Blume) and coax him, instead, to marry a bride chosen by the same matchmaker who had facilitated the union of Meshulam's own parents.

This pursuit of a young man by his elders with the intent of repairing the dysfunctionalities that those same parents, or their ancestors, had caused in the first place, is a pattern that we noticed already in *Mr. Mani* and *The Lover*, but it comes across most clearly in *A Journey to the End of the Millennium*. Ben Attar travels with his two wives from Tangier to the heart of Europe to convince his nephew's Ashkenazi wife not to repudiate the long-standing business partnership between her new North African relatives. Her discomfort with this relationship stems from her fear of and distaste for the uncle's bigamous lifestyle. But behind the nephew's own new marriage lie memories of his former marriage, while his new wife too is a widow, which leaves both of them married to saddening memories that occasionally permeate into their new relationships. The nephew's first wife had drowned herself in despair because he, prompted by his mother, had rejected their baby with Down syndrome. Ashamed and contrite after his wife's suicide, the young widower Abulafia had tried at first to flee to the Holy Land, but his uncle had pulled him out of the ship, alleging that such a journey "would have atoned for nothing and might even in its holiness have embroiled the sinner in additional sins" (35). Instead, Ben Attar sends Abulafia northward to distribute their exotic merchandise in Ashkenaz. Ironically, several years later, the uncle himself embarks on a journey that certainly embroils him in "additional sins" and atones "for nothing."

The retinue that the uncle brings to Ashkenaz includes his two wives, his Muslim business partner (who captains their ship), and a Sephardic rabbi charged with persuading the nephew's new wife to honor her husband's commitments to his North African relatives. At the end of the novel, the sudden illness and death of Ben Attar's second wife—after a trial in which their bigamy is emphatically proscribed—not only fails to atone for the suicide of Abulafia's first wife but also reenacts the kind of situation that Abulafia's new wife had feared: a chain of ill-considered replacements that expose the young and vulnerable to periodic assaults on their well-being.

Ben Attar argues in court that Abulafia was pleased when his uncle decided to take a second wife, installing her in Abulafia's abandoned house;

LOVE UNDER THE BURDEN OF HISTORY   153

in this manner, Ben Attar claims, they could "honor the grievous memory of the wife who had departed for the depths of the sea" (126). In other words, the uncle's second wife is conceived a priori as a kind of atonement or replacement for the nephew's ruined family. However, with this argument Ben Attar also forestalls and contradicts any assumption that Abulafia's first wife had drowned herself out of fear of being superseded by a second wife; he discloses, on the contrary, that the desperate woman had begged him, an aging uncle, to take *her* as his second wife: "to make it easier for her husband to part from her for fear that she would give birth to another bewitched demon" (199). Ben Attar claims that this had kindled in him the idea of marrying the teenage daughter of his childhood friend instead.

We saw in the previous chapter how Yehoshua imbues his works with a symbolic level of signification by playing with the names of his characters. From this angle, it is interesting to note that in *A Journey to the End of the Millennium* Yehoshua turns Agnon's Minna (Hirshl's second love and only wife in *A Simple Story*) into an Esther Minna. Both Minnas are wealthy, well educated, and relatively progressive in their worldviews. Yehoshua's Esther Minna is ten years older than her husband and much more independently minded than Agnon's character, but both Minnas win the hearts of their young men, less through their personal charms than due to their willingness to work through their husbands' earlier attachments, until these are gradually superseded by a sense of gratitude toward the new partner.

Although the discarded sequel to Agnon's *A Simple Story* does not elaborate whether Minna would be joining Hirshl in pursuit of their son, by specifying that Meshulam will suck on Blume's breasts Yehoshua neverthe-less reminds us about the maternal sustenance that Meshulam had missed when his parents sent him away to grow up at his grandparent's estate. This leads to Meshulam's desire for a substitute mother, just as, according to Yehoshua's interpretation of Agnon's story, Hirshl too had searched for a substitute for his own cold-hearted mother, first through Blume, and finally by accepting Minna. In *A Journey to the End of the Millennium*, the young Abulafia is likewise heavily manipulated by his mother and maternal uncle, reinforcing the commonalities between Agnon and Yehoshua's novels.

In chapter 4, when we discussed the role played by vocational identity in Yehoshua's works, we noted that the Sephardic rabbi whom Ben Attar hires to make a case for bigamy in Ashkenaz argues in court that Ben Attar should not be regarded merely as a merchant, but rather as "a man *disguised*

154 THE RETROSPECTIVE IMAGINATION OF A. B. YEHOSHUA

as a merchant. . . . A loving man, a philosopher and sage of love" (133–34, my emphasis). The rabbi insists that Ben Attar's primary vocation is to love his wives—both of them—and that his mercantile ventures, which include the pursuit of his nephew, merely fulfill his contracted responsibilities toward all his partners in business and love. Due to the tragic outcome of Ben Attar's bid to keep both his wives *and* the business partnership with his nephew, it appears, ultimately, that the latter prevails over Ben Attar's bigamous love. In other words, it is not clear at the end whether the bigamous husband is a merchant disguised as a lover or the other way around.

As Amia Lieblich notes, among the many "doubled loves" of *A Journey to the End of the Millennium,* only Ben Attar and his wives are actually engaged in a triangular relationship in the present of the action, even if he always has sex with them separately.[23] Unlike the wild multigenerational orgy that takes place at the end of the novel, which I discuss at the end of this section, and which is the only actual instance of a simultaneous sexual relationship, Ben Attar shuttles diligently from one wife to the other every night, exhausted and carrying the smells of his most recent conjugal visit. But, in hidden ways, all the other erotic triangulations also carry a trace of former relationships or fantasies of potentially new liaisons. Esther Minna and Abulafia bring into their conjugal bed the bitter memories of their former liaisons—she with her first husband, who died in sorrow due to their childlessness, while he is traumatized by the unforgettable image of his drowned and naked wife. Ben Attar's young second wife, as we noted at length in chapter 5 in the context of this novel's holiday scenarios, fantasizes even on her deathbed on Yom Kippur about the widower Rabbi Elbaz; it is implied that she might have fought harder to surmount her illness if she had had some hope of fulfilling this passion.

A Journey to the End of the Millennium closes with two parallel sexual encounters: one that portrays an exorbitant proliferation of sexual adventurousness, and the other marking the sudden reduction of an erotic attachment. As Gilead Morahg demonstrates in an insightful analysis of these divergent scenes, after the death of his second wife, Ben Attar is willing to relearn how to love his single remaining wife, the wife of his youth, while simultaneously, and in a spliced crescendo, the ship's teenage slave is lured into an orgy with three women, who represent three generations—a young woman, her mother, and an elderly grandmother—in a wild excess of prohibited relations.[24] This finale to the novel offers a poignant contrast

LOVE UNDER THE BURDEN OF HISTORY   155

between a focused love and wild desires. The orgy is portrayed, furthermore, as a cruel experience, for even in the midst of his ecstasy the bewildered teenager "knew that to the end of his days he would have no rest from the fury of his longings" (289).

Most interpreters of this novel have concluded that what initially strikes us as Yehoshua's endorsement of a cultural relativism through his sensitive representation of bigamy emerges at the end as an indictment of social mores that disguise gendered power games as acts of love.[25] However, on a political level of signification, this chimes in once again with Yehoshua's ongoing preoccupation with the reconfiguration of a stable and moral Jewish identity in Israel. Even in his most diaspora-oriented narrative—only two of his works are set entirely in the diaspora—Yehoshua mocks his characters' lack of a consistent commitment to Zion. Every year on Tisha b'Av, the day that commemorates the destructions of the First and Second Temples, Ben Attar and his nephew would meet at the juncture between Europe and Africa in order to exchange the yearly profits for fresh merchandise, and to mourn and fast together for the ancient national loss prior to embarking on their respective ways for another year. After one such meeting, the uncle wonders "whether he had behaved correctly in extracting his nephew from the hold of the ship bound for the Holy Land, for the sanctity of the ancestral land *might possibly have* sucked some of the poison out of his innards and imposed order on confusion" (51, my emphasis).

Although by Yehoshua's standards the diaspora-Zion axis appears in an extraordinarily muted form here, it still hovers around *A Journey to the End of the Millennium*'s representation of the complicated love affair between Jews and their various homelands, old and new, as well as between different kinds of Jews (and others) embodying an assortment of bewildering beliefs. Through its ethnographic agenda, this novel also historicizes a meeting between civilizations—Ashkenaz and Sepharad; East and West; and Muslims, Jews, Christians, and even a pagan who transform each other in this novel. It is a dynamic that, as many reviewers hastened to point out, hints at Yehoshua's hope for a more harmonized relationship amongst the different ethnic and religious groups in his own contemporary milieu.[26] Still, his representations of these intimate relations are invariably fraught with a historicized baggage—whether coming from a meddling parent, a previous spouse, or some traumatic residue that threatens, at any moment, to spiral such triangulations out of control, endangering the most vulnerable creatures, such as Abulafia's drowned wife and Ben Attar's teenage second wife. Thus, like Agnon's *A Simple Story*, Yehoshua's *A Journey to the End of the Millennium* ends with an ambivalent reassurance of alleged harmony achieved at a rather high cost.

"SO HE'S NOT A SAINT. . . . BUT HE DOES HAVE A SENSE OF BOUNDARIES" (*THE LIBERATED BRIDE*)

In both his scholarly commentary to Agnon's *A Simple Story* and his archived sequel to it, Yehoshua emphasizes the precarious harmony that Hirshl achieves after casting off his firstborn and resolving to live happily ever after with Minna by emotionally dissociating himself from Blume and his resentment toward the mother who had driven Blume away.

Agnon's novel famously withholds a happy denouement for Blume, promising to tell her story in a sequel that Agnon himself never followed through. He always felt uncomfortable providing a conventional romantic ending to his narratives, in part because, at a time of grave and and unresolved problems for Jews and others, the conventions of the happily-ever-after European love story constituted for him "a major capitulation," as Dan Miron observes.[27] Still, this does not prevent Yehoshua from imagining a sequel in which Meshulam becomes infatuated with his father's youthful love, in a sequel that brings Blume and Hirshl to confront each other at the national center in Jerusalem. We shall never know how this conflation between the national and the personal might have fully played out in Yehoshua's imagination, but probably it would have included an oedipal showdown at the site of the *akedah* on the Temple Mount.

To deepen our appreciation of the ways in which Yehoshua internalized Agnon's love plots, let us finally turn to an example from the novel that Yehoshua composed right after completing *A Journey to the End of the Millennium*.[28] There, again, the plot revolves around a father in pursuit of a son whose romantic aspirations were damaged due to the shortcomings of previous generations. But, exceptionally, the pursuing father in *The Liberated Bride* (2001) is not responsible for his son's damaged love life, although he still feels guilty about it and takes it upon himself to repair this situation. He sniffs around for clues about the collapse of his son's marriage in a hotel that Yehoshua situates right next to the house in Jerusalem's Talpiot neighborhood, where Agnon lived and worked for almost fifty years; in other words,

LOVE UNDER THE BURDEN OF HISTORY   157

the family of the divorced wife inhabits what Ben-Dov calls "Agnon's back yard."[29] However, through this contiguity, Yehoshua not only acknowledges his debt to Agnon but, in this case, signals a departure from the Agnonian paradigm of dysfunctional love triangles passed down endlessly from one generation to the next.

Although Professor Rivlin, a historian, is never allowed to discover the cause of his son's divorce, he nevertheless succeeds in facilitating his son's liberation. What starts as annoying interference from a parent therefore advances here to the son's liberation, cutting short the Agnonian (and Yehoshuan) oedipal/akedaic entanglement. One wonders whether Yehoshua's aborted sequel to Agnon's *A Simple Story* would have ended with a similar liberation, or if the reader would have been left once more with a sense of impending catastrophe that debunks a facile illusion of redemption, both from a psychoanalytic and a national point of view.

The basic features of *The Liberated Bride*'s love plot are refreshingly simple: a young man parts from his wife and wants no substitute. His father, however, contrary to the requests of his son, and exclusively of his own volition, embarks on a quest to free the young man, whose ex-wife by now has remarried and is even pregnant by her new husband. Over the course of the novel, we learn that "the poison" that had "spread disorder and confusion" into this marriage had not come from major unresolved problems in Ofer's own parental background,[30] or even, arguably, from the shocking aberration that Ofer witnessed in Galia's parental home (an incestuous relationship between her father and sister); rather, Ofer and Galia's *illusion* of happiness had been squashed by Galia's refusal to prioritize their bond over her attachment to a childish dream of the perfect family background. When Ofer informs Galia that he had found her sister lying naked in a bed next to their father, Galia staunchly denies it.[31] It hurts her less to discard Ofer than to destroy her illusion of an idyllic family, and ultimately it is this propensity to hold on to an illusion that destabilizes Ofer's life for half a decade, because it leads him in turn to also mythologize the possibility of returning to live by Galia's side. Only when she finally agrees to meet him again, and admits the truth of what he had witnessed, is he freed from the delusion of their romance.

Yehoshua tantalizingly leaves Professor Rivlin in the dark about the circumstances of his son's divorce. But he reveals that *even* without full knowledge, Rivlin correctly intuits his son's inability to automatically overcome this unhealthy attachment on his own, and only by pushing the right buttons and pulling the right strings does Rivlin succeed in bringing the couple together for a heart-to-heart meeting that liberates Ofer to turn a new leaf in his emotional life. In fact, the original title of this novel—*Hakalah hameshahreret* (liberat*ing* bride)—indicates that the "bride" *liberates* rather than is liberated, but again, the foreign publisher, as sometimes happens, adjusted the name to a more marketable option. Ofer's real liberation, however, starts after he agrees to take responsibility for his own independence, and this is the crucial point: "Even if I'm still tied to her in my thoughts, and maybe in my feelings," he reassures his father, "I'm morally a free man" (560).

It is here that we see Yehoshua's departure from the typical Agnonian ending, in which the younger generation is tied to endlessly unsuccessful bids to repair the dysfunctionalities that it inherits from its elders. Here, instead, we have a younger generation that can and does begin to repair its own losses, even if aided by a genuinely caring parent. But, as Ranen Omer-Sherman has shown, in parallel to the unraveled love knot between Ofer and Galia, *A Liberated Bride* also depicts a hopeless affair between two Arab-Israeli cousins, Rashid and Samaher, the latter already married off to another man in her village.[32] The unfulfilled love between these cousins— who during an artistic festival perform together, in Arabic, a translation of S. An-ski's *The Dibbuk*, which is the canonical Yiddish drama of a thwarted love—is not brought to any resolution in Yehoshua's novel, but it does remind us of a historical time during which Yehoshua set and composed *The Liberated Bride*, in the aftermath of the Oslo Accords, which was, after all, a derailed political romance of sorts.

Unlike the disturbing endings of Agnon's love plots, Yehoshua's later novels offer a somewhat more optimistic repair of the messes inherited from the past. Their complicated triangulations of sexual and marital relationships do gesture, however, toward a historiosophic conversation about national identity and responsibility that goes back to biblical concepts of national redemption and repair, notably through the rabbinic interpretation of the Song of Songs as a poetic expression of Israel's frustration with an exilic condition.[33]

When Yehoshua vents his frustrations about the reluctance of diasporic Jewry to join the daily responsibilities of sovereign life in Israel,[34] he also employs a sexualized and domestic terminology to discuss this complicated national history. Reminding his American Jewish audience about his responsibilities as a Jewish Israeli citizen, he angrily expressed to the celebrants of the centennial meeting of the American Jewish Committee in Washington, DC, that "the difference between you and me [is that] I'm married, and you are . . . playing with the idea of marriage. I have to deal with daily work, daily decisions, small decisions. . . . Life is decisions every day about many things, and this is how Jewishness is done for good and for bad."[35] It is interesting that in both his fiction and politically, Yehoshua welcomes a partnership with the non-Jewish inhabitants of Israel, but the partnership with diasporic Jewry rather irritates him. This is, first of all, because he views the diaspora's historical ties to the Jewish homeland as empty promises that did not materialize promptly enough at crucial junctures in Jewish history—especially between the world wars, when the Holocaust may have been perhaps averted or at least mitigated, and secondly because, as we saw for example through our maps in chapter 2, he fears that the diaspora option may again pull Jews away from the ancient homeland, instead of helping Israel work through its still relatively new period of national reconfiguration.

I am curious to know how Yehoshua would have completed that Agnonian sequel in his not-so "Simple Story in the Land of Israel," which unfortunately he hardly remembers. How far would Meshulam have gone on with Blume? Would it have rekindled Hirshl's own interest in his old flame? Is Minna still alive during Yehoshua's sequel, and if so, would Blume's "return" generate a kind of bigamous marriage for Hirshl? We may expect that in Yehoshua's sequel, Blume would give Hirshl his comeuppance—but how would the young Meshulam get over his infatuation with the woman whose rejection and substitution had enabled his own birth? Perhaps the matchmaker Toyber would surprise us by changing his vocation in the land of his forefathers, and thus fixing that which still could be fixed in the lives of the next generation. Most importantly, why did Yehoshua think that he could bring these bourgeois characters to the Jerusalem of the pre-State era? Would they have adapted and stayed, or would they leave?

Having committed himself to a lifelong engagement with his national condition, Yehoshua assumes the position of a watchman over the house of Israel, a position from which he expects that every *bodily present* member of this house—whether Jew or Arab, young or elderly—will also participate in the moral and practical regeneration of life in the ancient Jewish homeland. The primary goal for Yehoshua is therefore to facilitate a reconfiguration of a national covenant that goes back to ancient times. And as we watch his characters surveying new options on their horizons, we too begin to imagine creative solutions to their problems, which perpetually slide from the personal to the national, and back down again, during a constant struggle between the present and the past.

Coda

A TELEPHONE CONVERSATION WITH THE AUTHOR OF *MR. MANI*

Givata'im & Montreal
9 P.M. / 2 P.M. on a wintry day

162 THE RETROSPECTIVE IMAGINATION OF A. B. YEHOSHUA

THE *CONVERSATION* PARTNERS:

⬆️ *A. B. YEHOSHUA*
⬆️ *YAEL HALEVI-WISE*

Yehoshua's half of the conversation is "missing."

⬆️ As in *Mr. Mani* (1990), Yehoshua's signature novel, this fictional conversation takes place between a figure of authority and a younger interlocutor who are connected through ties of mentorship, kinship, or professional responsibilities. Only the words of the younger conversation partner are displayed on the page, though the arguments of the conversation partner can be gleaned through them.

———

—But *why* do they keep circling around such questions?
—Yes, of course.
—Okay, fine.
—Fine, let's not argue today ...
—
—The weather?
—Good, it's quite nice here today.
—No, not snowing yet.
—And by you?
—So cold?
—Really?
—But wait, how come you're saying now that it is good for Israelis to be sometimes reminded of Europe, if just the other day you wrote that Israelis ought to orient themselves more toward the Middle East where they live, instead of looking all the time towards Europe?
—Yes ...
—Okay, fine, I'm sorry. Let's not argue today.
—
—Hmmm, but I was hoping to ask you about the Americans at the Jewish Committee, why you told them to stop changing jackets like national identities, I mean, the other way around, to stop changing national *identities* like jackets, as if their Jewish identity were just a partial commitment?[1]
—Yes, but what do you mean, from an Israeli point of view?

—Yes, but . . .

—Hmmmm.

—Well, I realize of course that you've said all this before . . . it's quoted in my book, I mean in the book about you . . . But did you have to get so angry with them?

—No no, there's a difference, at least in tone, I would say, between what you clarified calmly in the newspapers, and what you said right there at the event in Washington.

—Yes, it's on open access, along with the whole storm of responses. The one I particularly liked was . . .

—Sure, I can forward you the link right now.

—Probably . . .

—Maybe, it needed to be aired out . . .

—Tsk, but they *didn't* understand you! Even the chair of the Centennial Committee, I'm blanking out on his name . . .

—Yes, Alfred Moses was very gracious about the whole commotion. It seems he even liked it. But when he says he agrees with you that there is a genuine threat to "Jewish existence in the Diaspora"—an internal danger of "apathy" supposedly "greater than the external danger that threatens Jewish existence in Israel"[2]—he doesn't realize, I think, that you're not so worried about the physical dangers like terrorism and war that still threaten Israel, as much as about an internal Jewish apathy that could be taking root *even* there. That Israelis might stop searching for the best moral and practical solutions to their problems and seek instead to escape to the diaspora, again.

—I know!

—Still, they figured you were talking about them. Didn't they invite you to talk about *them*?

—I know you're worried about Israel's survival!

—Sorry, I mean the *content* of the survival.

—Because, it doesn't sound right, that phrase.

—A better one . . . ?

—Values maybe? Or moral content?

—I'll have to reread it more carefully, then . . .

—Because American Jews feel strange calling themselves Israel, even if it may be their original name.

—Never mind . . .

—How about Labor Zionists in danger of extinction?

164 THE RETROSPECTIVE IMAGINATION OF A. B. YEHOSHUA

—No, what I mean is that whole Labor Zionist ethos.

—I thought you admire Ben Gurion?

—Ummm, that's interesting.

—Ha, and by the way, how come almost all the reactions to your speech came from men? Or did the AJC select just their responses for its online collection?

—Only Shulamit Aloni and some other woman, but never mind, what I really . . .

—Yeah . . .

—Anyway, this Kahn guy, a political scientist, I think from New Jersey, says that he disagrees with you; but in many ways he actually spelled out exactly what you believe in.

—That's what I'm trying to get at, Boolie, your attempt to cut "to the bare bones of Jewish existence."[3]

—No, it's the question of whether Judaism is a religion or a nationality, or both.

—Yes, the two codes, two different codes, inextricably intertwined. When people talk about separating them, I'm reminded of that bad joke about the surgeon who announces that his surgery succeeded, but the patient unfortunately died.

—I know we cannot separate them.

—Well, I didn't imagine you were worried about whether Jews will continue to exist, or even how in a hundred years; but interested rather in whether sovereign Israelis will continue to consolidate their identity as a creative and pluralistic . . .

—No no no, the AJC backlash focused on the *second* part of your sentence, without paying enough attention to the first part.

—Well, but didn't you tell them that if you visit America in a hundred years and find no Jews here, you will not cry? Therefore they paid no attention to what you had said at first—that *if* Israel, חס וחלילה, would no longer exist in a hundred years, *then* you would hardly care either about whether any Jewish identity exists, elsewhere. They missed a crucial if.

—What's the hinge?

—Like a hook . . . ?

—But then, if more than half of the world's Jewry is in Israel, and technologically strong, and over two generations . . .

—You still feel they're attracted to the *golah* option?

—So many of them in L.A.?

—No, I didn't know ...

—Why? How can Israel disintegrate little by little?

—I thought you were worried about the relationship with the Palestinians.

—Could be ...

—But maybe a more positive synergy between Israel and the diaspora, especially if the Palestinian conflict is resolved?

—Uh, for instance, in your *Tikkun* article?

—No, I mean the one you wrote when Oslo was first announced: on the four gaps in Israeli society that have been overshadowed by the Arab-Israeli conflict.

—You don't remember?

—Well, never mind.

—Yes! I was glad Hillel Halkin agrees with you on this, especially being your main translator.

—And *Mr. Mani*!

—Did I mention to you that I visited him when we stayed in Zichron Yaakov?

—Yes, in front of that beautiful *wadi*.

—Uh-hum.

—He agrees with you that Israel is "the only place in the world in which Jews are totally responsible for the society they live in, for the environment that surrounds them, for the government that rules them;"[4] but shouldn't we say rather Israel is the only place in the world where *Israelis* are totally responsible for the society they live in?

—I mean, because it becomes clearer, then, that Israeli identity includes Muslims and so on, and if diaspora Jewry can't see itself as part of *am Israel*, then it is they who turn themselves into a different branch of the family.

—Ha, ha, ha.

—I feel it hard, especially during the holidays.

—Unless ... well, unless one chooses to get locked up in a ghetto, without any real interactions with others ...

—Yes and *davka* it's ironic that a Reform rabbi felt you don't sufficiently appreciate the resilience of Judaism in the diaspora, nor Israel's own vulnerability, if it continues to allow Judaism to be regulated by the orthodox parties.[5]

166 THE RETROSPECTIVE IMAGINATION OF A. B. YEHOSHUA

—What do you mean, to be expected?

—Really?

—Hmmm.

—But the organizers were happy anyway that you drew so much atten-tion to their centennial . . .

—You think so?

—And, I also wanted to ask you . . .

—No!

—Really?

—But, okay, if "a religious Israeli Jew . . . deals with a depth and breadth of life issues that is incomparably larger and more substantial than those with which his religious counterpart in New York or Antwerp must contend,"[6] then aren't you implying, actually, that religious Israeli Jews experience Israeli dilemmas more sharply and more deeply than their secular Israeli counterparts?

—So how does . . .

—And what about Israeli Arabs?

—Who calls them Palestinian when they are Israeli citizens?

—No, no, I'm saying the *opposite*. I agree with you they're an integral part of it.

—Well, because you feel threatened by what you call the "diaspora option" more than by any Arab arguments against Zionism.

—Umm.

—No, not religious! Just national.

—All right. Peoplehood.

—I know, I know, you're worried that Zion can become an abstract liturgical orientation, again, rather than a *living* center of responsibilities for Jews who might even settle on Mars, for instance, like you said in your keynote address.

—Very difficult!

—Or moral values, too, in terms of what you call the "conflicting codes" of Jewish identity . . . But hopefully it will not come to that!

—What do you mean . . . how does being a Jew automatically grant anyone a global passport to emigrate? I think that may be an exaggeration.

—And how is it different if you're an Israeli?

—Okay, fine, I see what you're getting at.

—But you emphasized moral ethical values more in your apology.

—And *those* are Jewish actions?

—Perhaps you mean responsibilities, rather than values?

—No, not really . . .

—That is why J Street supporters get so stressed and worked up . . .

—Why did some of the responders get so angry, then?

—Ummm.

—Only Yossi Sarid wrote that he was happy you were clarifying "what is a Jew" rather than "who is a Jew."[7] And maybe it was convenient for him to stir the conversation back in that direction, though evidently you were *trying* to explain "what is an Israeli"—at least what you'd like Israelis to be . . .

—So what is at stake in those definitions?

—Sharansky gets it.

—Natan Sharansky? Really? I'm sorry to hear that . . .

—And what about his remark that "there is no Zionism without Judaism?"[8]

—It may be worthwhile to discuss it with him directly.

—But aren't you divorcing religion from Israeli identity?

—Okay, okay, I'll let it go . . .

—I know! It's even the main argument in my chapter on holidays, that "religion is too important to be left to the religious."

—In that case, it should matter *less so* in Israel.

—Well, then maybe people still misunderstand you on that crucial issue . . . because if you want the conversation to move *away* from Jewish survival and toward taking fuller responsibility over Israeli identity formation . . .

—Why me, personally? I mean, all Israelis. And Palestinians, and ultra-orthodox, and foreign workers as *gerim toshavim*, and . . . and . . . what about the diaspora Jews?

—Okay . . .

—I explained that *sovereignty* is your key concept . . . as well as responsibility.

—And what about identity?

—Didn't you just say you're not interested in identity?

—Yes, that's exactly what I mean, *Israeli* identity . . .

—Okay, fine, let's not argue.

—

—What did you say about the weather?

BIOGRAPHICAL SUPPLEMENTS

Despite his advancing years and the loss of Ika, his beloved wife, **A. B. Yehoshua** has continued to write powerful works of modern Israeli literature while intervening in public discussions about Israeli identity.

Yael Halevi-Wise continues to teach about the art of the novel in a variety of cultures.

NOTES

Chapter 1

1. The four men in this famous *aggadah* of the *pardes* are Ben Azzai, Ben Zoma, Elisha Ben Avuya ("Acher"), and Rabbi Akiva (Babylonian Talmud, *Masechet Hagigah* 14b).

2. Gershon Shaked, "Hatzel haparus 'aleinu" [The shadow covering us: On A. B. Yehoshua's *The Lover*], *Yediot Achronot*, February 25, 1977, 48–49, 51. See also Shaked's *Gal hadash besiporet ha'ivrit* [A new wave in Hebrew fiction] (Tel Aviv: Sifriat Poalim, 1971).

3. A. B. Yehoshua, "The Literature of the Generation of the State," trans. Yvonne Wohlgelerenter, *Israel Review of Arts and Letters* (January 7, 1999), http://www.mfa.gov.il/MFA/MFAArchive/1999/Pages/A%20B%20Yehoshua%20-%20The%20Literature%20of%20the%20Generation%20of.aspx. This lecture was originally delivered during commemorations of Israel's fiftieth anniversary in 1998; it was later included in Yehoshua's *Ahizat moledet* [Homeland grasp: Twenty articles and one story] (Tel Aviv: Hakibbutz Hameuchad, 2008), 171–80.

4. Yehoshua, in conversation with Bernard Horn, in *Facing the Fires: Conversations with A. B. Yehoshua* (Syracuse: Syracuse University Press, 1997), 56–58.

5. Nitza Ben-Dov's *Vehitehilatekha: 'Iyunim beyetzirot S. Y. Agnon, A. B. Yehoshua ve'Amos Oz* [And she is your praise: Studies in the writings of S. Y. Agnon, A. B. Yehoshua, and Amos Oz] (Jerusalem: Schocken, 2006), 13–43.

6. Ben-Dov quotes Amos Oz's fascination with a twilight atmosphere that he experienced in Agnon's home during the closing hours of the Shabbat, when Oz visited with his family as a child. Ibid., 42–43.

7. Menachem Peri and Nissim Calderon, "Sihah 'im A. B. Yehoshua" [In conversation with A. B. Yehoshua], *Siman Kriah* 5 (February 1976): 276. On the implications of this statement, see Avraham Balaban, *Mar Molkho: 'Iyun baromanim Molkho veMar Mani shel A. B. Yehoshua* [Mr. Molkho: A study of the novels *Five Seasons* and *Mr. Mani* by A. B. Yehoshua] (Tel Aviv: Hakibbutz Hameuchad, 1992), 19; and Avner Holtzman, *Mapat drakhim* [Road map: Hebrew fiction today] (Tel Aviv: Hakibbutz Hameuchad, 2005), 128.

8. A case in point is Anne Golomb Hoffman's appreciation of how Yehoshua continues to attend to the individual psyche, while increasingly engaging with the collective national experience. She elaborates in reference to *Five Seasons* (*Molkho*, 1987): "the reader's sympathetic response to the novel may be first engaged by the texture of mundane and bodily experience, but that microcosmic focus never loses its reference to the scale of the political-social macrocosm." "Oedipal Narrative and Its Discontents," in *Gender and Text in Modern Hebrew and Yiddish Literature*, ed. Naomi B. Sokoloff, Anne Lapidus Lerner, and Anita Norich (New York: JTS, 1992), 199–200.

9. Ziva Shamir, "Arba knisot lapardes" [Four gates into the garden: On *The Lover* by A. B. Yehoshua], *Yediot Achronot*, April 29, 1977, reprinted in *Sipur lo pashut* [Not a simple story: Readings in the works of A. B. Yehoshua, Amos Oz, and Haim Be'er] (Israel: Safra, 2015), 73.

10. Dan Miron, *Tesh'a vahetzi shel A. B. Yehoshua: Mabat "ashkenazi" 'al shnei*

NOTES TO PAGES 8–12

romanim "sefaradim" [A. B. Yehoshua's ninth-and-a-half: An "Ashkenazi" perspective on two "Sephardic" novels] (Tel Aviv: Hakibbutz Hameuchad, 2011), 26. In turn, Avidov Lipsker reminds us of Dan Miron's description of Mapu's *maskilik* narratives as a structure of "widening and shrinking circles, alternately referring to nature, land, people, family, human coupling, and political relations," a style that Lipsker ascribes also to Yehoshua. "Gvulot shel herut lelo gvul" [Limits of freedom without barriers], *Alei Siah* 47 (2002): 11–12.

11. Regarding this *gam vegam* philosophy (both/and), see Miron, *Tesh'a vahetzi*, especially 90–101.

12. Bernard Horn, "Sephardic Identity and Its Discontents: The Novels of A. B. Yehoshua," in *Sephardism: Spanish-Jewish History and the Modern Literary Imagination*, ed. Yael Halevi-Wise (Stanford: Stanford University Press, 2012), 205.

13. Gilead Morahg, "Bizkhut hanormaliut: *Mar Mani*" [In praise of normality: *Mr. Mani*], in *Hahemlah vehaza'am: 'Al hasiporet shel A. B. Yehoshua* [Compassion and fury: On the fiction of A. B. Yehoshua] (Or Yehuda: Dvir; Be'er Sheva: Ben Gurion University, 2014), 137–283.

14. ‏"הנורמליות אינה אלא פלורליזם עשיר‏ ‏ויצירתי שבה אדם ריבון למעשיו במידת‏ ‏האפשר ואופק אפשרויותיו גדול"‏ [hanormaliut einah ela pluralism 'ashir veyetzirati shebah adam ribon lema'asaiv bemidat ha'efshar ve'ofek efsharuyotaiv gadol]. A. B. Yehoshua, *Bizkhut hanormaliut* [In praise of normalcy] (Jerusalem: Schocken, 1980), 138; in Arnold Schwartz's translation, *Between Right and Right* (Garden City, NY: Doubleday, 1981), 145.

15. See A. B. Yehoshua, "Golah: The Neurotic Solution," in *Between Right and Right*, 21–74; see also Gilead Morahg's analysis of this important essay in "Facing the Wilderness: God and Country in the Fiction of A. B.

Yehoshua," *Prooftexts* 8, no. 3 (1988): 311–31.

16. A. B. Yehoshua, "From Myth to History," *AJS Review* 28, no. 1 (2004): 205–11.

17. Regarding this expectation from Hebrew writers, see, e.g., Michael Gluzman, *The Politics of Canonicity: Lines of Resistance in Modernist Hebrew Poetry* (Stanford: Stanford University Press, 2003), 6–9 and 16–35.

18. Ortsion Bartana argues, on the contrary, that "the Agnon school" lacks genuine followers, while "the Brenner school," which sought to overturn traditional Judaism more radically, includes such ostensible Agnonists as Yehoshua. "The Brenner School and the Agnon School in Hebrew Literature of the Twentieth Century," *Hebrew Studies* 45 (2004): 49–69.

19. As Ranen Omer-Sherman rightly observes, it is futile to reduce Yehoshua, including his most politically inflected novels, to any simplistic political platform. "'On the Verge of a Long-Craved Intimacy': Distance and Proximity Between Jews and Arab Identities in A. B. Yehoshua's *The Liberated Bride*," *Journal of Jewish Identities* 2, no. 1 (2009): 55–84 and "Guests and Hosts in A. B. Yehoshua's *The Liberated Bride*," *Shofar* 31, no. 3 (2013): 25–63.

20. A. B. Yehoshua, ‏"אקספרימנט צורני שבא‏ ‏לשרת תוכן אישי ולאומי עמוק וכואב"‏ [Experiment tzurani sheba lesharet tokhen ishi vele'umi 'amok veko'ev]. Privately circulated curriculum vitae, 2.

21. Nitza Ben-Dov, *Haim ktuvim: 'al autobiografiot sifruti'ot isra'eliot* [Written lives: On Israeli literary autobiographies] (Tel Aviv: Schocken, 2011), especially 184–85.

22. Yehoshua, privately circulated curriculum, 2.

23. Amir Banbaji, "Hakishlonot shel Molkho: Realism, Modernism, Mizrahiut" [The failures of Molkho: Realism, modernism, orientalism], in *Mabatim mitztalvim* [Intersecting perspectives: Essays on A. B. Yehoshua's oeuvre],

ed. Amir Banbaji, Nitza Ben-Dov, and Ziva Shamir (Tel Aviv: Hakibbutz Hameuchad, 2010), 176–77.

24. Todd Hasak-Lowy, *Here and Now: History, Nationalism, and Realism in Modern Hebrew Fiction* (Syracuse: Syracuse University Press, 2008), 48.

25. Robert Alter, *The Invention of Hebrew Prose: Modern Fiction and the Language of Realism* (Seattle: University of Washington Press, 1988); see also Shachar Pinsker, *Literary Passports: The Making of Modernist Hebrew Fiction in Europe* (Stanford: Stanford University Press, 2011), 323–24.

26. On the subject of Israeli-Palestinian relations, see the article that Yehoshua published in *Ha'aretz* on April 19, 2018, shortly after completing this novel. https://www.haaretz.com/israelnews /.premium.magazine-time-to-nix-the -two-state-solution-and-stop-israel-s -apartheid-1.6011274.

Chapter 2

1. Fania Oz-Saltzberger, "Hahistoria veha-historionim etzel A. B. Yehoshua" [History and historians in A. B. Yehoshua], in *Mabatim mitztalvim* [Intersecting perspectives], ed. Amir Banbaji, Nitza Ben-Dov, and Ziva Shamir (Bnei Brak: Hakibbutz Hameuchad, 2010), 570–76.

2. In a series of interviews with Yehoshua, Elaine Kalman Naves reviewed with him the compulsion to respond to history at different junctures in his life. "Talking with A. B. Yehoshua," *Queen's Quarterly* 112, no. 1 (Spring 2005): 76–86; see also https://www .elainekalmannaves.com/essays-articles -radio-interviews/item/50-talking-with -ab-yehoshua.

3. Within Israel studies, Gabriel Zoran pioneered a structuralist interpretation of narrative space in "Likrat theoria shel hamerhav basipur" [Toward a theory of space in narrative], *Hasifrut* 30, no. 31(1981): 20–34. This approach has greatly expanded to address literary-historical questions in stimulating intersections between literary fiction, philosophy, and social studies, as in Zali Gurevitch and Gideon Aran's "'Al hama-kom—ethnografia israelit" [On the place: An Israeli ethnography], *Alpayim* 4 (1991): 9–44; Barbara Mann's *A Place in History: Modernism, Tel Aviv, and the Creation of Jewish Urban Space* (Palo Alto: Stanford University Press, 2006); Karen Grumberg's *Place and Ideology in Contemporary Hebrew Literature* (Syracuse: Syracuse University Press, 2011); and Nili Scharf Gold's *Haifa: City of Steps* (Waltham: Brandeis University Press, 2017). Within the broader field of Jewish studies, see especially Shachar Pinsker's *Literary Passports: The Making of Modernist Hebrew Fiction in Europe* (Stanford: Stanford University Press, 2011); and the essay collections by Vered Karti Shemtov and Charlotte E. Fonrobert, "Jewish Conceptions and Practices of Space," *Jewish Social Studies* 11, no. 3 (2005); as well as Julia Bruch, Anna Lipphardt, and Alexandra Nocke's *Jewish Topographies: Visions of Space, Traditions of Place* (Hampshire: Ashgate, 2008); and Barbara Mann's *Space and Place in Jewish Studies* (New Brunswick: Rutgers University Press, 2012).

4. Preceding Franco Moretti's *Atlas of the European Novel, 1800–1900* (London: Verso, 1998) and *Graphs, Maps, Trees: Abstract Models for Literary History* (London: Verso, 2005), this spatial turn in the humanities and social sciences can be traced back to Henri Lefeb-vre's *La production de l'espace* (Paris: Anthropos, 1974); Michel Foucault's

I am grateful to Yael Faitelis for preparing the maps in this chapter under the auspices of a summer internship granted by McGill's Faculty of Arts and supplemented by the Department of Jewish Studies. She was guided in this endeavor by our specialist in geographic information systems, Ms. Deena Yanofsky, who provided invaluable support which greatly facilitated our progress.

172   NOTES TO PAGES 18–19

1967 lecture "Des espaces autres, Hétérotopies," eventually published in *Architecture, Mouvement, Continuité* 5 (1984): 46–49; Pierre Bourdieu's *La distinction: Critique sociale du jugement* (Paris: Minuit, 1979); and Mikhail Bakhtin's "Forms of Time and of the Chronotope in the Novel" (originally from 1937, later included in *The Dialogic Imagination* [Austin: University of Texas Press, 1981]).

5. This dovetails notably with Yigal Schwartz's cartographic analysis of works by Herzl, Oz, and other Zionist writers in *Hayad'at et ha'aretz sham halimon pore'ah: Handasat ha'adam umahshevet hamerhav basifrut ha'ivrit hahadashah* [Do you know the land where the lemon blooms: Human engineering and landscape conceptualization] (Or Yehuda: Devir, 2007); published in English, though unfortunately without the illustrative maps originally commissioned for this project, as *The Zionist Paradox: Hebrew Literature and Israeli Identity* (Waltham: Brandeis University Press, 2014).

6. Avidov Lipsker, "Mahsomim: Ezorei-sfar bageografia ha'etit shel A. B. Yehoshua" [Barriers: Liminal thresholds in A. B. Yehoshua's ethical geography], *Tarbut Demokratit* 11 (2007): 107; see also his "Gvulot shel herut lelo gvul" [Limits of freedom without barriers], *Alei Siah* 47 (2002): 9–19, and "A. B. Yehoshua—Retrospectiva: Mimetaphysica shel ro'a le'etika shel matzavim" [From a metaphysics of evil to an ethics of circumstances], *Mikan* 14 (2014): 311–26.

7. See notably the 2006 speech that Yehoshua delivered at the American Jewish Committee and the heated responses published as *The A. B. Yehoshua Controversy: An Israel-Diaspora Dialogue on Jewishness, Israeliness, and Identity*, ed. Noam Marans and Roselyn Bell (New York: American Jewish Committee, 2006), https://www.bjpa.org/content/upload/bjpa /abye/ABYehoushua_Controversy _2006.pdf.

8. On the fiction of S. Yizhar, see Amit Assis, *Lenohah 'erev stav mahrish—S. Yizhar vehuledet hatzabar meruah hasifrut* [S. Yizhar and the birth of the Sabra from the spirit of literature] (Ben Gurion University of the Negev: Heksherim Institute, 2017).

9. Amos Oz, "Hapatish vehasadan: 'Al 'Mot hazaken' me'et A. B. Yehoshua" [The hammer and the anvil: On *Death of the Old Man* by A. B. Yehoshua], *Min hayesod* (January 17, 1963).

10. Africa appears already in one of Yehoshua's earliest short stories, "A Long Hot Day, His Despair, His Wife and His Daughter," and in the play *A Night in May*, in regard to which Avraham Balaban observes that "Africa portrays the encounter between a calcified Western culture, torn from its roots, and a native culture still aware of the power of its primal sources." *Mar Molkho* (Tel Aviv: Hakibbutz Hameuchad, 1992), 9. Amos Levitan further acknowledges the importance of far-flung locations across Yehoshua's oeuvre in "Mehodu 'ad kush" [From India to Africa], *Iton 77* (May–June 2007): 34–36, and so does Yaakov Yuval's "Lesham uvehazarah: Galut yerushalayim asher besefarad" [There and back: Jerusalem's exile in Spain], *Ha'aretz Literary Supplement*, February 11, 2011, 1, 4.

11. Indeed, Hannah Naveh's *Nos'im venos'ot: Sipurey mas'a besifrut ha'ivrit hahadashah* [Voyagers: Travel stories in modern Hebrew literature] analyzes travel in Hebrew literature as a deepening of the "relativity and fluidity" of the concept of home (Tel Aviv: Ministry of Defense, 2002), 10. This same dynamic of homecoming and exile plays a central role in the development of all of modern Hebrew literature, as emphasized by Dan Miron in the case of Abramowitz ("Mendele") in *A Traveler Disguised* (Syracuse: Syracuse University Press, 1996); by Anne Golomb Hoffman in

NOTES TO PAGES 21–30   173

the case of Agnon in *Between Exile and Return* (Albany: SUNY Press, 1991); and from a comparative perspective in Sidra Ezrahi's *Booking Passage: Exile and Homecoming in the Modern Jewish Imagination* (Berkeley: University of California Press, 2000).

12. James Joyce, *A Portrait of the Artist as a Young Man* (New York: B. W. Huebsch, 1916), 299.

13. A. B. Yehoshua, *Bizkhut hanormaliut* [In praise of normalcy] (Jerusalem: Schocken, 1980), 138; trans. Arnold Schwartz in *Between Right and Right* (Garden City, NY: Doubleday, 1981), 145.

14. Yigal Schwartz's *The Zionist Paradox* includes an excellent discussion of diaspora as "no place" in Herzl's *Altneuland*, 57.

15. A. B. Yehoshua, *Hakala hameshahreret* [The liberating bride] (Bnei Brak: Hakibbutz Hameuchad, 2001), trans. Hillel Halkin as *The Liberated Bride* (Orlando: Harcourt, 2004), 118.

16. See, for example, the *A. B. Yehoshua Controversy*.

17. A. B. Yehoshua, *Hashiva mehodu* [Return from India] (Bnei Brak: Hakibbutz Hameuchad, 1994), trans. Dalya Bilu as *Open Heart* (San Diego: Harcourt Brace, 1997), 497.

18. Yehoshua, *Open Heart*, 496.

19. Ibid., 300.

20. For a refutation to a revisionist denial of this national history, see Derek Penslar's "Shlomo Sand's *The Invention of the Jewish People* and the End of the New Historians," *Israel Studies* 17, no. 2 (2012): 156–68, and David Nirenberg's "Anti-Zionist Demography," *Dissent* (2010): 103–9.

21. A. B. Yehoshua, *Esh yedidut: Duet* (Bnei Brak: Hakibbutz Hameuchad, 2007), trans. Stuart Schoffman as *Friendly Fire* (New York: Houghton Mifflin Harcourt, 2009), 56.

22. Yehoshua, *Friendly Fire*, 337–38.

23. A. B. Yehoshua, *Geirushim meuharim* (Tel Aviv: Hakibbutz Hameuchad, 1982), trans. Hillel Halkin as *A Late*

Divorce (San Diego: Harcourt Brace, 1993), 319, 321.

24. The murderer's agitation in reaction to Yehuda's ambiguous identity exemplifies what Yehoshua describes elsewhere as an identity crisis triggered by "ambiguous" Jewish behavior. A. B. Yehoshua, "An Attempt to Identify the Root Cause of Antisemitism," *Azure* 32 (2008): 48–79.

25. Rina Cohen Muller, "Ceux qui partent de la Terre Promise: Les émigrants Israéliens," *Les cahiers du Judaisme* 11 (2002): 109.

26. Gilead Morahg, "From Madness on to Sanity: A. B. Yehoshua's Shifting Perspective on the Diaspora," *Shofar* 11, no. 1 (1992): 50–60.

27. Vered Shemtov, "Boundaries and Crossings: An Interview with A. B. Yehoshua," *Sh'ma: The Journal of Jewish Ideas*, March 4, 2004, http://shma.com/2004/03/boundaries-and-crossing. David Herman, "A. B. Yehoshua: The Writer Still Shaping Israel's Identity," *Jewish Chronicle Online*, February 28, 2013, https://www.thejc.com/lifestyle/features/a-b-yehoshua-the-writer-still-shaping-israel-s-identity-1.42311.

28. Regarding Yehoshua's engagement with Spanish-Jewish history in this novel, see Yael Halevi-Wise, "Where Is the Sephardism of A. B. Yehoshua's *Hesed sefaradi / The Retrospective*?," in *Sephardic Horizons* 4, no. 1 (Winter 2014), http://www.sephardichorizons.org/Volume4/Issue1/WhereSephardism.html.

29. Dan Miron analyzes the relationship between these groups in *Tesh'a vahetzi shel A. B. Yehoshua: Mabat "ashkenazi" 'al shnei romanim "sefaradim"* [A. B. Yehoshua's ninth-and-a-half: An "Ashkenazi" perspective on two "Sephardic" novels] (Tel Aviv: Hakibbutz Hameuchad, 2011), 9–106.

30. Nitza Ben-Dov assesses this novel's autobiographical dimension in "Diokan shel ha'oman ke'ish zaken" [A portrait of the artist as an elderly man], in *Hayim ketuvim: 'al autobiografiot sifrutiot israeliot* [Written lives: Israeli

NOTES TO PAGES 31–34

literary autobiographies] (Tel Aviv: Schocken, 2011), 183–200.

31. On the role played by the desert in Yehoshua's oeuvre, see Ranen Omer-Sherman, *Israel in Exile: Jewish Writing and the Desert* (Urbana: University of Illinois Press, 2006), 84–85; and Yael Zerubavel, *Desert in the Promised Land* (Palo Alto: Stanford University Press, 2018).

32. A. B. Yehoshua, *Hesed sefaradi* [Spanish charity] (Israel: Hakibbutz Hameuchad/Kinneret Zmora-Bitan, 2011), trans. Stuart Schoffman as *The Retrospective* (New York: Houghton Mifflin Harcourt, 2013), 246.

33. Regarding a mutually validating relationship among cultural groups as a core aspect of Yehoshua's worldview, see Bernard Horn, "Sephardic Identity and Its Discontents: The Novels of A. B. Yehoshua," in *Sephardism: Spanish-Jewish History and the Modern Literary Imagination*, ed. Yael Halevi-Wise (Stanford: Stanford University Press, 2012), 189–211.

34. To Marshall Berman, Yehoshua replied, "If asked to define the concept of Zionism in one word, I would choose 'borders'; allowed one more word, I would add 'sovereignty.'" "Brief Reply to Marshall Berman," *Dissent* 52, no. 1 (2005): 103.

35. A. B. Yehoshua, "Hebrew Literature and *Dor Hamedina*: Portrait of a Literary Generation," trans. Emily Miller Budick in her *Ideology and Jewish Identity in Israeli and American Literature* (Albany: SUNY Press, 2001), 48. Yehoshua first delivered this essay as a lecture at Tel Aviv University and published it in *Ma'ariv* on June, 6, 1998.

36. "Five Recommendations to Historians from a History Lover," trans. Yael Halevi-Wise and Vas Gogas, *Sephardic Horizons* 4, no. 1 (2014), http://www.sephardichorizons.org/Volume4/Issue1/recommendations.html#sthash.VzLt4piA.dpuf. The lecture was originally delivered to historians in Jerusalem at the President's House

in 1998, and then included in A. B. Yehoshua, *Ahizat moledet* [Homeland grasp], 115–23.

37. Yehoshua, "Attempt to Identify the Root Cause," 48–79. Originally published in Hebrew in *Alpayim* 28 (2005): 11–30.

38. Earlier, in *Bizkhut hanormaliut* [In praise of normalcy], Yehoshua's definitions of "Zionism," "Jew," and "Israeli" did not emphasize boundaries, but in his recent iterations of these core definitions he adds that clear borders are an essential component of Zionism; see his three installments in *Ha'aretz:* "Defining Zionism: The Belief That Israel Belongs to the Entire Jewish People," May 21, 2013, "Defining 'Who Is a Jew,'" September 4, 2013, and "Defining Who Is an Israeli," September 12, 2013.

39. Yehoshua, "Brief Reply to Marshall Berman," 101.

40. Risa Domb, "Crossing Borders: The Clash of Civilizations in *The Liberating Bride*," in *Identity and Modern Israeli Literature* (London: Vallentine Mitchell, 2006), 84–85.

41. *The Liberated Bride* brought increased attention to Yehoshua's focus on boundary issues as a political problem and as a trope: see especially Ranen Omer-Sherman's "Guests and Hosts in A. B. Yehoshua's *The Liberated Bride*," *Shofar* 31, no. 3 (2013): 25–63; and Vered Karti Shemtov's "Merhav sifruti vegvulot geografim be*hakala hameshahreret shel* A. B. Yehoshua" [Literary space and geographic boundaries in A. B. Yehoshua's *The Liberated Bride*], in *Mabatim mitztalvim* [Intersecting perspectives], 272–82.

42. Yehoshua, *Liberated Bride*, 191.

43. On the increasing difficulty of separating Israel and Palestine, and the consequences of not separating them, see Yehoshua's more recent article in *Ha'aretz*, April 19, 2018, https://www.haaretz.com/israelnews/.premium.magazine-time-to-nix-the-two-state

NOTES TO PAGES 35–42   175

-solution-and-stop-israel-s-apartheid-1
.6011274.

44. A. B. Yehoshua, *Mar Mani* (Tel Aviv: Hakibbutz Hameuchad, 1990); translated by Hillel Halkin as *Mr. Mani* (San Diego: Harcourt Brace, 1992), 190. On boundary tropes in this novel, see Avi Gil's "Gvulot metushtashim be*Mar Mani*" [Blurred Boundaries in *Mr. Mani*], in *Bakivun hanegdi* [In the opposite direction], ed. Nitza Ben-Dov (Tel Aviv: Hakibbutz Hameuchad, 1995), 223–35; and Gilead Morahg's "Borderline Cases: National Identity and Territorial Affinity in A. B. Yehoshua's *Mr. Mani*," *AJS Review* 30, no. 1 (2006): 167–82.

45. Horn, *Facing the Fires*, 27; Carmela Saranga and Rachel Sharaby discuss in greater detail Yehoshua's ambivalent attitude toward the city of his birth in "Space as a Demon and the Demon in the Space," in *The Divergence of Judaism and Islam*, ed. Michael Laskier and Yaakov Lev (Gainesville: University of Florida Press, 2011), 276, 286; see also Ziva Shamir's comparative analysis of Yehoshua's, Oz's, and Beer's representations of their native city in *Sipur lo pashut* [Not a simple story: Readings in the works of A. B. Yehoshua, Amos Oz, and Haim Beer] (Israel: Safra, 2015), 38–49.

46. Yehoshua Cohen, "Yerushalaim—'ir dmuyot rabot" [Jerusalem—city of many characters], in *Bakivun hanegdi* [In the opposite direction], 392–96. See also Yasuko Murata, "A. B. Yehoshua's *Mar Mani*: A Sephardic World with Jerusalem as a Focal Point," Center for Interdisciplinary Study of Monotheistic Religions, http://www.cismor.jp/uploads-images/sites/2/2014/01/c1f7 25ea5f14a770a63f9322c338fff4.pdf.

47. A notable exception is Yehoshua's most recent novel, *The Tunnel* (*Haminharah*, 2018), which bypasses Jerusalem. Even in *A Journey to the End of the Millennium*, which is set entirely outside the Land of Israel, the characters pray traditionally in the direction of Zion and mourn the destruction of the ancient temples on Tisha b'Av. However, *A Journey to the End of the Millennium* does contain the seed of an alternative plotline oriented toward Zion: Ben Attar's bereaved nephew wishes to travel to the land of Israel, but Ben Attar sends the young man westward toward France and Germany, thus enabling the novel's medieval encounter between Sephardim and Ashkenazim.

48. An echo of Shulamith Hareven's *City of Many Days* [Ir yamim rabim] (Tel Aviv: Am Oved, 1972).

49. See Yehoshua's discussion of multiculturalism in *Ahizat moledet*, 83–98.

50. Yehoshua, *Mr. Mani*, 43. For a deeper analysis of this scene, see chapter 3 in this book. Further references to *Mr. Mani* in this chapter will be given parenthetically.

51. Halkin's introduction of the word "ecumenical" into his translation is helpful, not only because it highlights the subsuming of ideological differences under a collective good—which is Yehoshua's core attitude—but also because the Christian connotation of this term enhances Yehoshua's attention to Christian Jerusalem, as we will see later in this discussion.

52. By contrast, *The Tunnel* returns to the site of Ben Gurion's tomb in Sdeh Boker, weaving around it a multicultural interaction between Israelis and Palestinians that spirals out of control.

53. For further background on *Mr. Mani*'s Jerusalem, see Natanel Lifshitz, "Yerushalaim, 'Ir mitna'eret me'afarah" [Jerusalem—a city shaking off its dust], in *Bakivun hanegdi* [In the opposite direction], 380–85.

54. On the akedaic references of this episode and the critical response Yehoshua himself generated by claiming that in *Mar Mani* he "acted out" the biblical threat to Avraham's son, see Yael Feldman, *Glory and Agony: Isaac's Sacrifice and National Narrative* (Stanford: Stanford University Press, 2010), 21–24.

NOTES TO PAGES 45–51

55. Morahg, "Borderline Cases," 177–78; and Morahg, *Hahemlah vehaza'am: 'Al hasiporet shel A. B. Yehoshua* [Compassion and fury: On the fiction of A. B. Yehoshua] (Or Yehuda: Dvir; Be'er Sheva: Ben Gurion University, 2014), 179.

56. Saranga and Sharaby, "Space as a Demon," 279, 274.

57. In this interview with Bernard Horn, Yehoshua adds, "As you know, I have had a strong ideological position to Jerusalem ever since 1967, and especially in the late 1970s and the beginning of the 1980s when the American Jews were coming and playing with the Old City, as if it were a kind of sacred toy." *Facing the Fires*, 27–28. However, "Three Days and a Child," from which I quote below, was written prior to this 1967 demographic upheaval, yet it already displays this impatience with Jerusalem.

58. A. B. Yehoshua, "A Nation That Knows No Bounds," interview by Ari Shavit, *Ha'aretz*, March 19, 2004, http://www.haaretz.com/a-nation-that-knows-no-bounds-1.117161.

59. A. B. Yehoshua, "Shloshah yamim veyeled" [Three days and a child], in *Kol Hasipurim* (Tel Aviv: Hakibbutz Hameuchad, 2006), 137–38, my translation; an English version can be found in A. B. Yehoshua, "Three Days and a Child," in *The Continuing Silence of a Poet: Collected Stories* (Syracuse: Syracuse University Press, 1998), 45–46.

60. Yehoshua, A. B. *Shlihuto shel hamemuneh 'al mash'abei enosh: Passion bishloshah prakim* [The mission of the human resources manager: A passion in three parts] (Bnei Brak: Hakibbutz Hameuchad, 2004), trans. Hillel Halkin as *A Woman in Jerusalem* (Orlando: Harcourt, 2006), 3.

61. Yehoshua, *Retrospective*, 1.

62. Yehoshua, *Friendly Fire*, 302, 92.

63. Regarding Yehoshua's references to Jerusalem as a cultural womb, see Anne Golomb Hoffman, "The Womb of Culture: Fictions of Identity and

Their Undoing in Yehoshua's *Mr Mani*," *Prooftexts* 12, no. 3 (1992): 245–63; and Avraham Balaban, *Mar Molkho*, 25–26.

64. A. B. Yehoshua interviewed by Maya Jaggi, "Power and Pity," *Guardian*, June 24, 2006, http://www.theguardian.com/books/2006/jun/24/featuresreviews.guardianreview11, my emphasis. Yehoshua's proposal recalls the 1947 UN Partition Resolution, where Jerusalem was designated as an international area, but Yehoshua's version cordons off a symbolic space around the holiest Christian, Muslim and Jewish sites. Since 2006, new political developments have caused Yehoshua to reconsider his recommendations about such a partition.

65. Yehoshua is especially attracted to the French model of *laïcité*, to which he was exposed in the 1960s when his wife studied at the Sorbonne.

66. Lipsker, "Mahsomim," 115–16; and "A. B. Yehoshua—Retrospectiva," 324–26.

67. A. B. Yehoshua, "Hakir vehahar" [The wall and the mountain], in *Hakir vehahar: Metziuto halo sifrutit shel hasofer beyisrael* [The wall and the mountain: The extraliterary reality of the writer in Israel] (Tel Aviv: Zmora Beitan, 1989), 216.

68. Vered Shemtov, "Boundaries and Crossings," http://shma.com/2004/03/boundaries-and-crossing.

69. See Dana Amir's discussion of the contrast between a mythic and real Jerusalem in her review of *A Woman in Jerusalem*, "Miyerushalayim shel mata leyerushalayim shel ma'alah" [From terrestrial to celestial Jerusalem], *Alei Siah* 54 (2005): 25–30.

70. A. B. Yehoshua, *The Lover* (New York: Harcourt Brace, 1993), trans. Philip Simpson, 142; for the original Hebrew wording, see *Hame'ahev* (Jerusalem: Schocken, 1977), 149.

NOTES TO PAGES 52–56   177

Chapter 3

1. Literary chronotopes "materialize time in space" by channeling plot and meaning into an architectonic or geographic space. Mikhail Bakhtin, "Forms of Time and Chronotope in the Novel," in *The Dialogic Imagination*, ed. Michael Holquist, trans. Caryl Emerson and Michael Holquist (Austin: University of Texas Press, 1981), 250.

2. Mikhail Bakhtin, *Problems of Dostoevsky's Poetics*, trans. Caryl Emerson (Minneapolis: University of Minnesota Press, 1984), 172.

3. Mikhail Bakhtin, "The Bildungsroman and Its Significance in the History of Realism," in *Speech Genres and Other Late Essays*, ed. Caryl Emerson and Michael Holquist, trans. V. McGee (Austin: University of Texas Press, 1986), especially 40–43; and *Problems of Dostoevsky's Poetics*, 176.

4. On this aspect of Yehoshua's worldview, see Avraham Balaban, *Mar Molkho: 'Iyun baromanim Molkho veMar Mani shel A. B. Yehoshua* [Mr. Molkho: A study of the novels *Five Seasons* and *Mr. Mani* by A. B. Yehoshua] (Tel Aviv: Hakibbutz Hameuchad, 1992), 25; and Bernard Horn, *Facing the Fires* (Syracuse: Syracuse University Press, 1997), 113–14.

5. In his analysis of *Mr. Mani*, Gabriel Zoran confirms this multidimensional "reversal of time and space," where "time acquires spatial characteristics and functions, while physical spaces adopt functions from the axis of time. This reversal has an effect on the structure, ideology, psychology and historiosophy of *Mr. Mani*." "Zman kemerhav umerhav kezman: mivneh utfisat metziut be*Mar Mani*" [Time as space and space as time: Structure and the representation of reality in *Mr. Mani*], in *Bakivun hanegdi* [In the opposite direction], ed. Nitza Ben-Dov (Tel Aviv: Hakibbutz Hameuchad, 1995), 71.

6. A. B. Yehoshua, *Bizkhut hanormaliut* [In praise of normalcy] (1980; Jerusalem: Schocken, 1984), 138, my translation

and emphasis: "Hanormaliut einah ela pluralism 'ashir veyetzirati shebah adam ribon lema'asaiv bemidat ha'efshar *veofek efsharuyotaiv gadol.*" (In this case, Arnold Schwartz's translation of this passage does not capture the relevant vocabulary: *Between Right and Right* [Garden City, NY: Doubleday, 1981], 145.) I discuss this passage in greater detail in chapter 1.

7. Gilead Morahg, *Hahemlah vehaza'am: 'Al hasiporet shel A. B. Yehoshua* [Compassion and fury: On the fiction of A. B. Yehoshua] (Or Yehuda: Dvir; Be'er Sheva: Ben Gurion University, 2014).

8. Zehava Caspi emphasizes a voyeuristic tendency in Yehoshua's plays. "Mekomo shel ha'aher: Yetzer veyetziratiut badrama she A. B. Yehoshua" [The place of the other: Desire and creativity in the plays of A. B. Yehoshua], in *Mabatim mitztalvim* [Intersecting perspectives], ed. Amir Babaji, Nitza Ben-Dov, and Ziva Shamir (Tel Aviv: Hakibbutz Hameuchad, 2010), 453–68.

9. A. B. Yehoshua, "Flood Tide," in *The Continuing Silence of a Poet: Collected Stories*, trans. Miriam Arad (Syracuse: Syracuse University Press, 1998), 185.

10. A. B. Yehoshua, "Yatir Evening Express," in *Continuing Silence*, 142, 144.

11. Yael Zerubavel, "The Forest as a National Icon: Literature, Politics, and the Archaeology of Memory," *Israel Studies* 1, no. 1 (1996): 68–69.

12. See Michel Foucault, "L'oeil du pouvoir," in *Dits et écrits* (Paris: Gallimard, 1977), 3:190–99; and Dorrit Cohn's "Optics and Power in the Novel," in *The Distinction of Fiction* (Baltimore: Johns Hopkins University Press, 1999), 163–80.

13. Gershon Shaked had already pointed to *Facing the Forests* as a pivotal development in Yehoshua's career and more broadly in modern Hebrew literature in *Gal hadash besiporet ha'ivrit* [A new wave in Hebrew fiction] (Tel Aviv: Sifriat Poalim, 1971), 125–48. The title of Bernard Horn's volume of conversations with Yehoshua, *Facing the Fires*,

178   NOTES TO PAGES 56–60

draws special attention to the iconic position of this story in Yehoshua's opus and ethos.

14. In an excellent survey of the scholarship on *Facing the Forests*, Amir Banbaji highlights the analogies drawn between Yehoshua's watchman (*Hatzofeh*) and the biblical motif of the "watchman over the house of Israel," a connection that early on captured the attention of Uri Shoham and Mordechai Shalev. See Banbaji, "Yehoshua bere'i bikoret hasifrut ha'ivrit" [Yehoshua in the critical mirror of Hebrew literature], in Babaji, Ben-Dov, and Shamir, *Mabatim mitztalvim*, 19–24. "What is the mission of the student-prophet?," Shalev asks, and argues that the student-watchman rejects the national forestation project because he despises his father figures and is therefore ready to incite the Arab caretaker against their mission. "Ha'aravim kepitaron sifruti" [Arabs as a literary solution], reprinted in Babaji, Ben-Dov, and Shamir, *Mabatim mitztalvim*, 58–60, 63.

15. Hannan Hever, "Rov kemi'ut le'umi mesiporet israelit mereshit shnot hashishim" [Minority discourse of a national majority], *Siman Kriah* (July 1991): 328–39; and Gilead Morahg's extension of this line of analysis in "Shading the Truth: A. B. Yehoshua's 'Facing the Forests,'" in *History and Literature: New Readings of Jewish Texts in Honor of Arnold J. Band*, ed. William Cutter and David C. Jacobson (Providence: Program in Judaic Studies, Brown University, 2002), 409–18.

16. Dan Miron addresses the controversy surrounding modern revivals of this "watchman over the house of Israel" motif in *The Prophetic Mode in Modern Hebrew Poetry* (Milford, CT: Toby Press, 2010); also Reuven Shoham, *Poetry and Prophecy: The Image of the Poet as a "Prophet" and Artist in Modern Hebrew Poetry* (Leiden: Brill, 2003).

17. A. B. Yehoshua, *Esh yedidutit: Duet* (Bnei Brak: Hakibbutz Hameuchad, 2007), 373, trans. Stuart Schoffman as

Friendly Fire (New York: Houghton Mifflin Harcourt, 2009).

18. Yehoshua, *Friendly Fire*, 9.

19. On this device, see Boris Uspensky, *A Poetics of Composition*, trans. Valentina Zavarig and Susan Wittig (Berkeley: University of California Press, 1973), 64.

20. Virginia Woolf, *Mrs. Dalloway* (London: Granada, 1983), 5.

21. Yehoshua, *Friendly Fire*, 173, 182.

22. Ibid., 323.

23. See Adia Mendelson-Maoz's study of "The Bereaved Father and His Dead Son in the Works of A. B. Yehoshua," *Jewish Social Studies* 17, no. 1 (2010): 116–40; and for a broader illumination of Israeli literature in the shadow of war, Nitza Ben-Dov's *Hayey milhamah* [War lives] (Tel Aviv: Schocken, 2016), which focuses on *Friendly Fire* in chapter 10, 311–36.

24. Yehoshua, *Friendly Fire*, 60.

25. Ibid., 87.

26. Ibid., 357.

27. Yehoshua, *Esh yedidutit*, 348, my emphasis.

28. Adia Mendelson-Maoz surveys rooftop scenes in Israeli literature between the two intifadas (1987–2007) and takes *Friendly Fire* as a key example that bookends this era. "On a Hot Tin Roof," chap. 1 of *Borders, Territories, and Ethics: Hebrew Literature in the Shadow of the Intifada* (West Lafayette: Purdue University Press, 2018), 14–24 and 90–96.

29. Yehoshua, *Friendly Fire*, 221.

30. Ibid., 320.

31. Bernard Horn bravely addresses this question in "Sephardic Identity and Its Discontents: The Novels of A. B. Yehoshua," in *Sephardism: Spanish-Jewish History and the Modern Literary Imagination*, ed. Yael Halevi-Wise (Stanford: Stanford University Press, 2013), 201–3.

32. Ziva Shamir, "Molkho basar vedam: Sipur pashut ubetzido shovar politi vehistoriosophi ('al harealism habifocali baroman *Molkho*)" [Molkho flesh and blood . . . (on the bifocal realism of

NOTES TO PAGES 61–67   179

Molkho / Five Seasons)], in *Nekudot tatzpit* [Perspectives on society and culture in Israel], ed. Nuritz Gertz (Tel Aviv: Open University, 1988), 286.

33. Risa Domb, *Home Thoughts from Abroad: Distant Visions of Israel in Contemporary Hebrew Fiction* (London: Vallentine Mitchell, 1995), 48.

34. On Molkho's attitude toward this opera, see Avraham Balaban, *Mar Molkho* [Mr. Molkho], 101–4; and Dorit Hop, "Be'ikvot Euridikah" [In pursuit of Eurydice], in Babaji, Ben-Dov, and Shamir, *Mabatim mitztalvim*, 195–210.

35. This eyeglass motif has received considerable attention from scholars: Hillel Barzel, for example, compares the Manis' "passion for glasses" to the myopia of the student-watchman in *Facing the Forests*. "Keter ha'ahdut veketer haribuy" [Pluralism and singularity], in Ben-Dov, *Bakivun hanegdi*, 126; Gilead Morahg describes parallel cases of military duties "with impaired vision" in "Borderline Cases: National Identity and Territorial Affinity in A. B. Yehoshua's *Mr. Mani*," *AJS Review* 30, no. 1 (2006): 169. Nurith Gertz in *Hirbet hiz'ah vehaboker shelemaharat* [Hirbet Hiza and the day after] (Tel Aviv: Hakibbutz Hameuchad, 1983), 78, and Chaviva Shohat-Meiri, 'Al hatzhok besifrut haisraelit [On laughter in Israeli literature] (Merhavia: Sifriat Poalim, 1972), 28–29, also discuss this impaired-vision motif in Yehoshua's fiction. Yehoshua himself, in response to Yaakov Besser's question about the role of the eyeglasses in *Mr. Mani*, explained it is as "a metaphor for the option of seeing things from different perspectives, dimmer but also broader." "Ma ani betokh haviku'ah hagadol" [What am I within the big debate?], *Iton 77*, nos. 124–25 (1990): 27.

36. Isaiah 43:5, Jeremiah 5:21, Ezekiel 12:2. See note 16 above.

37. Gil Hochberg, "A Poetics of Haunting: From Yizhar's Hirbeh to Yehoshua's Ruins to Koren's Crypts," *Jewish Social Studies* 18, no. 3 (2012): 60.

38. Hanan Hever analyzes this dynamic through the faculty of speech rather than sight in "Rov kemi'ut le'umi mesiporet israelit mereshit shnot hashishim," 328–39, and in "Minority Discourse of a National Majority: Israeli Fiction in the Early Sixties," *Prooftexts* 10, no. 1 (1990): 147.

39. Nitza Ben-Dov, *Vehitehilatkha: 'Iyunim beyetzirot S. Y. Agnon, A. B. Yehoshua ve'Amos Oz* [Studies in the writings of S. Y. Agnon, A. B. Yehoshua, and Amos Oz] (Jerusalem: Schocken, 2006), 214–15. See below for further discussion of this paradigm.

40. Rachel Albeck-Gidron, "Totem ve'ivaron: Tahalikhei breyrah tarbutiyim hameyutzagim baroman *Hakala hameshahreret shel A. B. Yehoshua*" [Totem and blindness: Processes of cultural choice in Yehoshua's *Liberated Bride*], *Mikan* 4 (2005): 5–19.

41. A. B. Yehoshua, *Hesed sefaradi* [Spanish charity] (Israel: Hakibbutz Hameuchad/Kinneret Zmora-Bitan, 2011), trans. Stuart Schoffman as *The Retrospective* (New York: Houghton Mifflin Harcourt, 2013), 233.

42. On the negotiation of old and new in this novel, see Yael Halevi-Wise, "Where Is the Sephardism of *Hesed sefaradi / The Retrospective*?," *Sephardic Horizons* 4, no. 1 (2014), http://www.sephardichorizons.org/Volume4/Issue1/WhereSephardism.html.

43. Yehoshua, *Retrospective*, 15.

44. Yehoshua, *Hesed sefaradi*, 171; *Retrospective*, 152.

45. Yehoshua's reliance on Faulkner has been noted by Bernard Horn in "William Faulkner in Haifa," in *Facing the Fires*, 51–65; and by Nehama Ashkenasy in "Yehoshua's 'Sound and Fury': *A Late Divorce* and Its Faulknerian Model," *Modern Language Studies* 21, no. 2 (1991): 92–104.

46. Henry James, *The Art of the Novel* (New York: Scribner, 1934), 46.

47. William Faulkner, *The Sound and the Fury*, ed. M. Gorra, 2nd ed., Norton

180   NOTES TO PAGES 68–80

Critical Edition (New York: W. W. Norton, 1994), 234.

48. A. B. Yehoshua, *Geirushim meuharim* [*A Late Divorce*] (Tel Aviv: Hakibbutz Hameuchad, 2010), 439. (This edition includes the initially omitted tenth chapter.) See also Carmela Saranga and Rachel Sharaby's analysis of this scene in "Space as a Demon and the Demon in the Space," in *The Divergence of Judaism and Islam*, ed. Michael Laskier and Yaakov Lev (Gainesville: University of Florida Press, 2011), 270–87.

49. Yael Feldman, *Glory and Agony: Isaac's Sacrifice and National Narrative* (Stanford: Stanford University Press, 2010), 21–25, 284–300.

50. Elizabeth Deeds Ermarth, *Realism and Consensus in the English Novel* (Princeton: Princeton University Press, 1983), 20–21.

51. Zoran, "Time as Space," 72.

52. A. B. Yehoshua, *Mar Mani* (Tel Aviv: Hakibbutz Hameuchad, 1990), trans. Hillel Halkin as *Mr. Mani* (San Diego: Harcourt Brace, 1992), 43, my emphasis.

53. Ibid., 315.

Chapter 4

1. Yotam Reuveni, *A. B. Yehoshua: Diokan 2* [*A. B. Yehoshua: Portrait 2*] (Tel Aviv: Nimrod Press, 2003), 53–54.

2. Public interview with Avner Holzman at the Van Leer Institute in Jerusalem, January 20, 2016.

3. A major exception is Yehoshua's semiautobiographical künstlerroman *Hesed sefaradi / The Retrospective*, discussed by Nitza Ben-Dov in "Diokan shel ha'oman ke'ish zaken" [Portrait of the artist as an elderly man], in *Hayim ktuvim: 'al autobiografiot sifruti'ot isra'eliot* [Written lives: On Israeli literary autobiographies] (Tel Aviv: Schocken, 2011), especially 184–87; see also Gilead Morahg's analysis of this aspect in *Hahemlah vehaza'am* [Compassion and fury] (Or Yehuda: Dvir; Be'er Sheva: Ben Gurion University, 2014), 352–414; and Miron, *Tesh'a vahetzi*.

4. A. B. Yehoshua in conversation with Paul Holdengräber at the New York Public Library, March 28, 2011, audio, http://www.nypl.org/audiovideo /ab-yehoshua-conversation-paul -holdengraber.

5. Franco Moretti, *The Way of the World: The Bildungsroman in European Culture* (London: Verso, 1987). On feminist variations of this important genre, see *The Voyage In: Fictions of Female Development*, ed. Elizabeth Abel, Elizabeth Langland, and Marianne Hirsch (Hanover: University Press of New England, 1983).

6. Alan Mintz, *George Eliot and the Novel of Vocation* (Cambridge: Harvard University Press, 1978), 6.

7. On the bildungsroman as a form of national expression, see especially Jed Esty, *Unseasonable Youth* (New York: Oxford University Press, 2012).

8. Ilana Pardes, *The Biography of Ancient Israel: National Narratives in the Bible* (Berkeley: University of California Press, 2002).

9. Avraham Balaban, *Mar Molkho* [Mr. Molkho] (Tel Aviv: Hakibbutz Hameuchad, 1992), 99.

10. A. B. Yehoshua, *Hame'ahev* (Jerusalem: Schocken, 1977), trans. Philip Simpson as *The Lover* (San Diego: Harcourt Brace, 1993), 32, my emphasis. Ironically, again, the Labor Zionist ideologue A. D. Gordon had a similarly conspicuous beard, which made him look like an ancient prophet among the young pioneers.

11. Yehoshua, *Lover*, 87.

12. Eric Zakim, *To Build and Be Built: Landscape, Literature, and the Construction of Zionist Identity* (Philadelphia: University of Pennsylvania Press, 2006).

13. "Tardemat hayom" [Sleepy day], which was first published in 1959, has not been translated into English; it is included in Yehoshua's *Kol Hasipurim* [All the stories] (Tel Aviv: Hakibbutz Hameuchad, 1993), 21–30.

14. A. B. Yehoshua, *Shlihuto shel hamemuneh 'al mash'abei enosh: Passion*

NOTES TO PAGES 80–85   181

bishloshah prakim [The mission of the human resources manager: A passion in three parts] (Bnei Brak: Hakibbutz Hameuchad, 2004), trans. Hillel Halkin as *A Woman in Jerusalem* (Orlando: Harcourt, 2006), 5.

15. Yehoshua, *Woman in Jerusalem*, 6.
16. Ibid., 9, 237.
17. Ibid., 72. About the role of Jerusalem in this novel, see Dana Amir, "Miyerushalayim shel mata leyerushalayim shel ma'alah" [From terrestrial to celestial Jerusalem], *Alei Siah* 54 (2005): 25–30, and our earlier discussion in chapter 2.
18. Yehoshua, *Woman in Jerusalem*, 3.
19. A. B. Yehoshua, *Hakala hameshahreret* [The liberating bride] (Bnei Brak: Hakibbutz Hameuchad, 2001), trans. Hillel Halkin as *The Liberated Bride* (Orlando: Harcourt, 2004), 346. Gilead Morahg argues that the historian's quest for truth here mirrors the author's vocational commitment. "Portrait of the Artist as an Aging Scholar: A. B. Yehoshua's *The Liberating Bride*," *Hebrew Studies* 50 (2009): 179.
20. For an overview of all the different types of historians in this novel, see Ranen Omer-Sherman, "Guests and Hosts in A. B. Yehoshua's *The Liberated Bride*," *Shofar* 31, no. 3 (2013): 25–63. On a desirable conciliation between Israel's so-called Old and New Historians, see Yehoshua's "Five Recommendations to Historians from a History Lover," trans. Yael Halevi-Wise and Vas Gogas, *Sephardic Horizons* 4, no. 1 (2014), http://www.sephardichorizons.org/Volume4/Issue1/recommendations.html#sthash.VzLt4piA.dpuf.
21. Yehoshua, *Liberated Bride*, 514.
22. The proliferation of judges, lawyers, and allusions to "the law" in Yehoshua's fiction is noted by Avidov Lipsker, "Gvulot shel herut" [Limits of freedom], *Alei Siah* 47 (2002): 13.
23. Morahg, "Portrait of the Artist," 181, and for an updated Hebrew version, *Hahemlah vehaza'am*, 320–21.
24. Karen Grumberg, as mentioned, expands this question to consider

Gothicism as a longstanding artistic means of challenging conventional historiography. Although her *Hebrew Gothic* applies this analysis to *Mr. Mani* in Yehoshua's case, it would be interesting to extend it further to *The Liberating Bride*, or indeed any of Yehoshua's narratives. Regarding Yehoshua's representations of politicized historians in this novel, see Ranen Omer-Sherman's "Guests and Hosts in A. B. Yehoshua's *The Liberated Bride*," which thoroughly showcases this novel's representation of orientalism and authorial politics.

25. Yehoshua, *Liberated Bride*, 346.
26. Nitza Ben-Dov, *Vehitehilatekha:'Iyunim beyetzirot S. Y. Agnon, A. B. Yehoshua ve'Amos Oz* [And she is your praise: Studies in the writings of S. Y. Agnon, A. B. Yehoshua, and Amos Oz] (Jerusalem: Schocken, 2006), 167–77.
27. Yehoshua, *Liberated Bride*, 315–16.
28. Rachel Albeck-Gidron focuses on the oedipal dimension of this scene in "Totem ve'ivaron: Tahalikhey breyrah tarbutit hameyutzagim baroman Hakala hameshahreret shel A. B. Yehoshua [Totem and blindness: Processes of cultural choice in Yehoshua's *Liberated Bride*], *Mikan* 4 (2005): 5–19.
29. Yehoshua, *Liberated Bride*, 318.
30. Reuveni, *A. B. Yehoshua: Diokan 2*, 54.
31. Yehoshua, *Liberated Bride*, 286–87.
32. Note that the published translation does not preserve key professional terminology here, such as Yehoshua's use of the legal term "verdict." A. B. Yehoshua, *Hakala hameshahreret*, 162–63; *Liberated Bride*, 167–68.
33. On borders as a major theme in this novel, see especially Vered Karti Shemtov, "Boundaries and Crossing: An Interview with A. B. Yehoshua," *Sh'ma* (March 4, 2004), http://shma.com/2004/03/boundaries-and-crossing; as well as her "Merhav sifruti vegvulot geografim baroman Hakala hameshahreret she A. B. Yehoshua" [Literary space and geographic boundaries in A. B. Yehoshua's *The Liberated Bride*], in *Mabatim mitztalvim* [Intersecting

182 NOTES TO PAGES 85–92

perspectives], ed. Amir Banbaji, Nitza Ben-Dov, and Ziva Shamir (Tel Aviv: Hakibbutz Hameuchad, 2010), 272–82. More recently, Adia Mendelson-Maoz's *Borders, Territories, and Ethics: Hebrew Literature in the Shadow of the Intifada* (West Lafayette: Purdue University Press, 2018) devotes a chapter to Yehoshua's engagement with this concept. As Ranen Omer-Sherman points out in "Guests and Hosts in A. B. Yehoshua's *The Liberated Bride*," Yehoshua explained to the cultural critic Marshall Berman, "If asked to define the concept of Zionism in one word, I would choose 'borders'; allowed one more word, I would add 'sovereignty.'" See A. B. Yehoshua, "Brief Reply to Marshall Berman, *Dissent* 52, no. 1 (2005): 103.

34. Yehoshua, *Liberated Bride*, 105.

35. Yehoshua, "Five Recommendations," http://www.sephardichorizons.org /Volume4/Issue1/recommendations .html#sthash.GjbLQAG7.dpuf.

36. Yehoshua, *Liberated Bride*, 306–30. In an analysis of one of Yehoshua's earlier novels, *Molkho* (*Five Seasons*), Amir Banbaji constructs a similar argument regarding the uneasy overlap between Yehoshua's attitudes toward daily life, history and cultural interactions, "Hakishlonot shel Molkho: Realism, Modernism, Mizrahiut" [The failures of Molkho: Realism, modernism, orientalism], in *Mabatim mitztalvim* [Intersecting perspectives], especially 176–77.

37. Yehoshua, *Liberated Bride*, 220.

38. A. B. Yehoshua, *Hashiva mehodu* [Return from India] (Bnei Brak: Hakibbutz Hameuchad, 1994), trans. Dalya Bilu as *Open Heart* (San Diego: Harcourt Brace, 1997), 379.

39. Yehoshua, *Open Heart*, 178.

40. Ibid.

41. Mintz, *George Eliot*, 178.

42. Yehoshua, *Open Heart*, 211.

43. A. B. Yehoshua, "Israeli Identity in a Time of Peace: Prospects and Perils," *Tikkun Magazine* 10, no. 6 (1995): 39.

44. A. B. Yehoshua, "The Place of the Hebrew Writer in the Revival of Zionism," *Center for Interdisciplinary Study of Monotheistic Religions*, http://www.cismor.jp /uploads-images/sites/2/2014/01 /b63baddoca1d12d45af139d98fcf6dfb .pdf.

45. As mentioned in chapter 3, Amir Banbaji offers an excellent exposition of Yehoshua's representation of prophetic discourse in the iconic novella *Facing the Forests*. "Yehoshua bere'i bikoret hasifrut ha'ivrit" [Yehoshua in the critical mirror of Hebrew literature], in *Mabatim mitztalvim* [Intersecting perspectives], 19–21. Regarding modern adaptations of prophetic discourse, see especially Dan Miron, "Meyotzrim ubonim levney bli bayit" [From creators and builders to homelessness], in *Im lo tehiyeh yerushalayim* [If Jerusalem ceases to exist: Hebrew literature in a cultural and political context] (Tel Aviv: Hakibbutz Hameuchad, 1987), 11–89; and Yael Halevi-Wise, "Agnon's Conversation with Jeremiah in *A Guest for the Night*: 'Aginut in an Age of National Modernization," *AJS Review* 38, no. 2 (2014): 395–416.

46. Mordechai Shalev, "Ha'aravim kepitaron sifruti" [Arabs as a literary solution], in *Mabatim mitztalvim* [Intersecting perspectives], 63.

47. A. B. Yehoshua interviewed by Vered Shemtov, "Boundaries and Crossings," http://shma.com/2004/03/boundaries -and-crossing.

48. Robert Buffington, "Allen Tate: Society, Vocation, Communion," *Southern Review* 18, no. 1 (1982): 62.

49. Bernard Horn, *Facing the Fires: Conversations with A. B. Yehoshua* (Syracuse: Syracuse University Press, 1997), 89.

50. Yehoshua, "Place of the Hebrew Writer," 119.

NOTES TO PAGES 94–98   183

Chapter 5

1. A. B. Yehoshua, "Hagolah—hapitaron hanevroti," in *Bizkhut hanormaliut* (Tel Aviv: Schocken, 1984), 27–73, trans. Arnold Schwartz as "Golah: The Neurotic Solution," in *Between Right and Right* (Garden City, NY: Doubleday, 1981), 21–74.

2. Arnold Schwartz's translation renders *dat* as "religion" and *le'om* as the "national" component of Israeli identity. Unfortunately, Yehoshua too simply repeats this vague vocabulary when he reads in French and English from these published translations. His point is actually that these conflated markers of identity have jointly informed the behavior and definition of the Jewish nation both in exile and as a sovereign entity, and therefore to speak of a religious code as if it were separate from the "national" identity obfuscates the actual argument. A more accurate translation of *dat* vs. *le'om* is "religious" vs. "*civic*" (or ethnic) elements of a national Jewish identity, and this is the terminology that I use in this essay. However, for a recent update of Yehoshua's position on this distinction, see note 34 below.

3. Michael Bell, *Literature, Modernism and Myth: Belief and Responsibility in the Twentieth Century* (New York: Cambridge University Press, 1997); and Pericles Lewis, *Religious Experience and the Modernist Novel* (New York: Cambridge University Press, 2010).

4. Regarding the uneasy integration of religious and antireligious tendencies in Agnon's fiction, see especially Gershon Shaked, *Shmuel Yosef Agnon: A Revolutionary Traditionalist* (New York: New York University Press, 1989); and on Yehoshua's indebtedness to Agnon, see Nitza Ben-Dov, *Vehitehilatkha: 'Iyunim beyetzirot S. Y. Agnon, A. B. Yehoshua ve'Amos Oz* [Studies in the writings of S. Y. Agnon, A. B. Yehoshua, and Amos Oz] (Jerusalem: Schocken, 2006).

5. Ariel Hirschfeld notes the centrality of religious motifs in modern Hebrew literature despite its secular slant in

"Shivat ha'eloh: 'Al mekomo shel haelohim bashira ha'ivrit bador ha'aharon" [Return of the divine: On the return of God in Hebrew poetry of the last generation], in *Ha'agalah hamele'ah: me'ah'esrim shnot tarbut Israel* [The full cart: A hundred and twenty years of Israeli culture], ed. Israel Bartal (Jerusalem: Magnes, 2002), 165–76. See also David C. Jacobson's extensive work on religious motifs in Hebrew poetry, for instance in *Creator, Are You Listening? Israeli Poets on God and Prayer* (Bloomington: Indiana University Press, 2007). For an analysis of Yehoshua's integration of biblical materials rather than religious motifs per se, see Yedidya Itzhaki's *Hapsukim hasmuyim min ha'ayin: 'Al yetzirot A. B. Yehoshua* [The concealed verses: Source material in the works of A. B. Yehoshua] (Ramat Gan: Bar-Ilan University Press, 1992).

6. For a comparison of Yehoshua and Faulkner's novels, see Nehama Aschkenasy, "Yehoshua's 'Sound and Fury': A Late Divorce and Its Faulknerian Model," *Modern Language Studies* 21, no. 2 (1991): 92–104; and Bernard Horn, "William Faulkner in Haifa," in *Facing the Fires* (Syracuse: Syracuse University Press, 1997), 51–65, 125.

7. A. B. Yehoshua, *Geirushim meuharim* (Tel Aviv: Hakibbutz Hameuchad, 1982), trans. Hillel Halkin as *A Late Divorce* (San Diego: Harcourt Brace, 1993), 1. Yehoshua's epigraph to this novel is from the opening section of William Faulkner's *The Sound and the Fury*, originally published in New York by Cape and Smith in 1929.

8. Horn, *Facing the Fires*, 63.

9. Gilead Morahg, "Facing the Wilderness: God and Country in the Fiction of A. B. Yehoshua," *Prooftexts* 8, no. 3 (1988): 311–31; for an updated version, see *Hahemlah vehza'am*, 123–32.

10. A. B. Yehoshua, "Golah: The Neurotic Solution," 57 (originally in *Bizkhut hanormaliut*, 58.)

11. Yehoshua, "Golah: The Neurotic Solution," 46.

NOTES TO PAGES 96–106

12. Yehoshua, *Between Right and Right*, 67; *Bizkhut hanormaliut*, 66.

13. Secular adaptations of Jewish holidays into a kibbutz environment have been discussed for instance by Aryeh Ben-Gurion in "Shavuot, Back to the Sources: An Agricultural Holiday," *Kibbutz Trends* 2 (1991): 22–27; and Ze'ev Soker in "Dat hilonit bazionut hasotzialistit ubakibbutz" [Secular religion in socialist Zionism and the kibbutz], in *Tahalihei hilum batarbut hayehudit* [Secularization processes in Jewish culture], ed. A. Bar Levav, R. Margolin, and S. Feiner (Tel Aviv: The Open University, 2000), 2:717–24.

14. Yehoshua, *Between Right and Right*, 68; *Bizkhut hanormaliut*, 67.

15. Yehoshua, *Late Divorce*, 4–5, my italics.

16. Second Kings 23:21–22 and 2 Chronicles 35:17–19 tell about the sudden discovery of a "Book of the Law" during Josiah's reign in 622–23 B.C.E. The king reads about Passover celebrations, which had been neglected, and decides to revive them.

17. Gilad Gevaryahu and Michael Wise, "Why Does the Seder Begin with Karpas?," *Jewish Bible Quarterly* 27, no. 2 (1999): 104–10.

18. Yehoshua, *Late Divorce*, 258.

19. Ibid., 301.

20. Ibid., 305–6.

21. Ibid., 293.

22. Ibid., 294.

23. Although theology is the only "machine" at the command of this Russian rabbi, he represents a variation of *Adon Kanaut* (Mr. Fanaticism), a recurrent figure in Yehoshua's fiction, which Yigal Schwartz connects intuitively to the Sinaitic covenant in "Deus Ex Machina: Elohim, mekhonot uvnei adam basiporet shel A. B. Yehoshua" [God, machines, and humans in A. B. Yehoshua's fiction], in *Mabatim mitztalvim* [Intersecting perspectives], ed. Amir Banbaji, Nitza Ben-Dov, and Ziva Shamir (Tel Aviv: Hakibbutz Hameuchad, 2010), 507–15. Schwartz argues that religious symbolism is expressed through different kinds of machines in Yehoshua's literary imagination.

24. Yehoshua, *Late Divorce*, 296.

25. Ibid., 270–71.

26. Ibid., 294.

27. Ibid., 296–97.

28. Yehoshua, "Attempt to Identify the Root Cause," 48–79, originally published in Hebrew in *Alpayim* 28 (2005): 11–30 along with high-profile responses by Shlomo Avineri, Israel Yuval, and others.

29. Harold Bloom, "Domestic Derangements," *New York Times*, February 19, 1984, http://www.nytimes.com/1984/02/19/books/domestic-derangements.html.

30. In Yehoshua's own screenplay adaptations of *A Late Divorce*, Yael Kedmi muses, "This boy, my spooky little brother a timeless gravity to him . . . dark, brooding eyes. . . . Did he blame all of us?" In an earlier version of this screenplay, the toddler sits on the carpet, "doesn't say a word; now silently pushing a toy tank between his mother's feet, aiming at her, shooting . . ." (unpublished manuscripts shared with me by the author).

31. Genesis 32:28.

32. See Yehoshua's blunt remarks together with the discussion that followed his comments at the 2006 centennial celebrations of the American Jewish Congress. *The A. B. Yehoshua Controversy: An Israel-Diaspora Dialogue on Jewishness, Israeliness, and Identity*, ed. Noam Maranss and Roselyn Bell (New York: American Jewish Committee, 2006), https://www.bjpa.org/content/upload/bjpa/abye/ABYehoushua_Controversy_2006.pdf.

33. In one of his position papers, "Israeli Identity in a Time of Peace: Prospects and Perils," Yehoshua recommended that "the secular-hedonistic appetite" restrain itself and "address religiously rooted social and political issues unique to the Jewish State, such as the character of the Sabbath and the

NOTES TO PAGES 106–116   185

34. In a 2003 interview with Yotam Reuveni, Yehoshua added, "today I feel something deeper must be corrected in our society to *really* separate religion from our national identity"—not merely to separate "church" from state, but religion from nationalism, under which non-Jewish Israelis might participate more deeply in Israeli identity. *A. B. Yehoshua: Diokan* 2 [A. B. Yehoshua: Portrait 2] (Tel Aviv: Nimrod Press, 2003), 27.

35. Regarding the figure of the bereaved father across Yehoshua's works, see Adia Mendelson-Maoz's excellent overview of this theme in *Borders, Territories, and Ethics: Hebrew Literature in the Shadow of the Intifada* (West Lafayette: Purdue University Press, 2018), especially 80–86.

36. A. B. Yehoshua, *Esh yedidutit: Duet* (Bnei Brak: Hakibbutz Hameuchad, 2007), trans. Stuart Schoffman as *Friendly Fire* (New York: Houghton Mifflin Harcourt, 2009), 55–56.

37. Yehoshua, *Friendly Fire*, 386.

38. Ibid., 40–41.

39. Ibid., 224.

40. Ibid., 161.

41. Ibid., 75.

42. Ibid., 109.

43. Ibid., 335.

44. Amos Oz, *The Silence of Heaven: Agnon's Fear of God* (Princeton: Princeton University Press, 2012), 8; the original episode can be found in S. Y. Agnon, *'Tmol Shilshom* [Only Yesterday] (Tel Aviv: Schocken, 1953), 386.

45. On Agnon's lifestyle and the midrashic volumes he composed to accompany the liturgy of the High Holidays and Shavuot festival, see Dan Laor, *Hayey Agnon* (Jerusalem: Schocken, 1998), 281–88, 504–8.

46. Yehoshua has written about his upbringing in Jerusalem during the

holidays, as well as the assimilation of the foundations of ancient Hebrew law into the presently evolving judiciary constitution." *Tikkun Magazine* 10, no. 6 (1995): 38.

1940s and '50s in "Behipus ahar hazman hasefaradi ha'avud," in *Hakir vehahar* (Tel Aviv: Zmora-Beitan, 1989), 228–41, trans. Gilead Morahg as "Finding My Father in Sephardic Time," *Moment* 22, no. 5 (1997): 54–57, 85–92. More recently, he contrasted the chauvinism of the late Sephardic chief rabbi Ovadia Yosef with the openness of Yehoshua's own grandfather, who headed Jerusalem's Sephardic Beit Din in Ottoman and Mandatorial Palestine. See his op-ed in *Tribune* (November 15, 2013), http://www.liberation.fr/planete/2013/10/15/quand-les-funerailles-du-grand-rabbin-yossef-deviennent-happening_939725.

47. On the role of the Bible in modern Hebrew culture, see the special issue guest edited by Nehama Ashchkenasy, "Recreating the Canon: The Biblical Presence in Modern Hebrew Literature and Culture," *AJS Review* 28, no. 1 (2004).

48. A. B. Yehoshua, *Hesed sefaradi* [Spanish charity] (Israel: Hakibbutz Hameuchad/Kinneret Zmora-Bitan, 2011), trans. Stuart Schoffman as *The Retrospective* (New York: Houghton Mifflin Harcourt, 2013), 292.

49. Gidi Weitz and Dror Mishani interviewing Yehoshua, "Hard Talk," *Haaretz*, February 14, 2008, http://www.haaretz.com/hard-talk-1.239315.

50. Yehoshua, *Between Right and Right*, 67; *Bizkhut hanormaliut*, 67.

51. Shachar Pinsker, *Literary Passports: The Making of Modernist Hebrew Fiction in Europe* (Stanford: Stanford University Press, 2010), 337–50.

52. "The Religious Issue," in Yehoshua, *Between Right and Right*, 68; *Bizkhut hanormaliut*, 67.

53. A. B. Yehoshua, *Mar Mani* (Tel Aviv: Hakibbutz Hameuchad, 1990), trans. Hillel Halkin as *Mr. Mani* (San Diego: Harcourt Brace, 1992), 338.

54. Mordechai Shalev wrote extensively about the relationship between this episode and the biblical binding of Isaac. "Hotam ha'akedah be 'Shlosha

186 NOTES TO PAGES 116–122

yamim veyeled,' 'Bethilat kayitz 1970,' vebe *Mar Mani*" [The imprint of the *Akedah* in "Three Days and a Child," "At the Beginning of Summer 1970," and *Mr. Mani*], reprinted in *Bakivun hanegdi* [In the opposite direction], ed. Nitza Ben-Dov (Tel Aviv: Hakibbutz Hameuchad, 1995), 399–448; and see also Yael Feldman, *Glory and Agony: Isaac's Sacrifice and National Narrative* (Stanford: Stanford University Press, 2010), as well as Yehoshua's own exposition of his attempt to "Levatel et ha'akedah 'al yedei mimushah beMar Mani* [Cancel the *akedah* by enacting it in *Mr. Mani*], in *Bakivun hanegdi* [In the opposite direction], 394–98, trans. as "From Myth to History," *AJS Review* 28, no. 1 (2004): 205–11.

55. Wendy Zierler illuminates this intertextual conversation with the biblical Tamar in "Hagar veTamar: *Mar Mani* vektivah nashit" [Hagar and Tamar: *Mr. Mani* and feminine writing], in *Bakivun hanegdi* [In the opposite direction], 286–99.

56. On the role of suicide in *Mr. Mani*, see Rachel Harris, *An Ideological Death: Suicide in Israeli Literature* (Evanston: Northwestern University Press, 2014), 122–33.

57. Avraham Balaban, *Mar Molkho* [Mr. Molkho] (Tel Aviv: Hakibbutz Hameuchad, 1992), 43; and see Yehoshua, *Mr. Mani*, 306; *Mar Mani*, 291.

58. Yehoshua, *Mr. Mani*, 256, 258.

59. Ibid., 276.

60. Ibid.

61. Yehoshua does not embrace this post-Zionist position, but sometimes he comes close to it, as Laurence J. Silberstein notes regarding Yehoshua's tendency to argue "against the grain." *The Postzionist Debates: Knowledge and Power in Israeli Culture* (New York: Routledge, 1999), 229n10.

62. Yehoshua, *Mr. Mani*, 278; on the representation of Auschwitz in this novel, where the Shapiros are killed, see Balaban, *Mar Molkho*, 42–44 and Nitza

Ben-Dov, "In the Back Yard of Agnon's House: Between *The Liberated Bride* by A. B. Yehoshua and S. Y. Agnon," *Hebrew Studies* 47 (2006): 237–51.

63. A. B. Yehoshua, *Masa el tom ha'elef* (Bnei Brak: Hakibbutz Hameuchad, 1997), trans. Nicholas de Lange as *A Journey to the End of the Millennium* (San Diego: Harcourt, 2000), 257.

64. Already in antiquity, the mishnah's rabbis explained that dying at the end of Yom Kippur should be considered a sign of purity on grounds that the holiday had atoned for all sins (Babylonian Talmud, *Ketubot* 103b).

65. Yehoshua, *Journey to the End of the Millennium*, 249.

66. Adia Mendelson-Maoz discusses this moral dimension in "Koha hanorah shel ha'etikah: Kriah etit baroman *Mas'a el tom ha'elef leAvraham* B. Yehoshua" [The terrible power of ethics in Yehoshua's *A Journey to the End of the Millennium*], *Dapim: Research in Literature* 18 (2011): 61–86.

67. Yehoshua, *Journey to the End of the Millennium*, 249.

68. Ibid., 240, 244.

69. Ibid., 245.

70. Many commentators have assessed the relationship between North and South, or rather East and West, in this novel; see in particular Eddie Zemach, "Yehoshua bein tzafon ledarom" [Yehoshua between north and south], in *Masot 'al tom haelef* [Essays on *A Journey to the End of the Millennium*], ed. Ziva Shamir and Aviva Doron (Tel Aviv: Hakibbutz Hameuchad, 1999); Bernard Horn, "Sephardic Identity and Its Discontents: The Novels of A. B. Yehoshua," in *Sephardism: Spanish-Jewish History and the Modern Literary Imagination*, ed. Yael Halevi-Wise (Stanford: Stanford University Press, 2012), 189–211; and Gilead Morahg, "Testing Tolerance: Cultural Diversity and National Unity in A. B. Yehoshua's *A Journey to the End of the Millennium*," *Prooftexts* 19, no. 3 (1999): 235–56.

71. Yehoshua, *Journey to the End of the Millennium*, 237.

72. Ibid., 247–48.

73. Ibid., 238.

74. Ibid., 236.

75. Ibid., 239.

76. Ibid., 250.

77. A. B. Yehoshua, "Le'ayen berosh sikhah" [To examine the head of a pin], in Shamir and Doron, *Masot 'al tom ha'elef*, 224–30.

78. Yehoshua, *Journey to the End of the Millennium*, 254.

79. Ibid., 254–55.

Chapter 6

1. For a masterful analysis of literary strategies of naming, unnaming, and renaming, see Michael Ragussis, *Acts of Naming: The Family Plot in Fiction* (New York: Oxford University Press, 1986).

2. Although they are such small semiotic units, names in fiction, as in real life, perform a variety of denotative, connotative, and morphological functions. See Uri Margolin, "Naming and Believing: Practices of the Proper Name in Narrative Fiction," *Narrative* 10, no. 2 (2003): 107–27.

3. James Phelan and Peter J. Rabinowitz, "Narrative Worlds: Space, Setting, Perspective," in *Narrative Theory: Core Concepts and Critical Debates*, ed. D. Herman, James Phelan, Peter J. Rabinowitz, Brian Richardson, and Robyn Warhol (Columbus: Ohio State University Press, 2012), 84.

4. Boris Uspensky makes this claim when he examines name changes to track subtle shifts in narrative perspective in *A Poetics of Composition: The Structure of the Artistic Text and Typology of a Compositional Form*, trans. Valentina Bavarian and Susan Wittig (Berkeley: University of California Press, 1973), especially 20–31.

5. A. B. Yehoshua, *Mar Mani* (Tel Aviv: Hakibbutz Hameuchad, 1990), trans.

Hillel Halkin as *Mr. Mani* (San Diego: Harcourt Brace, 1992), 7.

6. For a brief discussion of the biblical Hagar, see Mordechai Shalev, "Hotam ha'akeda be 'Shloshah yamim veyeled,' 'Bethilat kayitz 1970' uve *Mar Mani*" [The imprint of the *Akedah* in "Three Days and a Child," "At the Beginning of Summer 1970," and *Mr. Mani*], reprinted in *Bakivun hanegdi* [In the opposite direction], ed. Nitza Ben-Dov (Tel Aviv: Hakibbutz Hameuchad, 1995), 440.

7. A. B. Yehoshua, *Nitzevet* [The extra] (Bnei Brak: Hakibbutz Hameuchad, 2014), trans. Stuart Schoffman as *The Extra* (London: Halban, 2016), 142.

8. In this vein, see Wendy Zierler, "Hagar veTamar: *Mar Mani* vektivah nashit" [Hagar and Tamar: *Mr. Mani* and feminine writing], in *Bakivun hanegdi* [In the opposite direction], 286–99. Regarding Honi in *The Extra* (*Nitzevet*), see Ziva Shamir, *Sipur lo pashut* [Not a simple story: Readings in the works of A. B. Yehoshua, Amos Oz, and Haim Be'er] (Israel: Safra, 2015), 179–89.

9. Replying to Paul Holdengräber's question about the absence of proper names in *A Woman in Jerusalem*, Yehoshua explained that when he names characters, he must give their particular background; but if he narrows their identity to a function (as in Kafka), the character can be presented "in a kind of abstract way, because I didn't want to give the reader an illusion that he will get more about this character than I want to give." New York Public Library, March 28, 2011, audio, http://www .nypl.org/audiovideo/ab-yehoshua -conversation-paul-holdengraber.

10. In "Madu'a bakha Yirmiyahu? Tanakh ve'intertextualiut be*Esh Yedidutit*" [Why did Jeremiah cry? Bible and intertextuality in *Friendly Fire*], Tehilla Shwartz Altshuler analyzes *Friendly Fire*'s intertextual engagement with the prophets. In *Mabatim mitztalvim* [Intersecting perspectives], ed. Amir Banbaji, Nitza Ben-Dov, and Ziva Shamir (Bnei

188 NOTES TO PAGES 129–136

Brak: Hakibbutz Hameuchad, 2010), 441–50. See also my opening arguments about *Friendly Fire* in "Agnon's Conversation with Jeremiah in *A Guest for the Night*: 'Aginut in an Age of National Modernization," *AJS Review* 38, no. 2 (2014): 395–416.

11. A. B. Yehoshua, *Hashiva mehodu* [Return from India] (Bnei Brak: Hakibbutz Hameuchad, 1994), trans. Dalya Bilu as *Open Heart* (San Diego: Harcourt Brace, 1997), 300.

12. Dan Miron discusses this name change in *Tesh'a vahetzi shel A. B. Yehoshua: Mabat 'ashkenazi' 'al shnei romanim 'sefaradim'* [A. B. Yehoshua's ninth-and-a-half: An "Ashkenazi" perspective on two "Sephardic" novels] (Tel Aviv: Hakibbutz Hameuhad, 2011), 48–51; and see also my engagement with this biblical referent in "Where Is the Sephardism of *Hesed sefaradi / The Retrospective*?," *Sephardic Horizons* 4, no. 1 (2014), http://www .sephardichorizons.org/Volume4 /Issue1/WhereSephardism.html.

13. Regarding this earlier literary history, see especially Gershon Shaked, *Hasiporet ha'ivrit 1880–1970*, vol. 1 (Tel Aviv: Hakibbutz Hameuchad, 1977), 84–89; and Dan Miron, *Bein hazon le'emet* [Between vision and truth] (Jerusalem: Mosad Bialik, 1979), 298–301.

14. Gary A. Rendsburg has recently expanded upon the Hebrew Bible's own tendency to play with proper names. *How the Bible Is Written* (Peabody, MA: Hendrickson, 2019), chap. 18.

15. A. B. Yehoshua, *Hame'ahev* (Jerusalem: Schocken, 1977), trans. Philip Simpson as *The Lover* (San Diego: Harcourt Brace, 1993). (The translation was first published 1985 by E. P. Dutton.) Further references to *The Lover* in this chapter will be given parenthetically.

16. Yehoshua considers *The Lover* the most Haifaian of his many novels set in this city. Nili Scharf Gold, *Haifa: City of Steps* (Waltham: Brandeis University Press, 2017), 182; 223–27.

17. Gilead Morahg, "A. B. Yehoshua: Fictions of Zion and Diaspora," in *Israeli Writers Consider the Outsider*, ed. Leon Yudkin (Rutherford: Fairleigh Dickinson University Press, 1993), especially 128.

18. A. B. Yehoshua, "Five Recommendations to Historians from a History Lover," trans. Yael Halevi-Wise and Vas Gogas, *Sephardic Horizons* 4, no. 1 (2014), http://www .sephardichorizons.org/Volume4 /Issue1/recommendations.html.

19. Ragussis, *Acts of Naming*, 6–7.

20. Anita Shapira, *Yigal Allon, Native Son: A Biography*, trans. Evelyn Abel (Philadelphia: University of Pennsylvania Press, 2008), 21.

21. Foreign transliterations of this name vary according to individual choices to drop or emphasize the *aleph* in יגאל. In Israel the name is pronounced either Yígal or Yigál, fudging its tenses, since Yiga'el means "will be redeemed," but Yigál suggest a more active redeemer.

22. On Israeli names, see Sasha Weitman, "Shemot pratiyim kemadadim tarbutiyim: Megamot bezehutam haleumit shel Israeliyim 1882–1980" [Proper names as cultural markers: Stages in Israeli markers of identity, 1882–1980], in *Nekudat tatzpit: Tarbut vehevrah be'eretz-israel* [Point of view: Culture and society in the land of Israel], ed. Nurit Gertz (Tel Aviv: Open University, 1988), 141–50.

23. According to David Ohana, Yehoshua is "the Mediterranean Israeli writer par excellence." *Israel and Its Mediterranean Identity* (New York: Palgrave Macmillan, 2011), 14; see also Alexandra Nocke's discussion of Yehoshua in *The Place of the Mediterranean in Modern Israeli Identity* (Leiden: Brill, 2009), 155–56.

24. S. Shifra, "Haratzon lehitmoded 'im hametziut (re'ayon im A. B. Yehoshua)" [The desire to engage with reality (An interview with A. B. Yehoshua)], *Davar*, July 18, 1975, 2.

NOTES TO PAGES 137–147   189

25. Personal discussion with Yehoshua on June 12, 2016. He also clarified the pronunciation of the character's name. I am thankful to Ralph Tarica for suggesting that Veducha is likely an affectionate form of Vida.

26. In *Mr. Mani*, Yehoshua uses his own given names, Avraham Gabriel, as well as the names of both his grandfathers—but he has always refrained from using the names of his parents (Ya'akov and Malka) or those of his spouse and children.

27. Yehoshua, *Hame'ahev*, 186–87.

28. In recent years, studies of Arab characters in Hebrew fiction have blossomed, most of them referencing A. B. Yehoshua among other authors; see, for example, Rachel Feldhay Brenner, *Inextricably Bonded: Israeli Arab and Jewish Writers Re-Visioning Culture* (Madison: University of Wisconsin Press, 2003); Yochai Oppenheimer, "The Arab in the Mirror: The Image of the Arab in Israeli Fiction," *Prooftexts* 19, no. 3 (1999): 205–34; the seminal work by Gila Ramras-Rauch, *The Arab in Israeli Literature* (Bloomington: Indiana University Press, 1989); Risa Domb, *The Arab in Hebrew Prose, 1911–1948* (London: Vallentine Mitchell, 1982); and recently, Lital Levy's *Poetic Trespass: Writing Between Hebrew and Arabic in Israel/Palestine* (Princeton: Princeton University Press, 2014).

29. Personal conversation with the author, June 12, 2016.

30. A. B. Yehoshua's remarks to the American Jewish Committee on May 1, 2006, published in *The A. B. Yehoshua Controversy: An Israel-Diaspora Dialogue on Jewishness, Israeliness, and Identity*, ed. Noam Marans and Roselyn Bell (New York: American Jewish Committee, 2006), https://www.bjpa.org/content/upload/bjpa/abye/ABYehoushua_Controversy_2006.pdf, 65.

31. Ibid., my emphasis.

32. For a discussion of this question from the perspective of the Song of Songs, see Yael Halevi-Wise, "Agnon's

Conversation with Jeremiah in *A Guest for the Night*"; and Ilana Pardes, *Agnon's Moonstruck Lovers: The Song of Songs in Israeli Culture* (Seattle: University of Washington Press, 2013).

Chapter 7

1. Yehoshua's archive, National Library in Jerusalem, AC-1841, Arc. 4* 1579 05 369.2819897–10.

2. Anne Golomb Hoffman, *Between Exile and Return: S. Y. Agnon and the Drama of Writing* (Albany: SUNY Press, 1991).

3. A. B. Yehoshua, "Nekudat hahAttarah b'alilah kemafteah lepeirush hayetzirah: Hadgamah 'al pi *Sipur pashut* le S. Y. Agnon" [The plot and its dénouement in *A Simple Story*], *Alei Siah* 10–11 (1981): 74–88.

4. A. B. Yehoshua, "A Father and a Daughter in an Unconscious Relationship: *In the Prime of Her Life* by S. Y. Agnon" (1998), in *The Terrible Power of a Minor Guilt*, trans. Ora Cummings (Syracuse: Syracuse University Press, 2000), 108–29.

5. See my companion articles on "'The Double Triangle Paradigm' in Hebrew Fiction: National Redemption in Bi-generational Love Triangles from Agnon to Oz," *Prooftexts* 26, no. 3 (2006): 309–43; and "Reading Agnon's *In the Prime of Her Life* in Light of Freud's *Dora*," *Jewish Quarterly Review* 98, no. 1 (2008): 29–40.

6. Yehoshua, "Nekudat hahattarah," especially 87.

7. Nitza Ben-Dov dialogues with Yehoshua's interpretation of Agnon's *A Simple Story* in *Agnon's Art of Indirection* (Leiden: Brill, 1993), 96–105.

8. Mordechai Shalev, "Hotam ha'akedah be'Shloshah yamim veyeled,' 'Bethilat kayitz 1970' uve*Mar Mani*" [The imprint of the *Akedah* in "Three Days and a Child," "At the Beginning of Summer 1970," and *Mr. Mani*], reprinted in *Bakivun hanegdi* [In the opposite direction], ed. Nitza Ben-Dov (Tel Aviv: Hakibbutz Hameuchad,

190 NOTES TO PAGES 148–151

1995), 399–448. Yehoshua's response appears at the end of that volume, 394–98.

9. A. B. Yehoshua, *Koḥa hanorah shel ashmah ktanah* (Tel Aviv: Yediot Aḥronot, 1998); trans. Ora Cummings as *The Terrible Power of a Minor Guilt* (Syracuse: Syracuse University Press, 2000).

10. Adia Mendelson-Maoz examines carefully this orchestration of moral rhetoric in Yehoshua's own narratives. "Kohah hanorah shel ashmah ktanah: Mehalakha lema'aseh" [The terrible power of a minor guilt: From prescription to action], in *Mabatim mitztalvim* [Intersecting perspectives], ed. Amir Banbaji, Nitza Ben-Dov, and Ziva Shamir (Tel Aviv: Hakibbutz Hameuchad, 2010), 550–69. She returns to this question in a somewhat more negative vein in *Borders, Territories, and Ethics: Hebrew Literature in the Shadow of the Intifada* (West Lafayette: Purdue University Press, 2018), which discusses moral responsibility during a time of military conflict, focusing on Yehoshua especially in chapter 4.

11. Private conversations with the author on June 14, 2017, and May 7, 2018. The folio merely shows the year in which it arrived at the National Library (2014). My guess is that Yehoshua toyed with this idea in the mid-1980s, prior to writing *Mr. Mani*.

12. I elaborate in "'The Double Triangle Paradigm' in Hebrew Fiction."

13. Yehoshua deals with this question in his essay on "Hamehapekha hatzionit—ha'im yesh lah hemshekh?" [The Zionist revolution—does it have a continuation?], in *Ahizat moledet* [Homeland grasp: Twenty articles and one story] (Tel Aviv: Hakibbutz Hameuchad, 2008), 46–59.

14. Such is Yehoshua's contention in "Hatimah: Levatel et ha'akedah 'al-yedey mimushah" [Closure: To cancel the *Akedah* by acting it out], in *Bakivun hanegdi* [In the opposite direction], ed. Nitza Ben-Dov, 394–98; translated

as A. B. Yehoshua's "From Myth to History," *AJS Review* 28, no. 1 (2004): 205–11; and *"Mr. Mani* and the Akedah," *Judaism* 50, no. 1 (2001): 61–65.

15. Yael Feldman in *Glory and Agony: Isaac's Sacrifice and National Narrative* (Stanford: Stanford University Press, 2010), especially 284–300.

16. Ibid., 284–300.

17. On the relationship between *The Liberated Bride* and Agnon's legacy, see Nitza Ben-Dov, "In the Back Yard of Agnon's House: Between *The Liberated Bride* by A. B. Yehoshua and S. Y. Agnon," *Hebrew Studies* 47 (2006): 237–51.

18. Although representations of love in Jewish literature and culture have been notably studied by Naomi Seidman in *The Marriage Plot; or, How Jews Fell in Love with Love, and with Literature* (Stanford: Stanford University Press, 2016); and David Biale, *Eros and the Jews: From Biblical Israel to Contemporary America* (Berkeley: University of California Press, 1997), this central feature in the history of Hebrew literature requires further work, especially a deeper assessment of the role of the Song of Songs and its midrashic history as a key intertext for Agnon and others, as Ilana Pardes has begun to show in *Agnon's Moonstruck Lovers: The Song of Songs in Israeli Culture* (Seattle: University of Washington Press, 2013), and more broadly, in *The Song of Songs: A Biography* (Princeton: Princeton University Press, 2019).

19. Karen Grumberg makes an argument for locating this process in the rise and widespread influence of the Gothic novel, defined as a historiographic challenge to authoritarianism; see her specific discussion of *Mr. Mani* in *Hebrew Gothic: History and the Poetics of Persecution* (Bloomington: Indiana University Press, 2019).

20. Historical romances that feature love affairs between representatives of opposed cultural backgrounds, including Jews and Gentiles, were highly popular and influential during the

NOTES TO PAGES 151–157   191

nineteenth century, especially after the publication of Walter Scott's *Ivanhoe* in 1819, as Michael Ragussis demonstrates in *Figures of Conversion: 'The Jewish Question' and English National Identity* (Durham: Duke University Press, 1995). In a similar vein, Doris Sommer has examined the politicized love stories of canonical Latin American novels in *Foundational Fictions: The National Romances of Latin America* (Berkeley: University of California Press, 1991); for a broader comparative context, see Tatiana Kuzmič, *Adulterous Nations: Family Politics and National Anxiety in the European Novel* (Evanston: Northwestern University Press, 2016). From a psychoanalytic point of view, the quintessential study of literary representations of triangulated desire is René Girard's *Deceit, Desire, and the Novel: Self and Other in Literary Structure*, trans. Yvonne Freccero (Baltimore: Johns Hopkins University Press, 1965).

21. Shachar Pinsker shows that, rather than the intergenerational oedipalized relations that I trace in this chapter, triangulations of homosocial and heterosexual relationships played a significant role in the earlier modernist construction of a Hebrew "poetics of fragmentation, fetishization, and voyeurism." "Erotic Triangulations and Homosocial Desire," in *Literary Passports* (Stanford: Stanford University Press, 2011), 188.

22. A. B. Yehoshua, *Masa el tom ha'elef* (Bnei Brak: Hakibbutz Hameuchad, 1997), trans. Nicholas de Lange as *A Journey to the End of the Millennium* (San Diego: Harcourt, 2000). Further references to *A Journey to the End of the Millennium* in this chapter will be given parenthetically.

23. Amia Lieblich, "'Al ma'aseh ha'ahavah hakfulah: Kri'ah bepsychologiah shel hagever veha'ishah" [On the doubled act of love: A reading in the psychology of man and woman], in *Masot 'al tom ha'elef* [Essays on *A Journey to the End of the Millennium*], ed. Ziva Shamir

and Aviva Doron (Tel Aviv: Hakibbutz Hameuchad, 1999), 34.

24. Gilead Morahg, "Testing Tolerance: Cultural Diversity and National Unity in A. B. Yehoshua's *A Journey to the End of the Millennium*," *Prooftexts* 19, no. 3 (1999): 249.

25. Unequivocally, Eddy Zemach reaches this conclusion in "Yehoshua bein tzafon ledarom" [Yehoshua between north and south], in Shamir and Doron, *Masot 'al tom ha'elef*, 25–33; as well as Adia Mendelson-Maoz, "The Question of Polygamy in Yehoshua's *A Journey to the End of the Millennium:* Two Moral Views—Two Jewish Cultures," *Shofar* 28, no. 1 (2009): 26–27; Morahg, "Testing Tolerance," 235–56; and Horn, "Ha'im hayehudim hem 'am ehad?," 323–40.

26. This clash between East and West, or North and South, in *A Journey to the End of the Millennium* has attracted considerable scholarly attention; see the essays by Dalia Ofir, Eddy Zemach, Yosef Toby, Nissim Calderon, and Gilead Morahg in Shamir and Doron, *Masot 'al tom ha'elef*; also Horn, "Ha'im hayehudim hem 'am ehad?"

27. Dan Miron, "Domesticating a Foreign Genre: Agnon's Transactions with the Novel," *Prooftexts* 7, no. 1 (1987): 10, 26.

28. A. B. Yehoshua, *Hakala hameshahreret* [The liberating bride] (Bnei Brak: Hakibbutz Hameuchad, 2001), trans. Hillel Halkin as *The Liberated Bride* (Orlando: Harcourt, 2004). Further references to *The Liberated Bride* in this chapter will be given parenthetically.

29. Nitza Ben-Dov, "In the Back Yard of Agnon's House: Between *The Liberated Bride* by A. B. Yehoshua and S. Y. Agnon," *Hebrew Studies* 47 (2006): 237–51.

30. We noted in chapter 4 how Hagit and Yohanan Rivlin's divergent attitudes toward their son's healing prospects lead them into a terrible fight along vocational fault lines. Nevertheless, they have a harmonious relationship, even if we accept Nitza Ben-Dov's

NOTES TO PAGES 157–167

categorization of Hagit as one of Yehoshua's domineering women—a pattern that Ben-Dov calls the "Astarte paradigm" after Yehoshua's Mrs. Ashtor (and the Canaanite goddess) in "Death and the Old Man." See Nitza Ben-Dov, *Vehitehilatkha: 'Iyunim beyetzirot S. Y. Agnon, A. B. Yehoshua ve'Amos Oz* [Studies in the writings of S. Y. Agnon, A. B. Yehoshua, and Amos Oz] (Jerusalem: Schocken, 2006), especially 214–15.

31. For an analysis of breached taboos in this novel, see Rachel Albeck-Gidron, "Totem ve'ivaron: Tahalikhei breyrah tarbutiyim hameyutzagim baroman *Hakala hameshahreret shel A. B. Yehoshua*" [Totem and blindness: Processes of cultural choice in Yehoshua's *Liberated Bride*], *Mikan* 4 (2005): 5–19.

32. Ranen Omer-Sherman, "Longing to Belong: Levantine Arabs and Jews in the Israeli Cultural Imagination," *Michigan Quarterly Review* 49, no. 2 (2010): 254–91.

33. On this topic, see Pardes, *Song of Songs*.

34. Although the "Canaanite" idea of severing Israel's connection with diasporic Jewry strikes Yehoshua as unrealistic, see his comments on this in *Ahizat moledet*, 176–77, trans. as "Hebrew Literature and *Dor Hamedina*" in Emily Miller Budick, *Ideology and Jewish Identity in Israeli and American Literature* (Albany: SUNY Press, 2001), 50–51. For a broader context, see Hannan Hever, *Producing the Modern Hebrew Canon: Nation Building and Minority Discourse* (New York: New York University Press, 2002), especially 105–9.

35. The transcript of A. B. Yehoshua's speech at the AJC's centennial meeting is available online as *The A. B. Yehoshua Controversy: An Israel-Diaspora Dialogue on Jewishness, Israeliness, and Identity*, ed. Noam Marans and Roselyn Bell (New York: American Jewish Committee, 2006), 64–65, https://www .bjpa.org/content/upload/bjpa/abye /ABYehoushua_Controversy_2006 .pdf.

Coda

1. Yehoshua's clarification, and the transcript of his comments at the American Jewish Committee's Centennial Celebration in Washington, DC (May 1–2, 2006), can be found at *The A. B. Yehoshua Controversy: An Israel-Diaspora Dialogue on Jewishness, Israeliness, and Identity*, ed. Noam Marans and Roselyn Bell (New York: American Jewish Committee), 7–13 and 61–66, https:// www.bjpa.org/content /upload/bjpa/abye/ABYehoushua _Controversy_2006.pdf. All subsequent citations in this coda refer to this compendium.

2. Interview by Yair Sheleg with Ambassador Alfred Moses, 47.

3. Gilbert N. Kahn, 43.

4. Hillel Halkin, 42.

5. Rabbi Eric H. Yoffie, 59.

6. Yehoshua, 10.

7. Yossi Sarid, 53.

8. Natan Sharansky, 56.

SELECTED BIBLIOGRAPHY

Works by A. B. Yehoshua

The A. B. Yehoshua Controversy: An Israel-Diaspora Dialogue on Jewishness, Israeliness, and Identity. Edited by Noam Marans and Roselyn Bell. New York: American Jewish Committee, 2006. https://www.bjpa.org/content/upload/bjpa/abye/ABYehoushua_Controversy_2006.pdf.

Ahizat moledet [Homeland grasp: Twenty articles and one story]. Tel Aviv: Hakibbutz Hameuchad, 2008.

"Ani Israeli!" In *Hakir vehahar*, 206–14. Tel Aviv: Zmora-Beitan, 1989.

"An Attempt to Identify the Root Cause of Antisemitism." *Azure* 32 (2008): 48–79. Originally published as "Nisayon lezihuy vehavanah shel tashtit haantishemiut." *Alpayim* 28 (2005): 11–30.

Between Right and Right. Translated by Arnold Schwartz. Garden City, NY: Doubleday, 1981. Originally published as *Bizkhut hanormaliut* [In praise of normalcy]. Jerusalem: Schocken, 1980.

The Continuing Silence of a Poet: Collected Stories. Translated by Miriam Arad and Marsha Pomerantz. Syracuse: Syracuse University Press, 1998.

"Defining 'Who Is a Jew.'" *Ha'aretz*, September 4, 2013.

"Defining Who Is an Israeli." *Ha'aretz*, September 12, 2013.

"Defining Zionism: The Belief That Israel Belongs to the Entire Jewish People." *Ha'aretz*, May 21, 2013.

The Extra. Translated by Stuart Schoffman. London: Halban, 2016. Originally published as *Nitzevet*. Bnei Brak: Hakibbutz Hameuchad, 2014.

"Facing the Forests." In *The Continuing Silence of a Poet: Collected Stories*, translated by Miriam Arad and Marsha Pomerantz, 203–36. Syracuse: Syracuse University Press, 1998. Originally published in 1963 as "Mul haye'arot." Collected in *Kol Hasipurim*, 81–98. Tel Aviv: Hakibbutz Hameuchad, 2006.

"Finding My Father in Sephardic Time." Translated by Gilead Morahg. *Moment* 22, no. 5 (1997): 54–57, 85–92. Originally published as "Behipus ahar hazman hasfaradi ha'avud." In *Hakir vehahar*, 228–41. Tel Aviv: Zmora-Beitan, 1989.

Five Seasons. Translated by Hillel Halkin. New York: Doubleday, 1989. Originally published as *Molkho*. Tel Aviv: Hakibbutz Hameuchad / Keter, 1987.

Friendly Fire. Translated by Stuart Schoffman. New York: Houghton Mifflin Harcourt, 2009. Originally published as *Esh yedidutit: Duet*. Bnei Brak: Hakibbutz Hameuchad, 2007.

"From Myth to History." *AJS Review* 28, no. 1 (2004): 205–11.

"Golah: The Neurotic Solution." In *Between Right and Right*, translated by Arnold Schwartz, 21–74. Garden City, NY: Doubleday, 1981. Originally published as "Hagolah—hapitaron hanevroti." In *Bizkhut hanormaliut* [In praise of normalcy], 27–73. Jerusalem: Schocken, 1980.

Hakir vehahar: Metziuto halo sifrutit shel hasofer beyisrael [The wall and the mountain: The extraliterary reality of the writer in Israel]. Tel Aviv: Zmora Beitan, 1989.

"Hebrew Literature and *Dor Hamedina*: Portrait of a Literary Generation." Translated by Emily Miller Budick. In *Ideology and Jewish Identity in Israeli*

194 SELECTED BIBLIOGRAPHY

and American Literature, edited by Emily Miller Budick, 45–55. Albany: SUNY Press, 2001. Originally published in *Ma'ariv,* June 6, 1998.

"Israeli Identity in a Time of Peace: Prospects and Perils." *Tikkun Magazine* 10, no. 6 (1995): 34–40, 94.

A Journey to the End of the Millennium. Translated by Nicholas de Lange. San Diego: Harcourt, 2000. Originally published as *Masa el tom ha'elef.* Bnei Brak: Hakibbutz Hameuchad, 1997.

A Late Divorce. Translated by Hillel Halkin. San Diego: Harcourt Brace, 1993. Originally published as *Geirushim meuharim* [A late divorce]. Tel Aviv: Hakibbutz Hameuchad, 1982. Extended ed., 2010.

The Liberated Bride. Translated by Hillel Halkin. Orlando: Harcourt, 2004. Originally published as *Hakala hameshahreret.* Bnei Brak: Hakibbutz Hameuchad, 2001.

The Lover. Translated by Philip Simpson. San Diego: Harcourt Brace, 1993. Originally published as *Hame'ahev.* Jerusalem: Schocken, 1977.

"Mah ani betokh haviku'ah hagadol" [What am I within the big debate?]. *Iton 77,* nos. 124–25 (1990): 27.

"The Meaning of Homeland." In *A. B. Yehoshua Controversy,* 7–13.

Mr. Mani. Translated by Hillel Halkin. San Diego: Harcourt Brace, 1992. Originally published as *Mar Mani.* Tel Aviv: Hakibbutz Hameuchad, 1990.

"Mr. Mani and the Akedah." *Judaism* 50, no. 1 (2001): 61–65. Originally published as "Levatel et ha'akedah 'al yedei mimushah be*Mar Mani*" [Cancel the 'akedah by enacting it in *Mr. Mani*]. In Ben-Dov, *Bakivun hanegdi,* 394–98.

Open Heart. Translated by Dalya Bilu. San Diego: Harcourt Brace, 1997. Originally published as *Hashiva mehodu* [Return from India]. Bnei Brak: Hakibbutz Hameuchad, 1994.

"The Place of the Hebrew Writer in the Revival of Zionism." Center for Interdisciplinary Study of Monotheistic Religions. http://www.cismor

.jp/uploads-images/sites/2/2014/01 /b63baddoca1d12d45af139d98fcf6dfb .pdf.

The Retrospective. Translated by Stuart Schoffman. New York: Houghton Mifflin Harcourt, 2013. Originally published as *Hesed sfaradi.* Israel: Hakibbutz Hameuchad / Kinneret Zmora-Bitan, 2011.

"Tardemat hayom" [Sleepy day]. First published in 1959. Collected in *Kol Hasipurim,* 21–30. Tel Aviv: Hakibbutz Hameuchad, 1993.

The Terrible Power of a Minor Guilt. Translated by Ora Cummings. Syracuse: Syracuse University Press, 2000. Originally published as *Koha hanorah shel ashmah ktanah.* Tel Aviv: Yediot Ahronot, 1998.

"Three Days and a Child." In *The Continuing Silence of a Poet: Collected Stories,* translated by Miriam Arad and Marsha Pomerantz, 35–94. Originally published in 1965 as "Shloshah yamim veyeled." Collected in *Kol Hasipurim,* 129–80. Tel Aviv: Hakibbutz Hameuchad, 2006.

"Time to Say Goodbye to the Two-State Solution. Here's the Alternative. A. B. Yehoshua, One of Israel's Staunchest Fighters for the Two-State Solution, Lays Out a Proposal for an Israeli-Palestinian Partnership." *Ha'aretz,* April 19, 2018. https://www.haaretz.com /israel-news.premium.MAGAZINE -time-to-nix-the-two-state-solution -and-stop-israel-s-apartheid-1.6011274.

The Tunnel. Translated by Stuart Schoffman. New York: Houghton Mifflin Harcourt, 2020. Originally published as *Haminharah.* Bnei Brak: Hakibbutz Hameuchad, 2018.

A Woman in Jerusalem. Translated by Hillel Halkin. Orlando: Harcourt, 2006. Originally published as *Shlihuto shel hamemuneh 'al mash'abei enosh: Passion bishloshah prakim* [The mission of the human resource manager: A passion in three parts]. Bnei Brak: Hakibbutz Hameuchad, 2004.

SELECTED BIBLIOGRAPHY   195

"The Yatir Evening Express." In *The Continuing Silence of a Poet: Collected Stories*, translated by Miriam Arad and Marsha Pomerantz, 141–62. Originally published in 1959 as "Mas'a ha'erev shel Yatir." Collected in *Kol Hasipurim*, 31–50. Tel Aviv: Hakibbutz Hameuchad, 2006.

Other Sources

Albeck-Gidron, Rachel. "Totem ve'ivaron: Tahalikhei breyrah tarbutiyim hameyutsagim baroman *Hakala hameshahreret* shel A. B. Yehoshua" [Totem and blindness: Processes of cultural choice in Yehoshua's *Liberated Bride*]. *Mikan* 4 (2005): 5–19.

Aloni, Shulamit, "An Israeli Without Hyphens." In *A. B. Yehoshua Controversy*, 14–16.

Alter, Robert. *The Invention of Hebrew Prose: Modern Fiction and the Language of Realism*. Seattle: University of Washington Press, 1988.

Altshuler, Tehilla Shwartz. "Madu'a bakha Yirmiyahu? Tanakh ve'intertextualiut be*Esh Yedidutit*" [Why did Jeremiah cry? Bible and intertextuality in *Friendly Fire*]. In Banbaji, Ben-Dov, and Shamir, *Mabatim mitztalvim*, 41–50.

Amir, Dana. "Miyerushalayim shel mata leyerushalayim shel ma'alah" [From terrestrial to celestial Jerusalem: On A. B. Yehoshua's novella *Shlihuto shel hamemuneh 'al mash'abei enosh*]. *Alei Siah* 54 (2005): 25–30.

Aschkenasy, Nehama, ed. "Recreating the Canon: The Biblical Presence in Modern Hebrew Literature and Culture." Special issue, *AJS Review* 28, no. 1 (2004).

———. "Yehoshua's "Sound and Fury": *A Late Divorce* and Its Faulknerian Model." *Modern Language Studies* 21, no. 2 (1991): 92–104.

Bakhtin, Mikhail. "The Bildungsroman and Its Significance in the History of Realism." Translated by V. McGee. In *Speech Genres and Other Late Essays*,

edited by Caryl Emerson and Michael Holquist, 10–59. Austin: University of Texas Press, 1986.

———. "Forms of Time and the Chronotope in the Novel." Translated by Caryl Emerson and Michael Holquist. In *The Dialogic Imagination*, edited by Michael Holquist, 84–258. Austin: University of Texas Press, 1981.

———. *Problems of Dostoevsky's Poetics*. Translated by Caryl Emerson. Minneapolis: University of Minnesota Press, 1984.

Balaban, Avraham. *Mar Molkho: 'Iyun baromanim* Molkho *ve*Mar Mani *shel A. B. Yehoshua* [Mr. Molkho: A study of the novels *Five Seasons* and *Mr. Mani* by A. B. Yehoshua]. Tel Aviv: Hakibbutz Hameuchad, 1992.

Banbaji, Amir. "Hakishlonot shel Molkho: Realism, Modernism, Mizrahiut" [The failures of Molkho: Realism, modernism, orientalism]. In Banbaji, Ben-Dov, and Shamir, *Mabatim mitztalvim*, 173–94.

———. "Yehoshua bere'i bikoret hasifrut ha'ivrit" [Yehoshua in the critical mirror of Hebrew literature]. In Banbaji, Ben-Dov, and Shamir, *Mabatim mitztalvim*, 14–29.

Banbaji, Amir, Nitza Ben-Dov, and Ziva Shamir, eds. *Mabatim mitztalvim* [Intersecting perspectives: Essays on A. B. Yehoshua's oeuvre]. Tel Aviv: Hakibbutz Hameuchad, 2010.

Band, Arnold J. "*Mar Mani*: The Archaeology of Self-Deception." *Prooftexts* 12, no. 3 (1992): 231–44.

Bartana, Ortsion. "The Brenner School and the Agnon School in Hebrew Literature of the Twentieth Century." *Hebrew Studies* 45 (2004): 49–69.

Barzel, Hillel. "Keter ha'ahdut veketer haribuy" [Pluralism and singularity]. In Ben-Dov, *Bakivun hanegdi*, 114–29.

Bell, Michael. *Literature, Modernism and Myth: Belief and Responsibility in the Twentieth Century*. New York: Cambridge University Press, 1997.

Ben-Dov, Nitza, ed. *Bakivun hanegdi* [In the opposite direction: Articles on

Mr. Mani]. Tel Aviv: Hakibbutz Hameuchad, 1995.

———. *Haim ktuvim: 'al uutobiografiot sifruti'ot isra'eliot* [Written lives: On Israeli literary autobiographies]. Tel Aviv: Schocken, 2011.

———. "Haomnam 'kav yashar vetiv'i lePalestina'?" In Ben-Dov, *Bakivun hanegdi*, 164–75.

———. *Hayey milhamah* [War lives: On the army, revenge, grief, and the consciousness of war in Israeli fiction]. Tel Aviv: Schocken, 2016.

———. "In the Back Yard of Agnon's House: Between *The Liberated Bride* by A. B. Yehoshua and S.Y. Agnon." *Hebrew Studies* 47 (2006): 237–51.

———. *Vehitehilatekha: 'Iyunim beyetzirot S. Y. Agnon, A. B. Yehoshua ve'Amos Oz* [And she is your praise: Studies in the writings of S. Y. Agnon, A. B. Yehoshua, and Amos Oz]. Jerusalem: Schocken, 2006.

Caspi, Zehava. "Mekomo shel ha'aher: Yetzer veyetziratiut badrama shel A. B. Yehoshua" [The place of the other: Desire and creativity in the plays of A. B. Yehoshua]. In Banbaji, Ben-Dov, and Shamir, *Mabatim mitztalvim*, 453–68.

Cohen, Yehoshua. "Yerushalaim—'ir dmuyot rabot'" [Jerusalem—city of many characters]. In Ben-Dov, *Bakivun hanegdi*, 386–92.

Domb, Risa. "Crossing Borders: The Clash of Civilizations in *The Liberating Bride*." In *Identity and Modern Israeli Literature*, 78–89. London: Vallentine Mitchell, 2006.

———. *Home Thoughts from Abroad: Distant Visions of Israel in Contemporary Hebrew Fiction*. London: Vallentine Mitchell, 1995.

Esty, Jed. *Unseasonable Youth*. New York: Oxford University Press, 2012.

Ezrahi, Sidra. *Booking Passage: Exile and Homecoming in the Modern Jewish Imagination*. Berkeley: University of California Press, 2000.

Feldman, Yael. "Between Genesis and Sophocles: Biblical Psychopolitics

in A. B. Yehoshua's *Mr. Mani*." In *History and Literature: New Readings of Jewish Texts in Honor of Arnold J. Band*, edited by William Cutter and David Jacobson, 451–64. Providence: Program in Judaic Studies, Brown University, 2002.

———. *Glory and Agony: Isaac's Sacrifice and National Narrative*. Stanford: Stanford University Press, 2010.

———. "Isaac or Oedipus? Jewish Tradition and the Israeli *Aqedah*." In *Biblical Studies / Cultural Studies*, edited by I. C. Exum and S. Moore, 158–89. England: Sheffield Academic Press, 1998. Updated Hebrew version in *Alpayim* 22 (2001): 53–77.

———. "The Jacob Complex and Zionist Masculinism in the Work of A. B. Yehoshua." In *Gendering the Jewish Past*, edited by Marc Lee Raphael, 49–65. Williamsburg: William and Mary College, 2002. Earlier Hebrew version in Ben-Dov, *Bakivun hanegdi*, 204–22.

Foucault, Michel. "Des espaces autres, Hétérotopies." *Architecture, Mouvement, Continuité* 5 (1984): 46–49.

———. "L'oeil du pouvoir." In *Dits et écrits*, 3:190–99. Paris: Gallimard, 1977.

Gil, Avi. "Gvulot metushtashim be*Mar Mani*" [Blurred boundaries in *Mr. Mani*]. In Ben-Dov, *Bakivun hanegdi*, 223–35.

Gluzman, Michael. *The Politics of Canonicity: Lines of Resistance in Modernist Hebrew Poetry*. Stanford: Stanford University Press, 2003.

Gold, Nili Scharf. *Haifa: City of Steps*. Waltham: Brandeis University Press, 2017.

Grumberg, Karen. *Hebrew Gothic: History and the Poetics of Persecution*. Bloomington: Indiana University Press, 2019.

———. *Place and Ideology in Contemporary Hebrew Literature*. Syracuse: Syracuse University Press, 2011.

Gurevitch, Zali, and Gidon Aran. "'Al hamakom—ethnografia israelit" [On the place: An Israeli ethnography]. *Alpayim* 4 (1991): 9–44.

Halevi-Wise, Yael. "Agnon's Conversation with Jeremiah in *A Guest for the Night*: 'Aginut in an Age of National Modernization." *AJS Review* 38, no. 2 (2014): 395–416.

———. "The 'Double Triangle' Paradigm: National Redemption in Bi-generational Love Triangles from Agnon to Oz." *Prooftexts* 26, no. 3 (2006): 309–43.

———. *Interactive Fictions: Scenes of Storytelling in the Novel*. Westport, CT: Praeger, 2003.

———. "Where Is the Sephardism of *Hesed sefaradi* / *The Retrospective*?" *Sephardic Horizons* 4, no. 1 (2014). http://www.sephardichorizons.org/Volume4/Issue1/WhereSephardism.html.

Harris, Rachel. *An Ideological Death: Suicide in Israeli Literature*. Evanston: Northwestern University Press, 2014.

Hasak-Lowy, Todd. *Here and Now: History, Nationalism, and Realism in Modern Hebrew Fiction*. Syracuse: Syracuse University Press, 2008.

Herman, David. "A. B. Yehoshua: The Writer Still Shaping Israel's Identity." *Jewish Chronicle Online*, February 28, 2013. https://www.thejc.com/lifestyle/features/a-b-yehoshua-the-writer-still-shaping-israel-s-identity-1.42311.

Hever, Hannan. "Minority Discourse of a National Majority: Israeli Fiction in the Early Sixties." *Prooftexts* 10, no. 1 (1990): 129–47.

Hirschfeld, Ariel. "Shivat ha'elohi: 'Al mekomo shel ha'elohim bashira ha'ivrit bador ha'aharon" [Return of the divine: On the return of God in Hebrew poetry of the last generation]. In *Ha'agalah hamele'ah: me'ah'esrim shnot tarbut Israel* [The full cart: A hundred and twenty years of Israeli culture], edited by Israel Bartal, 165–76. Jerusalem: Magnes, 2002.

Hochberg, Gil. "A Poetics of Haunting: From Yizhar's Hirbeh to Yehoshua's Ruins to Koren's Crypts." *Jewish Social Studies* 18, no. 3 (2012): 55–69.

Hoffman, Anne Golomb. *Between Exile and Return: S. Y. Agnon and the Drama of Writing*. Albany: SUNY Press, 1991.

———. "Oedipal Narrative and Its Discontents: A. B. Yehoshua's *Molkho* (*Five Seasons*)." In *Gender and Text in Modern Hebrew and Yiddish Literature*, edited by Naomi B. Sokoloff, Anne Lapidus Lerner, and Anita Norich, 195–216. New York: Jewish Theological Seminary of America, 1992.

———. "The Womb of Culture: Fictions of Identity and Their Undoing in Yehoshua's *Mr Mani*." *Prooftexts* 12, no. 3 (1992): 245–63.

Holdengräber, Paul. "In Conversation with A. B. Yehoshua." New York Public Library, March 28, 2011. Audio. http://www.nypl.org/audiovideo/ab-yehoshua-conversation-paul-holdengraber.

Holtzman, Avner. *Mapat drakhim* [Road map: Hebrew fiction today]. Tel Aviv: Hakibbutz Hameuchad, 2005.

Hop, Dorit. "Be'ikvot Euridikah" [In pursuit of Eurydice]. In Banbaji, Ben-Dov, and Shamir, *Mabatim mitztalvim*, 195–210.

Horn, Bernard. *Facing the Fires: Conversations with A. B. Yehoshua*. Syracuse: Syracuse University Press, 1997.

———. "Sephardic Identity and Its Discontents: The Novels of A. B. Yehoshua." In *Sephardism: Spanish-Jewish History and the Modern Literary Imagination*, edited by Yael Halevi-Wise, 189–211. Stanford: Stanford University Press, 2012.

Itzhaki, Yedidya. *Hapsukim hasmuyim min ha'ayin: 'Al yetsirot A. B. Yehoshua* [The concealed verses: Source material in the works of A. B. Yehoshua]. Ramat Gan: Bar-Ilan University Press, 1992.

Jaggi, Maya. "Power and Pity: Interview with A. B. Yehoshua." *Guardian*, June 24, 2006. http://www.theguardian.com/books/2006/jun/24/featuresreviews.guardianreview11.

198 SELECTED BIBLIOGRAPHY

Lewis, Pericles. *Religious Experience and the Modernist Novel.* New York: Cambridge University Press, 2010.

Lifshitz, Natanel. "Yerushalaim—'ir mitna'eret me'afarah" [Jerusalem—a city shaking off its dust]. In Ben-Dov, *Bakivun hanegdi,* 380–85.

Lipsker, Avidov. "A. B. Yehoshua—Retrospectiva: Mimetaphysica shel ro'a le'etika shel matzavim" [From a metaphysics of evil to an ethics of circumstances]. *Mikan* 14 (2014): 311–26.

———. "Gvulot shel herut lelo gvul" [Limits of freedom without barriers]. *Alei Siah* 47 (2002): 9–19.

———. "Mahsomim: Ezorei-sfar bageografia ha'etit shel A. B. Yehoshua" [Barriers: Liminal thresholds in A. B. Yehoshua's ethical geography]. *Tarbut Demokratit* 11 (2007): 107–16.

Mann, Barbara. *A Place in History: Modernism, Tel Aviv, and the Creation of Jewish Urban Space.* Palo Alto: Stanford University Press, 2006.

———. *Space and Place in Jewish Studies.* New Brunswick: Rutgers University Press, 2012.

Margolin, Uri. "Naming and Believing: Practices of the Proper Name in Narrative Fiction." *Narrative* 10, no. 2 (2003): 107–27.

Mendelson-Maoz, Adia. "The Bereaved Father and His Dead Son in the Works of A. B. Yehoshua." *Jewish Social Studies* 17, no. 1 (2010): 116–40.

———. *Borders, Territories, and Ethics: Hebrew Literature in the Shadow of the Intifada.* West Lafayette: Purdue University Press, 2018.

———. "Kohah hanorah shel ashmah ktanah: Mehalakha lema'aseh" [The terrible power of a minor guilt: From prescription to action]. In Banbaji, Ben-Dov, and Shamir, *Mabatim mitztalvim,* 550–69.

———. "Koha hanorah shel ha'etikah: Kriah etit baroman *Mas'a el tom ha'elef leAvraham* B. Yehoshua" [The terrible power of ethics in Yehoshua's *A Journey to the End of the Millennium*].

Dapim: Research in Literature 18 (2011): 61–86.

Mintz, Alan. *George Eliot and the Novel of Vocation.* Cambridge: Harvard University Press, 1978.

Miron, Dan. *Bein hazon le'emet* [Between vision and truth: Blossoming of the Hebrew novel in the nineteenth century]. Jerusalem: Mosad Bialik, 1979.

———. "Meyotzrim ubonim levney bli bayit" [From creators and builders to homelessness]. In *Im lo tehiyeh yerushalayim* [If Jerusalem ceases to exist: Hebrew literature in a cultural and political context], 11–89. Tel Aviv: Hakibbutz Hameuchad, 1987.

———. *The Prophetic Mode in Modern Hebrew Poetry.* Milford, CT: Toby Press, 2010.

———. *Tesh'a vahetzi shel A. B. Yehoshua: Mabat 'ashkenazi' 'al shnei romanim 'sfaradim'* [A. B. Yehoshua's ninth-and-a-half: An "Ashkenazi" perspective on two "Sephardic" novels]. Tel Aviv: Hakibbutz Hameuchad, 2011.

Morahg, Gilead. "A. B. Yehoshua: Fictions of Zion and Diaspora." In *Israeli Writers Consider the Outsider,* edited by Leon Yudkin, 124–37. Rutherford: Fairleigh Dickinson University Press, 1993.

———. "Borderline Cases: National Identity and Territorial Affinity in A. B. Yehoshua's *Mr. Mani.*" *AJS Review* 30, no. 1 (2006): 167–82.

———. "Facing the Wilderness: God and Country in the Fiction of A. B. Yehoshua." *Prooftexts* 8, no. 3 (1988): 311–31.

———. "From Madness on to Sanity: A. B. Yehoshua's Shifting Perspective on the Diaspora." *Shofar* 11, no. 1 (1992): 50–60.

———. *Hahemlah vehaza'am: 'Al hasiporet shel A. B. Yehoshua* [Compassion and fury: On the fiction of A. B. Yehoshua]. Or Yehuda: Dvir; Be'er Sheva: Ben Gurion University, 2014.

———. "Portrait of the Artist as an Aging Scholar: A. B. Yehoshua's *The Liberating Bride.*" *Hebrew Studies* 50 (2009): 175–83.

———. "Shading the Truth: A. B. Yehoshua's 'Facing the Forests.'" In *History and Literature: New Readings of Jewish Texts in Honor of Arnold J. Band*, edited by William Cutter and David C. Jacobson, 409–18. Providence: Program in Judaic Studies, Brown University, 2002.

———. "Testing Tolerance: Cultural Diversity and National Unity in A. B. Yehoshua's *A Journey to the End of the Millennium*." *Prooftexts* 19, no. 3 (1999): 235–56.

Moretti, Franco. *Atlas of the European Novel, 1800–1900*. London: Verso, 1998.

———. *Graphs, Maps, Trees: Abstract Models for Literary History*. London: Verso, 2005.

———. *The Way of the World: The Bildungsroman in European Culture*. London: Verso, 1987.

Muller, Rina Cohen. "Ceux qui partent de la Terre Promise: Les émigrants Israéliens." *Les cahiers du Judaisme* 11 (2002): 108–19.

Murata, Yasuko. "A. B. Yehoshua's *Mar Mani*: A Sephardic World with Jerusalem as a Focal Point." *Center for Interdisciplinary Study of Monotheistic Religions*. http://www.cismor.jp/uploads -images/sites/2/2014/01/c1f725ea5f14 a770a63f9322c338fff4.pdf.

Naveh, Hannah. *Nos'im venos'ot: Sipurey mas'a besifrut ha'ivrit hahadashah* [Voyagers: Travel stories in modern Hebrew literature]. Tel Aviv: Ministry of Defense, 2002.

Naves, Elaine Kalman. "Talking with A. B. Yehoshua." *Queen's Quarterly* 112, no. 1 (Spring 2005): 76–86. https:// www.elainekalmannaves.com/essays -articles-radio-interviews/item/50 -talking-with-ab-yehoshua.

Nocke, Alexandra. *The Place of the Mediterranean in Modern Israeli Identity*. Leiden: Brill, 2009.

Ohana, David. *Israel and Its Mediterranean Identity*. New York: Palgrave Macmillan, 2011.

Omer-Sherman, Ranen. "Guests and Hosts in A. B. Yehoshua's *The Liberated Bride*." *Shofar* 31, no. 3 (2013): 25–63.

———. *Israel in Exile: Jewish Writing and the Desert*. Urbana: University of Illinois Press, 2006.

———. "'On the Verge of a Long-Craved Intimacy': Distance and Proximity Between Jews and Arab Identities in A. B. Yehoshua's *The Liberated Bride*." *Journal of Jewish Identities* 2, no. 1 (2009): 55–84.

Oz, Amos. "Hapatish vehasadan: 'Al 'Mot hazaken' me'et A. B. Yehoshua" [The hammer and the anvil: On *Death of the Old Man* by A. B. Yehoshua]. *Min hayesod* (January 17, 1963): 271–73.

Oz-Saltzberger, Fania. "Hahistoria vehahistorionim etzel A. B. Yehoshua" [History and historians in A. B. Yehoshua]. In Banbaji, Ben-Dov, and Shamir, *Mabatim mitztalvim*, 570–76.

Peri, Menachem and Nissim Calderon. "Sihah 'im A. B. Yehoshua" [In conversation with A. B. Yehoshua]. *Siman Kriah* 5 (February 1976): 276–82.

Pinsker, Shachar. *Literary Passports: The Making of Modernist Hebrew Fiction in Europe*. Stanford: Stanford University Press, 2011.

Ragussis, Michael. *Acts of Naming: The Family Plot in Fiction*. New York: Oxford University Press, 1986.

Ramras-Rauch, Gila. *The Arab in Israeli Literature*. Bloomington: Indiana University Press, 1989.

Reuveni, Yotam. *A. B. Yehoshua: Diokan* 2 [A. B. Yehoshua: Portrait 2]. Tel Aviv: Nimrod Press, 2003.

Saranga, Carmela and Rachel Sharaby. "Space as a Demon and the Demon in the Space." In *The Divergence of Judaism and Islam*, edited by Michael Laskier and Yaakov Lev, 270–87. Gainesville: University of Florida Press, 2011.

Schwartz, Yigal. "Deus Ex Machina: Elohim, mekhonot uvnei adam basiporet shel A. B. Yehoshua" [God, machines, and humans in A. B. Yehoshua's fiction]. In Banbaji, Ben-Dov, and Shamir, *Mabatim mitztalvim*, 507–15.

200 SELECTED BIBLIOGRAPHY

——. *Hayad'at et ha'aretz sham halimon pore'ah: Handasat ha'adam umahshevet hamerhav basifrut ha'ivrit hahadashah* [Do you know the land where the lemon blooms: Human engineering and landscape conceptualization]. Or Yehuda: Devir, 2007.

Shaked, Gershon. *Gal hadash besiporet ha'ivrit* [A new wave in Hebrew fiction]. Tel Aviv: Sifriat Poalim, 1971.

——. *Hasiporet ha'ivrit 1880–1970.* Vol. 1. Tel Aviv: Hakibbutz Hameuchad, 1977.

——. "Hatzel haparus 'aleinu" [The shadow covering us: On A. B. Yehoshua's *The Lover*]. *Yediot Achronot*, February 25, 1977.

Shalev, Mordechai. "Ha'aravim kepitaron sifruti" [Arabs as a literary solution]. Reprinted in Banbaji, Ben-Dov, and Shamir, *Mabatim mitztalvim*, 54–70.

——. "Hotam ha'akedah be'Shloshah yamim veyeled,' 'Bethilat kayitz 1970' uve*Mar Mani*" [The imprint of the *Akedah* in "Three Days and a Child," "At the Beginning of Summer 1970," and *Mr. Mani*]. Reprinted in Ben-Dov, *Bakivun hanegdi*, 399–448.

Shamir, Ziva. "Hahoveh hu ha'avar shel ha'atid" [The present is the past of the future]. In Ben-Dov, *Bakivun hanegdi*, 139–50.

——. *Sipur lo pashut* [Not a simple story: Readings in the works of A. B. Yehoshua, Amos Oz, and Haim Be'er]. Israel: Safra, 2015.

Shavit, Ari. "A Nation That Knows No Bounds: Interview with A. B. Yehoshua." *Ha'aretz*, March 19, 2004. http://www.haaretz.com/a-nation-that-knows-no-bounds-1.117161.

Shemtov, Vered Karti. "Boundaries and Crossing: An Interview with A. B. Yehoshua." *Sh'ma* (March 4, 2004). http://shma.com/2004/03/boundaries-and-crossing.

——. "Merhav sifruti vegvulot geografim behakala hameshahreret shel A. B. Yehoshua" [Literary space and geographic boundaries in A. B. Yehoshua's *The Liberated Bride*]. In Banbaji, Ben-Dov, and Shamir, *Mabatim mitztalvim*, 272–82.

Shifra, S. "Haratzon lehitmoded 'im hametziut (re'ayon 'im A. B. Yehoshua)" [The desire to engage with reality (an interview with A. B. Yehoshua)]. *Davar*, July 18, 1975.

Sosnowski, Saul. "Latin American-Jewish Writers: Protecting the Hyphen." In *The Jewish Presence in Latin America*, edited by Judith L. Elkin and Gilbert W. Merkx, 297–308. Boston: Allen and Unwin, 1987.

Weitz, Gidi and Dror Mishani. "Hard Talk (Interview with A. B. Yehoshua)." *Haaretz*, February 14, 2008. http://www.haaretz.com/hard-talk-1.239315.

Yuval, Yaakov. "Lesham uvehazarah: Galut yerushalayim asher besfarad" [There and back: Jerusalem's exile in Spain]. *Ha'aretz Literary Supplement* (February 11, 2011): 1, 4.

Zakim, Eric. *To Build and Be Built: Landscape, Literature, and the Construction of Zionist Identity*. Philadelphia: University of Pennsylvania Press, 2006.

Zemach, Eddie. "Yehoshua bein tzafon ledarom" [Yehoshua between north and south]. In *Masot 'al tom ha'elef* [Essays on *A Journey to the End of the Millennium*], edited by Ziva Shamir and Aviva Doron, 25–33. Tel Aviv: Hakibbutz Hameuchad, 1999.

Zierler, Wendy. "Hagar veTamar: *Mar Mani* vektivah nashit" [Hagar and Tamar: *Mr. Mani* and feminine writing]. In Ben-Dov, *Bakivun hanegdi*, 286–99.

Zoran, Gabriel. "Zman kemerhav umerhav kezman: mivneh utfisat metziut be*Mar Mani*" [Time as space and space as time: Structure and the representation of reality in *Mr. Mani*]. In Ben-Dov, *Bakivun hanegdi*, 69–79.

INDEX

Agnon, Shmuel Yosef, 3, 18, 95, 112–13, 156–58, 183n4, 185nn44–45
   Nitza Ben-Dov on Yehoshua and Agnon, 4, 146, 156, 179n39, 189n7, 190n17
   Yehoshua's indebtedness to, x, 3–4, 113, 130, 145–47, 153–59
Albeck-Gidron, Ruth, 63
Altshuler, Tehilla Schwartz, 187n10
Amir, Dana, 176n69, 181n17
Arab-Israeli relations, 11, 49, 59, 165–66, 118, 141–42, 174n43, 175n52, 192n32
   See also diversity and cultural pluralism: Palestinians and Israeli-Arabs; Palestinians
Aschkenasy, Nehama, 179n45
Assis, Amir, 172n8

Bakhtin, Michael, 52, 172n4, 177nn1–3
Balaban, Avraham, 53, 169n7, 172n10, 177n4, 179n34
   on Five Seasons (Molkho), 75
   on Mr. Mani, 117, 186n62
Banbaji, Amir, 11, 178n14, 182n36, 182n45
Bartana, Ortsion, 10, 170n18
Barzel, Hillel, 179n35
Ben-Dov, Nitza, 4, 11, 63, 83
   Agnon's influence upon Yehoshua, 4, 147, 189n7, 190n17 (see also Agnon, Shmuel Yosef)
   on Friendly Fire, 178n23
   on The Liberated Bride, 190n17, 191n30
   on Mr. Mani, 186n62
   semi-autobiographical dimensions in Yehoshua's work, 11, 173n30, 180n3
   Yehoshua's "Astarte paradigm," 63, 83, 192n30
Ben-Gurion, David, 13, 114, 164, 175n52
Berman, Marshall, 32
biblical references in Yehoshua's fiction, 13, 128–29, 132–34, 183n5, 185n55
   in dialogue with the prophets, 25, 56–57, 61, 71, 91, 97, 143–44, 187n10

in relation to the akedah (binding of Isaac), 68, 116, 146–50, 175n54, 185n54, 189n8, 190n14
in relation to The Song of Songs, 143–44, 159, 190n18
See also historiosophic themes in Yehoshua's fiction; "watchman over the house of Israel" motif (Hatzofeh lebeit Israel)
bildungsroman, 36, 73–74, 78, 89, 92, 180n5, 180n7
Brenner, Rachel Feldhay, 189n28
Brenner, Yosef Haim, 10–12, 115, 170n18

Calderon, Nissim, 5
Caspi, Zehava, 177n8
Chronotope (definition), 52–53, 177n1
   across Yehoshua's fiction, 13, 53, 177n5

diaspora (Israel-Diaspora relations), 21–22, 27, 90, 98, 106–7, 142–43, 162–67, 192n34
   in "The Yehoshua Controversy," 7, 142–43, 159, 162–67, 192n1
   described as a neurosis, 97–98, 106–7
   See also national identity: and dispersion
diversity and cultural pluralism, xi–xii, 4, 9, 37–45, 49, 53–54, 155–56, 165, 191n26
   Arabs, Palestinians and Israeli-Arabs (interest in), 11, 21, 134, 171n26, 174n43, 178n14, 178n15, 185n34
   Arabs, Palestinians and Israeli-Arabs (representation of), 13, 31–35, 59–60, 118, 141–42, 158, 189n28; in "Facing the Forests," 56, 178nn14–15; in Friendly Fire, 59–60; in The Liberated Bride, 170n19; in The Lover, 141–42; in Mr. Mani, 39–45; See also Arab-Israeli relations
   Christians (representation of), 38, 49–50, 81, 110
   ethnic diversity within Judaism, xi–xii, 4, 9, 39–46, 89–90, 152–56, 186n70, 191n26; Sephardim, 9, 39, 116, 137, 173n28–29, 186n70; Mizrahim, 89, 122–25, 129, 186n70, 188n12; Ashkenazim, 42, 122–25,

202 INDEX

diversity and cultural pluralism (*continued*)
ethnic diversity within Judaism
(*continued*)
186n70; Mediterranean identity, 136,
188n23, 191n26
foreign workers in Israel (representation
of), 79–81, 110–11
mutual validation across ethnic and
religious differences, 31, 54, 124–25,
160, 174n33, 175n49, 175n51, 186n70; in
Friendly Fire, 178n31; in *Journey to the
End of the Millennium*, 124–25, 186n70,
191n26; in *Mr. Mani*, 40
pagans and paganism (representation of),
94, 123
Domb, Risa, 32, 61
Dostoevsky, Fyodor, 52

Esh yedidutit. See *Friendly Fire*
Extra, The (Nitzevet), 8, 15, 19

Facing the Forests (*Mul haye'arot*), 56, 61–62,
177n13, 178n15
watchman's stance, 56, 61–62, 178n14
family microcosms, 23, 29, 69, 86, 107, 111,
143–44, 158–59, 191n20
Faulkner, William, 7, 66–67, 96, 113, 130, 151,
183n7
Bernard Horn on Faulkner and Yehoshua,
179n45
Nehama Aschkenasy on Faulkner and
Yehoshua, 183n6
Yehoshua's indebtedness to, x, 4, 66–67,
96, 113, 130, 151, 183nn6–7
Feldman, Yael, 68, 150, 175n54, 185n54, 190n15
"Flood Tide," ("Ge'ut hayam"), 55–56
Five Seasons (*Molkho*), 74–75,
watchman's stance, 60–61, 63–64
Friendly Fire (*Esh yedidutit*), 25–27, 57–62,
108–13, 178, 187n10
fire imagery in, xv, 25, 108–9
Hanukkah in, 108–13
name symbolism in, xv, 25, 62

Geirushim meuharim. See *Late Divorce, A*
Gertz, Nurit, 179n35
Gluzman, Michael, 170n17
"Golah: The Neurotic Solution," 94–99,
106–7, 147
See also national identity: and dispersion
Gold, Nili Scharf, 171n3
Grumberg, Karen, 171n3, 181n24, 190n19

Haifa, 142, 188n16
Halevi-Wise, Yael, 173n28
on Yehoshua and Agnon, 187n10, 189n5,
189n32
Halkin, Hillel, 40, 165, 175n51
Hakala hameshahreret. See *Liberated Bride,
The*
Hakak, Lev, 42
Hame'ahev. See *Lover, The*
Haminharah. See *Tunnel, The*
Hanukkah, 109–10, 112, 114
in *Friendly Fire*, 108–13
Hashivah mehodu. See *Open Heart*
Harris, Rachel, 186n56
Herman, David, 27–28
Hesed sfaradi. See *Retrospective, The*
Hever, Hannan, 56, 178n15, 179n38, 192n34
Hirschfeld, Ariel, 183n5
historical novels, 17, 36–45, 68–69, 95, 115, 121,
151, 190n20
historiosophic themes in Yehoshua's fiction,
xiv–xvi, 70–71, 77, 111–13, 116, 126–30,
138–39, 159
definition, x, xiv, 113
myth vs history, xiv, xvi, 31–32, 51, 102, 126,
176n69
national normalcy, 9–10, 51, 136, 143
national redemption, xiv, 31–32, 77, 104,
135–36, 140–44, 149, 188n21
symbolic names and concepts, xv, 5–6,
13–14, 57, 62, 95, 126–44
history (Yehoshua's representation of), 10–13,
17, 26, 36–37, 68–70, 115, 171n2, 174n36
and anti-Semitism, 32, 173n24, 184n28,
186n62
of Arab-Israeli relations and conflict,
31–34, 56, 59, 90, 165, 171n26, 189n28
of Israel, xiv, 26, 30–35, 58, 90–91, 134–37,
163 (*see also* Zionist ethos)
in *The Liberated Bride*, 82, 85–87
and the responsibility of historians, 82,
85–86, 181n19, 181n20, 181n24
of other cultures, xiii, 6, 17, 21, 26–28,
48–50, 90–91; in Africa, 59, 64, 172n10;
in America, 163–64; in Europe, 60,
176n65; in India, 6, 23–24, 88; in Spain,
48, 173n28; (*see also* national identity)
Hochberg, Gil, 61–62, 179n37
Hoffman, Anne Golomb, 146, 169n8, 172n11,
176n63
Holdengraber, Paul, 187n9
Holtzman, Avner, 169n7

INDEX 203

Hop, Dorit, 179n34
Horn, Bernard, 4, 8, 36, 96, 177n13, 191n25
  on *Mr. Mani*, 8
  on mutually validating relationships
    among cultural groups, 174n33, 178n31,
    186n70, 191nn25–26
  on Sephardic themes across Yehoshua's
    work, 9, 186n70
  on Yehoshua's indebtedness to Faulkner,
    179n45, 183n6
humor, x, 16, 29, 47–48, 60, 68, 75, 102–4,
    123–24, 151, 179n35

Itzhaki, Yedidya, 183n5

Jacobson, David C., 183n5
Jaggi, Maya, 49, 176n64
Jerusalem, 18, 35–51, 69–70, 137–38, 176n64
  in Yehoshua's life, x–xii, 21, 30, 36, 46,
    175n45, 176n57, 176n64
  across Yehoshua's oeuvre, 35–36, 46–51, 68,
    145, 156, 175n47
  in *The Lover*, 137–43
  in *Mr. Mani*, 36–45, 69–70, 116–20, 175n46,
    175n53, 176n63
  in *Open Heart* (*Hashivah mehodu*), 24
  in *A Woman in Jerusalem* (*Shlihuto shel
    hamemuneh*), 46–47, 50, 80–81, 176n69
  See also Zion
Jordan, Hashemite Kingdom of, 30–31, 35
Journey to the End of the Millennium, A (*Masa
    el tom ha'elef*), 121–22, 152–56
  love plot, 152–56
  Yom Kippur in, 120–25
  Tisha b'Av and Zion in, 155, 175n47
Joyce, James, 21, 45, 95

Kafka, Franz, 10, 95, 130, 187n9
Kalman Naves, Elaine, 171n2
*Koha hanorah shel ashmah ktanah. See Terri-
    ble Power of a Minor Guilt, The*

Laor, Dan, 185n45
Late Divorce, A (*Geirushim meuharim*), 25–27,
    32
  Passover in, 96, 99–107
  watchman's stance, 67–68
Liberated Bride, The (*Hakala hameshahreret*),
    33–34, 63–64, 156–58
  boundaries and borders, 181–82n33 (*see
    also* national identity: and defined
    borders)

professional identities in, 81–85
  watchman's stance, 63–64
Lieblich, Amia, 154
Lipsker, Avidov, 18, 49, 170n10, 181n22
Lover, The (*Hame'ahev*), 28–29, 75–77,
    130–44, 149
  name symbolism in, 130–44, 149
*Masa el tom ha'elef. See Journey to the End of
    the Millennium, A*
Mendelson-Ma'oz, Adia, 185n35, 190n10,
    191n25
  on Yehoshua's representation of territorial
    boundaries, 182n33
  on the ethical dimension of Yehoshua's
    work, 148–49, 186n66, 190n10
  on *Friendly Fire*, 178n23, 178n28
Midrash, 1, 15, 128, 151, 169n1, 187n8
Mintz, Alan, 73–74, 89
Miron, Dan, 7–9, 156, 170nn10–11
  on *The Retrospective* (*Hesed Sfaradi*),
    188n12
  on Sephardic themes in Yehoshua's work,
    9, 173n29
  on the "watchman over the house of
    Israel" motif, 178n16, 182n45
  on Yehoshua's layers of composition, 7–8
Mr. Mani (*Mar Mani*) xi–xiii, 8–9, 68–70,
    115–20, 150, 175n54
  geographic and cultural borders (represen-
    tation of), 34–35, 175n44
  Jerusalem in, 36–45, 68–70, 175n46, 175n53,
    176n63
  narrative style, xvi, 9, 162–67
Molkho. See Five Seasons
Morahg, Gilead, 9, 27, 54, 134, 181n19,
    191nn25–26
  on empathy and alienation (Yehoshua's),
    54, 177n7, 178n15, 186n70
  on national ab/normality vis-a-vis *Mr.
    Mani*, 9, 175n44
  on Yehoshua's representation of a diaspora
    "neurosis" in *A Late Divorce*, 27, 97–98,
    106, 183n9
Moretti, Franco, 18, 171n4
Mul haye'arot. See Facing the Forests
Muller, Rina Cohen, 27
multilayered style, x, xiv–xv, 1–15
  in Hebrew literary history, 1, 12, 129–30,
    136, 170n10, 188nn13–14
  in world literature, 4, 7, 130
  Yehoshua's, x, xiv–xv, 1–15, 63–65, 86,
    92–93, 127–30, 144, 155–56, 158, 169n8,

204 INDEX

multilayered style (*continued*)
    Yehoshua's (*continued*)
        170nn10–11; Amir Banbaji on Yehoshua's
        juxtaposition of current reality/history,
        11, 182n36; Dan Miron on Yehoshua's
        five compositional facets, 7; Gershon
        Shaked on Yehoshua's "shadows of
        meaning," 3; Nitza Ben-Dov on Yehosh-
        ua's "twilight" dualism, 4; Yehoshua on
        his propensity to open "drawers" within
        his fiction, 3, 10; Ziva Shamir on Yehosh-
        ua's layers of meaning, 7
Murata, Yasuko, 175n46

name symbolism, 1, 12–13, 25, 105–6, 126–44,
    153, 187n9, 189n26
    in *The Tunnel*, 1–2, 12–14
    in *Open Heart* (*Hashivah mehodu*), 25
    in *The Lover*, 50–51, 130–44, 188n21
    Isra-el, 25, 163, 106, 126, 142–43, 163
    Moses, 105–6, 143
    Ruth, 129
    Yehuda, 25
    Yigal, 135–36, 140–44, 188n21
    See also historiosophic themes in Yehosh-
        ua's fiction
national identity, xi, 5, 9–11, 34–35, 41, 112–13,
    138–39, 162–68, 106, 126, 143, 160
    and anti-Semitism, 32, 174n37, 184n28
    and defined borders, xiii, 27–28, 31–35, 41,
        174nn41–44, 176n64, 181n33
    and dispersion, 10, 11, 17–25, 41, 69–70,
        89–90, 106–7, 119–20, 143, 160, 164–67
    and ethical responsibility, xiv, 35, 53–54,
        60–64, 67–71, 77–93, 119–20, 166–67
    and normalcy, 9–10, 21, 37, 51, 53–54,
        170n14, 177n6
    and psychological health, 9, 26, 105–7
    and religion, xvi, 24, 90, 94–99, 102–26,
        176n64, 183n2, 184n33
    and sovereignty, 9–10, 37–38, 77, 89–90,
        143, 159, 164, 167, 174n34
    in *The Yehoshua Controversy*, 143, 162–67,
        192n1
    in Yehoshua's essay, "Golah: The Neurotic
        Solution," 94–99, 183n2
Naveh, Hanna, 172n11
Negev desert, 41, 128, 174n31
    as a place for modern Jewish regeneration,
        13, 41, 128
    in *Mr. Mani*, 41, 128
    in *The Retrospective* (*Hesed sfaradi*), 29–31

in *The Tunnel*, 13
Nitzevet. See Extra, The

Omer-Sherman, Ranen, 158, 174n31, 181n20,
    181n24, 182n33
    on *The Liberated Bride*, 158, 192n32
onomastics, 136, 187nn1–2, 187n4, 188n14,
    188n22
    See also name symbolism
Open Heart (*Hashivah mehodu*), 5–6, 22–25,
    87–90
    name symbolism, 25, 87
    vocational identity, 87–90
Oz, Amos, 3, 4, 19, 112, 149, 175n45, 185n44
Oz-Saltzberger, Fania, 17

Palestinians, 13, 31–35, 59, 118, 141–42, 189n28
    See also Arab-Israeli relations; diversity
        and cultural pluralism: Palestinians and
        Israeli-Arabs; West Bank
Pardes, Ilana, 74, 190n18
Passover, 96–107, 184nn16–17
    in *A Late Divorce*, 96, 99–107
Peri, Menachem, 5
Pinsker, Shachar, 114, 171n3, 191n21
political reductionism (warning against), xv,
    11–14, 16–17, 36, 51, 128, 170n19
professional occupations and vocational
    identity of Yehoshua's characters, 72,
    74–77, 92–93, 119
    See also psychological development of
        Yehoshua's characters
prophetic mode and discourse, x, xv, 50,
    71–74, 91, 143–44, 160, 178n14, 178n16,
    182n45
    See also biblical references in Yehoshua's
        fiction; "watchman over the house of
        Israel" motif (*Hatzofeh lebeit Israel*)
psychological development of Yehoshua's
    characters, 4, 8–9, 187n9
    cognitive awareness, 61, 65
    Oedipal conflict (representation of),
        97–98, 145–51, 181n28, 191nn20–21
    parallels between psychology of individu-
        als and national development, 9, 53–54,
        73–74, 78, 97–98, 146–47, 169n8, 170n14,
        177n6
    professional identity of characters, 72, 74,
        92–93
    psychological realism, 11–12, 72, 128

Ragussis, Michael, 135, 187n1, 191n20

Ramras-Rauch, Gila, 189n28
redemptionist expectations. *See* historiosophic themes in Yehoshua's fiction
religion, xvi, 49–50, 94–95, 98–99, 106, 113–14
See also history: of other cultures; national
identity: and religion
Retrospective, The (Hesed sfaradi), 7–8, 19,
29–31, 33–34, 179n42, 188n12
high point vs. the abyss, 54, 64–65
Reuveni, Yotam, 72, 185n34
Rosh Hashanah, xvi, 117
in *Journey to the End of the Millennium*, 121
in *Mr. Mani*, 117–18, 121

Saranga, Carmela, 45, 175n45, 179n48
Schwartz, Yigal, 172n5, 184n23
Seidman, Naomi, 190n18
Shabbat, 184n33
in *A Late Divorce*, 96, 101
in *Open Heart (Hashivah mehodu)*, 24
Shaked, Gershon, 183n4, 188n13
on "Facing the Forests," 177n13
on *The Lover*, 3
Shalev, Mordechai, 56, 91, 128, 147, 178n14,
185n54, 187n6
Shamir, Ziva, 7, 60, 169n9, 175n45, 187n8
Shapira, Anita, 135
Sharaby, Rachel, 45, 175n45, 179n48
Shemtov, Vered Karti, 27, 49, 171n3, 181n33,
182n47
Shlihuto shel hamemuneh 'al mash'abey enosh.
See *Woman in Jerusalem, A*
Shoham, Reuven, 178n14
Silberstein, Laurence, 186n61

"Tardemat hayom" (Sleepy Day), 77–78
Terrible Power of a Minor Guilt, The, 148–49
"Three Days and a Child," 147–48
Jerusalem and, 46, 176n57
Tisha b'Av (commemoration of destruction
of the Temples), 107
in *Journey to the End of the Millennium*, 155,
175n47
translation (lost and gained in), 5–6, 40, 73,
67, 78, 130, 175n51, 181n32, 188n21
travel, 17–21, 27–30, 69, 172n11
Tunnel, The (Haminharah), 1–2, 12–14, 175n47

"watchman over the house of Israel" motif
(*Hatzofeh lebeit Israel*)
in the Bible, 56, 74

in modern Hebrew literature, 178n16,
182n45
in Yehoshua's oeuvre, xiii–xiv, 56, 67,
70–71, 178n14
See also prophetic mode and discourse
West Bank, 59
in *Friendly Fire*, 57, 59
in *The Liberated Bride*, 64, 87
in *The Retrospective (Hesed Sfaradi)*, 31
in *The Tunnel*, 13
See also Palestinians
*Woman in Jerusalem, A (Shlihuto shel hame-
muneh 'al mash'abey enosh)*, 46–47, 50,
79–81, 187n9
Jerusalem, 46–47, 50, 80–81, 176n69
vocational identity, 79–81

"The Yatir Evening Express" ("Masa ha'erev
shel Yatir"), 55
Yehoshua, Avraham
coming of age, xi–xii, 18, 30, 31–32
core ideological preoccupations, 11, 16–22,
39, 51, 77–78, 94, 114, 126 (*see also*
Zionist ethos)
literary generation, 3, 10, 31–32, 174n35 (see
also *Dor Hamedina*)
literary influences, x, 7, 10, 95, 130, 151 (*see
also* Agnon, Faulkner)
literary works, 193–94; bibliography, 193–
94; early short stories and novellas, xii,
11, 18–19, 30–31, 54–56, 118; novels (*see
individual titles*); theatre plays, scripts,
librettos, xii, 54, 107, 177n8, 184n30
marriage and widowhood, ix, 14, 159–60
places of residence, ix, 21
religious heritage, 112–13, 124, 176n65,
184n33, 185n46
Sephardic background, xi, 9, 113, 124, 134,
174n33, 185n46
speeches and essays, xiv, 31–32, 49,
53, 90–93, 106, 142–44, 148–49; on
anti-Semitism, 105, 173n24, 184n28;
his core definitions of Jewish identity,
143, 167, 174n38, 183n2, 184n33; on
geographic borders and Israeli identity,
31–35, 174n34, 174n38; on history and
historians, 86, 174n36; on Israel v. diaspora, 97, 159, 162–67, 174n38, 192n34 (*see
also* "Golah [diaspora]: The Neurotic
Solution"; national identity (dispersion); "The Yehoshua Controversy")

206 INDEX

"The Yehoshua Controversy," 159, 162–67,
    172n7, 192n1
  in relation to Israeli identity, 142–43,
    164–68
  in relation to Jewish identity, 142–43,
    163–67
Yizhar, S., 10, 18, 172n8
Yom Kippur, 114–25, 186n64
  in *Journey to the End of the Millennium*,
    120–25
  in *Mr. Mani*, 115–20

Zakim, Eric, 77

Zemach, Eddy, 186n70, 191nn25–26
Zerubavel, Yael, 55
Zierler, Wendy, 186n55, 187n8
Zion, 6, 18, 49–50, 68–71, 120, 145, 155, 166
  See also Jerusalem; Zionist ethos
Zionist ethos, 27–28, 31–32, 50, 77–78, 113,
    134–35, 172n5, 174n38, 180n10
  critique of, 77–78, 114, 140, 149, 155, 166,
    186n61, 190n13
  in Jewish tradition, 50, 56, 77, 91, 119–20,
    135, 143–44, 166–67, 174n38, 175n47,
    183n13
Zoran, Gabriel, 68, 171n3, 177n5

Printed in the United States
by Baker & Taylor Publisher Services